Betrayal of Magic

By Brian Dockins

DOMA Series

Book 1: Betrayal of Magic
Book 2: Shrouded Island
Book 3: Rise of the Witch
Book 4: Magic of Heroes
Book 5: Hounds of the Himalayas
Book 6: Second Exodus
Book 7: Hidden Relics (Forthcoming Winter 2013)

DOMA Origins
(Amazon Kindle Exclusive)

Winged Demon: Darius and Natalie
Circus Freak: Bryce
Brujeria: Rafe
Deviant Behavior: Jude & Madison
Secrets In Stone: Gabe

Betrayal of Magic

Book One of
DOMA: Department of Magic

By

Brian Dockins

Siege Tower Publishing

DOMA: Department of Magic Book One
Betrayal of Magic
A Siege Tower Book

Copyright © 2011 by Brian Dockins

Cover art by Tim Oliver-Grow
Cover design by Onaje Beal

ISBN-13: 978-0615481944
ISBN-10: 0615481949

First Siege Tower Trade Paperback Printing: June 2011

Printed in the United States of America

Chapter One

When he woke that Tuesday morning, Cadan Johnson had no idea that his entire life would come crashing down.

The alarm clock screeched in his ear as he rolled over and slammed the oversized snooze button with the palm of his hand. As his eyelids fluttered open, he saw that darkness still dominated the sky. The window was cracked and a cool crisp morning breeze breached the slight opening, the white linen drapery billowing up with each new gust.

His body still ached from a hard practice the previous day, and the last thing he wanted to do was leave the comfort of his plush, warm bed. Before the nine minute snooze could sound on the alarm, Cadan rolled out of bed and turned off the annoying contraption. Stretching the stiffness from his legs, he walked over to the chest of drawers and found an old, torn up t-shirt and gym shorts. After throwing on clothes and sneakers, he went downstairs.

Halfway down the stairs, the aroma from the kitchen below reached his nose. Hunger never set in for him in the mornings until reaching the dining room and smelling his stepmother's phenomenal cooking.

The small dining area was situated near the foot of the stairs and just outside of the large kitchen. He found his father seated at the table scraping the few remaining eggs from his plate, past his brown tangly beard, and into his mouth. Simon was for all appearance a giant; he was several inches past six foot and his body was a mass of muscle from many long years working at the steel yard.

Since his mouth was full of food, Simon greeted him with a smile and a nod. When his stepmother, Daphne, saw him enter the dining room, she appeared from the kitchen with a plate of food. She wore her usual brown apron and her bountiful crayon red hair was pulled up to the back of her head in a feeble attempt to tame the chaos. Her eyes were an emerald green, sparkling with perpetual pleasantness and resonating with motherly softness.

"Morning, Cadan," she said as she set the plate down at the spot across from Simon. He pulled the chair out and plopped down. "Did you hear your brother or sister stirring up there?"

"I think I heard Derrick." His slightly younger brother was always the last to the breakfast table, always the last out of bed.

"I'm surprised," Simon snorted into his food. His cantankerous father was not always an easy man to get along with. For the most part he was quiet and the words that passed from his mouth were always well thought out and important. Idle chatter was not his favorite pastime, and his one notorious pet peeve was tardiness. It just so happened that Derrick's most prominent trait was tardiness. That combination made for some tense meals at the Johnson table.

"Hey Papa!" Raney came bounding down the stairs two at a time, greeting her father as she hit the bottom floor. It always annoyed Cadan that she was just a little too perky in the morning, as if she had a constant stream of caffeine flowing through her veins.

"Hey my sweet little angel," his father said as he held out an arm and hugged his daughter. She had just turned thirteen, four years younger than Cadan. Since grades seven though twelve were piled into one campus, they went to the same school – there was no differentiation between junior high and high school other than school years.

2

She was still wearing her pajamas and her messy hair was pulled back into a ponytail. None of them bothered to shower in the morning until after practice.

Derrick sauntered into the room a few moments later, plopping down into the chair next to Cadan. His head was cocked to the side and his eyes were almost closed. As Daphne set his breakfast in front of him, he groaned a thank you that channeled a zombie movie. She returned quickly from the kitchen with her own plate and sat in the remaining chair between Simon and Raney.

Several times during their meal, Simon glared at Derrick, obviously unhappy at his lack of motivation, which was typical of mornings. It looked like any minute his father would break out into a lecture.

Cadan decided to lighten the tense mood and start some conversation. "So what are we going to practice this morning?"

Simon turned to Cadan with a smile. "I thought we could practice some spellwork."

In many aspects his family was very normal and average. His father worked eight hours a day, five days a week at a steel plant, while his stepmother tended to the home and took care of the kids. Simon got a meager raise and bonus every January, which they used to recover from the debt incurred buying holiday presents just a few weeks before.

Raney was popular at school and was a constant social butterfly, applying herself to her homework, and continued involvement in several extra-curricular activities. Both brothers were on the varsity soccer team and ran track and cross country. Cadan didn't have many friends and absolutely no social life, which left him quite a bit of time for his academic work; Derrick did only well enough to get passing grades and advance to the next year. While overall their parents were very pleased, Derrick still received lecturing for his mediocre grades.

They would go on inexpensive vacations like other families, which mainly consisted of camping trips to parks and forests that were just a few hours from home. They stayed away from larger cities because Simon had social anxiety in large crowds. They celebrated birthdays and the holidays at the end of the year like everyone else too.

There was one notable exception to their family – their home lives revolved around their magical abilities.

As far back as he could remember, they could perform spells and other magical feats. Simon had begun instructing them in the art of the ruhk-magic, along with other skills, such as sword fighting, the bow and arrow, and other survival techniques. He taught them about the origin of ruhk-magic and those who wield it. He explained that the gift of sensing, creating, and manipulating ruhk-magic was rare, and few people could perform the feats that they could. Cadan didn't know any others besides their small family; when he asked his father about it, he would say that there were probably other people out there, but he didn't know any.

One thing had always been clear though – they were under no circumstances permitted to use or talk about magic to anyone else other than their own family. They also knew that the consequences would be grave if they were to ever use ruhk-magic anywhere but in the privacy of their own land. Simon explained that if 'normal' people were to ever discover their spectacular abilities, they would all be locked up and studied. Cadan was terrified that he would be taken from the rest of his family and spend the remainder of his life inside some cell, where scientists would poke and prod at him day and night.

Growing up, he would have nightmares of this happening. His father would only laugh and tell him that it was the pressure of secrecy causing him anxiety. He could never talk about it to anyone at school, which had made it even more difficult to make friends. Simon would never allow a potential friend to come to their house, so inviting someone for a sleepover was out of the question. He had made a few friends in the first few years of school, but they began asking questions about his personal life. He was not sure what was okay to talk about, so he wouldn't say anything at all. The other kids found this annoying so he was ostracized.

Derrick and Raney were less anxious of secrecy. They were able to make a few friends much more easily, however they never judged Cadan for his lack of friends, and always included him when they went out socially.

Exercises in fighting techniques and ruhk-magic became a part of their daily routine. Their father always had them up at 5:00 A.M. so that they could eat their breakfast and practice for an hour before getting ready for school. He could only remember maybe a dozen mornings in his entire life that they were able to sleep late, and even on those occasions, it was only another hour or two.

Cadan had always wondered why their father drove them so hard. What were they practicing for? When they asked him, he would simply say that since the gods had granted them with the ability to perform such wonderful acts, it was their responsibility to hone their powers and perform them to the best of their abilities. He equated the idea of practicing ruhk-magic to someone who had an aptitude for medicine. It would be a waste for that person to pursue anything other than the healing of their fellow man.

He always had the impression that they were training for war. There was grave determination in his father's eyes during their sessions, and frustration in the lines around his mouth when one of them slipped up. A sense of urgency undergirded their time together, and he was judicious in his time management. Simon would scan the surrounding woods, as if he were paranoid that they were being watched. Sometimes Cadan thought that at any moment a cadre of magic wielders would swarm down on them from the tree tops and attack their quaint homestead.

Since it would have been awkward, even disrespectful, to ask their father about his constant worrying, Cadan decided one day, a few years ago, to ask his stepmother about Simon's behavior. Daphne seemed a little uncomfortable discussing her husband's actions, and excused them as part of his social anxiety. Cadan was completely unsatisfied with her explanation.

"Ah," groaned Raney. "I was hoping we would get to practice with the bow and arrow." She recently signed up for the school archery team, and counted on extra practice time at home.

"It will still be dark out behind the house and I want to take advantage of that," Simon answered as he stuffed more food in his mouth. He always liked to practice spellwork when it was darker, and other less noisy activities were done in the daylight. Most of the time their spells were simple, but occasionally a spell would go out of control and produce more light and noise than they intended. That was usually the case with Derrick and sometimes Raney. They seemed less interested in practicing, and it showed in their sloppy work.

On the other hand, Cadan dove headfirst into ruhk-magic. With almost no friends or planned social activities, there was nothing to keep his mind from magical endeavors. He progressed through his father's 'levels', showing weekly improvement.

"What spells are we going to work on?" asked Derrick. That question was the most initiative he would show in the entire day.

"Shields," answered their father. He used his last bit of biscuit to sop up the remainder of gravy on his plate, and pushed his chair back to stand. "Be out there in five minutes so that we can start."

He stopped by the kitchen sink to deposit his plate, came back into the dining area, kissed Daphne on the cheek and retreated through the back door.

Cadan hurried to finish his breakfast, as did Derrick and Raney. When his brother stood, he nearly hit his head on the simple, nickel-finished light fixture hanging from the ceiling. Like their father, Derrick was a giant; since Cadan was only six feet tall, there were times he felt like a miniature standing next to his father and brother.

They quickly followed after Simon. They found him in the small clearing a few dozen feet behind the house. He was already sitting on the old oak stump he had cut down a few years before.

"Cadan," he said as they approached. "Please stand to the south side. Derrick and Raney, please stand to the north." He motioned each direction as the three teens walked to their respective sides of the clearing.

Cadan took his place in front of a large oak tree and readied himself. He had only practiced producing shields a few times. The power required to produce them was not great, but precision was tantamount and if not brought forth correctly, shields were useless.

"I want you to begin by creating a small shield to surround yourself," Simon instructed them. "Be careful to make it large enough to fit around you in both circumference and height. Remember to sketch the parameters of the spell in your mind, before you draw the ruhk-magic to complete the task." Their father paused, so Cadan closed his eyes and began to concentrate.

The stillness of the clearing at dawn was the essence of pure tranquility. The only sounds were a few birds moving through the trees and a squirrel somewhere near – typical noises of the forest that did more to soothe the mind than confuse.

As he slowly worked the design of his spell out in his mind, the noises grew louder and deeper. Harnessing ruhk-magic heightened all five senses to such a degree that he could almost taste the crumbled leaves under his shoes.

The effect was strange, and even though the sounds and smells of the forest amplified, the symphonic chorus only aided his concentration.

After tracing the desired area of the shield, he tapped into the source of power near his heart and released a small quantity to complete it. Drawing the power was pure euphoria. It was a transcendent experience like none other. A few seconds later his shield was surrounding him, completed. Although their father did not specify, Cadan left his shield slightly permeable so that he could still hear.

After a few moments, Simon began instructing again. "Do not allow the lines of your spell to become bent or meander – keep them straight and clean. When filling your spell with the ruhk-magic, do not cross your parameters or your spell will become sloppy." He grunted. "Derrick, keep your spell tighter. A sloppy spell is more detectable to other magic wielders and also less powerful."

"Sorry, Father."

"Don't apologize, son. You are here to learn. You are an extremely powerful ruhk wielder, and I want you to have the skill to match your power." Simon turned to the other side of the clearing. "Now, Cadan, your shield is quite large. For the beginning exercise, you do not have to strain yourself so."

Cadan brought the parameters of his shield back, not realizing that it had extended out around him for over ten feet in all directions. Just a bit further and it would have enveloped his father. Despite what Simon had said, creating a shield was not really a strain at all.

"You may release your shield." They obeyed his command. "Now, Cadan your shield was very good, but a little large. Remember not to overtax yourself. Only use what power is needed to perform your desired spell. There may come a time when you need to perform consecutive spells, so reserve your energy where possible." He turned his head to the other side of the clearing. "Derrick, you must work on your precision. I could have detected you from miles away. Raney, continue to practice using larger quantities of the ruhk-magic so that you may create better shields and perform greater spells."

They each nodded as their father gave them advice.

"Now, let's see how well your shields hold up. Cadan, call forth another shield exactly as you just did. Derrick and Raney, you two will send a small barrage of ruhk-fire at his shield so that we can see just how strong it is." And by *it*, he meant both the shield and the ruhk-fire. Simon's method to setting up these exercises was so all parties involved would receive some sort of practice.

Cadan closed his eyes momentarily so that he could produce another shield, and once it was in place, he reopened them. He could feel Derrick and Raney drawing magic to create their ruhk-fire. Producing energy was one of the hardest spells to master, but once someone became proficient, Simon had promised that the task would become easier.

Derrick and Raney both produced gray ruhk-fire. The hue of their fire was identical to that of their irises. Simon shared the same eye color, so he produced gray ruhk-fire as well. For some reason, Cadan inherited the traits of his birth mother and had royal blue eyes with an even deeper blue ruhk-fire. He had asked his father about the correlation between eye color and the color of their magic once. He answered that it was just one of those universal truths.

Ruhk-fire, itself, was one of the most beautiful sights that he had ever witnessed. It resembled fire in that it was a gas-like substance that was nearly completely transparent, and crackled with several similar hues that complimented each other in an exquisite formless presence. If manipulated appropriately, it could behave much like regular fire, and it had boundless other uses. The size, shape, and intensity could be molded in many ways.

Both of Cadan's siblings pounded his shield with ruhk-fire, and each shot poured out around the invisible field that was protecting him. Gray energy covered the shield, but none of it was of sufficient power to penetrate his guard. He felt safe behind the security of his well constructed wall.

After several moments, the power they were sending his way decreased, and he could tell that his brother and sister were tiring.

"That is enough," Father called to them. "Good shield, Cadan."

He walked over to Derrick and Raney and stood between them. "You two did very well with your ruhk-fire, and I can see improvements. It is unfortunate for you that Cadan seems to be showing an aptitude for producing shields. I think most ruhk-wielders would have a difficult time penetrating his defenses."

Simon closed his eyes and called forth a shield that encircled him, Derrick, and Raney. "Now Cadan, I want you to attempt to break my shield with your ruhk-fire."

Cadan closed his eyes and pulled forth a vast quantity of magic to produce the blue colored energy of his ruhk-fire.

With his fists clenched tight, he threw first his right arm, and then his left, sending sprouts of blue incandescent energy at the dome, neither of which made purchase. He sent another round, and again his father's shield held.

This was so frustrating, Cadan thought. His father wasn't even sweating from the strain. Cadan shot both fists towards his family again, this time forming columns of blue fire that continued to pour against the shield. The surge in power began to heat his body, and sweat seeped from every pore.

His efforts began to show. First his father's legs began to wobble from the strain and then his arms began to shake. The strain of deflecting Cadan's power was weakening his father's defense.

Just before he felt Simon's shield give way, Cadan threw his arms down, quenching the ruhk-fire, knowing Simon couldn't hold up much longer. Clearly exhausted, his father dropped his shield. He would have fallen over, if not for Derrick and Raney grabbing each of his arms.

"Very good job," Simon's voice wavered. "Now help me back to the house, children. I need to rest up a bit before I have to go to work. You three should get ready for school."

Chapter Two

Cadan stepped out of the shower, dried the steam off the mirror, and looked at his reflection. He reached into the top drawer, found his hair gel and spread some between his palms. As he worked it through his tangle of sandy blonde curls, he looked into the mirror and almost gave up hope. Who was he trying to impress by styling his hair?

Derrick had several girls vying for his attention. Nearly half the male students and possibly a few female had the hots for Raney. It wasn't that Cadan wasn't attractive; his self esteem was not so low that he couldn't look at himself in the mirror and admit that he was an attractive guy. He was just different than the other guys.

He heard the names that people called him, especially the other boys. They thought they were clever with their muffled slurs and their snickering. Because of his secret, he felt completely disconnected from others his own age. When not around his own family, he was uncomfortable with being himself.

Despite the negative voice in his head, he fixed his hair anyway. He decided to go light on the gel, since it wouldn't mix well with sweat from soccer practice that afternoon. He threw on a t-shirt and a pair of light-colored denim jeans. He wore a pair of light brown sneakers and put his soccer cleats in his gym bag.

After making sure all of his things were in order, he walked over to his chest of drawers. He opened the small plain wooden box on the top and peered inside. Lying atop a soft cushion of fabric were two small gems – one diamond and one jade – each hanging from a silver chain.

These were no ordinary stones. They were numina stones. He only knew of a few variations, but each numina stone was special. These stones could increase the power of their wearer or even imbue them with special gifts. In appearance, they were mere gems like one might find at a jewelry store; only a wielder of the ruhk would be able to decipher the difference.

The jade numina was part of a collection of five that their family owned. The green stone's purpose was communication, and they typically came in sets there linked together. While their father had made them practice its use during one of their morning sessions, they had never come across the need to use them. Everyone had cell phones, so their father told them to only use the jade stones when absolutely necessary and their phones were not accessible. They were to have them on their person at all times.

The diamond was different. Other than the five jade numina, Simon kept a small collection hidden in a safe in his study. There were only two diamond numina in their family's possession: one was locked away in Simon's office, and the other one was sitting in his top drawer. Simon had told Cadan that his mother had bequeathed this to him prior to her death, which was all he would say on the matter.

The numina had prompted many questions about his mother, but it seemed to pain his father too much to discuss her, not to mention she was not a topic he was comfortable talking about in front of Daphne, his second wife. Their mother had died many years ago and Cadan had no memories of her. The diamond numina was all that he had left.

There were times when it deeply pained Cadan that he had never known his mother. He and his father had so little in common, and he had always explained this by telling Cadan that most of his personality and physical appearance were from his mother. Cadan wondered what she looked like;

Simon assured him that he had no pictures. With no photograph to go off of, he would often try to sketch what he thought she might have looked like.

Cadan never wore the diamond, because he was too afraid of losing it. It was bad enough that each of them had to wear the small round green stone around their necks at all times – including soccer practice, games, and even showers. He didn't want the hassle of two stones. He put them both on one afternoon after school, and Derrick had made a comment that he looked like Mr. T.

Something was telling him that he should wear it that day. It was like a voice in the back of his head, urging him to place the second silver chain around his neck. After fastening the jade around his neck, he reached down and grabbed the chain holding the diamond. He positioned the second chain around his neck next to the first.

When the diamond came to rest in the middle of his chest, he could feel a surge of heat through his body. The amplification of power with the numina was great, and even without opening himself to ruhk-magic, he could feel the awesome power gurgling just below the surface of his self control.

He had no idea that wearing the numina would be the end of everything that he had come to love. Doors of understanding would soon blast open, so painful, and yet so hopeful.

Moments later he grabbed the truck keys off the table by the front door. With a hug from Daphne, he bolted out the front door. He met Derrick and Raney at the old pickup. Their father had bought them the old beater a few years ago, so they could get to school and back. With Cadan driving, Derrick in the passenger seat, and Raney riding in the middle, they were off to school. The engine puttered rhythmically as they drove down the dirt road away from their house and towards the main county road that led into town.

When they pulled into the school parking lot, Raney, as usual tried to hide her face. Their truck smoked and jostled its way into a parking spot between a Toyota and Kia, both at least a decade newer than the old truck. Cadan grabbed his book bag and gym bag from the bed of the pickup and headed into the main building just as the first bell rang and everyone began sprinting to get to their respective classes.

He and Derrick stopped off at their lockers, which were next to each other, and shoved in some of their books. Cadan grabbed his math and chemistry books, since they were his first two classes. Before he could shut his locker, he heard Derrick clear his throat.

When Cadan turned to his brother, he saw him nod back up the hallway towards the principal's office. A group of three girls, decked out in their finest, were prancing down the hallway, eyes darting around, as if they were predators on the prowl. They were three of the most popular girls at school, and their reputation put them near the top of the cruel list. As they breezed past, Cadan ducked his head down to avoid any eye contact. Unfortunately, he caught the eyes of the center girl, Kristen, who smiled at him. It was a casual smile, so slight that anyone else observing would not have seen.

Except for Derrick. "Did you just see Kristen smile at you?" he asked, punching Cadan in the shoulder playfully.

"Whatever," Cadan mumbled, shutting his locker.

"She was totally eyeing you."

"I've also heard her call me names when all of her friends are around."

"You know how girls are," he chided. "She's worried about appearances and impressing her friends."

"At my expense."

"At plenty of people's expense. You aren't the only person she makes fun of. Just the other day, she embarrassed Raney and her little gaggle of mini-princesses."

"Whatever," Cadan repeated.

"Maybe you should try to find her alone one day and actually talk to her."

"Why would I try to talk to her?"

"Why wouldn't you? You are my brother and all, and you aren't a bad looking guy. I've heard a few girls say they think you're totally cute." He paused. "Just go talk to her."

"Really?" Cadan turned around and faced Derrick. "Really? Absolutely not. I don't need to give that Disney Princess any more ammunition than she already has on me."

Without another word, Cadan whirled around and walked off to his next class.

The day seemed to drag by so slowly. Even History, which was, by far, his favorite subject, seemed to creep. The teacher's lecture on the politics of Europe between the two World Wars seemed to flow through his right ear and out the left. He hadn't realized it until sitting down for his first class, but something about practice had left him frustrated. The source of his unease was still a mystery.

He was anxious to get to soccer practice. The physical exertion of practice always helped relieve tension.

The bell rang and before the teacher could assign last minute homework, the students grabbed their bags and were running out the door. Cadan took the still-empty pages he pulled out for notes and shoved them back into his history book. He slid the book into his bag and left the classroom.

As he walked down the hall towards his locker, he passed a girl on her cell phone pleading, "But mom!"

Like a sudden bolt of lightning on an otherwise clear day, the source of his problems flashed in front of his eyes.

His mother.

It all came down to this woman about whom he knew almost nothing. His father had told him that she had blonde hair, was beautiful and kind, and had loved Cadan dearly, but beyond that Simon had remained silent. Cadan built up the nerve to ask about her a few times, but was always met with anger or deep pain, depending on the day. He didn't even know her name.

But how was it possible to not ever know her name, or even hear Father or Daphne speak it? Neither Derrick nor Raney had bothered to ask; was he the only one who cared? He could check his birth certificate, but he had no idea where his father had stashed it. It was probably in the safe in his father's office or some other hidden place. Would he show Cadan the birth certificate if he asked?

Probably not, he but he realized there was one place that was bound to have a copy – the counselor's office.

He had just a few minutes until the next class started, so he bypassed his locker and headed to the administrative offices in the main building. As he entered the main hall, he saw three guys walking his way, each a few inches taller than him, and even wider. They all wore green and orange school letter jackets that were littered with football patches. He knew what awaited him, so he tried to slip past them unnoticed. Two of the guys walked to each side of him, and as they passed they threw their shoulders into his. As they walked off laughing, he tried to regain his balance and hold tight to his book bag.

He wanted nothing but to use ruhk-fire and burn them from existence. He would never have done such a thing, but it was so tempting. He turned back around and continued towards the offices.

Passing the secretaries, he went straight back to where the school counselor, Mrs. Tether, would be. As he rounded the corner and into her office, he found her sitting behind her desk writing furiously in a student's file. She was a heavy set woman and looked even heavier in her thick, forest green sweater. Her short brown hair was a curly frame around her round, pale face. Glasses hung off her nose, and her eyes showed the weariness of her job, desperate for a vacation. Her office was guacamole green with the annoying inspirational artwork hung everywhere; it was the kind of artwork that had one word below a picture, with a short phrase that was intended to inspire. Instead of motivating him, Cadan usually just stifled a gag.

"Hello, Cadan," she looked up from her writing and greeted him with a warm, motherly smile.

"Hello, Mrs. Tether."

"What can I do for you?" she asked.

"I was wondering if you had a copy of my file."

"Your file?"

"You know, the file that the school has on me that will have all of my personal information."

"Why, of course –," she stopped and her expression suddenly became very cold and lifeless. "Now that you mention it, I think your file has gone missing. I've been meaning to contact your father about getting copies of your papers to replace the records we lost."

"You lost my file?" This did not make a bit of sense. Why had her mood suddenly changed?

"I'm sure your father will be very agitated with me, but hopefully he will understand. We do have hundreds of files to keep up with, after all."

"So you don't have a copy of my birth certificate on file?" How did she know his file was lost? She hadn't even bothered to look for it.

"I told you Cadan, we lost your file. I am deeply sorry for the trouble this may cause you and your family."

The pulse of his heartbeat was met by a second pulse, almost identical to and in sync with the first. The heat radiating off the diamond was intense, so he reached down and used the fabric of his t-shirt to pull it slightly away from his chest.

"How do you lose a file?" Cadan asked, doing his best to ignore the burning gem under his shirt.

"I am deeply sorry for the trouble this may cause you and your family."

Why was she repeating the same phrase over and over?

"And how do you know my file is lost without even checking?"

"I am deeply sorry for the trouble this may cause you and your family."

There was something wrong with Mrs. Tether. It was almost as if she were a robot – or under some sort of trance. *That was it!* There was a spell at work here and the only person he knew capable of performing a magical feat that could alter an individual's brain to such a degree was his father. Cadan hated this form of magic, and his father had only taught him the basics that dealt with the mind. Messing with an individual's mind was worse than breaking open someone's diary and posting the contents on a blog for the world to see. The individual who had placed the spell was strong. There was no method he knew of to determine its origin, but his gut told him that his father was behind it. There was no other mage in their vicinity as far as he knew. Maybe his father was trying to prevent him from finding his birth certificate or some other bit of information.

He had dabbled in mind-magic a little with some guidance. He didn't think he could break the spell that had been cast on Mrs. Tether, but he would give it a try – especially if it meant being able to glean some information about his mother.

He placed both hands on Mrs. Tether's desk and leaned forward. Drawing a vast quantity of ruhk-magic, he began concentrating on the signature that was surrounding her brain. Reaching out with the power, he tried to gently touch the base of her spine, but found he harnessed more ruhk than he could handle.

He had forgotten about the diamond numina against his chest. His intent was to pull only enough power to find his father's spell, but the actual ruhk flowing from his hand was filling her mind, and he could not pull back. He was completely uncertain of the consequences.

Panic gripped him and he tried with all of his might to retreat, but his own spell had locked on to the spell that had been in her mind previously.

And then something snapped. Hard.

Cadan felt his body propel away from the counselor's desk and his head make contact with something behind him and then everything went black.

But the blackness quickly dissipated into something else entirely. He was lying on the ground but not in the counselor's office. In fact, he was not in any room he recognized.

As he looked up, he was staring at a set of knees. He wasn't lying on the ground at all; it was just his height. She wasn't a giant – but he was a child. He followed the body of the person standing in front of him and found that it was a slender, beautiful woman, with long blonde hair flowing down around her shoulders. From the sides of her hair, he could see slight, but pointy, ears protruding out. Her wide mouth displayed a smile, greeting him with more love and affection than he had ever known. Her almond shaped blue eyes were the same ones that stared back at him when he looked in a mirror.

He had never seen this woman before, but she seemed so familiar.

They were not alone; a man stooped behind her. He leaned down and stared at Cadan with a look of pride as he placed a hand on the woman's shoulder.

"He's such a sweet boy," the woman said.

"And strong," the man added. "And I have you to thank."

"His kindness comes from my side," she said, as she rested her head against the man's shoulder. "But his strength definitely comes from your side, husband."

His mother!

But who was the man who stood beside her, claiming to be his father? Even without the beard there was no way the man was Simon. Their build was different, their features even more so.

Was this some sort of hallucination brought on by the conflicting spells or the power of the diamond numina?

The image faded leaving only blackness, a void of nothingness, as if he hung somewhere between the world of the living and the abyss that must be death.

He felt hands on his shoulder shaking him awake. When he opened his eyes, he stared up at the face of his brother. Behind Derrick, Raney and Mrs. Tether were watching intently with their hands over their mouths. The school principal was standing behind Mrs. Tether, speaking with someone on the phone.

Cadan tried to pull himself up, and heard the principal tell the person on the other line that he was awake. The principal nodded and then hung up the phone.

"Are you okay?" Derrick asked.

"I think so."

"What happened?" Raney asked frantically. The question was not directed at him.

"He just came in here to talk to me about something," the counselor explained. "Before he could tell me what he came to me about, he began fumbling around and then fell over. I assume that he fainted."

"Fainted?" Derrick asked Cadan. "What caused you to faint?"

"I don't know?" he lied.

"We almost called an ambulance," the principal informed him. "I called your father and he asked that your brother and sister take you home. He is leaving work now and will meet you there." The principal did not look happy. "I do not agree with that plan. I think you should be going to the hospital, but your father strictly forbids me to call them."

"My father," Cadan heard myself mumble. As he said the words he could feel an acrid taste on his tongue, as if they were expired cough syrup.

"What Cadan?" Derrick leaned closer.

"Nothing," he said, shaking his head. "I just want to go home."

Chapter Three

The truck came to a stop in front of their house, and Derrick jumped out from behind the wheel. Raney saw that Cadan wasn't moving any time soon, so instead of asking him to let her out, she just slid out the driver's side. His brother stared at him wordlessly, as if looking for the right thing to say. Finally he shut the door and walked into the house, leaving Cadan to sit in the truck by himself.

He sat there pondering the possibility of confronting Simon with the vision from the counselor's office. There was no way to be certain if the vision was something brought on by the stress of losing his mother at an early age or if the vision was legitimate. Considering Mrs. Tether and her unusual repetition of the one phrase, he had a feeling that something was wrong.

How would Simon react? If the vision was not true, he would be deeply upset. And Daphne would definitely be heartbroken if the subject was broached. But he knew that he had to say something.

Cadan stared at the house in front of him. The large two story dwelling with a beautiful wraparound front porch had always been the place he called home. He remembered learning to ride a bike in the driveway, and would always cherish the day that Simon brought home the old beater pickup he purchased for the three of them. Despite the bright sunny day, he could almost see his emotional attachment to the house burning away, as if acid had been poured overhead.

Another thought came to mind, hurting almost as much as the first. If Simon wasn't his father, then that meant that Derrick and Raney were not his siblings. There was no mistaking the familial resemblance of those three, with their inhuman height, dark brown hair, and steel grey eyes. He was the odd one out, with lighter colored hair, slimmer build, and bright blue eyes.

He finally opened the truck door and stepped outside. His legs were still a little wobbly from fainting less than an hour before, and he had the feeling of being drained of all energy or willpower. Raney was watching through the front window of the house to make sure he could climb the four steps. Gripping the banister, he was able to slowly navigate up to the front door, and into the house.

Before Raney could say anything, he continued straight upstairs to his room. He set his book bag on the floor near his desk and was about to sit down when he heard the front door open again. He knew it was Simon by the sound of his hurried footsteps.

Should he wait or confront him now? As the nausea of passing out had begun to recede, he was left with only anger. Actually, anger was not the best word to describe his emotions. *Rage* seemed a better fit.

For the first time ever, the safety and security of his family was crumbling away, and he was left with nothing but a vague dream of his *real* family. Everything he had come to know and love was nothing more than fraud. It left his chest feeling hollow, and he nearly collapsed again. The vibrant colors of his home and his life had suddenly dulled to a melancholy gray.

Like a switch, something clicked in his mind – he bounded down the stairs two at a time. When he got to the bottom, he found Simon and Daphne sitting on the couch in the living area, with Derrick and Raney sitting on the smaller sofa directly across from their father.

Simon stood when he entered, slowly walking towards him.

"Don't," Cadan demanded as he threw a hand up.

The tone and shortness of his voice took Simon by surprise. Normally he would have never spoken to his father in such a way. Respect was something Simon had always demanded from his children. Cadan guessed he didn't have to worry about that now, since he was no longer Simon's child.

"What has come over you?" Simon asked.

"I want answers," Cadan replied plainly. "Tell me about my mother. Describe her to me."

"Why are you asking about her?" Simon pleaded.

"Just answer me. I want to know."

"She was beautiful. One of the most beautiful women that has ever lived."

"No," Cadan shook his head. "Describe her in more detail."

"What do you mean, Cadan?"

"Tell me about her ears."

"Her ears were small and delicate—"

"You lie!" In his vision her ears were larger and pointed.

"What is the matter, Cadan? Where is this coming from?" He could see it in Simon's eyes. The past that he had long buried was resurfacing, bubbling up out of the dirt he had spent over a decade piling up.

"Tell me about the counselor. Did you place a spell over her?"

Simon didn't say a word for several moments. The room was silent except for the tick-tock of the ancient grandfather clock. Finally he spoke. "I did."

"Why?" Cadan asked.

"To protect you."

"Protect me? From what? Your spell knocked me unconscious! How is that protection?"

"There are things about your past – our past – which you are not ready to learn. The school counselor is the one hole I discovered in keeping these secrets from you. I had to place the spell on her when you were just a child."

"Why the counselor? Because she keeps my birth certificate?"

Simon nodded in understanding. "So that is why you went to see her? You wanted to see your birth certificate?"

"Yes."

"You don't have a birth certificate."

"How could I not have a birth certificate?"

"Well, there may be one out there somewhere, but I have no idea where it is."

"That makes no sense."

"Cadan, I wish I could tell you more."

"Then tell me more! Tell me whether or not you are my father."

Simon's silence answered his question. He stared at Cadan and his grey eyes began to water. Tears streaked down his cheeks, running into his beard. His mouth finally opened.

"I am not your father."

The revelation hit the room like a barrage of gunfire. Derrick and Raney gasped in unison and stared in bewilderment at their father. No one said a word for several minutes. Daphne held a tissue at her face and was crying. Simon searched the room, looking for the right thing to say.

Cadan's family had disintegrated before his eyes. He no longer had a mother, a father, or even a brother or sister. They were still a family unit; he was the outcast. He was some random kid that they had picked up to add to their little collection.

Finally, Simon spoke. "What happened when you were unconscious?"

"I saw my mother and father. It was like old memories were coming back to me. Ones that I had repressed or something." And then it hit Cadan. He had not repressed the memories on his own. There had been an outside force. "Did you place a spell on me too?"

"When you were a young child, I helped you forget the painful memories of your parents. I wanted you to feel loved and accept me as your father. I thought it was the best way to cope with the loss of your mother and father."

"So they're ... dead?" The word was acrid coming off his tongue.

"Yes, they died when you were just a child. Derrick and Raney's mother had died around the same time, and Daphne and I took you in as our own. We wanted you to feel the love of parents despite losing yours."

"You lied to me. You lied so many times."

"I know, and for that I cannot apologize enough. I just hope you understand why we did what we did."

"You lied to me!" Cadan screamed. The tears began pouring from his eyes like a fountain. Daphne stood up to come towards him, but he held his hand up. The last thing he wanted was for anyone to touch him.

"I'm so sorry, Cadan. I never meant to hurt you."

"But you could have told me something about my parents. You could have told me the truth."

"There is so much that you don't know. Things I'm not prepared to tell you. There are certain things that are just too painful."

"I broke your spell. I wore my diamond numina to school and when I touched Mrs. Tether's mind, I couldn't handle the backlash of your spell."

"You are powerful like your father."

"In my vision, they said that they were proud of me."

"They were proud of you. Daphne and I are proud of you, as well."

"You're not my father – that means nothing to me."

"Don't say that, Cadan! I have always loved you like a son. I have never made you feel any less than my own child."

"But I am not your child."

"I didn't have any part in creating you, no. But in my heart, you are just as much my child as either Derrick or Raney."

"You are still my brother," Raney said quietly. Cadan turned to see her sitting on the couch with her legs pulled up and her knees in front of her nose. She was crying.

His sense of family wasn't the only one that was shattering. Derrick and Raney were also being lied to. He could tell by the baffled looks on their faces. If their father could completely fabricate everything he had said about Cadan's mother, even lying about being his father, then by the same token, all descriptions of their mother were false, too.

Cadan looked over at Derrick, and he could tell his mind was following the same logic. His brother's face was contorted in rage and pain, and his eyes kept darting over to his father.

Derrick turned and faced Simon. "So, who is our mother?"

"She died around the same time as Cadan's parents."

"So everything you have ever said about her was false, then?"

Clearly, Simon wasn't sure how to respond to this. By admitting his mistake, he would be ostracizing all three children.

Simon spoke after a thoughtful few moments. "Your mother's name was Glenda. She loved you both very much, and like me, wanted the best for you. If she were alive today, she would be so proud of both of you."

"Where are the pictures of her?" Raney asked. "You've never shown us pictures of our mother."

"I don't have any."

"How could you not have pictures of our mother?" Derrick asked.

"It is complicated," Simon explained. "We were in a place where pictures were not common, and after your mother's death, I had to leave quickly. My priority was to make sure you were both safe. And you too, Cadan. I had to make sure that our children were safe."

For some reason this last statement upset Simon the most. His head fell into his palms, and he began crying again.

"Tell me about my parents," Cadan asked finally.

"I can't."

"Why?"

"This is bigger than you or me, Cadan."

"Why are you being so cryptic, so secretive?"

"I wish I could tell you everything."

"Then why don't you?"

"Because I cannot."

He wanted to scream. Why was Simon being so persistent in not telling him anything?

"So my last name is not Johnson?" Cadan asked.

"No, it is not. Your last name is Stone."

"Cadan Stone," He mumbled, trying to see how it sounded. The name didn't sound right.

"How did my parents die?"

"That is a conversation I am not ready to have right now."

"Can you at least tell me where my parents are from? Where did they meet and get married? Where was I born? Do I have any other family out there?"

Simon studied him, probably surmising the potential results of revealing more information. "You were born in New York – Manhattan Island, to be specific."

The discovery of his birthplace was nearly as surprising as learning that Simon was not his father. He had always assumed he was born in Iowa Park, Texas. The largest city he had ever been to was a suburb of Dallas, and that was on their way to a campground for vacation one time. Wichita Falls seemed like a metropolis to him. He had seen New York City on the television, and it had always been impossible to imagine a place where so many people were piled into one area.

"What are my parents' names?"

"Gordon and Michelle."

Hearing their names brought a new wave of sadness. He felt a weight press down on his chest. As the two simple words sunk in, that pain intensified. Two names of people he would never know.

"So do we have a secret, other last name, too?" Derrick asked.

"Mercer."

"Mercer? So I'm Derrick Mercer – not Derrick Johnson?"

"Yes."

"So both mine and Cadan's jerseys and letter jackets are wrong? Are you going to pay to get new patches and jerseys?"

"Is that really what you are concerned about right now?" Raney said, as she hit him in the shoulder.

"You cannot tell anyone about our real last names. Not for any reason. It must stay as secret as the knowledge that we can perform magic. There are people who would hurt us if they knew the truth. It is bad enough that we kept our first names."

"Why would anyone care about our last name?"

"The people that our family fled from would know that name. You must never tell anyone."

"Will you tell me anything else about my parents?" Cadan asked Simon.

"Your father and mother were the two best people I have ever known. I would have died for your father, if the occasion had presented itself. They were good people and they loved you so dearly. Your father had a powerful presence, and was even more powerful with ruhk-magic. He was a formidable opponent but a very likable person. Your mother was the essence of class and grace. She was one of the most beautiful women I have had the pleasure of laying eyes upon. Her heart was almost too big to be contained by her slight body."

Hearing the description of two people who he had never met, yet had seen just an hour before in his dream, helped to fill in the picture. It also made him thirst for more knowledge.

"I need to be alone now."

He turned and walked towards the stairs.

"Cadan, stop."

Cadan turned to face Simon, who had already crossed half the distance separating them.

"I'm very sorry about this. I wish there was something I could do or say that would make it better."

There wasn't anything he could say to Simon, so he turned and walked up the stairs. Even before he made it to his room, he knew what he had to do.

He couldn't face Simon again. He had lied for years, pretending to be his father. How could he have done such a thing? And then to say he had good intentions? Daphne never pretended to be his mother, but she did go along with Simon's lies.

Cadan knew that he still loved them all – especially Derrick and Raney. They had always been his family, despite the lies. But he could no longer stay in Texas – he had to find more information on his parents, and since Simon was not willing to provide that information, he would go off of what he had been given. He would travel to Manhattan; he wasn't sure how he would get there, but he would try.

Gordon and Michelle Stone. He had names to go off of, and assuming his date of birth was accurate, he could find something by going to a local library there. He had a computer in his room, and considered looking online for some record of their existence. For some inexplicable reason, that just did not feel satisfying. He needed the cathartic act of leaving what he knew. He would travel to the vicinity of where his parents had lived.

He knew he had to wait until they went to bed to sneak out. It was still early, so it would be several hours before they went to their rooms. He decided to try and sleep, since he knew he might not get another good night's rest any time soon.

Sleep came upon him before he realized he was drowsy. Instead of peaceful slumber, his mother's face returned. She came and went in flashes, usually smiling, but a few times crying. His father was with her at times. He didn't recognize where they were, and he couldn't recall the details of the locations. His focus always seemed to settle on the love and compassion pouring from his mother's crystal blue eyes. Somehow, even in his dreams he felt safe.

Had the feeling of needing to relieve himself not crept up, he would have slept through the night. In fact, when he awoke, the sun had already set. It was near midnight. He slipped into his bathroom out of necessity, and while he was in there, grabbed several of his hygiene and hair care products and threw them on the bed. From the closet he pulled out his backpack and removed all of his school books and binders so that he could make room for the essentials.

With limited space, he had to make concessions on what he could take with him. Since he was wearing a pair of blue jeans, he decided to throw a pair of cargo shorts and a pair of soccer shorts in the bag. He chose four of his favorite shirts, several pairs of socks, and some underwear. He retrieved his journal and two pens from a desk drawer. Under his bed, he had a metal box that held all of the money he had saved. They made a meager allowance for doing odd jobs over and above their daily chores, and, as he had no social life, had saved every penny. His last count put him at somewhere near a thousand dollars. That seemed like a lot of money, but if television shows had any shred of truthfulness, the money wouldn't last him very long in New York City.

In the bottom drawer of his dresser, he found a small gold box that contained a dagger. The dagger had a small but intricately carved hilt. Simon had told him once that it was sentimental, but said that the story behind the weapon would have to wait for another day. Now, he guessed it had been his father's. He slid the dagger into his bag as well.

He was still wearing the diamond numina. He pulled the chain over his head and slipped the stone into one of the backpack's side pockets. He retrieved the jade numina stone from its place on his dresser and stashed it away as well.

In just a few minutes, he had finished packing, only taking what few items he could not live without. When he zipped up his backpack, he stared around the room. Suddenly the thought that he may never see the room again hit him. Would he come back?

He didn't feel like he could answer that question. But for now, Simon was the last person that he wanted to see.

He slipped out his bedroom door and found the entire house pitch black. As he passed Derrick and Raney's rooms, he had to resist the urge to stop and peek in one last time. Would he ever see them again? He loved them dearly, but this was something he had to do. He fought the tears back, mumbled a goodbye and continued on.

Downstairs, the open windows let in enough moonlight that he could see the living room was empty. Without making any loud noise, he slipped from the front door, down the steps, and trotted along the dirt driveway towards the main road. Cadan never even turned around to take one last look at the house he had grown up in.

Chapter Four

The cracking of thunder erupted in the night sky, reverberating off of the buildings that lined the river also known as 52nd Street in Manhattan. The rain had not let up for three hours and had collected along the city streets so much that now the curbs were barely visible beneath the swirling maelstrom.

A smattering of lamp posts was all the light that Cadan had to find his way to the next awning. As he crossed the street, he attempted to leap over the stretch of water, but his black boot landed just short, splashing another wave onto his already soaked clothes.

Cursing to himself, he decided to forgo the next awning and continue on his path through the city. There was no sense in trying to stay dry at this point – the weight of his wet pants and hoodie felt suffocating. By the damp feeling on his skin underneath, he knew that the water had permeated through every thread on his body. He glanced at the large sentinel-like building in front of him, attempting to get his bearings. He did not recognize any of the locations from his afternoon ventures in the city, but according to the street sign, he knew he was close. The hostel's sign had said they close their doors at 11:00 PM sharp. According to his watch, which he synchronized with the hostel clock, he had four minutes remaining.

He would not have considered himself someone who was scared of the dark, but this particular night was an exception. Cadan could not shake the feeling that someone or something was following him. Paranoia had plagued his mind since the sun had set, and it was a feeling he was not accustomed to.

It was strange to see the varying heights of the buildings. One would be two stories tall, and then right behind it, one with twenty sets of windows to the top. Back home in Texas, a three story structure was tall.

He missed the stars. The twinkling lights of the sky were a permanent sight at home except on those rare occasions when it was cloudy. In the city, there was not a cloud in the sky, yet there were no more than a dozen stars visible. He would never have thought there were places on Earth that the stars weren't allowed to shine.

When he reached the intersection of 50th Street, he turned his head each way. The hostel was not in sight, and he couldn't remember in which direction it lay. He had spent many hours searching this area of Manhattan earlier, but now the streets began to blend together in ceaseless uniformity. He was accustomed to the simplicity of his little Texas hometown. He was not at all adept at navigating such a confounding assortment of roadways.

He checked his watch again and saw that he had less than two minutes before the hostel closed its doors. He was trying to decide which direction to try first, when suddenly he heard a commotion behind him. He spun around to look for the source of the noise and saw that two large metal trash cans had fallen over. Garbage had spilled from the lips of the overturned cans, united with the flowing water nearby, and began a trek downstream. He instinctively thought that the wind must have been the reason the trash cans capsized, but the dread flooding his heart told him otherwise. The feeling of being followed weighed even heavier on his mind.

Quickly gauging that Times Square was to his left, he turned and bolted right. He made quick time for three or four blocks and then finally stopped. The hostel was nowhere in sight and the lamp posts became more scarce as he travelled westward.

Suddenly a howl ripped through the air. It sounded like a dog, but not quite. There was something hungry about the sound, and he had no desire to see the mouth from whence the scream had erupted. He could not turn back around, as the source of the sound had come from that direction, so he decided to head north to try to circle around whatever had made that noise. Hopefully he would find the hostel, with a nice warm – and dry! – bed waiting for him.

He travelled several more blocks and then stopped. No more loud noises and no mysterious overturned trash cans could be seen, but he couldn't see more than five feet in any direction. Only one street light glowed some several hundred yards up the street. He found an outstretched awning attached to a large building that appeared to be some sort of old hotel, and quickly ran underneath it to get out of the constant bombardment of rain.

Cadan checked the time again, and found that it was already 11:05. He was so angry he nearly punched the side of the concrete building. "It would serve you right, Cadan Stone," He grumbled to himself. The last name sounded strange coming from his own mouth. Up until a week ago, he had been Cadan Johnson. Now he had a new name. He had foolishly continued his search even after the sun had set, and now he would have to find a place to sleep on the street – all because of his impatience.

Cursing his wet clothes again, he decided to do something about it. He closed his eyes and began to concentrate his thoughts inwardly, drawing on the power of the ruhk-magic. The ancient power soon filled his body. Harnessing the energy, he evoked a spell that would heat the area around his body. In seconds, his clothes dispelled all moisture – including the dampness from his bunching underwear. He opened his eyes again and found a tangle of now dry curls in his face. As he pushed his hair back, he noted the smoke emanating from his mouth, a byproduct of the use of the magic. The elation that came with using the ruhk-magic remained with his body – he had once heard Simon describe it as a marijuana high. When he had originally heard that statement, he asked Simon if he had ever smoked pot, which the old man quickly denied, then stormed off.

In any other circumstance, Cadan would find humor in the memory, but this night and the past several days had drained any hint of humor from his mind. He had replayed the argument with Simon over and over in his mind, and on more occasions than not, that memory had brought tears.

Something about the final conversation with Simon had bothered him ever since he left home. Simon seemed scared of something. As angry with him as Cadan was, there had to be a reason he wouldn't reveal anything about his parents. Cadan got the impression that Simon was protecting him.

He had left his home several nights before and had made his way to Manhattan. He found a trucker off of Interstate 287 who was bound for Little Rock, Arkansas. The trucker was suspicious, but agreed to give him a ride after a lengthy lie about trying to make it home to his parents in Little Rock. At the truck stop in Arkansas, he purchased some food and then walked to the nearest Greyhound station, where he bought a bus ticket to New York City.

Once he arrived in Manhattan, he found a travel center with a listing for hostels. He and Derrick had always planned on taking a backpacking trip through Europe and had read up on hostels, so Cadan knew that they would be cheap, simple accommodations, with staff who asked very few questions. He had to share the room with three strangers, but it provided the perfect base of operations to find out more about his parents.

Abrupt laughter up ahead brought his mind back to the present. He fumbled through his backpack to make sure everything was still safe and dry, and then he looked around again. From around the corner of the next intersection, three girls walked quickly by, with an enormous umbrella over their heads, giggling about something the three of them had shared. Cadan stopped just short of the corner to let them pass. As they hurried west, he glanced down the street in their direction.

A club was set off in one of the buildings just a hundred feet or so down the street. The building was as black as the night sky, with a simple façade and red carpet spanning the hundred feet across the front. The velvet carpet was framed by gold rails in a poor imitation of some Hollywood club he had seen on television once. The large, but shoddy lights on the front sidewalk were not quite as big as spotlights, but it was obvious that the club owner wanted people to think they were. It was almost tempting to see if he could get in to the club despite his appearance – he figured most clubs were for people who were eighteen or older, and since he was still seventeen, it seemed like a challenge to see if he could get in.

One of the girls screamed. As the other two looked towards the building they were next to, they joined the first in perfect harmony. Dropping their umbrella, they began running towards the club. Despite the towering heels on the back of their boots, they were making quick time.

He ran in their direction to see what had caused the alarm. He knew it was a foolish choice the minute his feet left the pavement, but he was overcome with an unhealthy mixture of curiosity and bravery.

Arriving at the location from where the girls had bolted, he turned to his left to see a dark alleyway. At first he could not see anything that would have elicited such a reaction, but soon his eyes adjusted and what he had previously thought of as darkness suddenly moved. He quickly gauged the person or thing he was looking at – and it was looking right back at him. It was almost human in appearance, but at least ten feet tall. The stench of blood – and a lot of it – permeated Cadan's nose, and he could hear a faint growl, almost inaudible, coming from the creature.

He froze there on the sidewalk, his mind racing, grappling for options. Should he run away like the girls? Surely the girls would call the police or animal control to come deal with the problem. For some strange reason, he felt the impulse to approach the creature, but the smell of blood kept him back. Another thought came to mind. If the police were coming to the scene, he did not want to be anywhere around. For all purposes, he would be considered a runaway, and more than likely be sent home. He refused to accept that fate.

He was about to turn around and leave, when the darkness of the creature came closer. The growl deepened and became louder until finally a snout appeared in the small light from the street lamp down the street. Under the snout he could make out a large row of teeth at least as long as his hand and as sharp as the swords that Simon used during training. A troll!

He had heard stories from Simon, but always thought they were legends. Despite his own powers, he found it hard to believe that creatures from old stories could physically walk the earth in modern times. But one big, ugly troll was staring at him on the streets of Manhattan, probably deciding which end of his body he would start eating first.

The monster lurched forward, diving for him. He took three nimble steps back and watched the clumsy creature fall to the pavement. It only took seconds for the troll to regain its footing and return his attention to Cadan. Back up on both feet, the troll swiped his large trunk of an arm towards him. Cadan pushed himself to the ground to dodge the blow. He crawled back on his hands and knees a few feet, lifted back up, and began running to the other side of the street.

He turned just in time to see a bright yellow cab stop just in front of the troll. The cab's horn blared, the driver frustrated that there was something in his way. A few other cars stopped behind the cab, but took a little more care venting their frustration as they were preoccupied by the ten foot tall, green nightmare in view of their windshields.

The troll howled in frustration and slammed a fist down on the front of the cab. The hood detached from the vehicle on all sides and was pulverized into the engine block. The engine erupted in a myriad of noises and the front two tires popped. The back of the cab came off the ground at least five feet. As it slammed back down, the driver inside stuck his left arm out and shook a fist at the troll, screaming in a language with which Cadan was not familiar.

The troll kicked the remnants of the cab as if it were just a soccer ball, sending it careening into the mini-van behind it. Then, the monster turned its attention back to Cadan. Wishing to put as much distance as possible between him and the troll, he turned and bolted down the nearest alleyway.

Cadan rounded a dumpster and continued running down the center of the alley, taking a brief glimpse behind him to see the troll push the dumpster away as if it were an empty soda can. Without even bothering to look both ways, he crossed over a street and continued down the alley. Behind him brakes squealed; he knew the troll must be gaining distance on him.

Suddenly the alley forked – it continued on straight, but also curved to the right. He turned quickly to see that the troll's face had been blocked by a sign hanging from one of the buildings. Hoping to change directions without the monster noticing, Cadan took the fork on the right and made his way eastwards.

He ran another hundred feet and stopped, thankful that the night had become quieter. The only sounds were rain beating down on the concrete and an occasional clap of thunder. Leaning against the wall, he tried to catch his breath. He saw that the troll had stopped at the fork, studying it to determine which way to pick up his pursuit.

Cadan allowed his muscles to relax momentarily, and his shoulders slid back against the wet brick of the building. He leaned his head back and felt the rain pound his face and run down his neck. He fought the urge to run, but stopped to wait on the troll's decision. If the troll continued forward, the pursuit would be over and Cadan could disappear. If the troll turned right, the chase would resume once again.

Cadan opened his eyes and leaned his head back up. He was about to peer around the small column of brick to check on the troll when a force shoved him to the ground. He fell on the pavement and his face nearly met the ground. Taking in a mouthful of filthy water, he tried to regain his footing. Before he could move too much, someone kicked him in the side, sending him tumbling.

Recalling his training, he used the force of the tumble to gain some footing. He nimbly slipped up to a crouch and searched for his new attacker.

Standing in front of him was a large man – nearly as ugly as the troll – with a large sword brandished in his hand. At first glance, he appeared human, but Cadan quickly took in the grotesque features. The bottom half of the newcomer's face, encompassing his mouth and nose, stuck out about an inch too far to look normal – almost like a snout. His nose, which was covered in warts, took up the majority of his face, and the top seemed to twist around to the right. Yellow eyes peered back at Cadan with an intense hatred.

He assessed the situation. Behind him a lumbering troll waited to have him for dinner; in front of him stood someone nearly as ugly as the troll.

The ugly man's intentions became quickly clear, as the sword came slashing towards him.

Cadan ducked as the sword whizzed just over his head. The sound of the blade as it passed within an inch of his ear nearly paralyzed him with fear, but instead of freezing, he stepped back. The ugly man prepared for another swing. Cadan tensed the muscles in his legs, and as the sword swept towards him, he danced backwards two steps and twisted slightly to the right.

The point of the sword passed just in front of his stomach. Reacting quickly, Cadan balled his fist and planted it on the man's elbow. He grunted in pain and pulled his hand back, but the strike accomplished its task by sending the broadsword to the ground, skidding across pavement and stopping against a building.

His attacker was equally as fierce without a sword, wasting no time in coming towards Cadan, both fists up level with his chest. He lunged his arms towards Cadan with a mechanized ferocity, and had Cadan not been agile, the punches would have found purchase somewhere on his slight frame.

"What are you doing, Jason?" a voice growled from behind the ugly man. Cadan stopped and backed up a few feet to respond to the newcomer.

"Mind your business or help me, Clay," he replied.

As his assailant's ally stepped from the shadows, Cadan was taken aback. The newcomer was equally as hideous as the yellow-eyed menace, with one notable exception – he was no taller than four feet. In his right hand, he carried what looked like a medieval battle axe. On his head, he wore a steel helmet that extended down over his too-large ball of a nose. A small part of his ugly face was exposed as was the reddish-black beard that hung nearly to his chest.

Cadan found the situation a bit humorous despite the danger that he was obviously facing. He could not hold back. "So what is this, the attack of the uglies or something?"

"You think you're real funny," the tall one spoke. Cadan remembered that his name was Jason. "We'll sever that pretty little elf-head from your shoulders."

Elf-head? Cadan had never been called an elf before. He had been told at school that his features were sometimes feminine. Often, the insults the jocks directed at him related to his features. But why had they called him an elf? If trolls existed, then maybe elves did as well.

Which reminded him – he wheeled around momentarily to see the troll had begun his pursuit down the alleyway in their direction. Both Jason and Clay seemed to have noticed as well. They were shifting uncomfortably as their gazes passed between the troll and Cadan, as if they were trying to figure out what to do.

Cadan took advantage of their confusion and dove for the tall one's broad sword. He turned just as his back made contact with the wall, and the sword found its way into his hands. Jason and Clay both reacted to the maneuver and came towards him. The dwarf stepped in front of his unarmed ally and lifted his axe.

Cadan held the sword up to deflect the blow. When the two pieces of steel made contact, the force almost ripped the sword from his hands. It felt as if his shoulders would be pulled from their sockets. When he stabilized the force in his arms, he swung backward, nearly knocking the axe from Clay's hands.

Since the dwarf's head was chest level, it was easy to send a leg up and kick him in the side of the face. Cadan made sure that his foot made contact directly on the exposed skin, just inside the little man's helmet. Clay tumbled

36

backwards, losing the axe, and holding his face in pain. The troll was very close then. Instead of attacking Cadan, Jason watched the troll anxiously and stooped down to help his companion up.

Cadan gripped the sword tightly and soared past his attackers, who were now preoccupied with escaping the troll. He continued down the alleyway, leaving his three opponents to fight amongst themselves.

As he raced through the rain, his mind began reeling at what he had just seen. He was being pursued by a troll, a dwarf, and some other half breed that looked like something between a troll and a human, all three of which looked like they were ripped from the pages of a fantasy novel. He wished desperately that he could call Simon, but he knew that was impossible at the moment.

After Cadan made another turn in the alley, the noises behind him were silent. The only sounds were that of the rain and his feet moving quickly through the water. Fatigue had yet to set in – he had always had high endurance – but he had the sudden urge to stop and get his bearings. He hesitated only slightly before two more dark shapes were upon him.

A dark skinned female stepped into his path. Both of her hands were outstretched and glowing, and she was preparing to use ruhk-fire against him. Before Cadan could build a proper shield to counteract the attack something even darker fell from the sky, landing on top of him.

He fell under the weight of the dark form. He couldn't free himself from its grasp. He peered down at the arm that was pinning him by the neck and saw dark skin. Based on the direction of the arm, he estimated the location of the attacker's head, and using the hilt of the sword, he slammed it backwards into his new assailants face. With a shriek of pain, the man dropped his hold and fell off of him. It was then that Cadan first noticed the tangle of black feathers all around the guy.

"Move, Darius!" the woman shouted as she hurled ruhk-fire in his direction.

Cadan was always quick with shields, but knew that he did not have enough time. He jumped aside as the violet iridescent energy blazed past him, contacting the feathered creature on the ground.

Taught never to hit a woman unless absolutely necessary, he charged the dark skinned beauty, who cringed back from what she had assumed would be an attack. As he passed, he slipped a foot under one of her ankles, sending her tumbling to the ground, caught up in her own black cloak.

Before he could make it very far, another man stood in his way. As if the nightmares could not get any worse – or any weirder – the man had four arms, two on each side of his torso. Not only did he have extra appendages, but he was at least two feet taller than Cadan and his arms were at least as large as Cadan's waist was round.

All four arms tried to wrap Cadan up in a cocoon, but the big man was slow to move. Cadan simply ducked around him, with two of the arms barely grazing his back, and bolted down the alleyway.

But again his way was blocked. This time there were three people, two boys and a girl, standing in his way. The one in the center had dark hair and wore a contorted grimace on an otherwise handsome face. The boy to his right was no older than Cadan – he had a mess of curly hair that was more blond than brown and features that made him think he was the real "elf-face." It would have been an understatement to call the girl beautiful, her silky hair fell in curls behind her head, and while she was tiny, her stance displayed a power and grace that could only be taken for perfection on the battlefield.

The three opponents in front of him did not look as easy to bypass or take down. The man in the center held a sword as large as the one that Cadan held in his right hand. The boy on the right held a staff as long as he was tall and the girl already had an arrow knocked and drawn in her bow. The tip of the arrow was clearly aimed directly at him.

"You must come with us," the man in the center finally spoke. "My name is Nate. We mean you no harm. We are only here for your own safety."

"Then why have you sent all of your goons to attack me?"

"Some of my team are less than graceful when it comes to rescue missions."

Cadan gestured to the blade in his right hand. "Then why did one of your team members use this sword against me? Rescue was the last thing in that big ugly head."

The boy on the right chuckled, but stopped short when he received a glare from his leader.

"I apologize for their rude behavior," he nodded. "But I must insist that you lay down your weapon. It is a fact that you will be coming with us, but it is completely up to you whether you are conscious or unconscious for the trip."

The girl on the left must have predicted Cadan's response. The arrow was loosed from the bow and made contact with the blade just above the hilt. The sword flew from Cadan's hands and landed against a dumpster far behind him.

Nate came towards him with his own sword drawn, and Cadan immediately recognized the fighting stance. His right hand moved behind his back, slipped under his shirt, and found the only defense that he had brought with him from home. In one quick motion, he flung the dagger at Nate and buried it in his right shoulder. The broad sword fell with a racket to the ground with Nate not far behind, screaming and clutching his bleeding shoulder.

The boy on the right hesitated for a moment and then charged. Cadan was able to dodge the first swing of the staff, but was not so fortunate on the second swing. The end of his staff made contact with the small of Cadan's back, and his vision blurred from the pain. He regained his footing and dodged a third swing. On the fourth swing, he found a hole. The boy had extended himself just a bit too far, and it was enough that he sent a kick to his side. It did not stop him completely, but gave Cadan enough time to send a punch to his pretty face.

Feeling the weariness of the struggle begin to overcome him, Cadan staggered and tried to find something to grab on to. The girl with the bow had another arrow knocked, ready to fire, but something held her back.

Cadan glanced over in time to see Nate lift his left arm, which was now glowing with green ruhk-fire. Green fire was all Cadan saw before passing out.

Chapter Five

The dreams were not very pleasant. When he first lost consciousness, Cadan remembered falling into blackness for what seemed like days. Finally the blackness faded and he was surrounded by monsters of the worst sort. Clay, Jason, and the troll took turns beating him. So much blood flowed from his wounds that he figured he should run out soon. Still the beatings continued. The four-armed man was there along with the dark skinned girl, who kept laughing at him. He tried to trip her again, but she brought ruhk-fire down on his feet, and they disappeared. The boy with the staff and the girl with the bow laughed as their leader, Nate, pummeled him with more of his green fire.

His family was somewhere in the distance, and they were looking for him. He could neither see nor hear them, but Cadan knew they were there and he knew that they were calling out to him. He could not explain it, but he knew that if he acknowledged their search, the monsters would turn their attention away from him and devour his family.

But somewhere, behind all of the chaos of the scene, there was a dark, lurking figure. The figure was behind something, but he could not tell what the object was that hid it.

The dream faded and he felt the twitch of his eyes opening. Focusing his vision took longer than it did when simply waking up from sleep. There was a fog that had settled over his mind, as if he had taken a half-dozen allergy pills. He could tell immediately that the room was nearly all white – stark walls surrounded him, and a white and silver framed ceiling reflected in an off-white marble floor.

He was lying in a small bed with his head propped up on two pillows. The only furnishings in the room were two chairs at his feet, a table to his left, and a small double door cabinet over to his right. The after-smell of ruhk-magic burned in the room as if it were incense. Someone had performed several powerful spells here.

He sat up in bed and pulled the covers back. He was wearing the navy blue tank top that he had on earlier and the same dark denim pants. His boots were missing, as were his jacket and backpack. There was no sign of his dagger and the jade and diamond numina were also gone. He glanced around and saw no sign of any of them. He was surprised that there were no binds keeping him in place; he had to assume that he was a captive.

But then another thought occurred to him. What if the previous night had been some elaborate dream? Men with four arms and black wings? Trolls and half-trolls? What had he eaten the night before? Maybe he injured himself somehow and this was a hospital in New York.

There was a knock on the door and he felt his muscles tense in anticipation.. The sight of the newcomer answered all of his questions. The previous night was no dream. Monsters were indeed alive and roaming the earth.

The man – or creature – appeared human at first glance. He had rough, wiry, reddish-brown hair that sprayed from the top of his head in wild wisps and continued down over his ears into sideburns and nearly met on each side of his mouth. He wore a short, white lab coat as if he were some sort of doctor. That was where all sense of normalcy ended. He wore pants that followed the strange backwards contour of his legs and stopped midway where his calves might be. There erupted more of the reddish-brown hair. Cadan realized the hair may actually be fur because instead of feet, the creature had hooves as large as a Clydesdale horse.

"Hello, young man," the creature greeted him. "I am Hadrian, the Chief Medical Officer of this facility."

"Um, not to be rude," Cadan stammered. "but what the hell are you?"

Hadrian chuckled. "I am a faun. It may be easier for you to think of me as half man, half-goat. Although it is rude to equate my race with goats." He dropped the subject as he mumbled to himself and did not seem happy that he had mentioned the association.

"Where am I?"

"Please, do be calm. Agents will be coming momentarily to check on you and brief you on your current situation."

"Situation?" he almost screamed. "You call being kidnapped in the middle of the night a situation? This is illegal!"

"What a rude little boy," said a female voice. He searched around the room but did not see another person. The door had closed behind the faun, and Cadan did not see anyone else enter.

"Who said that?" he asked, searching the room.

"Me, you dolt," came the voice again.

And then he saw the origin of the voice. A tiny woman, no larger than the palm of his hand was sitting atop Hadrian's shoulder.

The faun and the little woman shared a laugh, and then wings sprung up from behind her as she fluttered closer. He could see that she wore a simple purple tunic with a slit just big enough for her wings to fit through. As she came closer to his face, he fought the urge to swat at her.

"This is my nurse, Estelle," Hadrian explained. "She is a pixie."

Cadan was speechless. He knew that asking questions would only bring more questions. He was afraid to leave the room because there was no guessing at what freak show waited in the hallway.

"You seem to be healing quite nicely from your injuries," Hadrian noted without moving any closer. "Estelle and I will leave now. An agent should be here any minute."

As the faun and pixie turned and left, Cadan got the urge to bolt. There had to be a way out of this hospital. He stood up from the bed, only to realize that his muscles were weak. His body suffered from the same malady that had made it hard for him to wake.

Before the door was fully closed, the blond boy from the night before appeared. Now that Cadan could see him in better lighting, he could definitely make out the elf-like features. A defined jaw framed his tanned face. Cadan wondered if he really was an elf. He had always assumed the elves in fairy tales were pale. His features were pretty – by his demeanor it was obvious that he was very aware of this fact. His eyes were a striking Caribbean blue; it was impossible not to stare.

He swaggered into the room. His gate spoke confidence, matching the half grin that appeared to be a permanent fixture on his face. His age was hard to determine, but Cadan assumed it was roughly the same as his.

"Hello," the boy said as he nodded his head.

Cadan fought the urge to attack him. He was surprised that he didn't feel sore on his back from where the staff had hammered into him, but he could still remember the intensity of the pain. But then he calmed down when he remembered that he had kicked the elf-boy in his ribs hard enough to break a few, and had gotten in another good punch. It should have left a bruise, but there as not sign of a scuffle on the elf-boy's face.

"What am I doing here?" Cadan asked.

"You know the answer to that question," the boy replied. "Let me start by introducing myself. I'm Jude Bishop. What is your name?"

He thought about lying, but then decided against it. "My name's Cadan Stone. And I would really like to leave."

Jude smiled. "You will have to ask the Administrator about that. That is where we are going first."

"Where are we? Why is everyone so mysterious?"

"I will let Josiah fill you in on the details. Your boots are under the bed. The remainder of your things have been put in your room."

Cadan decided to give up with the questioning. It was futile to ask any of these maniacs anything. Wordlessly he found his boots and slipped them onto his feet. He followed Jude from the white room and into a hallway. The width of the hallway spanned no more than eight feet and the walls were metallic. Coldness washed over him as he trudged across the marble floors. There were several doors exactly like the one of the little room he had been in, but there were no other breaks in the monotony of the gray tones. He could see an elevator at the end of the hall in the direction they were headed.

He took a few minutes to get a better gauge of his opponent from the previous night. Jude was nearly the same height as him, and wore a very simple white dress shirt that fit snuggly on his thin, yet muscular frame. He had a thin black tie and black pants and shoes. He seemed dressed like he was at a prep school. Cadan was sure that if the need arose, he could easily take down Jude in a fight.

When they entered the elevator, he stared upwards to see that the ceiling of the compartment was nearly twenty feet high. He opened his mouth to ask about it, but then decided it would be as futile as all of his questions so far.

The buttons on the door were marked with combinations of letters he guessed were acronyms, and Jude pressed one towards the middle of the array. Again, Cadan fought back the urge to question.

Seconds later the doors opened into a vast room. The cold feeling from the hospital wing evaporated, and he immediately felt warm. They were in a large ante-chamber of some sort with soft, hay-colored walls framed by large mocha-colored wood beams that stretched to the ceiling. All around were lush couches and chairs, tables and shelves filled with a wide range of artifacts. He immediately thought of a museum. Most of the items looked ancient and priceless. There was a cabinet with a glass front that was filled with vases of all materials and colors. He recognized a Greek painting on the front of one. History had always been his strongest subject in school.

Paintings from all periods adorned the wall. He even noticed a stele from the Ancient Near East period. The floor looked like one giant slab of gray and white marble and it glowed as if it had just been buffed.

On the far side of the chamber, double doors swung open. An unremarkable man limped forward with the assistance of a black cane. He had short black hair that was peppered with gray, almost as if he had been out in the snow. He wore a simple black suit with a white shirt underneath and no tie. His round spectacles were pushed as far up his nose as they would go.

"Josiah," Jude called out to the old man. "I present you our newest recruit, Cadan."

Newest recruit, Cadan sniffed to himself. He tried not to respond out loud and used this time to size up the situation. He kept his eyes focused on the old man, but hoped he would have the chance to search out an escape route from the building.

"Welcome to our facility, Cadan," Josiah beamed at him. He seemed to be pleasant, hardly the attitude of a kidnapper. He gestured behind him. "Please step into my office, where I hope to answer all of your questions."

Cadan silently followed Josiah and Jude into the office. The office was shaped like an octagon, and seemed to be an extension of the ante-chamber outside the elevator. Enormous shelves occupied most of the room, along with the scattered paints, various wall art, and more tables littered with artifacts. An empty hearth was positioned on the floor to his right. Books lined the shelves; most of them were so old that he was afraid to touch one for fear that they would fall apart in his hands.

A desk sat at the back of the room, directly opposite of the door, containing a computer monitor in the midst of countless stacks of the old, dust-ridden books. As he eyed the room, he saw a fireplace implement that was used for poking logs, and two swords mounted on one wall, as his only possible weapons. He could sense that the other men were both magic-wielders. There was no way to be certain if he could make it to the wall of swords before one of them brought him down. He decided to wait it out to see if he could talk himself out of this problem first.

In the center of the room, set over a thick, large rug, were two short sofas. Josiah hobbled over to the faded red couch and stood. He beckoned to the matching soft blue couch in front of him, indicating he expected them to sit.

As Cadan took his seat on one end of the couch, Jude sat just a few feet away. Josiah set himself into the center of his sofa. "I imagine you have many questions," he smiled solemnly. Before Cadan had a chance to ask any of those questions, Josiah continued. "I am not quite sure where to begin on my typical speech about the program. We usually locate ruhk-wielders when they are much younger. From what I hear from my agents, you have already mastered fighting techniques, use of medieval style weaponry, and seem to be at least somewhat adept at using ruhk-magic. I would like to pose a question first. How do you come to us with such knowledge of the magic you possess?"

Cadan had not thought of this until now. He surmised that whomever had kidnapped him seemed to specialize in capturing magic-wielding individuals like himself. If they discovered the truth of his knowledge, it would certainly put his family at risk.

"I taught myself," Cadan finally answered. "I used my abilities in front of my foster parents one day, and they were so scared that they kicked me out of the house. They feared that I would harm one of them or one of their other foster children. I've been living on the streets since then."

"You are self-taught?"

"Of course," he nodded. "It wasn't easy, but I eventually learned some tricks. I can't do much really."

"But what about your fighting skills? I hear you excel at sword combat. What child of the streets has access to swords?"

"I have never used a sword," he lied. His hands had held a sword every day of his life. It was a rule that Simon never negotiated – he had practiced at least two hours a day every day. Even holidays. "I had to defend myself occasionally, usually with boards and such, so I just naturally translated that to the sword last night."

Cadan noticed that the old man didn't ask about the dagger. Either Josiah was choosing to ignore the fact that he had a weapon on him or the dagger was still lying on the ground back in the alleyway.

His response seemed to satisfy the prying old man. Josiah nodded and waved a hand as if to beckon a new topic. "Then I shall share with you some of the history behind the magic that you have been using all of these years. But first I would like some refreshments."

As if on cue, the door swung open. A tiny creature no more than two feet tall came walking in, carrying a tray over its head. As the little grayish green creature approached, Cadan could tell that she was female.

Josiah must have noticed him staring. "This is Gladiola. She is a gnome on staff here at the facility."

"Pleased to meet you," she curtsied after setting the tray on a table in between the two couches. Her voice was slightly squeaky and timid.

He noticed that her tiny little face did not have a nose, just two little slits that must have served as her nostrils. Her eyes were too large for such a tiny face, and they stared at him almost affectionately, with just a hint of wonderment. Under the nostril slits was a mouth that stretched the entire width of her face. The smile she gave him seemed to be a permanent fixture. He decided immediately that he liked her.

She curtsied to the three of them, before hustling from the room. Josiah leaned forward and grabbed the carafe of dark brown liquid. He poured a tiny amount into a small glass tumbler and handed it to Cadan, and but Cadan kept his hands in his lap. Josiah grinned and set it down in front of him anyway, as if to say this would be a long conversation and he would surely get thirsty later. He poured another for Jude and then one final glass for himself. He settled back into his couch.

"So, are you familiar with the Gods and Goddesses of the Pleroma?" Josiah began. Cadan shook his head. That was a lie, but he had to maintain that he had no knowledge of the magic he possessed. He had heard the legend so many times he could probably recite it better than the old man. "Well long ago, the great unknown deity, who was later named Dyas, and his consort Parthivi created two separate worlds – one to be ruled by magic and one to be ruled by science. After creating these worlds, they set them apart and placed a veil between them, so that the residents of each would not be able to travel to the other. To aide them during the creation process, they created 'children,' or lesser deities as we would think of it. When the creation was completed, these twelve lesser deities were placed on the side of the veil which contained the world of magic. Dyas and Parthivi created ruhk-magic, the life force of that world, then remained on the side of the world ruled by science, separated from the lesser deities."

Cadan actually did have a question – one he had never thought to ask Simon. "What does the word 'ruhk' mean?"

Josiah took a swig from his drink and explained. "We do not know the original meaning of the word as it is very old. The ancient Hebrew people took the word into their own language, and its literal translation is 'breath.' It is used many times in the Hebrew Bible, what you may know as the Old Testament, and its most common usage is to describe the 'breath' or 'spirit' of Yahweh."

Josiah did not seem to care if Cadan was satisfied with that answer, because he continued with his story. "It is possible that their design of separation with the veil worked for some time, but at some point in the distant past, the veil began to fail in small increments, and ruhk-magic began slipping through these tiny fissures and holes in the veil. There is extensive evidence that creatures, and even humans, passed through the veil, as well. We can see this evidence in the culture of the ancient civilizations of Earth, in the artwork, and in our own legends that have sprung up over time."

"You mean like trolls and gnomes?" Cadan asked.

"Yes, although I would not let them hear you refer to them as creatures. They consider themselves on par with humans, and as I have friends among them, I would have to agree as well."

"I meant no offense."

"And I don't think they would take any offense, young man. They would understand that you are new to this element of the world. But you are correct about the legends. There are stories that date back many centuries that tell of monstrous creatures that humans could barely describe. Trolls are a great example. Many of the magical creatures migrated north into the Scandinavian Peninsula in Europe, and that is the reason most of the legends of 'mythical creatures' are found in ancient Norse writing. That is but one of many examples. We could spend days discussing that topic alone."

He took another drink. "Many living organisms and much magic passed through that veil. Earth still functioned as it always had, but with one new element – magic. This magic entered into our world at various points; most periods of history are littered with evidence."

He set his drink down and sighed heavily. "And this is where we come in. It was during World War II, when the US government was fighting Hitler's army that they finally realized what was happening. I say the government recognized, but it was more like a bureaucrat and a few scientists discovered it. Not only was Hitler rapidly researching technology, he had an insatiable interest in the occult and fantastic. The dictator had found several ruhk-wielders and was using them for purposes of war. They brought this before President Roosevelt, who was still in the midst of the New Deal, the program that helped America recover from the Great Depression. The President immediately recognized the need for more research into the area of magical affairs. Using several of his new programs that were created in the New Deal, he was able to secretly funnel money into a new clandestine department of the government. And thus was born the Department of Magic, or as it was nicknamed: DOMA. That is the agency in which you are now an operative."

"Whoa!" Cadan flung his hands up. "I did not sign up for this. I am no operative and have no desire to be one."

"Frankly, you don't have a choice in the matter. All magical beings and all beings with magical abilities are by law a part of DOMA. You are either with us as an operative, in the field doing good for your own kind, or you will remain here as our prisoner. The choice is yours. You cannot be allowed to roam completely free with all of the power you possess. If you fell into the wrong hands, terrorists for instance, what do you think they would be able to accomplish? Unchecked in the world, you could be a great weapon of destruction if not trained properly and sufficiently protected."

"What about my civil liberties? Isn't this illegal to hold me if I have done nothing wrong?"

"Well, there are laws that apply to this, but they are known only to a very, very select few outside of the Department. And they fully support all that we do within DOMA. You will have all of your rights with one notable exception: DOMA now controls where you are able to go and how you use your magic. But I always encourage members of our group to view it in the positive light. You are here to help others who are born with special gifts like yours. You have already met Hadrian and Gladiola. Do you think that society would ever accept them? Of course not. When magical beings are brought into this world, we make sure that they have a safe place to reside – away from fear and persecution."

For all purposes Cadan was a prisoner. He could protest, fight back, do something to change his situation here, but he instinctively knew that any action on his part would be futile. Trying his best to keep a cool head, he decided to play along and see how this turned out.

"So magical creatures pass through the veil? How is that possible?" He had never had this in-depth of a conversation with Simon. For some reason he had never felt the urge to doubt the man who he once thought was his father. In retrospect that had been a mistake.

"Magic passes through the veil in two ways," Josiah explained as he held up two fingers. "The first way is the easiest for us to handle. Tiny gateways, if you will, suddenly burst open in random locations across the globe. In some instances, a magical being passes through that gateway. Thankfully they only stay open for a brief time, otherwise more magic would pass through than does now. Using a combination of ruhk-magic and modern technology, we can monitor these gateways and react to the situation in a rapid manner. In the past decade, we have had excellent success in collecting those beings that have passed through."

"What do they say this other world is like?"

"Well, that is the most interesting part of it. It seems that their memories are not fully intact after crossing over. Sometimes they remember fragments from their previous lives; most times, they remember nothing. There are recordings in our library of some of these fragments. We have learned that the world of magic is called Andaloria. As for specific details, they are scarce and fragmented at best."

Josiah set his glass down. "The second way that magic passes through is the most troubling for us. You see, ruhk-magic is what creates and sustains the cycle of life in Andaloria. When ruhk-magic passes through the veil, it interacts with the natural life cycle of biology. Its effects are seen most often during the birth of a baby. A woman may suddenly give birth to a baby goblin, with no other explanation than that she has at some point come into contact with a slight trace of ruhk-magic. It is an unseen force to the naked eye, therefore it's hard to track exactly how this occurs. It is how most of the magic-wielding humans are born."

Well that was interesting, Cadan thought, but he couldn't quite get the whole prisoner business out of his mind. He needed more information if he were ever going to get out of this. "So do I have to work here for a certain period of time and then I get to leave?"

"I am sorry to bring you this news, Cadan, but your life is now forever entwined with DOMA. It is not as bad as it may sound to you now, though. Our agents, such as Jude here, are perfectly content with their lives. This is not a bad place and this is not a bad job to have. You will be paid handsomely and there are many fun activities in which you will participate.

"We try to imitate a normal life as much as possible here. You will begin as both a student and an agent. The day starts off with general classes, with curriculum similar to that of an average American high school. Math, history, and literature play a large part in that educational piece. Following lunch each student is given the time to work in their chosen area of specialty, similar to a graduate school. We have one student who is currently studying the product of combining technology and ruhk-magic. You may choose your own specialty with a little guidance, but it must be something to which a senior staff member can serve as your mentor.

"This is not just about working all of the time. You will be expected to train in the afternoon following your classes. You will have time to settle in, but then you must join your team to begin training for future missions."

"What team?" Cadan asked, glancing over at Jude.

"The Department has various facilities around the US, and a few outside the borders. You are currently in our Rocky Mountain Facility. I cannot be any more specific than that as our exact coordinates are known to less than a handful of people. At this Facility, we have one main team of operatives who have fulfilled enough training requirements and have proven capable of completing missions with little supervision. We refer to them as Paladins, and each Facility has their own team just like ours. You will be placed on our Knights team, the same team in which Jude is a member. All Knights train to become Paladins."

"Which team attacked me last night?"

"I should probably tell you that the incident in Manhattan was not last night. You have been asleep for three days. The leader of the Knights, Nate, is one of my advanced students. He was the one that attacked you with ruhk-fire. That should not have happened and he will receive due punishment for his actions. He knows better than to use that level of magic against another living being unless circumstances call for it. I think that you angered him by plunging a dagger into his shoulder, but he should have realized that his injury was minor considering we have Healers in this facility."

"Great, so I've already made one friend."

Josiah chuckled. "He will get over it. Nate is brash and arrogant, but he is a great instructor and was a powerful Paladin when he was on their squad. Give him some time to recover from his wounded pride, and I'm sure the two of you will get along famously. To answer your previous question, the group that was sent to apprehend you was a composite of Paladins and Knights. In recent months, we have had many sightings to deal with. DOMA is relatively short handed and our resources too spread out to sufficiently deal with every problem. Everyone here is overtaxed, and we have had to rely on the Knights a little more than I feel is proper. I am sure once everyone has a chance to get to know you, they will be happy that you are here, if just for the simple fact that you are an extra, helping hand on missions."

There was silence for a moment. Josiah sat back comfortably in the faded sofa, staring at Cadan as if sizing him up. There were definitely some questions the man had regarding his new recruit, but he seemed unable to find a way to voice them. His eyes trailed Cadan up and down and once he even glanced over at Jude. It was a strange, awkward silence.

Finally Josiah spoke. "Do you have any more questions for me?" He continued his stare as if trying to bore holes through his face with his eyes.

Cadan met the old man's stare, and spoke plainly. "We would be here all day."

"Well then," Josiah slapped his knee as if he were about to stand. "I'm sure that once your training and classes begin, most of your questions will start receiving answers. You and I will have regular meetings so that we can assess your progress. We will follow up in about a week during one of our sessions to go over any lingering questions you may have. How does that sound?"

"Perfect." Cadan hoped that he had laid just the right amount of sarcasm down in his tone. He did not want to anger Josiah, but he definitely did not want the old man to think he was buying this whole routine.

He truly did have questions. His emotions and thoughts were running around like stirred up ants, and he wasn't sure if he wanted to scream in anger or burst into tears. Both responses were on the verge of breaking loose. He thought of Simon – he would know what to do. Cadan could contact him if he still had the jade numina.

Another thought occurred to him. Maybe he could talk to Josiah about the images of his parents. Was it possible that he would know something of them? After all he surely inherited his magical abilities from them. This DOMA place may have some record of them. What if his parents had been a part of the program? He had no idea what his father and mother had been like, but by the kind and honest faces in his dream, he could not imagine them participating in something as hideous as this.

His mind returned to the present when Josiah spoke. "Jude here will show you around the Facility as your tour guide. He is both a great student and significant contributor to his team."

Josiah stood with the aid of his cane and beckoned for the two of them to stand and exit. He quickly stood and waited for Jude's cue. The other boy nodded and smiled at Josiah and they left.

Cadan glanced at Jude as they left the room, and he wondered just how much he could trust his new 'friend.'

Chapter Six

They returned to the elevator without a word. Cadan decided that he would try and remember the buttons that Jude was pressing to reach their destination. He had no idea where they were headed, but he would remember the button that was pressed to get there.

Once the door was closed, Jude finally spoke. "So what do you think about all this?"

He wasn't sure what Jude meant by 'all this.' "Do you mean the facility or this whole kidnapping business?"

He knew there was no way to disguise the river of anger that flowed from his mouth with the last words. He hadn't meant to lay it on so thick, but he was frustrated – and even a little scared.

"In time you won't think of it as kidnapping," Jude explained rather matter of fact, ignoring Cadan's insolence. "It is for your own good. While here, you will be doing some good for other magic-wielders."

"So in other words, I will participate in the kidnapping next time?"

"Of course," Jude chuckled.

He was surprised by the directness of the response. Was Jude trying to make fun of him? Cadan decided for the direct approach. "Was my question funny or something?"

Jude waited a minute to respond, but the smile never left his mouth. "Relax. You know, you are really uptight. I was just laughing because we have heard that question on several occasions. You find this whole thing strange because of your perspective. Once you see what we do, you will understand more and not be so angry."

"How long before I go on my first mission?"

"That depends on two very important factors: your success in training and your attitude. They don't let incapable Knights with bad attitudes anywhere outside of this facility. Josiah needs to know that he can trust all of his operatives."

He would have to start faking a good attitude. Apparently Josiah would only let him out of the building if he played nice and pretended to be a good boy and a good little agent. That shouldn't be too hard. If they let him go on a mission, then he could find some way to escape. The other night, he was able to take on several of the agents; it had taken eight of them and a troll, to bring him down. Surely he could get away from whatever team he was sent out with.

The elevator door opened into a long wide hallway. The walls were textured and painted khaki, with a dark wood trim along the bottom and top of each side. Paintings and wall art hung amidst an array of doors, and some distance off, the hallway split and veered in two different directions.

"This is the dormitory level," Jude explained as they walked down the hall. "The Knights and Paladins both stay on this level." They passed an opening in the hall that formed an alcove. Inside were large plush couches, a television, a few tables, and some vending machines along one side. "This is the lounge. We can come here and relax late at night. Lockdown is almost always 10:00 pm, but we can stay up later as long as we are on this level. So sometimes we'll come up to the lounge and watch TV."

"Lockdown?" Cadan asked. He had heard that term on a prison movie once.

"You have to remember that we technically live on a military base," Jude pointed out. "Lockdown applies to most of the soldiers that are stationed here as well. They have a night guard that patrols the Facility to keep us safe."

"Guards?" he asked. "As in regular soldiers from the Army?"

"Yes. The US Armed Forces provide DOMA with soldiers."

"How do the guards handle the whole magic people thing?"

"They rotate the guards every couple of years. Josiah says that after they leave and before they get to go home, they go through a debriefing program which basically erases their memories of their time here. Most leave here thinking they were on some sort of low-risk mission in whatever current war the US is in."

"That shouldn't be too hard of a task, since the US seems to be at war with someone all of the time."

"Exactly."

Despite the conversation, he kept careful note of their route, through a series of twists and turns, passing nearly a dozen doors before finally stopping. "This is our room," he said as he slipped a tiny key into the door. The key looked like a flash drive. He pulled another one from his pocket and handed it to Cadan.

"*Our* room?"

"Yes, nearly everyone has a roommate, and I'm yours. I promise that I do not snore and I don't smell too bad on a typical day."

The room looked like a fancy hotel suite. They walked into a small sitting area with a couch and a large flat-screen TV mounted on the opposite wall. Jude flung his key down on the table in front of the TV and continued further into the room. The walls were painted a soft blue and the couch was cream-colored. It looked broken in and comfortable. Cadan noticed three different video game systems on the table under the flat screen and there were piles and piles of video game cases all around the table and wall. It was not really messy, but it was still clutter enough that Daphne would have had a fit. He made a mental note that if he were here more than a few days, he would have to convince Jude of the benefit of a tidy space.

He followed Jude into the room, as his roommate flicked the lights on. There was short hallway that led into what appeared to be the bedroom. Along the hall, there was a small alcove that held the tiny little kitchen – more like a kitchenette. There were black and white tiles on the ground, white cabinets, gray walls, and dark gray granite counter tops. The only appliances were a mini-fridge, a stove/oven combination and a microwave taking up a good deal of the already-tiny amount of counter space. Hopefully they wouldn't have to cook at the same time. There was barely enough room for both of them to fit into the galley-style kitchen, and neither of them would be preparing any gourmet meals here.

The bedroom was the largest of the rooms in the apartment, but not by much. It was sparsely furnished, but the intensity of the cluttered decorations made up for that. There were two beds on the wall to the left with a large end table separating them. On the end table there were two bedside lamps, one for each bed. On the opposing wall, there were two giant chests of drawers, one on each side of the large walk in closet. He wasn't sure if Jude bothered to use any of the drawers, or even the closet. Most of his clothes were on the floor around the bed and in the doorway to the closet. Cadan did catch sight of his backpack leaning against one of the beds.

A sudden shiver ran up his back as he thought about what was in his backpack. He crouched down on the ground and rummaged through the large compartment. Both the dagger and the journal were gone! The dagger's absence was more an issue of sentimentality, but the absence of the journal was far more critical. It contained information on Simon and the rest of his family. He could not betray their location to the crazy government program he was now entangled with.

He checked the smaller pouch on the outside, where he had stashed his diamond and jade numina stones – they were both gone. So Josiah must be a pickpocket. Should he ask about them? But then he couldn't plead ignorance if questions were asked. If Josiah was really that curious or suspicious of what he found, then Cadan was certain he would ask.

"Sorry it's a little messy," Jude shrugged, as he threw himself onto the far bed, which was of course, not made.

"No problem," Cadan shrugged too. "It wasn't like either of us was expecting a new roommate." Cadan hoped that his new 'friend' got the point of his comment. "So what are all of these posters for?"

There were posters hung up all over the room. He recognized that many of them were of the band Cobra Starship. Jude must be a fan. Surprising, the Femme Fatales were on a few. As always, the famous pop group was wearing as little clothing as they could get away with and not be considered naked. Their expressions of ecstasy were entirely inappropriate for anything except a dirty movie, and their eyes were darting in all different directions as if they were looking for someone with talent to join their group. Cadan rolled his eyes and kept looking around.

"Well, you can guess that I love Cobra Starship," Jude explained. Cadan had guessed correctly, although that was no feat of brilliance. "And the Femme Fatales are kind of cool."

"They're cool, but can't sing their way out of wet paper bag."

Jude burst out laughing. "I've never heard it put quite that way, but that's hilarious. You're right, though."

"Then why do you have their poster up there?"

"There's a secret about them that I guess you can know now since you're a DOMA agent. You see, they're actually fairies."

"Like real fairies? Or is that just some expression?"

"No they're real fairies. We have one here at the Facility you'll meet soon, especially if you go on a mission. They are magical beings – they appear human and usually have deep red hair. On some occasions, they have crazy colored hair, like green or purple."

"And the Femme Fatales are allowed outside of the Facility? How did they manage that?"

"They all trained at different DOMA facilities and ended up meeting each other at one of our program-wide meetings, and they got the idea to start this group. The only reason the powers that be allowed them to do it is because they make so much freaking money. Josiah says that almost all government programs are underfunded and the Department of Magic is no exception. The Fatales pay DOMA about a third of all of their profit and they keep their true nature a secret. In exchange, they get to live outside the base. They have to check in with us every few days and to get permission to travel outside of California."

"Hmmm." Cadan didn't know what else to say. Jude made it sound like the Fatales were completely free, but they actually hadn't received too fair of a trade. They weren't free at all – just remote prisoners.

On the opposite wall from the doorway, there were large brown curtains pulled closed. He walked over and pulled them back to reveal a window. It was completely black outside, but he could not see a single star in the sky. Very unusual, if they were out away from any cities, Cadan thought as he studied the darkness.

Jude saw the confused look on his face. "That's not the kind of window that you're used to. It's a monitor-window."

"A what?"

"We call it a monitor-window. It's actually a giant LCD screen. The controls are over there to the right of the screen; you can choose what you want to view on the screen."

Cadan found the control panel and pressed a random button. On the screen a jungle appeared, complete with the lush green foliage and insects buzzing by. A sloth swung from a tree far in the background. Close to the front, a frog made its standard *ribbit* sound. He was surprised at how real the monitor looked on the wall. The resolution was so high he actually felt as if he were staring out a glass pane in the jungle. The desired effect actually worked on him; he immediately felt a soothing sensation.

"That's pretty cool, huh?" Jude smiled. "I usually only turn it on at night, when I try to go to sleep. I try all of the different ones, just to keep things interesting."

"What's wrong with a real window? Surely we have a nice view if we're in the mountains."

"Well, that's the thing. We're actually *in* a mountain."

"As in underground?"

"Sort of. We're not below the ground in a sense, but we are inside a mountain – the entire base is inside the mountain. We've pretty much stayed in the center of the base – the infirmary is the lowest you've been so far and Josiah's office is just a few floors from the top. Right now we're in between those two floors."

"So the screen just gives the effect that we're outside."

"Yes, and it works. They have to hide the base inside a mountain to help make our location a secret. Nobody would even know to look for us here, but they are afraid that people may stumble upon us accidently. Josiah told me that a group of campers found the base once by accident. They were actually climbing the side of the mountain and saw one of the hangar doors. He said that they had to erase that part of their minds and drop them off in another location."

"It doesn't seem right to play with people's minds like that."

"He said that he doesn't enjoy that aspect of the job, but that it's a necessary evil. Our secrecy is of the utmost importance."

"What, is he afraid that the government will kidnap us and perform experiments on us?"

The irony was not lost on Jude.

"You really are uptight, Cadan. If you keep throwing out comments like that, you will never get to go on a mission with us."

Cadan had forgotten his pledge to play this game. "I'm sorry," he lied. "It's just all so scary to me, and that's my coping mechanism."

"No worries. So how old are you?"

"Seventeen. I'll be eighteen in three months. How old are you?"

"I'll be eighteen in four months. I want to have a cool birthday party."

"They let you have parties?"

"Of course. We just have to get it cleared. We usually have little parties, either in the cafeteria or in the lounge down the hall."

"What are parties here like?"

"It depends. If it's just our Facility, they're usually fairly boring. Except when we fight, which seems to happen often enough. But if we time it right and some of the other agents from the other Facilities are here, then we have a great time."

"How many other Facilities are there?"

"Not sure exactly. I know of seven other than this one. Six of those have agents and most of them are our age. There are some jerks in each of them, but a few of the agents are my friends. You'd like them."

"I'm sure," Cadan lied again. He sat down on his bed, which was actually made. Jude had thrown some of his clothes on the center of the bed, and there were a few books laid on top. Cadan noticed *The Hunchback of Notre Dame* and *The Complete Works of Shakespeare*. He could not see a connection between the two, so he asked. "You like these?"

"Yes," Jude nodded. "I don't get a chance to read much, but I like books about Europe. I've always wanted to go. We have a library upstairs that has a really good selection."

Cadan had never been to Europe either – in fact, he had not travelled more than a few hours from home. The little town of Iowa Park, Texas just west of Wichita Falls, was where he had spent most of his childhood years. His family had been to several states and national parks no more than a few hours from home and that was the extent of their travels.

"So have you travelled much?"

"We do get vacations, but DOMA regulates the when and where. It's usually at the camp grounds in Oklahoma. We get a few shopping excursions if we're good, but that's about it."

"What about before you were taken by DOMA? Did you travel then?"

"There was no Before-DOMA for me. I was born here and have been here ever since."

"Where are your parents?"

That seemed to be a sore subject for Jude. "They died when I was younger. Josiah has been like my father ever since."

So they had something in common, Cadan thought. He wanted to ask Jude more about his parents, but decided against it. The topic seemed to take him out of his ever present jovial mood and onto the precipice of some dark place.

Jude's eyes returned to their usual luster as he continued. "I spent most of my time at the Great Lakes Facility, which has always been nicknamed 'The Nursery.' If DOMA finds a child that is too young for training, or if a magic-wielder already in DOMA has a child, they are raised at the Nursery. It's one of the prettiest Facilities, nestled somewhere between Lake Huron and the Georgian Bay on a little peninsula. I was relocated to the Rocky Mountains when I was eleven; Josiah began training me then." From the look on his face, those seemed to be happy memories. "So what about you?"

"What about me?"

"Well, where were you born and all that? What are your parents like?"

Was he asking this out of sheer curiosity and just trying to get to know Cadan, or did he have an ulterior motive? Cadan knew that Josiah was a father figure to Jude, and this seemed to be information that Josiah would love to possess. A simple lie wouldn't work with Jude, Cadan knew. He would have to fabricate a larger story for this to work, and the larger the story was, the harder it would be to maintain. He had to think and think fast. Jude seemed quick enough to catch contradictions.

"My parents both died when I was a baby, too," Cadan admitted. That part was at least true. "My uncle took me in, but he was abusive, so when I was seven I ran away and have lived on the streets ever since."

"How did you learn to use the ruhk-magic?"

"Like I told Josiah, I had to learn to defend myself. People tried to mess with me, and I just learned how to deal with them the most efficient way I could."

"And that's how you learned to be such a good sword fighter?"

"Yes."

"You had a sword?"

"Um no, I used boards, poles or whatever else I could find."

"But if you used a pole, that's completely different from the sword. I have practiced and practiced on the sword, but can never quite get the hang of it like I can with the staff. I thought sword fighting was just one of those things that you had to pick up with an actual sword."

"I don't know," Cadan shrugged. "I guess I'm just naturally good. I'm not sure."

"Was your mother or father an elf?"

"What?"

"I can tell you're half-elf like I am. My father was an elf, and my mother was human. See." He pulled his hair back, and Cadan noticed a slight, upturned point of the top of each ear. It wasn't actually a fine point like the elves he had seen in books, but it rose up a little higher than a normal human ear. He pointed to his eyebrows. "See how our eyebrows have a slightly higher arch and go up a little higher on the sides than regular humans?"

"I've never noticed that." That was an honest response. Cadan had never paid attention to the slight difference. He walked over to the mirror next to Jude's bed. Just as Jude said, his eyebrows were higher. He lifted a giant tangle of curly hair from the sides of his head and studied his own ears. Sure enough, he had the slightly raised point. Was that why Simon had always cut his hair, but never seemed to take much off? Derrick always had shorter hair, but not Cadan. Daphne often commented on how his blonde curls were beautiful, and how Simon should never cut them off. Was this their reason? How could he have missed this?

"Elves almost always have really light blonde hair and sharp pointed ears," Jude explained. "They are usually thinner than humans because of their physiology. Sometimes, elven features in men make them appear effeminate."

Cadan remembered the dream of his parents and his mother's face. She had long, light blonde hair, and he vaguely remembered thinking that her ears looked odd. Her eyebrows were well manicured, so it was difficult to say if they were arched or not, but she did have very delicate features on a narrow face. His mother must be an elf.

"I guess my mother was," he finally answered. It was another statement he could make without lying. Maybe this wasn't going to be as hard as he thought. "I don't remember them very well at all, but if one of them was an elf, then it would have to be my mother."

"So you had no idea you were part elf?"

"No, not until now."

"What about your features? You never noticed those before?"

"No, I didn't."

"To human eyes we look very different."

When Cadan started junior high, the other boys had begun calling him names. They said that he looked like a girl or just ridiculed him for looking strange. At the time, he thought they were just being mean. Derrick had approached the ring leader of the group and hit him in the face several times, and the name calling had stopped for a time. Cadan never made many friends after that, but at least there was a respite to the name calling. Derrick could be scrappy enough when necessity dictated, and everyone was scared of him after that.

Jude could tell that the direction of the conversation was not a happy one, so he tried to lighten the mood. "There are positives to being an elf. Have you ever noticed that you have more stamina that a regular human?"

Cadan knew immediately what Jude was talking about. He had run cross country in high school and always won. He was the fastest of anyone at his school and could run the longest without tiring. He took first place in every competition in his district and always won a place at the State competition held in Austin each year. With little explanation provided, Simon would never let him go. He had just learned to accept it. Soccer was another of his favorite sports, and he was the only member of the team who could play the whole hour long game without needing a substitute to take his place on the field.

"Yes, now that you mention it." He told Jude about his cross country meets and soccer games.

"You are definitely half-elf. That's awesome! See, we do have a lot in common. We'll be good roommates."

He was not as hopeful. He glanced around the room and groaned inwardly.

"Have you ever met a full elf?"

"Of course. There are a few here and there are even more in the other facilities. Do you remember the girl the other night with the bow and arrows? Her name is Madison, and she's full blooded elf."

"She had good aim." He remembered the sword popping from his hand.

"Oh yeah, very good aim. You didn't even see her at her best. It's a natural talent with most elves, and Madison is one of the best. She is even good with a gun, but much prefers the bow and arrow. You'll get to officially meet her in just a bit. Don't be put off by her gruff demeanor, she's actually pretty cool."

"I'm sure we'll get along great." This time the sarcasm was neither fake nor sign of a bad attitude. Jude rolled back in the bed laughing.

"So what keeps people from using their crazy powers and busting out of here?" Cadan asked. He didn't want to make Jude suspicious, but thought the question was innocent enough.

"Do you feel any pain in the back of your neck?"

"A little," Cadan admitted. He hadn't thought about it yet, but there had been a tiny pain at the base of his neck when we woke earlier. He had thought it was just the lingering effects of the fight that night in Manhattan.

"It's a tracking beacon. They can find us no matter where we are. Anyone involved with DOMA has one. All individuals, all levels. Josiah told me that even he has one. The Femme Fatales have one, and even the soldiers who are stationed here have one. If you are strong enough, smart enough, and lucky enough, you could possibly break out of here. But DOMA would know where you are. Every facility administrator has access to the tracking system, so even the other Facilities could find you. There would be no point in trying to run."

"Can the beacons be disabled?"

"No one has ever tried. I wouldn't even know how to disable them. They're microscopic and can't be seen without a magnifying device, so it's not like there's a switch inside. They're water proof since they're in our bodies, so you can't just throw water on them. Are you already planning a prison break?" He laughed again, this time more from discomfort than humor.

"Just wondering," he shrugged. "To tell you the truth, I think I may like it here after all. Talking to you has made me feel a little better about this." That was not a lie. Cadan did feel very comfortable with Jude – possibly a little too comfortable. He had to remember who they were working for, and that anything he said would likely find its way back to Josiah. "I lived on the streets before, so this can't be any worse."

Jude looked very pleased. "I'm glad to hear that. I think we can be good friends. Just give this place a chance, okay?"

"Sure," he nodded. He wasn't sure if Jude's words were propaganda brought on by Josiah's brainwashing or if they were genuine. Jude seemed to be a nice and interesting guy, and Cadan made a mental note to give him a chance. He remembered something that had been nagging at him since he woke up that morning. Well, he assumed it had been morning, but since they were underground with fake windows, he had no way of knowing. "Can I ask you something?"

"Shoot."

"How were you all able to track me that night in Manhattan?"

"We didn't."

"But you all followed me for a while until that troll showed up. How did you find me? Was it just a coincidence that the troll showed up?"

"We weren't following you. The computers here showed a gateway opened in Manhattan, and since the New York agents and the Paladins here were occupied with another mission, Josiah sent Nate and the Knights to apprehend the troll. We found you by accident."

"But someone or something was following me before I ever saw the troll."

"Maybe you're just a paranoid person. Did you ever see anyone?"

"No, just weird noises and stuff. And I'm not a paranoid person. I swear there was someone following me."

"Well, it wasn't us. We were laying a trap for the troll, and trying to stay off the busy streets. We were getting ready to send our own bait, when you came along and played the part nicely for us. We didn't expect to find a skilled ruhk-wielding warrior waiting for us. We were as surprised your presence there as you were of ours."

So it wasn't the DOMA agents following him before the troll happened along. That left three alternatives: Jude was lying, he was going crazy, or there was indeed someone else following him. At this point his roommate was his only friend, leaving none of the options optimal. His mind wandered to the dark figure from the dream. Was there any connection? At least he was now locked behind solid walls with armed forces everywhere.

"So Jason and Clay seem like real charmers," Cadan noted sarcastically.

"You'll find that those two goons are always in trouble. If they weren't so strong and such good fighters, they would never have made Paladin status. They're hard to control and very stupid, but some of the best fighters DOMA has. Josiah made them stay back when the Paladins went out on their mission, so when the troll threat came on the screen, he reluctantly let them go with us. Manhattan is so densely populated that it's much harder to deal with those situations."

"How did you contain the troll?

"We used a little device called a numina stone," Jude explained. Cadan wanted to comment, but knew that he had to feign ignorance to maintain his ruse. Jude continued the account. "The numina stones can aid a ruhk-wielder to accomplish certain spells or can enhance abilities. The one that Nate used was called a garnet, and it can control certain species and some animals."

He had heard of a normal garnet, but never heard of a garnet numina. "Can it control humans?"

"No," Jude shook his head. "For some reason, it can't control humans. But they have been used to control trolls, goblins, or griffins."

"Goblins and griffins?!" It was a storybook come to life.

"Oh yes, we have a few goblins here but the griffins are held elsewhere. They are too large and need too much space to be kept inside a mountain."

"So what do you do about all of those people that saw the troll?"

"What do you think?"

"More mind scrambling?"

"Of course."

"Sounds fun."

"It's not that difficult of a spell to perform. It's painless for the people we perform it on, and it only affects the memories that the spell caster specifies."

Maybe the spell could work the other way. Was it possible that someone could perform the reverse on him and unlock memories of his parents?

Chapter Seven

Jude checked the watch on his wrist. The small gold clock was mounted on a thick band of leather – Cadan liked the watch and thought it look rustic, but sophisticated at the same time.

"Lunch was served for agents about two minutes ago. We should probably get up there."

The mention of food reminded him that he was starving. He did not know if they had fed him while he was asleep, but the noise in his stomach indicated that if they had, it hadn't been much.

"You'll get a chance to meet the Knights and Paladins."

"I've met the Knights." Well not really, but he had tussled with them already.

Jude smiled. "Well, now you'll have a chance to get acquainted with them better. Hopefully they won't hold the fight against you for too long."

"Why would they hold it against me?"

"Um, let's see. We train and train and then some random magic-wielder we find on the streets somehow nearly bests the whole team. Nate had to take you down with a blast of ruhk-fire – which I should mention was entirely out of line. I was pretty pissed at him for doing that. He could have hurt you with all of the power he packed into it. But they didn't like the fact that you took everyone down. Especially Jason and Clay. They'll do everything they can get away with to make your life miserable."

"Great."

"But don't worry. The Knights stick together. The two teams are competitive by nature, and I'm sure the other Knights will stick up for you, even if it's for the simple fact that they don't care much for the Paladins."

"Well, that's some consolation." Cadan forced a laugh.

"You can change first if you want to."

Cadan realized that he was still wearing the same clothes he wore from the other night. "I don't have any other clothes."

"You're about the same size as me. Dig through my stuff and see if there's something you like."

He decided that borrowed clothes – even dirty clothes from the floor of their room – would be better than what he had been wearing for days now. He rummaged around and found a dark blue shirt and a pair of cargo pants. Luckily he had been smart enough to pack a few pair of extra underwear, so he could change out of the ones that he had been wearing for far too long. He stepped into the kitchen for some privacy and removed his dingy garments and replaced them with the new outfit that Jude provided. When he went back into the room, Jude had found a pair of simple brown shoes similar to the ones that he was wearing.

"Thank you," Cadan smiled.

"No problem," Jude nodded. He was actually trying to put some of the clothes into a drawer, as if tidying up for five seconds would make a bit of difference with the cluster he allowed his room to degrade into. "We'll talk to Josiah about letting you make a special shopping trip so that we can get you a wardrobe. They'll deliver some standard issue uniforms. Our first class of the week is tomorrow, so you can borrow one of my uniforms."

"I don't have any money."

"Um, you work for the government now. We got government plastic," he smiled as he rubbed his thumbs against his fingers, indicating that there was a lot of money at their disposal. "And we have laundry service. Every morning, a bag is left outside, and we have to fill it up with dirty laundry before we leave for breakfast. The clothes are returned that evening before dinner."

"Cool," was all Cadan said, as he slid the shoes on his feet. They were a perfect fit.

They left the room, and Jude inserted the key back into the door before leaving. Apparently re-inserting the key locked the door. Cadan checked his pocket to make sure that his key was in there. He didn't anticipate venturing off on his own, but one could never be too prepared, especially after being nabbed by magic-tracking, experimenting, deranged government types.

The cafeteria was only one floor up from the dormitory level, so the elevator ride was short. Once the door opened, Cadan saw the first sign that there was other life at the Facility – and a lot of it. People of all kinds were walking to and fro in a bustle around the foyer outside the elevator. Already several had finished their meal and were waiting on the elevator to get there. The ones standing outside the elevator were all human. He guessed that they were the soldiers Jude had told him about. Two fauns near one wall were talking in hushed tones. Neither of them were Hadrian, whom he had met earlier, although he had to admit that it would be hard to tell the difference. They all had the same color hair and styled in much the same way. One of the fauns appeared female because of her features and that fact that the hair didn't come down as far on her face.

Jude nodded to the soldiers – three men and two women – as they stepped off the elevator and towards a door that led into the kitchen. The kitchen had the typical appearance of a high school cafeteria with a rack for the trays to slide on. There was a long metal buffet with several cooks and servers on the back side, waiting to hand food choices to their customers. Jude grabbed two trays and handed one to Cadan. They slid them on the conveyor in front of the buffet.

Behind the buffet line, the kitchen was active. There were sinks against the back wall and stoves and ovens against the right one. The entire wall on the left was packed with various boxes, cooking implements, and other supplies.

Cadan noticed the cooks for the first time. Out of the six individuals standing behind the counter, only two were human. He recognized the little gnome Gladiola standing on a stool and stirring a pot laid over one of the burners. She glanced back and saw them enter and greeted them with a smile and a brief wave before continuing her work. The creature in the back was a goblin – or so Cadan guessed – from his trademark green, leathery skin and permanent scowl. His eyes were deep yellow like – well the first thing that came to his mind was urine. *That's kind of gross,* Cadan thought to himself, trying not to laugh.

First they had to pick their choice of meat: chicken, beef, or pork. There was a tall man standing behind the counter at that point, waiting to serve. Cadan could not stop staring; the individual standing in front of him was human from the waist up. Where his waist ended, a horse started. It was like someone took the head and neck off of a horse and stuck the top half of a human there. He remembered reading about creatures like this, and knew that the legends called them centaurs. He made a mental note to ask Jude, and make sure that was what they were called. Jude talked to the centaur as they passed, and Cadan learned that his name was Irion.

Cadan smiled at the centaur as he took his chicken and set it on the tray. The next part of the line was for the side dishes. A faun took their orders and handed them their choices. Jude talked to the faun as well, but Cadan could not catch his name.

They picked out beverages themselves and were able to choose from a small assortment of desserts. After setting their cups down on the tray, Jude made for the door, and Cadan followed right behind. He could hear from the noise ahead that there was quite a crowd in the eating area, and he was more than a little intimidated.

As they walked into a room filled with tables, he quickly estimated about twenty people were in the room. There were over a dozen tables placed in four rows. The first table was close to the kitchen door, and he immediately recognized two people. How could anyone forget such faces? And those grotesque faces were sneering at him.

Six people sat at the table, three on each side. Jude leaned over and told Cadan their names in a hushed tone. Jason's ugly face towered over the other five, while Clay's equally disturbing face was now missing its helmet and was level with everyone else's chest. Those two weren't the only ones staring at him; the other four at the table were watching as well. On the side with Clay was another guy, Anthony, with buzz cut short hair and a stern expression across his well-defined face. The girl sitting next to him, Carmen, had long, curly blonde hair and distinctly elven features. Her eyes were large and pretty, giving her the appearance of someone with a bubbly demeanor, although Cadan detected and undercurrent of cruelty behind them.

Across from them were another guy and girl. Russell looked like a typical gothic guy: his clothes were all black, with a silver detail here and there, his hair was cut short in the back and fell down his face in the front, and there was even a trace of eyeliner and possibly concealer on his face. His expression spoke pain, cruelty, and anguish; his eyes made you feel like he could and would transfer those emotions to any victim at any given moment. The girl, Heather, did not look like she belonged. Her skin was naturally tan, and long straight brown hair framed a pretty face. She stared at him the same way as her tablemates, but her demeanor was different. It made Cadan feel even more uncomfortable.

They passed another table with two fauns and two gnomes sitting across from each other. The table across from them had four Pixies sitting on the tabletop and eating from miniature plates.

They sat opposite each other at an empty table. Jude sat on the end of one bench, and Cadan took the place directly across from him.

"Where are the Knights?" he asked.

"They will be here shortly," Jude answered. "We're late to everything." He smiled.

Cadan had just bit into his chicken when a tray slammed down next to Jude. The blonde girl from the other night was sneering down at him. Even with her nose wrinkled, she was beautiful. Her skin was pale, and her eyes were the shape of large almonds, her irises, the color of a clear sky, outlined by a little too much eyeliner. Her wavy blonde hair fell behind her shoulders, revealing her pointed ears. She was wearing tight blue jeans that accentuated her curves and a shirt that hung off her shoulders and didn't quite make it down to the top of her jeans. The excessive amount of bracelets she wore clanked as she moved her arms.

Jude began the introductions. "This lovely young scorpion is Madison Taylor." He motioned to the elf girl.

"Nice to meet you, Madison."

She sneered again and began eating her food.

There wasn't much time to worry about awkward silences, as the other three arrived shortly. The girl sat next to Cadan, and the two guys took their places on the opposite end.

"These two are the twins Darius and Natalie Gibson." Jude indicated the girl sitting next to Cadan and the guy on her other side. He was a few inches taller than Cadan, and his smooth, cleanly shaven head gleamed in the light while Natalie had jet black braids that hung halfway down her back. The smooth dark complexion of their skin was interrupted only by the light violet of their irises, giving them both an exotic look. In any other setting, he would have assumed they were colored contact lenses, but in this place, he was sure they were natural. Both were very slender but muscular. When Jude said their names, they both nodded in Cadan's direction and went back to their plates.

"Our big man here is Bryce Beck." He was actually the kindest of all. He smiled and said a soft hello; it was a strange voice from such a large guy. And then he remembered why Bryce was so large. Underneath his arms was another set of arms. Those extra appendages and the massive bulk of muscles added an extra two feet to his height.

When Cadan turned back from meeting Bryce, a lone figure at a far table caught his eye. It was Nate.

Jude must have followed his gaze. "Grumpy over there is our fearless leader Nate Carter." He leaned in closer and whispered. "He is still a little sore about the whole knife-in-the-shoulder debacle."

Natalie leaned over and added in a hushed tone. "But I thought it was brilliant."

"Thanks," he quietly responded.

"Don't get the wrong impression, boy." Madison stopped eating for a moment. "She is not saying that out of respect for you, but more disdain for him. So please don't believe that was a compliment."

"I can speak for myself." Natalie said.

Madison never bothered to turn her head, but simply cut her eyes in the other girl's direction. "Only on the rare occasion your brother is not speaking for you."

"I don't speak for my sister," mumbled Darius.

"No, you just control her," Madison shot back.

"I'm just protective," he explained. "You would be too in a place like this."

"If that's what you have to tell yourself to sleep at night, little raven, then keep at it."

Jude saw the puzzled expression on Cadan's face, and shook his head as if to tell him not to say anything. *Do not ask about the raven comment. I will tell you later.*

Hearing Jude's voice in his head startled him. Mental conversations were one of the many tricks that Simon had taught them when they were much younger and had encouraged its use for practice. He would never admit it to anyone out loud, but he and Derrick had used the trick on more than one exam in school. He was about to respond in the same manner, but then thought twice. If he were to communicate with Jude in such a manner, it would reveal that he knew a more refined use of the ruhk-magic that could not be learned on one's own. But Jude was watching him and by the other boy's expression, he knew that the voice in Cadan's head was no big surprise.

He decided to place a small deal of trust in his new friend. *Your team seems to get along fabulously.*

They shared a smile. *Don't you mean* our *team?*

I guess you're right. But seriously, out of all of the staff here, there isn't one therapist that can help us?

They chuckled out loud.

Madison head darted between the two of him. "So you've already taught him to talk in your head?" She did not look too happy.

Jude spoke out loud. "Madison is a little upset that she can't talk mentally very well. She was born with enough ruhk-magic ability to set a piece of paper on fire."

She huffed at him and glared. "I couldn't have it all. With all of this intelligence and gorgeousness in one package, there wasn't much room for anything else."

"If that's what you have to tell yourself to sleep at night," Darius quipped, turning her own line against her.

She shrieked, reached down and grabbed one of her rolls, and hurled it at his face. They both laughed.

See, they can get along. He and Jude laughed.

"You did some mighty fine sword work the other night, Cadan," Madison smiled. Her compliment actually seemed genuine. "Now we finally have someone who can take Anthony on in the competitions."

"Competitions?" Cadan asked.

"Once a week we have a scrimmage. The Knights versus the Paladins. The winners get some sort of privilege or reward."

"How does your – err, I mean our – team usually fare?"

"I've been on this team for three years now, and we haven't won once," she revealed with a somber expression.

Cadan was not able to hide his horrific expression. "When is our next competition?"

"In three hours," said Jude.

"What? I don't think I'm ready for that."

"You won't have to participate. You usually get to observe one first," Jude explained.

"So why do we lose all of the time?" Cadan asked innocently, immediately regretting the decision. He was afraid that it was a bad question to ask with this volatile group.

"Where do I begin? We only have another half hour of lunch, so of course that's only time enough for half the reasons." Madison turned her head quickly to Nate, and then back again. Her voice went softer. "With better leadership, we might have a shot."

"He's not a good leader?"

"He just has a bad attitude about his position," Jude explained, and his tone said that he was trying to relieve some of the blame from their leader. "Up until six months ago, he was a full fledged member of the Paladins and went with them on missions. He advanced in his training, and Josiah wanted to give him the chance to show his leadership."

"Why couldn't he lead the Paladins?"

"Have you seen Anthony?" Jude asked sarcastically. "That boy is like the epitome of a military man. He gets his team out on the field and he bosses them around like they're his own arms. Grueling taskmaster stuff. He's successful as a leader, but he would never be a follower. He would rather eat troll crap than take an order from someone. I've seen him roll his eyes at taking orders from Josiah."

"So why not let them take turns, or let Anthony be our team leader instead?"

"Because Anthony is DOMA's golden boy. He gets the results. He has never failed on a mission."

Cadan turned to Natalie, Darius, and Bryce. "I meant to apologize for the other night. About the whole fight thing."

Darius turned to him with eyes so serious, he thought he might get punched right there. "If it had been me in your shoes, I would have put up a fight too. Don't worry about it, man. Seriously."

Natalie turned to him. "My brother and I were taken much like you, but without all of the fighting."

"When were y'all taken?" Cadan asked. He thought better of his question. "Actually it's none of my business. I'm sorry for asking."

"It sucks to talk about, but as teammates it is best if we get to know each other, so we can understand where everyone is coming from." She paused and stared at her brother for an instant. Then she took a deep breath. "In the span of a few days, both my gift and Darius's wings manifested themselves. This was about two years ago."

Darius interrupted briefly. "Imagine the problems of puberty, and on top of that you got two giant black wings that keep popping out of your back at random times."

Natalie continued. "Our parents found out, and they were pissed. They were both very into their church, but not in the good Christian way. They were more interested in the parts of the Bible that spoke of God's judgment. My dad beat the ever loving fire out of Darius. When I saw my brother go down and the blood started pouring from his mouth, I had had enough. I used ruhk-magic against my father. I slammed his sorry butt into the wall."

Darius picked up the story, as he could tell this part was too hard for his sister. "I can remember the looks on their faces. It was hatred mixed with anger. My mother finally quit crying long enough to try and make excuses for our father. We ran away from home, and within a week, DOMA had apprehended us."

"Did you ever find out what happened to your parents?" Cadan asked.

"That's the messed up part," Natalie chimed back in. "We found out later from Josiah that our parents went to the press for attention. There was a news article printed in the local paper where our parents warned everyone that we were demon children. My father survived his fight with the drywall that I sent him through and continued in his arrogant ways. We haven't heard asked about them since."

"I'm sorry to hear that," Cadan said.

"Don't be sorry," Darius shook his head. "They didn't understand what was happening to us. She and I had time to adjust the supernatural things going down, so we were prepared. My dad was introduced to it all when he accidentally walked in on me in my bedroom."

"It doesn't excuse his behavior, though," Natalie told him. It was obvious that the discussion had come up many times before.

"No it doesn't, and I'm sure that deep down he has had to live with the consequences of his actions every day."

Don't ask about Bryce's past. Sensitive topic. Jude shook his head so slightly that Cadan barely noticed.

Nate had finished his meal and left his table in a huff, without a single word to any of his teammates. Everyone watched him briefly and then turned back to their food.

Cadan asked, "So why doesn't Nate sit with the Paladins? Wouldn't he be happier there?"

"They won't let him," Madison explained. "They've given him a hard time ever since he was transferred to the Knights. Plus, he's held this secret grudge against Anthony ever since."

"This place has a lot of drama," Cadan noted with a chuckle.

Madison laughed too. "And you came in with some, my dear. Nate and the Paladins don't like you. Heck, I'm not even sure about you." She winked at him.

"Why would all of the Paladins dislike me?"

"A myriad of reasons." She took a swig of her soda. "For starters, Clay and Jason hate you because you made them look like complete idiots the other night. No loss there for anyone because they are, in fact, complete idiots. Secondly, Anthony won't like you because you show promise. You come in here with all of this knowledge and skill, and from what Josiah says, you are very powerful. Anthony will see you as future competition."

"What about the others?"

"Russell is the guy dressed in nothing but black, and he hates anything that moves, as well as most things that don't. Carmen is one of the most recent additions to DOMA. She was a late bloomer, and actually kept her elven heritage and magical abilities a secret until she was fifteen. She was captain of her cheerleading team and all around Miss Popular at her high school. DOMA, suspicious of her stamina and strength, investigated and found out that her father could use ruhk-magic and her mother was an elf, so they were all brought into DOMA."

"How is she already a Paladin?"

"She was a Knight for about two months. Her father had already taught her much of what she should know before she even got here, so it didn't take long for her to advance."

"Where are her parents now?"

"Dead. They tried to break out and shot several guards. They were both executed," Madison explained.

"That's horrible."

"You say that, but you never met them. They were horrible people. Very nasty. They used their powers to gain a bunch of wealth and were total snobs. If you ask me, Carmen is much better off without them."

The worst part was that Cadan found their situations somewhat similar. If Simon and Daphne had been taken along with Derrick and Raney, their father would not have hesitated to try and break them out. Wouldn't any parent who unconditionally loved their child do the same?

Madison continued. "Now Heather, that's a completely different story. She is the strangest one. Looks real normal, but there's just something not right with her. She is always quiet and just sort of stares at everyone."

"She has a thing for Cadan," Natalie threw in.

"What?" Madison turned and looked at her with a smile. "How do you know?"

"Did you see the way she was checking him out as he walked in?"

"Maybe she was checking out Jude," Cadan spoke quickly.

"That's who she usually stares at," Darius chuckled. "But maybe she has a new victim for her stalking."

Cadan needed to change the subject fast. The last thing he needed right now was some girl stalking him. "So is it hard to advance to Paladin? I mean, it seems like all of you are as good, if not better, than some of the Paladins." He wasn't sure how they would take it after he finished the sentence. There wasn't an easy way to say that, but he was honestly very curious. For a moment after he asked the question everyone looked around at each other as if looking for someone to respond.

Natalie laughed and answered. "Baby, you are looking at the cream of the DOMA crop here. But we at this table have one quality that DOMA hates."

"What is that?"

"Unpredictability," answered Madison. "We are the bad seeds in the garden."

"You all seem fine to me."

"Oh, we're definitely fine," Darius winked as he finished his desert.

Madison continued. "But we have what Josiah calls 'bad attitudes.' We suck at following orders, especially if they're from Nate. Natalie would rather spend her time playing with computers, Darius here has a temper unmatched by anyone, and even though Bryce can lift a car with three arms tied behind his back or punch you so hard that your brain would fall out the back, he'd rather be in his room playing with his teddy bear."

"I would not!"

"Bryce, my dear, who has a night light?"

"Madison, leave him alone," Jude put a hand on her shoulder. He turned to Cadan. "And Madison is cruel and thoughtless."

"Entirely," she smiled, as if proud. "And Jude here is impetuous and arrogant."

"I am not. I'm just good looking and aware of that fact."

"Yes, my dear you are definitely that, but being aware of your own looks detracts from said looks."

To sum it up, Darius said, "So, Cadan, you are basically hanging with the freaks."

Jude spoke up, lifting his glass in mockery of a toast. "We're like the Bad News Cubs."

Cadan considered correcting him, but knew it would burst his ego a little. No, he decided to let him have his moment.

They all laughed together.

Chapter Eight

He had mixed feelings about his team. On one hand they seemed crazy and as dysfunctional as a daytime soap opera. With personalities as large as a troll and even bigger egos, he wasn't sure if he cared to get to know them at all. Why waste the time when he planned on breaking free from this bizarre nightmare the first chance he got? They didn't seem completely happy with being here either, but were apparently content with their lot. On the other hand, they were like one big family, but with a few extra arms and some wings thrown in to make it more interesting. They were weird, but in the same vein, so was his own family. He was always surrounded by the freaks in life.

DOMA scheduled a short period for their food to digest in between lunch and the training session. He and Jude bid farewell to the Knights and went back to the elevator. Jude wanted to show him the Library, the next stop on the tour. They had to wait in a short line.

"So what do you think of the Knights?" Jude asked.

Cadan wasn't quite sure what to say. "They seem ... entertaining."

Jude laughed. "Definitely that. A lot of attitude, but a lot of heart."

"I can tell," he shook his head. "It sounds like they're at each other's throats all of the time, but underneath all of that, they love each other."

"Well said," agreed Jude.

"So are bad attitudes the real reason the Knights haven't been promoted?"

"That is one of the larger problems, yes."

"What are the others?"

"Each of the Knights has some sort of block," Jude explained. His voice had lowered so that only Cadan could hear. There were some soldiers a few feet away at the elevator. "Take Bryce for instance. We were joking with him at lunch, but everything we said was true. He's as strong as ten oxen, but scared of his own shadow. Absolutely zero self esteem. And he really does have a teddy bear in his bed. Natalie has some sort of block on her mind when it comes to using ruhk-magic. Josiah has tried working with her individually, but I think it's much the same as Bryce. She just needs a little confidence boost."

"What about Darius?"

"That's a long story," Jude explained. "The facility in Florida is known as the Aviary, and it's where DOMA sends all of the seraphs."

"What's a seraph?"

"A seraph is a specialized group of elves," he explained. "Every so often an elf is born with large plush white wings on their back. Their training usually involves a lot of fighting techniques in the air, so DOMA has always kept them at a separate Facility. When there's a dragon to apprehend, they're great to have."

"Dragon?!"

"Shhh," Jude hissed as he looked around. "Yes, DOMA has taken down a couple dragons over the past few decades. Not common at all, but they show up occasionally. Now, would you quit interrupting, or you'll never get the first question answered."

"Sorry."

Jude smiled. "No worries. You see, before Darius, all seraphs were elves, which meant that they were blonde haired, blue eyes, and always beautiful. You can imagine that a big group of pretty people can carry quite a bag of pretentiousness with them. Well, DOMA originally tried to reassign Darius to the Aviary, but he was transferred back two weeks later."

"What happened?"

"He won't say much about the specifics, but it couldn't have been pretty. Natalie said that he was never the same after that. Apparently they did not accept him and ridiculed him at every turn. No one would be his roommate and no one would train with him."

"What a bunch of jerks."

"Oh, they are so much more than jerks. You'll meet some of them eventually, and they are the worst sort. They are cruel to other non-seraph elves, and they especially despise half-elves. They're so nasty; you'd be better off having lunch with the Paladins instead."

"So that makes the two of us high up on their favorites list?"

"We're real close to the top of *a* list ... their hit list."

They both laughed, and then it was their turn to get in the elevator.

Just one floor up, the elevator opened into the Library. The foyer was much like the one outside of Josiah's office; it had the same style of decorations and furnishings. However, while they his office look sparse, here it seemed like every inch of space was taken up. Shelves of books and artifacts of all sizes and shapes, and from different historical periods, covered every surface. In the middle of the foyer area, there were mounds of books stacked up next to each other as if the place had suddenly run out of shelf room.

"The kid that works down here is a little odd," Jude warned.

"Odd how?"

"Just wait," Jude smiled and led Cadan into the library proper.

Once through the main entryway, he was greeted with the most spectacular sight since arriving at the Facility. He never knew that so many books existed! The room they entered was a perfect square, every space of wall lined by dark wood shelves. The only break in the shelves was the other three archways, one on each wall. There were dark oak tables scattered about the room, and each was littered with even more books. The floors were covered in yet more wood, but adorned with drab rugs of various colors.

Through the trio of archways, he could see identical rooms in every direction, three more opposite the elevator and one on each side.

Instead of a ceiling, there was a large opening in the center. He moved to the center of the room and stared up; there was another room above with shelves surrounding those walls. One floor with twelve rooms was just not enough to hold it all – they had to have twelve more above. He wondered if someone had attempted to count the collection.

The Library was quiet, the quietest area he had encountered so far in the Facility. It wasn't until he had walked into the Library that he noticed all of the other rooms had the hum of machinery behind the walls. But in the library, he could not hear a single sound.

He took a moment to look at the nearest shelf. From their appearance, the books ranged in age. One book looked so ancient that he was afraid if he touched it, it may fall into a pile of dust in his fingers. The next book was a new release best seller that Simon had recently read. It was quite an odd arrangement.

"What do you think?"

"This is marvelous. I love this room."

"I figured you would. I like it down here too because it is so quiet. It's a nice place to come and think. Some of the back rooms have reading chairs and couches."

"There are so many books. Is every room this full?"

"Yes, and the back areas are even more crowded."

"So where is this weirdo that runs the library?"

"I don't so much run the library," a voice came from behind them. Jude smiled as Cadan whirled around. "It's more like I try to keep it tidy and organized."

"I'm sorry, I –"

"No, it's quite alright," the boy said as he came closer. "I really am quite the strange one."

There was nothing remarkable about his appearance. He was a few inches shorter than Cadan, with a very thin build. His hair was black and cut close to his head, and eyes were a light orange. Thick black framed glasses sat atop his face, and as he entered the room, he pushed them further up on his nose. An olive skin tone gave him the appearance of Latin or Middle Eastern heritage, but Cadan couldn't quite place it. Both his sweater and khaki pants were dirty, which Cadan guessed was dust from the Library. He was pushing a loaded book cart into the room with him.

"Cadan, this is our resident librarian, Tomas Reis,' Jude introduced them. "Tomas, this is the new recruit, Cadan."

"Pleased to meet you," Tomas nodded, without extending a hand to shake. It was obvious that he wasn't very socially adept, but he didn't seem to be offended by Cadan's name calling.

"And I should come to Cadan's defense," explained Jude. "I told him that you were strange, and him calling you a weirdo was only a reference to my earlier statement."

"Why would I be offended by something that was true?"

They both laughed, and Cadan watched in confusion.

"I wanted to bring Cadan down here so that he could see the Library."

"Well, here it is," Tomas beckoned around him. "Doesn't look like anything special, but once you start perusing the titles, the importance of this place becomes quite clear."

"What do you mean?" Cadan asked.

"We have some very ancient and some very important books here."

"Like?"

"Why, you're quite the inquisitive one," Tomas said to Cadan, but darted his eyes over to Jude, where he was directing the comment. Suspicion laced the words.

"He's very inquisitive," agreed Jude. "He is just curious about all of this, trying to understand."

"Of course," Tomas nodded, looking a little relieved. He continued. "We have many ancient documents which have been lost for centuries, ones that modern scholarship has only postulated upon. For instance, we have one of the original copies of the Greek Septuagint."

"The Greek what?" asked Jude. This bit of information seemed to confound even the tour guide.

"The Septuagint was created sometime between the 3rd and 1st centuries BCE. It was the first translation of the Hebrew bible into Koine Greek, and would have been the scripture quoted by the early Christians. There are fragments that have passed down through the centuries, but no original. But in this library, you will find one of the original copies from the lost Library of Alexandria."

"I remember reading about that in school," Cadan nodded. "How did the original go from a two thousand year-old library in Egypt to the middle of a mountain in Colorado?"

"That would be a very long story, and one that we do not have time for. The short version is that we here in DOMA are actually part of a long tradition of magical folk that have protected knowledge of both our magical heritage and the history of the world which we inhabit."

"I just wish they had kept better records of all the battles our magical heritage has participated in," Jude chuckled.

Tomas glared at him. "One, your use of the word *heritage* is appalling. Two, there is much more to the ruhk-magic than its purposes in combat. But you are correct in that it seems from the Andalorian archives, the mages in the other world were more skilled and more powerful than anyone on earth, save some of the members of the Ogden family. And it seems that line will die out with Josiah, since he has no descendants."

From the somber expression on Jude's face, that last comment seemed to have stung. With the death of his parents, he looked to Josiah as a father figure. Tomas's comment was a reminder that this was not in fact a truth. Cadan decided that the bookworm was definitely a little lacking on the social skills.

"I am a student of history," Tomas explained. "And I wish that my fellow ruhk-wielders were as interested in our traditions and our collective past as I am."

"At least you have Wendell to talk to," Jude laughed.

"Who is Wendell?" Cadan asked.

"Wendell Winters is the Chief Archivist of DOMA," Tomas explained. "And in a manner of speaking, my boss. He doesn't spend much time here anymore since Josiah has started placing him on random assignments."

"He's a crazy old man," said Jude. "With white hair that sprouts out of his head like his scalp were a garden. He looks like an Einstein knock-off."

"That is not very nice," Tomas tried to stifle a laugh.

Jude sighed and patted Cadan's arm. "We need to get downstairs to the Training Room for our session."

"One more thing," Tomas took two steps closer to Cadan and lowered his voice. "I'm sure you're questioning the program and what DOMA is asking of you, and I want to do my part to help you. There are definitely issues of ethics and morality when it comes to the apprehending and detaining of magical people. I was born in the Department so I do not have first-hand knowledge of life outside, but I do believe that my studies have given me some insight into the general human condition. I feel strongly that what we do here is not only a necessity, but it is the right thing to do for humanity."

Cadan nodded. He wasn't sure if there was an appropriate response to a speech such as that, but he understood, and for some inexplicable reason, it seemed a sound argument. Until then he had the feeling that everyone – except maybe Jude – was all part of one large conspiracy against him. Everyone under the mountain was concocting a plan to maintain his captivity and, quite possibly, bring about his very destruction. But maybe that was wrong, he thought. Tomas seemed a very simple, yet genuine, soul.

Despite not knowing where he was and surrounded by dozens of armed soldiers and creatures from a fantasy novel, he felt a ray of light. Tomas was surely one of the most socially inept people that he had ever met, but his comment seemed selfless and instinctual.

"I am usually always here in the library or in my dorm room, which is two doors down from yours. If you need anything or have any questions, please do not hesitate to seek me out."

"Thank you," Cadan nodded.

Jude turned to leave and Cadan followed on his heels.

When they were out of ear shot, Jude spoke. "I don't know what that was all about. He got all serious for a minute. I thought it was going to turn into an episode of Oprah."

"You watch Oprah?" Cadan asked.

"Of course," said Jude. "We never miss an episode in the lounge."

"Well, Tomas was just being nice," Cadan said quickly.

"Whatever," Jude mumbled, as they stepped back into the elevator.

Chapter Nine

After a brief stop at their room so that Jude could change into his training session uniform, they quickly made their way to the Training Room floor. He had expected a large gymnasium like the one at his school, but instead he and Jude walked out into a cavernous, metallic room. Windows lined one side and gave a view of an even more spacious room beyond. Computers and other equipment were positioned under the windows that extended the entire length of the far wall. There were various swiveled seats bolted to the steel floor.

Jude beckoned as they entered. "Welcome to the observation deck."

"It's about time." They turned to see Madison and the other Knights waiting in a huddle on one side. "We're about to start."

Each of the Knights was wearing the same suit that Jude had changed into. The top was a dark blue and the pants black, and their boots were black as well. Two large brown leather straps went across each shoulder and formed a tilted cross over their chests. Jude explained that this was to sheath their weapon of choice; his roommate's was the staff. They were also given a helmet of dulled silver, which covered their head, and other than the piece that covered the front of the nose, the face was open. On top of each helmet was a set of clear goggles. The Paladins had matching uniforms except their color was red.

Nervous anticipation made the group's interaction a bit strained. Even after years of preparation and weekly bouts in the arena, the Knights' trepidation on the battlefield was evident. Cadan only experienced this on the final games of a soccer tournament and could not imagine having to cope with the feeling on a regular basis.

Natalie nervously twirled her braids as she stood between her brother, whose arms were folded in his permanent stance of disdain for his surroundings, and Bryce, who seemed so nervous that he was a sneeze away from the shakes.

Nate did not speak once. Cadan expected some sort of pep talk or speech from the leader's mouth or at the very least some sort of quick strategy discussion. Instead Nate's eyes darted around the room, from the arena to his team, and then back into the arena. Despite Josiah's pride in his pupil, Cadan still had yet to see any leadership qualities displayed. If he were the captain of the soccer team back home, they would have had a vote and removed him quickly.

The door opened and two men – well, one man and one centaur – came walking out of the elevator. The man was dressed in a uniform similar to the ones that the non-magic soldiers wore around the base. His skin was a shade darker than Darius's and the only hair on any part of his head was the well trimmed goatee around his mouth.

The man immediately turned to Cadan. "I am Colonel Nieson, and this is Tregellos," he indicated the centaur. "You will observe this session while the Paladins and the Knights spar in the arena. Take careful note of the rules of combat, as we do not tolerate any deviation from the combat restrictions."

Nieson turned towards the center of the room and held a hand out to each group. "Paladins and Knights, prepare for your session. Please enter your side of the arena and await my command."

Double doors on each side of the room hissed open. The Paladins gallantly and confidently glided through their door, while the slump-shouldered Knights shuffled awkwardly through theirs. With a short wave to Cadan, Jude disappeared last through the door, before it hissed closed. A loud and distinct clicking sound, like that of a locking mechanism, echoed through the room.

Nieson noticed Cadan jump. "That noise was our security – so that no ruhk-magic leaks from the room," the colonel explained. "It can get very intense in there. If some of it were to leak in here, the consequences would be disastrous."

Cadan moved closer to the observation windows so that he could get a better look inside. The viewing platform was actually raised from the floor of the arena by about a dozen feet. The arena was the largest room that he had seen in the facility so far – he estimated that it was at least two hundred feet in every dimension.

There were two platforms on each side, one for each team. On the Paladin side, Anthony stood in the front with his arms folded and his chest held high in a posture fit for a war general. He stared out at the opposing team, eyeing each one as if he were mechanically plotting out their demise. Jason and Clay held their respective weapons, hunched over and ready to lunge at their foes. Carmen looked bored.

On the other side, the Knights were standing in a disheveled mess. Natalie and Darius were fighting over something while Bryce just shook his head and watched them. Madison tried to break them apart and finally gave up. Nate simply stared ahead and ignored his entire team. Only Jude was preparing for the battle ahead by stretching his legs and arms and readying his weapon.

"What are the rules of combat?" Cadan finally asked Nieson. It would be best if he knew these before the match for a better understanding of what was happening.

"For starters, those are not their own weapons. We let them use the weapon of their choice, but we have modified them to be less deadly, such as greatly dulling the blades of the swords and battle axes, or blunting the tips of Madison's arrows. This makes fatalities in the arena very unlikely."

"Shouldn't they wear some kind of armor?"

"They are," he replied flatly. "The fatigues they are wearing are made from a synthetic compound of cotton and steel, and then warded with magic that prevents piercing by any weapon. They also deflect most forms of magical spells."

"So what is the point of combat if they can't get hurt?"

"Oh," Nieson chucked. "They can definitely be injured. I've seen Jason swing his sword with enough force to break an arm. Just because the armor cannot be pierced doesn't mean the body underneath is invulnerable. We also provide them objects in the room on which to use their powers." He pointed into the arena.

At various places on the vast floor, small platforms were lifting boulders up and into the room. He was not sure what they were for other than to use for cover.

Nieson leaned forward and flicked a switch near one of the monitors on the table. A microphone extended from the wall and stopped just a few inches from his mouth. "You will have ten seconds before we start." Even through the thick walls and glass that separated the observation room from the arena, he could hear Nieson's voice booming inside. "Please use this time wisely to prepare for combat."

Immediately a glow formed around Anthony, Carmen, Heather, and Russell. Even through the warded walls Cadan could feel the tingling sensation that came with other magic-wielders harnessing the ruhk. Anthony and the two girls were moderately powerful, but Russell was, by far, the most powerful. Cadan turned to the Knights to see Nate, Jude, and Natalie draw ruhk-magic, yet not nearly the quantity of their opponents. All participants pulled their goggles down over their eyes.

Darius leaned forward and his large black wings sprung from an opening in the back of his suit. This was the first time that Cadan had seen them in the light and had only one thought – they were beautiful. How could Darius be ashamed that his wings were not white like other seraphs? Now he could see how Darius got the nickname *Raven*. Cadan noticed that the moment his wings sprung forth, his eyes, and then his head, dropped down, as if shame came along with the wings.

Nieson eyed the watch on his wrist before finally dropping his right hand to his side. He leaned forward and spoke one word: "Begin."

Jude was the first to move. In a display of quickness like Cadan had never witnessed, Jude was off the platform with his staff drawn, moving towards the far side of the arena. He had placed a small shield of ruhk-magic up around himself and was taking cover. Madison held her bow in her right hand and pulled an arrow from its sheath with her left. She leapt from the platform across from Jude and took cover behind a boulder.

On the opposite side, Jason and Clay descended and moved through the center of the room. Russell stepped forward and raised both hands. With one swift movement, he had placed an enormous shield over Natalie and Nate, preventing both from performing any spells of significance. Simon had taught him and Derrick how to create these, and Cadan had learned well. He was able to prevent his brother from wielding the ruhk-magic, but had never been able to fully block Simon.

From the looks on Natalie and Nate's faces, Russell's shield was successful. Without use of the ruhk, Nate unsheathed his sword, motioned for Bryce to follow, and descended the platform into the center of the room, moving towards Jason and Clay. Natalie was weaponless without the ruhk, so she stayed where she was. The look on her face said this was a typical outcome.

Carmen and Heather slowly descended their platform, while Anthony pulled his sword free and joined Jason and Clay in the center. With the ruhk-wielding Knights cut off from the power, hand to hand combat was all that remained.

The Paladins still had control of their ruhk-magic.

They would use whatever advantage they could find. Anthony and his two men met Nate and Bryce in the center of the room. Anthony and Nate lunged forward and their swords met in the air. For a brief moment, they were the only two in the room moving. Steel met steel as the sounds of battle were heard, even in the observation room. For the Paladin it seemed to be effortless, but Nate was struggling by the second swing.

Darius took to the air above. Before he could make it very far, a bolt of ruhk-fire shot from Russell's outstretched right hand and struck Darius on one of his wings, sending him tumbling down behind the platform where he had started.

Tired of being just spectators, Jason and Clay circled the sword fight on each side and came around to face Bryce. The big man held his battle axe in front of him in preparation, but his face showed the unmistakable expression of grim apprehension bordering on sheer horror.

The dwarf held his axe and prepared to charge, but stopped short when he was met by a scream from Madison. She leapt from behind her boulder. She knocked her arrow, but before she could loose it, several small stones came flying from her left. Carmen strolled forward from around one of the large rocks with her right hand extended, ruhk-magic emanating all around her. She was levitating and hurling rocks at her opponents. That was another trick that Simon had taught Cadan, and one that he had actually perfected more fully than the shield. He had eventually worked his way up to lifting Simon's truck.

One of the rocks found purchase on the side of Madison's head and sent her flying. She met the ground ten feet further down the arena floor. Her unconscious form didn't move for the remainder of the session.

Cadan could see the ruhk-magic itself that comprised the spell Carmen had formed to levitate the rocks, and was surprised by how messy it was. Simon had taught him to keep the energy "inside the lines." His adoptive father was so obsessed with clean spells that he had started his three children on coloring books at a very early age. Part of their homework was to color pages upon pages of pictures. If they veered outside of the lines, they were forced to start over. This paid off later when their training in the art of the ruhk began. Simon taught them that when a spell formed, there were certain invisible boundaries that were set. If one could keep the ruhk within those boundaries as opposed to letting it roam free, the spell was vastly more powerful and also more untraceable to an opponent. Much of Carmen's ruhk-magic that she held was within that boundary, but there was a good deal more being released than a properly trained mage should have allowed.

On the other side of the dueling leaders, Jude leapt from behind his rock. Cadan watched his lithe roommate glide across the floor towards Jason. In just three long strides, he closed the gap. His staff shot forward, clipping Jason hard on the side of the knee. With a loud snap of bone, the half-troll dropped his weapon, fell to his side and clutched his knee, a shard of bone now protruding through the skin.

Heather was there in a moment. In a similar fashion to her teammate Carmen, she pummeled Jude with rocks. He anticipated the maneuver and was able to dodge the first few. Sensing her opponent's propensity for avoiding her bullets, she reached out with the ruhk to the boulder on her right, lifted it from the ground, and sent it directly for Jude. He turned to run, but the object clipped him hard in the back, sending him flying.

"That boy is undisciplined," Tregellos commented to the Colonel in a deep voice. "I have spent more time than I care to working with him, and yet he turns his back to his foe and runs."

"With a leader like Nate, I'd run too," Nieson sniffed. "I don't understand what Josiah sees in that boy. I can't remember the last time I've seen him exhibit anything resembling leadership."

Anthony and Nate continued their sword fighting, ignoring the surrounding commotion. Clay and Bryce faced off on one side, as the metal on metal scraping of their axes meeting echoed against the glass in front of Cadan. With several quick thrusts of his smaller axe, Clay knocked the weapon from two of Bryce's four hands. He held his top row of arms up in the air in a sign of surrender.

Seeing this out of the corner of his eye, Nate stepped back from his parlay with Anthony and dropped his sword, also surrendering. Cadan shook his head in disgust; Simon would never have allowed one of his children to surrender a match because their opponent had the upper hand.

"The session is completed," Nieson told the participants through the intercom. "Please stand down and sheathe all weapons. The Healers will be here momentarily."

He switched the microphone off.

"When Helena arrives, you may enter the arena with her," Nieson informed Cadan.

"Who is Helena? I thought Hadrian was the doctor here."

"Helena Lang is the Chief Healer at this Facility. Hadrian is the doctor. She uses ruhk to heal while Hadrian's methods are non-magic, but most of the time they work together."

As if on cue, the door slid open and a middle-aged woman glided through. Her fierce dark eyes found him and she stopped. As she flipped her long straight black hair behind her shoulders, she continued past him and towards one of the doors. He found her beautiful in a statuesque kind of way. Her long navy dress clung to her upper body, but the material below her waist billowed out behind her as she made her way through the sliding door into the arena. As Cadan followed, Hadrian clopped through the elevator and joined them, followed by the ever chipper Estelle, flitting her wings just inches above the doctor's shoulder.

As they entered the room, Jude was using a nearby rock as leverage to pull himself up slowly, wincing all the while. Madison was already on one knee and trying to stand. Jason, however, was not moving. He lay on the ground groaning softly while holding his leg where the bone had broken through.

Without uttering a word, Helena leaned down next to Jason's leg and placed both hands on each side. When he didn't move his own hands off of the injured area, Helena slapped them and the injured leg. He screamed out in agony and removed his hands. After just a few seconds, she stood back up, the healing spell complete.

"You two," she motioned towards Nate and Anthony who were standing closest. "He is healed now, but will need to rest. Please take him to the infirmary and see that he gets a bed."

Cadan reached down and offered Jude a hand, which he gladly accepted. Cadan reached his left arm under Jude's shoulder for support.

"You okay?"

"Just hit my back pretty good," he replied. "Going to be sore for a day or two."

"If you let me heal that, I can cut the time in half." Helena glided over to them and waited for a response to her offer.

"I'll be okay," he shook his head.

"Nonsense," she said flatly and wrapped her left hand around his back. Before Jude could pull away, she was already retracting her hand and had a triumphant smirk on her face. "See, that wasn't so bad."

Cadan could feel Jude shiver – he wasn't sure if it was from the healing process or from fear of the cold woman in front of them. He squeezed Jude's right shoulder for emotional support.

Madison left before she could receive any healing. Natalie, Darius, and Bryce had followed her out. None of them seemed interested in a post-game pep talk.

"Want to go the infirmary?" he asked Jude quietly.

"No," mumbled Jude. "Just take me back to our room so that I can lie down."

"Got it."

Several minutes later, Cadan was laying Jude down on his bed. He went into the small kitchen area, found a bag and filled it with ice from the miniscule freezer. He found a dish cloth in one of the drawers, wrapped it around the bag of ice and took it back into the room. Jude turned over and Cadan helped him remove his shirt before setting the ice down on the small of his back.

There was a knock on the door. Cadan opened it to find Madison glaring at him. Without uttering one word, she stormed past him into the room where Jude was resting.

She threw herself on Cadan's bed. "How do we constantly get beat by those a-holes?"

"Great to see you too, Madi," Jude mumbled from his pillow.

The room was silent for an uncomfortable moment. "You two were good out there," Cadan finally spoke. He couldn't think of anything else to say.

"Jude and I were taken down before we could do anything. How is that good?"

"The brief moment you were in battle, I think you were awesome."

"Really?" Jude lifted up from his pillow and shook his head. "We were awful. Half our team doesn't even bother to make an effort and our leader doesn't say a word to us. I'm surprised we haven't been shipped off to the Nursery."

"There's a nursery here too?"

"No, *the* Nursery. As in the Great Lakes Facility," he answered. "It's where all of the adolescent and teenage ruhk-wielders live. That was where most of us grew up."

"Is it like this Facility?"

"Sort of, but it feels a lot warmer and more comfortable, with not quite so many guards running around."

"So how –"

"Now you're trying to distract me. I want to complain some more about my team."

"They have promise."

"That's giving us a little too much credit," Madison moaned.

"Not at all."

"How do you figure?" she asked.

"Take you and Jude for example. Both of you are well-trained warriors with a natural fighting ability that would be hard to match. Your problem is your lack of a leader who both wants the job and is qualified for it."

Jude smiled at the compliment. "You're right, I am a naturally excellent fighter."

"No," Cadan corrected. Jude's smile disappeared. "I said you had natural fighting ability. That alone does not make you an excellent fighter."

"What's the difference?" Cadan could tell that he was on the verge of wounding his roommate's pride.

"The difference is that you fight for yourself. You forget that you have five other people who are depending on you. You also have their power and their skills at your disposal, but the way you all fight, it's lost. By combining your powers, you can accomplish much more."

"As in linking our powers?"

"No, not that kind of combination. For instance, how come no one covers Darius when he attacks from the air? I would think that an airborne teammate could come in handy in a fight."

Jude and Madison stared at him for a moment as it all sank in. He could tell that she finally understood. On several occasions, Simon had set up a scrimmage specifically designed to teach them the value of teamwork. Although they never had any real enemies to face, he was sure that he and Derrick would be able to face down the entire Paladin team together.

"What about Natalie and Bryce? They are worthless on the field." Jude looked exasperated.

Cadan had an idea. "Have you ever noticed the way Bryce stares at Natalie?"

"Of course," Jude chuckled. "We joke about it all of the time. Well, if Darius isn't around. He gets a little protective of his sister. Old Four Arms likes him some Natalie."

"Have you tried to use that to motivate him to fight? I haven't been here long, but there has to be some pent up aggression in there somewhere. Find a way to make it appear that Natalie is in some kind of danger in the arena, and he may just enter the battle swinging."

"That's not a bad idea," smiled Madison.

"It's worth trying. From what I saw today, you don't have much to lose."

"We need a new leader," Jude suggested.

"Why don't you do it?" Cadan asked Jude.

"I could never be a good leader," said Jude. "Like you said, I'm a good fighter, but I'm out for myself, and I know that."

"What about Darius or Madison?"

"No," Jude shook his head. "I think you should be our leader."

"I agree," Madison said quickly.

"No way," Cadan said immediately. "None of the others would go for it."

"Sure they would. Everyone likes you well enough. In fact I'm surprised that they're as okay with you as they are. Normally they won't even talk to new people for a while. At least they'll have a conversation with you."

"What about Nate?"

"Forget what that little creep has to say," Madison snorted. "He can take a flying leap for all I care."

"I'll talk to Josiah. He'll listen to me. I'm sure he'll let you take Nate's place on a trial basis at the least."

"But I just got here, Jude. I don't know the first thing about all of this stuff you all do."

Jude laughed and shook his head. "This may be your first few days with DOMA, but I can guarantee this is not your first time around ruhk-magic."

"Why do you think that?"

"A non-magic human would be freaking out right about now. You didn't seem the least bit surprised having a faun for a doctor and a pixie for a nurse. You already have skills with the sword, and I'm going to guess that you know a little something about ruhk-magic as well."

"Just different spells I picked up on my own."

"Well, however you learned them, you probably know more than the rest of the Knights. I still see no reason you shouldn't be our leader."

Chapter Ten

Eventually Jude and Madison gave up on the team leader discussion, and Madison retreated to her quarters. Jude lay on his bed, with the ice pack on his back, while the two of them talked. Cadan found that they had more in common than he originally thought. The fact that Jude knew nothing of his birth parents was the beginning of a bond between them. They were both raised by adults who loved and cared for then, but were missing one key thing – a genetic link.

Cadan was reminded of the evening two weeks before when he said those horrible things to Simon and Daphne. He was angry at learning that much of his life had been a lie, but he didn't take any time to sort through their perspective before attacking. Simon tried to explain his motives, sure, but he remained so secretive even when Cadan's parentage was revealed. Actually Simon and Daphne had never treated him any differently than Derrick or Raney. If anything, Simon had always seemed to approve more of Cadan than his own biological son.

Simon and Daphne had always loved him and provided a great home for him. Derrick and Raney were everything he could have ever wanted in siblings, and they got along better than most families. But reflecting back on his childhood, he could see that there had been something missing. There had been some deep-seated feeling of isolation. While he was surrounded by those who loved him, there was still a piece of his soul missing.

He had even been given something else that other children had not received – access to a magical world of spell casting and weapons training. Simon rarely went into detail about why he insisted on practicing, but had made two things clear to them: they were never to talk to anyone outside of their small family unit about what they participated in, and that there was a small chance that the training could come in handy one day.

Maybe Simon knew of DOMA and feared that one day they would find his children and take them. Would Simon know where to find him now? Surely he wouldn't risk Derrick, Raney, and Daphne to come and save him from this place.

Other than appearances, his former home back in Texas probably wasn't all that different from the Nursery that Jude was raised in. Maybe Cadan fit in perfectly with the Knights – they were all orphans.

It was an unusual fact about his team, once he voiced it. The reality that none of them were in the care of their biological parents was either a strange coincidence or the very reason they were all put together. He made a mental note to ask Tomas about that idea when he next saw him.

Dismissing the subject, Cadan laid back down, but it was futile. He wanted to talk to Tomas as soon as possible. Glancing over to see that Jude had fallen asleep, he grabbed his access key to the room and made his way to the Library.

After checking a few of the rooms of books, he found Tomas on the floor sorting through stacks of old, dusty volumes.

"Cadan," Tomas said. By his uplifted eyebrows, he was clearly shocked to find a returning visitor so soon.

"Hey Tomas," he said, plopping down next to the archivist.

"What can I do for you?"

"I need some help. Or rather, I have a few questions."

"I'll do what I can, but I'm not quite as good with answers as Wendell might be. He should be back tomorrow."

Cadan didn't know how to voice his concern. With the whole government imprisoning magic people thing and all, he didn't feel that there were many in the Department he could trust. For some reason, he felt that he could trust Tomas implicitly. "I'd rather ask you first."

"Sure. What is it that you wanted to ask me about?"

"I don't know anything about my parents. I thought that since you have access to the histories, there may be information available."

"What would make you think that DOMA would have information about your parents?"

He realized that this was the closest to revealing more of his past than he had told anyone since being captured – including his own roommate. He would have to tread carefully as he did not want even Tomas to know of his family back home.

"Just a hunch. I don't know for sure, but since I can safely assume that they were able to use the ruhk-magic, and that one of them must have been an elf, the odds that they were affiliated with DOMA are very likely."

"But if they were affiliated with DOMA, wouldn't they still be here, and wouldn't you have been raised in DOMA?"

"I'm not sure. Maybe they retired or got out somehow."

"No one retires, and no one gets out. Your service for the government is indefinite. At best, you get a nice little desk job like Wendell or Helena."

"Then maybe they weren't a part of DOMA. But is there any way to check the histories and rule that theory out?"

"Sorry, but that's classified."

"Classified?"

"Yeah, for some inexplicable reason, everything from the past fifty years is always classified. As far as I know, only Josiah and Wendell have access to the histories from the past fifty years."

"Why would they make it classified?"

"Although the government doesn't know of our existence, we're still a part of their structure and have to follow similar rules to that of other agencies, like the CIA or the FBI."

"I get that, but to classify only the past fifty years of history? It's almost as if they have something to hide."

Tomas eyed Cadan suspiciously for a few moments, but he could also see the gears turning behind those glasses. For all of his analytical prowess, Tomas had never stopped to take a critical view at what was being asked of him.

"Maybe you're right, Cadan, but there's nothing that we can do about that. What do you know of your family? What facts?"

What should he tell Tomas? The truth? He decided to be as honest as possible. "I am fairly certain that my mother was an elf and my father was human—"

"And I would guess by your level of power, that they could both wield the ruhk-magic."

"How do you know my power level?"

"You can't sense other people's power levels?"

"No." And that was the truth. Simon had never taught his children that spell.

"It's simple, really. You have to hold a small quantity of the ruhk with your mind, and then reach out and graze the mind of an individual near you. You cannot really see the actual power itself, it's more a feeling you get when looking at their mind. Power levels are hard to quantify and measure, so gauging relative power of individuals is more of a greater than, less than type of equation." He set the book he was holding down. "Try it on me."

Cadan closed his eyes and allowed the ruhk to flow through his body. He knew from the warmth that he pulled more than was necessary, but he wanted to be prepared for his first time performing this spell. He let the power flow through both arms, and then gently reached out towards Tomas. Like a glowing fog of iridescent light, ruhk-magic flowed from his fingertips, and brushed along Tomas's temples.

He only had to search for a few seconds before he found what Tomas was referring to. There, inside of his mind, almost in his brain itself, he could see the potential for ruhk-magic. Tomas was very powerful – but for some reason, one that he couldn't quite explain, Cadan knew that he was more powerful. There wasn't anything tangible about how he knew; he just knew.

"You did it," Tomas smiled. "And I'm sure you can tell that you are much more powerful than I am."

"You are still quite powerful."

"Oh, I know," Tomas smiled even bigger. "In raw power, I'm one of the most powerful at this facility, but you are much more powerful than me, and possibly even more powerful than Josiah."

"Wow," was all he could say. Simon had never told him this before.

"Do you know how to mask your ability to use the ruhk-magic?"

"No."

"You just have to create a shield around your mind. The only difference from a normal shield is that you smooth out one side of the shield and invert it. The spell sounds quite complicated but once you try it a few times, it becomes very easy and almost second nature."

"So people can mask their ability? Then how can DOMA be certain they find everyone?"

"Because a mage of any significant power can see through that, especially if they are looking. The spell would work if you were standing in a crowd and another mage just glossed over everyone quickly."

"That's interesting."

"Not really," Tomas shook his head, dismissing the conversation. "I'm more interested in getting back to your parents."

Cadan had almost forgotten.

"What else do you know about them?" he asked.

"I know that they're from New York City."

"How do you know this?"

"I'm not sure," Cadan lied. "Must be some kind of latent memory or something like that. I can vaguely recall an image of them as well."

"Was that why you were in New York when they found you the other night?"

"Yes. I was looking for information on them. I don't even know their names."

"That's not much to go on. Without names and without access to the classified section of the archives, I don't think there is any way to trace your parents."

Cadan felt defeated. "No way at all? Is there anything you can research?"

"The only idea that comes to mind is the DOMA Facility located in New York. If your parents were indeed involved with DOMA, then maybe they were at that Facility. But that doesn't explain why they aren't in DOMA now."

"What if they are?"

"It's not possible. I know every single ruhk-wielding operative in DOMA, and I would know if there was a couple who had lost their child seventeen years ago. I'm sorry Cadan, but they are not in DOMA. And I doubt that they ever were. Once you're in DOMA, you don't ever get out."

"I appreciate you taking the time to talk to me about it."

"No problem," Tomas smiled warmly. Cadan felt the tear fall down his cheek before he even realized it was there. He tried to wipe it away before Tomas saw it. Too late. "I'll tell you what. I'll do my best to look through any recent documents that I have access to, and if I come across anything, I will let you know immediately."

"That would be very nice."

"You know, another avenue that you may want to try is Josiah himself. He is a very helpful and caring man. I would imagine that if you asked him for assistance, he would be more than happy to answer your questions. I'm not sure how much of the classified information he could reveal, but I'm sure he'd do his best to help you find peace with this topic."

"You really think so?"

"At this point, Cadan, what could it hurt? Josiah has a sensitive spot for parentage. He lost his as well. He won't say what happened to them and neither will any of the other elder mages. All I know is that they are gone. Just as with your family, I don't know anything about the generation before Josiah, but unlike you, his family's history is told in great detail."

"The Ogdens."

"Yes," Tomas shook his head. "The Ogdens were a legendary family on Andaloria and there are hundreds of stories of their greatness."

"Why are they so wonderful?"

"It is said that they descended from a man named Ogden and a Witch-Priestess named Doriana. During the time that a great empire reigned over most of Andaloria, the Ogdens sat on the throne. Once the empire collapsed, the Ogden line disappeared into obscurity for some time. Later, they returned as kings of a great land. One of the most notorious of all Ogdens was Adam. Alongside his brother and two sisters, they returned the lost goddess Achama to the Pleroma."

"They did what?"

"Achama was the goddess that was ripped from the heavens in ancient times. Through the heroic efforts of the Ogdens, she was returned. It's a long story."

"Sounds like a myth to me."

"It may be," Tomas shrugged. "Then again, it may not be. How can you be certain when you eat lunch next to a man with goat hooves for legs?"

"You have a point. How do you know so much about the Ogdens?"

"Their stories are all over the books that have come from Andaloria. Some of the previous immigrants from that realm were interviewed and many had things to say about the Ogdens."

"Is that classified as well?"

"Of course not," Tomas said as he began looking around the stacks of books. He moved a few old dusty volumes around before settling on a small, brown, leather-bound book. "Here it is," he declared. He handed the book to Cadan. "This is one of the best books on the Ogdens. It details many of their exploits. It's a chronicle-style history book but a page-turning read."

The book was the size of a spiral notebook, but much thicker. The cover was hard brown leather with beautiful blue and gold etching of a lion's head across the front.

"I can take this out of the library?"

"Sure. I'll just update the catalog to show that you checked it out and there won't be a problem. We're are allowed to check the books out from here."

"But it's old."

"Almost all of the books are old. Just take care of it."

"I will."

"Promise me. That's one of my favorites."

"I promise."

"And I promise to let you know if I find any clues on your family."

"Thank you."

"It's the least I can do for you for visiting me down here. It gets kind of lonely sometimes, and I don't get many visitors."

"Why don't you come up more?"

"I'm not exactly Mr. Popular," said Tomas. He avoided Cadan's eyes. "I know that everyone finds me boring. I catch them rolling their eyes when I talk, even though they think I don't notice. Sometimes I hear the comments they make behind my back."

"They give each other a hard time, I think. That's how they must show their love."

"That's a funny way of showing it. I have never once been invited to do anything."

"Well, now I'm inviting you."

"We'll see."

"What about the scrimmages? Why don't you participate in those either?"

"I get a special dispensation from the scrimmages since I cover for Wendell when he's out of the Facility."

"But don't you want the practice?"

"For me the ruhk is about so much more than battling."

"But what if you ever need the fighting skills?"

"I doubt that the fighting skills will ever come in handy down here."

"I'm about to participate in my first one. Maybe you should join us."

"It's been a while since I created any spells that could be of use in battle."

"Well, think on it."

"I will. Tell everyone I said hi."

Cadan left the Library with more questions than he had when he had arrived. At least he knew that his parents weren't involved with DOMA in any way. Therefore, Simon and Daphne had not been involved with DOMA either. There was some reassurance in that fact.

He thumbed the brown leather book in his hand. The stories sounded interesting, and he couldn't help but be a little envious of Josiah. The Administrator knew his lineage for the past several centuries or more. Cadan would give anything to know one thing about his mother other than her name. Somehow that didn't seem fair.

If Tomas said anything that Cadan took away from the conversation, it was his advice on the next course of action Cadan should take in his search. There was one person that he needed to speak with – Josiah.

The elevator took him back to the dormitory level. He had expected the hall to be empty. Instead, he found two of the Paladins – Carmen and Heather. The former was standing in the middle of the hall as if to block his way, and the latter slumped against the wall.

He tried to ignore them as he veered to the right to pass, but Carmen's small, but not too delicate, hand stopped him. This was worse than any high school experience, Cadan groaned inwardly.

"Not so fast, pretty boy," she muttered.

"Can I help you with something?"

"We just want to talk to you for a minute," she said.

"Carmen, just let him go," Heather sighed. Her reluctance was apparent.

"Talk about what?" Cadan asked.

"Do we have to have a particular reason? Maybe we just want to get to know the new guy and help him feel more welcome here."

"For some reason I doubt that's why you stopped me."

She laughed – a deep, throaty noise that spoke of malice. "I guess I'm fairly obvious. I actually don't like you and probably never will."

"What did I do to you?"

"Oh, it's just this little air of entitlement that you have about you. You look at us like you are better than we are. I heard you have some experience with ruhk-magic and I watched you size us Paladins up. I can see the wheels turning behind your eyes and I know that you have something up your sleeve."

"I'm wearing short sleeves."

She didn't laugh. "But honestly I'm not here for myself. Heather here has a slightly different opinion of you. In fact, our opinions couldn't be more different. She thinks you're … what did you call him, Heather? Dreamy?"

"Carmen, stop it," Heather stood up from the wall and walked towards her friend.

"Sorry, sorry." Carmen smiled and backed away. "I was here only for the ice breaker. I'll leave you two alone now."

The blonde girl whirled and started for her room.

Heather turned and looked at Cadan. "I'm so sorry for my roommate. She's a little over the top sometimes."

"No problem," he shrugged. What was going on here?

They were silent for a moment, until Heather finally spoke again. "I never called you dreamy. I told Carmen that I thought you were cute and nice, and it would be cool to talk to you."

"We're talking now," he said flatly.

He could see the pain in her eyes, and she turned to follow Carmen. "Maybe this was a bad idea," she mumbled.

The whole set up was annoying beyond words, but he was being a jerk to her, and she wasn't the one who had been rude earlier. "Wait, Heather. Stop."

"I really didn't mean to bother you," she turned back around. "I really just wanted to formally introduce myself and welcome you."

"I know, and I'm sorry for being so nasty to you. It's just that the contact I've had with the other Paladins has been anything but positive, and I was just associating you with them. I'm really sorry."

"Yeah, I know my team is a little difficult."

"Difficult?"

"Okay, they are downright horrible – most of the time. But once you get to know them, they aren't so bad."

"I'll have to just take your word for it." he forced a smile.

"So, I would ask you about yourself, but I'm sure you're tired of talking about your past and everything that happened before you got here."

"A little tired of it," he exaggerated. "There's not much to tell. My parents died when I was younger, and I lived on the streets until DOMA found me."

"Oh, you poor thing."

"I got by."

"Well, you're in a better place now. Living here is tough sometimes, but we get to have fun every once in a while. And the food isn't bad."

They both chuckled.

"So, have you grown up in DOMA?"

"Yes, I lived at the Nursery until I turned twelve and then I was transferred here. Not much to tell."

"Seems to be a common story."

"Most of us were born here. Other than watching television and the very rare opportunity to communicate with a regular human on a mission, we have little contact with the outside world."

"That must be tough."

"You get accustomed to it. There's some really good shows on the television. Maybe one night we could go to the lounge and watch some together."

It was phrased more as a question. Was this girl asking him out on a date? He wasn't the least bit interested in a date at the moment. He'd been kidnapped and locked into a super secret government agency, and now a girl was asking him out on a date? He had no idea how to let her down easy. She was the only Paladin who was even speaking to him in a civilized manner, so he didn't want to make her angry.

All he could think of was, "Sure."

She smiled and said good bye, retreating down the hall towards her room.

Chapter Eleven

The next morning at breakfast, the Paladins jeered at the Knights as they passed their table. Cadan thought that victories over their younger opponents would have become mundane by now, but that was apparently not the case. Initially, he felt pity for his teammates. That quickly dissipated. It was replaced with anger, and anger was something that he could easily funnel into a healthy determination. The danger with the anger portion of emotional evolution was that the duration of anger tended to last longer than what might be healthy. It was during that period that something bad could happen. He had to fight the urge to hit each one of the Paladins in their face.

Heather still seemed to find him intriguing for some unknown reason. As he passed the Paladin table, five of the Paladins sneered or threw something at him, but Heather sat with her arms folded and stared deeply into his eyes. It was somewhere between creepy and nuts, but he wasn't quite sure where. Sure, she was beautiful, but where she abounded in looks, she was severely lacking in etiquette. Last Cadan checked, it wasn't nice to stare. Just the night before, she had asked him on a date to watch television. Her invitation was still a little strange.

The mood at the Knight's table wasn't much of an improvement. Darius was even more standoffish, if that was possible, and Natalie just glared at her food. A day had passed since the scrimmage, yet had he not been there, he would have sworn they had just come from it. Bryce acted the same as always, wordlessly eating his food. Today, his brow was furrowed in a frown, and Cadan noticed the big man's eyes dart over to Natalie on more than one occasion. By the way all of his arms were shifting, Cadan could tell that Bryce was not happy that the Paladins had thrown a wadded napkin at Natalie.

Permanently-scowling Helena sat at a table eating her breakfast with two other people. One was an old man who was balding on top of his head. His jowls seemed to hang low enough to touch his chest. The eyes behind his glasses seemed hard as if the life he had lived had become too much for one person to handle.

The other was a younger woman with thick, reddish-brown hair cut close around the nape of her neck. Her glasses were in the style of a previous decade, with the outside of the frames meeting in a point. She seemed bubbly and happy, laughing at something Helena said.

"Who are those two?" Cadan asked Jude.

"The man is Benton, one of the senior mages here at the base. He is the person responsible for most of the technology you see."

"Like the arena?"

"He created that some time back. His main discovery was the ability of combining ruhk-magic with certain technology, creating a machine that locates significant spells all around the world. DOMA is able to monitor all gateways that spontaneously appear from Andaloria. It's how we knew that troll appeared in New York. They can also find a mage if he or she performs a large spell."

"How does that work?"

Natalie answered. "It's a combination of a GPS program and a few other bits of software and hardware combined with a heavy dose of ruhk."

Jude added. "Natalie here studies with Benton. She is great with computers and nerdy stuff like that."

"The other one," Madison indicated the red head with funky glasses. "That's Hazel. She is one of the youngest of the elder mages and although she pretends to be all sweet, she is actually a hardcore bitch."

"Pot calling the kettle black," Darius laughed to himself.

Madison grunted and pushed her hair behind her ear, doing her best to ignore his comment.

"Observe her nice outfit," Jude whispered as he leaned towards him, pointing across the dining area towards her. Cadan hadn't noticed before, but it was quite odd. "She always wears a sleeveless vest over her shirt and flowing skirt. The colors and combinations change, but the style is always the same."

"Be nice," Natalie urged him.

"She needs to find some bigger vests," Madison pointed out. "The buttons over her bosom are screaming for help."

Natalie giggled. "She has a perfect hourglass figure."

"Um, that's a pretty thick hourglass," Jude added.

"She's also a big Trey Piper fan," Madison explained.

"Trey Piper?" Cadan asked, surprised that someone her age would listen to that kind of music.

"Yeah," she said. "The little kid pop star with the lesbian haircut?"

"That's a little weird," he smiled.

"Not really," said Natalie. "Trey Piper is actually a half-elf, half-fairy employee of DOMA, much like the Femme Fatales. He helps finance this facility. Hazel is his guardian and manages some of his career from here."

"His whole life story that his fans have memorized is actually something that Josiah created himself," Jude explained.

Cadan laughed and returned to his breakfast.

Jude and Madison began quietly talking about the next scrimmage. Cadan was close enough to hear them, but he quite honestly didn't pay them much attention. As soon as breakfast was over, he planned to head straight for Josiah's office. Hopefully the Administrator would have answers to some of his questions.

What plagued his thoughts most as he swished the spoon through his lukewarm oatmeal was the expanding lie that he would have to maintain for Josiah. He felt more comfortable with Tomas than anyone so far except maybe Jude, and Josiah was closer to the bottom of that list. Something about the old man made Cadan as nearly as uncomfortable as Heather had. Josiah would be observant and suspicious just by nature of his occupation. He knew that his lie had to be tighter, with no room for prodding questions that would reveal unwanted details. Whatever he said or did, he could not ever betray his family.

"So where did you go last night?" Jude finally asked.

"Down to the library."

"For what?"

"To talk to Tomas," Cadan answered. "You fell asleep and I just wanted someone to talk to."

"Sorry about that, man," Jude said. "If you needed someone to talk to, you could have woken me up."

"I don't think I'd have been able to wake you up."

"Why's that?"

"You snore so loud, I thought I was being attacked by a troll again."

The whole table burst out in laughter. Even Bryce, who Cadan had assumed was not as quick as the others, was laughing hard, slapping all four hands on the table. Natalie rolled her head back in a cruel cackle. Jude tried to deny it, but after a clasp on the back by Darius, he just sat and shook his head in defeat.

"Is it that bad?" he asked finally.

"Definitely."

"Sorry."

"Tell that to the people next door," said Madison.

From the next table over, Nate threw his spoon down into his unfinished cereal and stormed out of the room.

Madison shrugged and leaned forward, beckoning everyone else to do the same.

"We have a plan for the next scrimmage."

"Does this plan include not getting our asses kicked?" Natalie asked. There was no sarcasm in her voice.

"In fact, that is the central focus," said Jude.

"Who came up with this plan?" asked Darius.

"Cadan."

"What?" Natalie and Darius said at the same time. He finished, "how can this newbie come up with a plan for a scrimmage that he has never been in? How does that work?"

"We can debate his credentials later," said Madison. "But the fact is, he has some pretty good ideas."

"No, I think his credentials are actually very important when it comes to our well being in the arena," Darius shot back.

"Really?" Madison tilted her head and glared at him. "We haven't had a scrimmage where our well being *wasn't* at serious risk."

"Exactly," agreed Jude. "So we don't really have much to lose."

"Look, everyone," Natalie waved her hands. "I don't mean to sound like my arrogant brother, but shouldn't Cadan have a little more training before he goes making plans for us and all?"

They continued the conversation as if Cadan weren't sitting at the table. He was happy that he didn't have to talk, since Jude and Madison were nicely coming to his defense.

"Cadan has had some practice with the ruhk-magic already," said Jude. "And his ideas are good."

"Name one," Natalie said.

"For starters," Jude began, "we need to provide cover for Darius so that he can actually get off the ground, and provide a distraction when he makes an attack from the air."

"There is nothing wrong with my flying skills."

"I'm not saying there is. We just need to act more like a team and cover you so that you can get off the ground, and then you can assault the Paladins from the air."

"I don't think getting Darius in the air will make that much of a difference," Natalie said. She turned to her brother. "No offense."

"None taken," he mumbled.

"They shield us every time. That basically takes me out of the fight," Natalie said. "I don't have any hand to hand combat skills."

Jude turned to Cadan. "How do you propose we solve that problem?"

"We shield them first," he answered nonchalantly.

"Shield them first?" Natalie laughed. "How? None of us are as powerful as Russell."

"Maybe not, but I am." They all stared at him in disbelief.

"Are you sure?" asked Jude.

"Yes," Cadan answered. He couldn't be certain that he was more powerful than Russell, but he knew that he could get a shield up much faster, and speed in that case was worth more than power.

"Have you ever constructed a shield before?" Madison asked suspiciously.

"Yes." He had to lie. "The first time was by accident. I threw a shield up instinctively once when a rabid dog attacked me in an alley."

"The spell for a shield is quite complex," Madison informed him. "Not to mention that a shield to cut someone off from ruhk-magic is much more complex than a simple barrier shield. How do you 'discover' it by accident?"

"I don't know."

"Uh hum," she mouthed quietly, while she watched him with her arms folded. "My theory on you is that there is much more than meets the eye. But I don't care. We all have our secrets here. What I do care about is that you might be the key to us finally beating the Paladins."

"The point is," Jude said, changing the subject. "He says he knows how to produce a shield, and I believe him. This may just be our chance to beat them for once."

They finished their breakfast quickly after that, and then departed the cafeteria. As they were leaving, Cadan grabbed Bryce's arm, holding him back.

"Bryce," he said quietly so the other couldn't hear. "Can I talk to you for a second?"

"Sure," the big man answered. "What did you want to talk about?"

"About the upcoming scrimmage," Cadan answered. "I know you're scared when the fighting starts, but I wanted you to know that I think you are capable of so much more."

"Josiah tells me that all the time."

"But I don't think you believe it yourself."

"Why do you say that?"

"Because nothing ever changes. You are the strongest person in this whole facility, and you should be able to mow down anyone that comes near you."

"I don't like fighting."

"I know you don't, but we're training for the occasion that we need to use those skills to save our lives or someone we love." Cadan paused, took a deep breath, and then asked the next question. "What is it about fighting that scares you?"

"I just don't like it." Bryce said quietly but firmly.

"No, I mean what *specifically* about it do you not like?"

Bryce studied Cadan for a moment without saying a word. Each set of arms were folded over his broad chest, and he watching Cadan as if wondering whether or not he should answer. Maybe he didn't know the answer to the question. Was it possible that he hadn't actually thought about the specifics to his problem?

Finally he answered. Bryce's voice sank as deep as his despair. "I don't want to hurt anyone."

Cadan was no psychologist, but it was clear that Bryce had injured someone before. That was the reason for his trepidation. His instinct was to pry further and get to the bottom of things, but then he made himself stop. The reason for his reluctance to swing his battle axe was neither any of Cadan's business nor of any importance. What was important was for Bryce to realize his full potential and assist his teammates in the next match.

"Bryce," Cadan said as he put a hand on the big man's shoulder. "Scrimmages are pretend battles. You can't hurt anyone, and if you accidentally do, the healers can take care of it."

"That doesn't mean they won't feel pain. I won't be the cause of pain in anyone's life."

"But Jason and Clay wouldn't mind causing you pain. In fact, they'd likely enjoy it."

"Does that make it right?"

Well of course it doesn't, Cadan wanted to say, but that wouldn't help Bryce break out of this psychosomatic shell he had encased himself in.

"It's not about right or wrong, Bryce," he said instead. "I believe the Knights are a worthy group, but for some reason you all haven't been able to prove yourselves in battle. There is so much untapped potential within the group, and within you. I can see it. I want Josiah and Nieson and everyone else to see it. Everyone dismisses you as a possible threat, but I know that you are much more than they think."

"I will repeat, I don't want to cause anyone pain."

So they had come full circle. Cadan obviously wouldn't get much further than a loop back around to the same argument, so he decided to give up.

"Just remember what I said, okay?"

"I will," Bryce nodded.

Cadan turned to leave, but Bryce stopped him.

"Thank you, Cadan."

"For what?"

"Everyone else yells at me for not fighting hard enough or complains about me behind my back where they don't think I can hear. You're the first person to ever approach me in a reasonable way and want to talk about it."

"Think nothing of it, Bryce. I may be the new guy, and you don't know me that well, but I like you and the rest of the Knights. Being holed up in some government facility is the last thing I want to be doing, but now that I'm here, there is nobody I would rather spend that time with than the Knights."

"What do you think you're doing?" a voice said from behind him.

He turned around and Nate was standing there with his arms folded over his chest and a scowl smeared across his face like dirt.

"We were just talking," Cadan explained.

"Please leave us, Bryce," Nate flipped a hand a few times, gesturing for the big guy to leave them.

Bryce hung his head and walked to the elevator. Most of the guards were back on duty and the foyer leading to the cafeteria was deserted.

"Nate, what is your problem?"

"What is your problem?"

"Where is this coming from? I haven't said or done anything to you."

"Just you being here offends me. You come into our facility and get placed on the Knights' team, and within days, you think you have what it takes to be the leader?"

"I'm not trying to take your spot," Cadan tried to explain.

"Oh, yes, you are. I heard Jude and Madison talking about it in the hall."

"I just had a few suggestions."

"You have been here for days. I have been with DOMA for almost two decades. You come in, start at the bottom and work your way up. If it were up to me, you would be in the back of the kitchen washing greasy pans and cleaning troll shit off the guards' shoes."

"Well, it's a good thing that Josiah decides that type of stuff."

"Josiah doesn't always make the best decisions," Nate said angrily.

"Like the decision to take you off of the Paladin team and let you lead the Knights?"

"That was a mistake, and he knows it. He just can't admit he's wrong."

"I really thought you were smarter than this, Nate. Josiah wanted to test your leadership abilities so he gave you a team with a lot of issues to see what you were made of."

"The Knights are an insolent group of DOMA rejects. None of them would hack it on a Paladin team."

"You are absolutely correct. They are horrible at what they do. But you know what? With a little bit of confidence and just a little bit of guidance, they could be amazing. They have something that the Paladin team will never have."

"What is that?"

"Heart," Cadan said. "It sounds cliché and cheesy, but the Knights express human emotion, some good and some bad. The Paladins are stoic, inhuman machines."

"Be careful. Those are my teammates you're talking about."

"No, they're not," Cadan said, raising his voice. "You just don't get it. That's the problem. You are not a Paladin anymore. You are a Knight. I think I have the power and skill to take any Paladin out. Based on that fact alone, I deserve a spot on that team. But Josiah placed me on the Knights, which by the way suits me just fine, and I will do everything in my power to help my team. That's what a team is for."

"I tried, but they are just too difficult to manage."

"Did you really?" Cadan doubted his statement.

"Of course I did."

"What did you do?"

"I tried leading them."

"No, specifically, what did you do?"

"Well..."

"Did you coach them one on one? Did you give them a pep talk? Did you hold a meeting after a scrimmage and go over what went wrong?" Nate was silent and refused to look at him. "I didn't think so."

"They are beyond hopeless. I mean Bryce just stands there and looks stupid and refuses to do anything."

"Sure that's a weakness, but his weakness has a weakness."

"What do you mean?"

"The thing with Natalie."

"What thing with Natalie? What does she have to do with Bryce?"

"See, you don't even know your own team members. You are completely oblivious to a very obvious fact about Bryce. You're a selfish and indignant person."

The color of Nate's faced turned a fiery red and his mouth twitched, itching to come up with something with which to come back. He knew Cadan was right.

"Nate, I'm not trying to take your place, but the Knights are my friends. If you cannot help them keep from getting their own tails served to them in scrimmages, I will. And if that means I usurp you as team leader, then I think it's a small price to pay for success."

"If I wouldn't get in trouble, I would take you down now. You're in need of a lesson."

"Really?" Cadan smiled coyly, egging him on. He knew that was mean, but if Nate did decide to fight him, it would be best if he were angrier, which would make him sloppier. Cadan used Tomas's trick and knew that in sheer power he bested the Knight's leader by nearly double.

"Josiah made a mistake with you as well," Nate finally said. "You should have been sent to the Nursery, or, better yet, the Lower Pens. I just hope he doesn't come to regret his decision."

With that, Cadan turned and made his way towards the elevator. He knew from the moment that Jude suggested he become the leader, a confrontation with Nate was imminent. Enemies were something that Cadan had plenty of here, despite his wish to at least stay on neutral terms with as many people as possible. Adrenaline was still pumping in his veins, and he knew that he would have to watch his back.

His thoughts turned to his teammates. The Knights were a surly group of teens and there were many reasons on the surface to dislike them. But there was something about them that drew Cadan closer. Was it the fact that they were the underdogs? He knew what it was like to be picked on and ridiculed when you'd rather be a recluse and not noticed at all. Was it that simple?

Did it have anything to do with the fact that now he didn't have to hide who he really was? Back home in Texas, he could only be himself at home where magic was understood and taught on a daily basis. But at school and anywhere else off of the farm, he had to hide such a big part of himself. Derrick and Raney had always been more popular at school, which seemed to make it easier for them. Cadan simply retreated into himself anytime he left the farm, causing the other kids at school to make fun of him. Here at the facility, he didn't have to hide that part of himself – he now had to hide where he came from. And for some reason that was an easier aspect of his life to hide.

With a tiny ding, the elevator doors opened onto the floor that housed Josiah's office. Cadan wasn't sure if Josiah was in his office or if he was available, but he hadn't learned the procedures for making appointments. If this were the principal's office, there would be a secretary with a desk in front of the door, but Josiah didn't appear to have a secretary.

Cadan hesitated before approaching the dark oak double doors. After a few seconds of deep breathing, he finally knocked. At first there was no response or noise from behind those doors, but finally, they opened.

Josiah was standing there on the other side, several feet back. His hand was outstretched. Cadan could feel that he was holding the ruhk, and assumed that he had used the power to open the doors. He clung to his cane with the other hand.

Another man sat on the chair between the two couches. Cadan had not yet seen him around the facility. He stood up as Cadan entered the room, and, even from a distance, he could tell that the man was several inches over six feet. His long brown hair was pulled into a ponytail on the back of his head, and his eyes were a startling red.

"Cadan," the administrator smiled. "What brings you here?"

"Sorry to come unannounced, but I wanted just a minute of your time. I can come back later."

"That is no problem," he smiled. "Come inside, and you may have as much of my time as you like." He motioned towards the other man. "This is Nolan Burrell; he is the Administrator of the Los Angeles Facility."

"Nice to meet you, young man," Nolan said sternly. Where Cadan grew up, it was customary and polite to extend a hand in greeting, but Nolan must have grown up somewhere else.

Cadan simply nodded and took his place on the couch opposite from Josiah. On the table in the middle, Josiah had several books open, which may have been research that his impromptu arrival had interrupted.

"So what can we do for you?"

Cadan took a deep breath. "I wanted to talk to you about my parents." He would have to maintain some degree of deception with his story, and be careful not to reveal anything of his family back home in Texas. "I don't know who they are, or their names, but I do have very vague memories of them. I want to know more."

"Well, that is very interesting," Josiah sat back. Cadan noticed a momentary glance in Nolan's direction. "We must first discuss everything that you do know of them, even down to the minor details. Then we can play detective and try and glean more information from what scattered information we have. Now, describe them physically."

"I believe that my father is human and my mother is at least part elf. That is the memory I have of their faces. For some reason that I cannot explain, I believe they were both ruhk-wielders. I also believe that they were from somewhere in New York City."

"Ah," Josiah understood. "So, was that the reason we found you in Manhattan?"

"Yes," Cadan nodded. "I wanted to search the library records and find some trace of them. My last name is Stone, so I don't think that there would be too many."

"What happened to your parents?"

"I don't know."

"Are they dead or did you run away?"

"I know I didn't run away from home, and I believe that they are dead."

"How old were you when you found yourself without them?"

"I don't know that either. I just have vague memories of them, and then memories without them. I don't know when I lost them."

Nolan grunted. Cadan turned to see the LA Administrator stare down at his folded hands. He couldn't tell if the man was ignoring the conversation or analyzing everything that he said.

"That is not much to work with, Cadan. Are you sure that there is not some detail that you are keeping from me?"

"I promise."

"Well there's not much to go off of here."

"Do you know if they were a part of DOMA?"

Josiah studied Cadan for a minute, as if thinking of something that he was not ready to tell him. He glanced at Nolan again, this time their expressions were both confused. "I don't recall ever having an agent that was married to an elf that also had a child. Doesn't fit anyone I remember, and I remember just about everyone. But it perplexes me that there were possibly two ruhk-wielders, one elven, who were living in Manhattan, so close to one of the DOMA facilities. Unless they hid their magical abilities very well and never once used them, the operatives there would have caught them. And if you have memories of them using the ruhk, then I would assume that they had."

"Are there records that I could look at?"

"There are indeed records, but those are top secret. When DOMA was initiated between the World Wars, one of the policies was to protect all files on individuals in the program for the past few decades of any given year. Just last year we were able to take records from the early 50s out of the highest classified status. Granted, they are still classified enough that not even the President has access to them – in fact, he doesn't even know they exist."

"Why is that?"

"It is mainly to protect the individuals who participate in the program. Most of what we do is controversial. Considering we take individuals such as yourself into custody, we don't want you held responsible for similar actions that you may have to take in the future. It is also to ensure that non-magical government employees do not discover DOMA. The world would erupt in chaos if our existence ever got out."

"I really wish I could find my family," he mumbled.

"I know you do, Cadan," Josiah comforted. "And I wish that there was something that I could do. I do have access to the most secret of archives in the facility and at DOMA headquarters in Nebraska. I promise you that I will peruse them to see if there is something that might lead us to them."

"So are all ruhk-wielders and other magical creatures a part of DOMA? Is it possible that there are some out there who have escaped DOMA's notice?"

Josiah and Nolan both laughed as if sharing an inside joke. "That is a very sensitive topic among the upper echelons of DOMA. Our official stance is that there are absolutely no ruhk-wielders or magical creatures that have escaped our notice. The truth is – and don't tell any of the other senior staff that I admitted this out loud – that there are possibly hundreds that have escaped our notice. And even if we were able to find them, I don't think we have the resources to detain and control them all."

"So then it is possible for my parents to have escaped, unnoticed from DOMA?"

"Quite possible," Josiah answered. "Although highly unlikely, given where you think their location was. I will research this for you."

"What about your family?"

"My family?"

"I heard you were part of the great Ogden family," Cadan answered. "Do you have any relatives still alive?"

Again, Josiah and Nolan shared a look.

"No, sadly they have all departed. I was an only child, and my parents are no longer with us. The Ogdens have a great family legacy that will likely end with me."

"How did the Ogdens cross over?"

"The details are sketchy at best, but we believe that they came through on what Andalorians would refer to as an airship."

"An airship? Like a ship for the air?"

"Precisely. They have the ability to fly. They look very similar to a 17th century seafaring vessel, except the bottom is much wider. An airship is seaworthy, but it is primarily designed for flying."

"How does an airship fly?"

"There are certain numina stones that have specialized powers. One of these stones, called an amethyst, can levitate an inanimate object, such as a ship. Of course, the proper spells are required. Apparently, the Andalorians utilized this type of transportation frequently. It was on one such voyage, the one on which my ancestors sailed, that a storm surge occurred, a portal opened, and they found themselves on Earth."

"When was this?"

"It was my great-grandfather that came over to earth in 1894. There was a rather large group that came over with him. They founded a community where they lived for some time. There is much more I could tell you about them, but unfortunately that would take quite some time."

"Sounds interesting," Cadan smiled. He would have to check the book that Tomas gave him to see if there were any good stories about this period in the Ogden history. "When did your family become involved with DOMA?"

"My grandfather was the first Ogden born on earth and was one of the original founders of DOMA. He and several others were Roosevelt's main advisers in setting up the Department of Magic; many of the traditions we recognize today were created by the original group."

"It would be awesome to see an airship!" He said with genuine sincerity. "Did your great-grandfather's airship survive?"

"If it did, we don't know where it is. Some of the records he kept were damaged, but there is another airship that survived." Josiah leaned back and crossed one leg over the other. He continued. "My mother came over from Andaloria in 1947, when she was only 10 years old. Her family came through a portal in an airship and they crashed in a desert in Nevada."

"That's the same year as the Roswell alien crash conspiracy in New Mexico," Cadan observed.

Josiah chuckled. "That was no mere coincidence, my boy. You see, my mother's ship crashed in June of that year, and DOMA had to act quickly. It occurred at night, so the ship's entry into earth's sky and the subsequent crash made quite a bit of commotion. The first DOMA heard of the situation was on a local news report. The agents had to move in fast." His voice changed slightly; the emotional impact was evident. "They found the ship buried in the dirt some ten or so feet down. My grandfather was a responding agent, and he was able to get inside and rescue my mother and the few people who came with her. My mother's parents had come along for the trip, but did not survive the crash. Once all of the survivors and bodies had been removed, my grandfather went to check on the ship, only to find it sealed tightly. My mother was near the door of the ship, but she denied knowing anything about how the ship had closed, and claimed that she had no idea how to get inside. The Roswell conspiracy was created to distract the public from the truth of what would later be called Area 51."

"So your grandfather rescued his future daughter-in-law?"

"Yes, in fact, he did. My father and my mother met not long after that and ten years later, they were married."

"You have such an interesting family."

Josiah could read the expression on Cadan's face. His reaction to the stories was two-fold: they were entertaining, but they also made him realize just how lacking his life was. He had no interesting stories to tell of his family.

"Cadan, I will do what I can to find information on your family. Please do your best to remain positive; I will keep you apprised of anything I can locate."

"Thank you, Josiah," He nodded and stood to leave. Cadan merely glanced at Nolan, and regretted it immediately. For the entire story, the man had watched him intently, as if trying to discern if he were hearing the truth

"Anytime, Cadan," Josiah nodded back.

Cadan turned and left. The conversation was pleasant, but there was something that still bothered him. He would have figured the more time he spent with Josiah, the more comfortable he would feel. The conversation about Josiah's family had made him feel even more uneasy and he didn't have the first clue why.

Chapter Twelve

Cadan only had six days until he had to participate in a scrimmage against the Paladins. Initially he was excited about the opportunity to display his skills and help his new underdog friends beat the cool kids.

As the days grew closer, his mood went from trepidation to mortification.

Class started promptly at 8:00 AM following breakfast in the cafeteria. Even though there were only thirteen students at the facility, classes were still similar to his high school back home. A collection of a half dozen uniforms were brought to his room the day after his meeting with Josiah, and surprisingly, everything fit nicely.

History, their first class, was with Wendell Winters, the Chief Archivist that he had already heard about. Wendell was even odder than Jude described. His most notorious feature was his hair. The top of his head was bald, but snow white hair shot out from the sides as if reaching for something around him. His eyes were a little crazy and darted all over the place as he lectured about the early Mesopotamian civilizations and the evidence of the presence of ruhk-magic in their beginnings. His mood seemed to shift erratically; one minute he would be chuckling, the next he was screaming. He became especially upset when Clay began nodding off.

The classroom itself was mundane; it embodied the classic preparatory school look. The walls were old paneling with trim everywhere, the floors were an aged cherry wood, and the chalkboard was black with a stain of white puffiness that only comes from years of use. The dark wooden look was interrupted only by three LCD view screens along the far wall of the room. The images on the screens depended on which teacher occupied the room. Wendell chose three different scenes – the Library of Congress, the British National History Museum, and the Castle Sant'Angelo. *Wow, this guy needs to get out more often,* Cadan thought as the lecture droned on.

Their second class was Biology, taught by the beautifully fierce Helena. Even lecturing on different bone fractures the human body could receive and methods of healing them, her voice remained curt and monotone. Her black hair framed a pale, delicate face that was interrupted only by dark violet eye shadow and black eye liner. Her black skirt swished around the room as she walked. Her three view screens showed rotating images of the human body. It was a like some morbid power point with pictures that ranged from real images of a particular organ to diagrams of certain systems. It was tough to decide if he was more scared of Wendell or Helena. At least monotone Helena was more predictable.

Two more classes followed, and they were both short, which Cadan guessed was the Department's way of placing less importance on the two subjects. While Literature and Math played an integral role in the typical education system, for DOMA operatives, they were not too handy in the field. The seemingly bubbly red haired Hazel taught Literature with the passion of a typical high school teacher, and DOMA students were just as equally bored. She went on and on about *The Lord of the Flies* and its allegorical themes of civilization, or some such. Cadan would have thought a few minutes on the topic would have been more than sufficient, but she found enough to fill up an hour. He was distracted by her taupe vest with green lacing and long violet skirt.

The interesting aspect of Literature class was that, apparently, actual books made of paper were old news. DOMA had issued all of the students e-readers.

Hazel had pulled a flat, bright white console from one of her desk drawers and handed it to him, introducing the new device before they began their discussion. Cadan had seen an e-reader once at the local bookstore, but had never actually spent any time with one. From the main menu, he found the folder that contained his library, which was pre-loaded with several classics the class must have been studying for this term. Just a few lines down, he found The Lord of the Flies. With a click of the button, the words appeared on the screen. He was amazed.

Cadan was also issued a Link. Smaller than the e-reader, it looked more like a cell phone. With the device, he could send messages to another person's Link. He sent Jude a message to pay attention. A few minutes later, a message popped up on his screen, but not from Jude. The names were mean, but nothing he hadn't already heard a dozen times before at his high school. Clay and Jason were snickering behind their machines. Cadan deleted the message and stared straight ahead, which seemed to make them a little angry.

Hazel's three screens were just as unusual as the others: a view of Shakespeare's theater in London, Walden Pond, and Poenari Castle. Thankfully they were labeled because he couldn't have picked any of them out of a line up. He had no clue what the castle was, so he looked it up and found that it was the inspiration for Bram Stoker's *Dracula*.

Another female ruhk-wielding instructor named Sheila Brown taught Math. She was at least fifty years old and her hair was a mixture of gray and white. The pencil that was holding the bun of hair on top of her head made it snug, and it didn't once budge as she wrote furiously on the chalk board. She was covering basic algebraic expressions and solving for one variable, material which he had covered in junior high. Jason and Clay, who were both at least a year older than him were having quite a bit of difficulty. It was odd that the view screens were turned off in her class. Occasionally someone asked a question regarding the subject, and Sheila answered it with little patience in her tone.

By the end of the first day of classes, Cadan knew that grades at DOMA would never present a problem.

Classes were followed by a brief lunch. Afterwards each person was given a two hour session to focus on their respective areas of concentration. Natalie left to go to Benton's office, where they were working on computers or something, while Jude and Madison trained with Nieson. Bryce needed more one on one time, so he trained with Tregellos individually. Darius was completely silent on where he went, and the others didn't seem too forthcoming on the details.

Sheila advised him that he was given a one week reprieve on choosing a concentration. He decided to spend that time reading the book about the great Ogden family.

He found a comfortable reading chair in the lounge near their room, kicked off his shoes and curled up with the dusty old leather-bound book.

The first story was about the gods and goddesses of Andaloria. The youngest goddess Achama, who was curious and sometimes troublesome to the others, was wooed by the evil Archon Kronak. Because of her curiosity, she was pulled from the Pleroma and died in the manner of a goddess. The whole story sounded like a mash up of a fairy tale and Greek mythology. He was entertained, and that seemed to be the point. He wasn't sure what an Archon was, but he filed it away in his mind to remember to ask Tomas later.

The man named Ogden, which later relatives would use as their last name, was a leader of a small city in the south of the main continent of Andaloria. He was charged by one of Achama's priestesses, Doriana, to take up the mantle of the goddess Achama. The two were later married and begat offspring who harnessed the power of the lost goddess. Cadan actually chuckled out loud. The story almost read as if it were actual history. The Ogdens were an egotistical bunch to pander to such a story. Somebody must have gotten a little heavy handed when they were tracing the Ogden family tree.

At some point towards the end of the first chapter, Cadan must have dozed off. He found himself back on the streets of New York City. The sky was dark, but there were no street lights as there had been the first night. He held up his hand and could barely make out the faint shape of his fingers in front of him. Lightning flashed overhead, but there was no sound. It was an eerie feeling. Goose bumps popped up on his arms and the hair on the back of his neck was sticking straight up.

He knew from the beginning that this was a dream, but there was no way to wake himself. Something clawed at his mind, forcing him to lie in the deep slumber that had become an urban nightscape of despair. He cried out and while he could feel the vibrations of his vocal chords, no sound came from his mouth.

He started moving forward, down what he assumed was a street. There was a faint light coming from a window a few blocks ahead. Even though his feet hit the pavement, he heard nothing.

Behind, some leaves crushed under the weight of a footstep. He whirled around, but in the vast nothingness, there was no movement.

He heard it again, only this time it was a little to the right. He turned, and, in the slight bit of light emitted from the window, he could see the silhouette of a man. He appeared to be wearing a robe with the hood pulled low over his face to conceal his identity.

Cadan tried screaming, but no sound came out.

The dark figure was still, but then all at once, it was moving. Quickly, it made its way towards Cadan, with one hand lifted, outstretched as if reaching for him.

His body started convulsing. He awoke and found Jude and Madison standing over him, worried looks on their faces.

"Are you okay?" asked Jude.

Cadan was sweating profusely. The book had fallen onto the floor in front of him. He shook his head in an attempt to bring his mind out of its stupor. He wiped his brow and looked around.

"We heard you scream from down the hall," said Jude. "Do we need to take you to Dr. Hadrian?"

"No," Cadan answered, shaking his head. "I think I just had a bad dream."

"Okay," Jude said finally. He ruffled Cadan's hair and then sat down next to him. "What are you doing?"

"Reading this book that Tomas gave me."

"What book?"

"The history of the Ogdens," Cadan answered.

"How fun," Jude chuckled as he leaned back in the chair. "We had to hurry back so that Madison could watch her game."

She sat on the sofa not far from them and used the remote to turn on the flat screen TV. With the punch of a button, she found ESPN.

"What game?" he asked. Cadan actually crossed his fingers that it would be soccer.

Madison didn't answer. Instead, her eyes lit up when she found the right channel. Girls – or people that looked like girls, were roller skating around a rink that was raised on the outside and beveled towards the center. Most of the women were skating around in a cluster, holding their arms up to block each other. There were two teams, and the girls on each team wore the same colored shirts and helmets. From there, the similarities ceased. Stickers and paint adorned their helmets and arms. They all wore tights on their legs and a bigger variety of accessories than he had ever seen. Their elbows and knees were protected by pads, and just when he was about to ask why, a small girl came barreling through the crowd.

The crowd screamed as the tiny girl ducked and jumped her way through the mess of tangled limbs. Her green helmet was adorned with a star on each side. The other girls in green helmets blocked the red helmets from taking out Star Helmet Girl.

As she made it past the last one, Madison jumped up and yelled triumphantly. It was apparent that she was a green helmet fan.

"Chupacabra is my girl!"

"Chupacabra?" Cadan mouthed to Jude.

He shrugged and smiled. "She's Madison's favorite player."

"And only the best in the entire league."

"What is this?"

"It's roller derby," Madison said exasperated, as if he should have been born with this knowledge. "Only the best sport there is."

He immediately understood a little more about Madison. The raving lunatic girls on the screen were her role models for life. No obstacle was too large for Madison, throwing adversaries to the ground as she pummeled her way through. The similarities carried as far as her dark make up.

"Someday, I want to leave here, move to Austin, and join the Cobras." He assumed that was the green team.

Another thought came to mind. There had to be a way to motivate her to use that same strength and aggression on the battlefield.

Darius and Natalie returned from their individual sessions, followed quickly by Bryce. The twins sat on the couch on each side of Madison. Bryce sat in the chair next to Jude. Darius looked angrier and more frustrated than Cadan had seen him yet.

What's wrong with Darius? Cadan asked Jude telepathically.

Don't bring it up, Jude cautioned.

Is it because of his training? What does he study?

We have no idea and the one time that I asked, I almost got the living crap beat out of me. Whatever it is, he doesn't like to talk about it or have it mentioned.

Thanks for the warning.

Each of the next five days followed much the same routine. Cadan was given a week to determine his concentration of study, which meant that the first day after his first bout with the Paladins, he would have to make the decision.

There were no classes on the day of the scrimmage. Cadan wished that there had been, so that he'd have had something else to occupy his mind. His stomach churned worse than a hurricane in the Gulf. The black and blue standard uniform fit more comfortably than he thought it would, and he was surprised by the range of motion his body could still maintain despite the tightness of the outfit.

He and Jude met the rest of the Knights on the Training Level. The door to the elevator hissed open to the large monitoring area. The Paladins were already in one corner, suited up and ready for battle. They burst into laughter as the Knights entered, and though they weren't looking at Cadan and his teammates, he was sure the timing was a little too coincidental.

Nieson and Tregellos were busy at their respective terminals, preparing the simulation. Josiah stood just behind them watching their progress. When he noticed them enter, he smiled and waved in their direction.

"Boys," he nodded. "I came for your first session, Cadan."

"Great," Cadan shrugged. "Just one more thing to make me nervous."

"I don't want to make you nervous, Cadan. Just pretend that I'm not here."

Cadan knew that his skills could match any of the Knights or Paladins. From the past few days of conversation, the Knights had finally settled on the fact that he would lead their team. Jude wasn't sure how to break the news to Nate, but he didn't really seem to care. Cadan wasn't nervous that his team would fail. He just didn't want to fail his team.

Failure had been such a big part of their lives, and they had grown accustomed to the idea that they would never beat the Paladins. He could see it in their utter lack of confidence. Sure, he was an outcast at school, but he had always excelled at both soccer and track events. That had given him a certain level of confidence. The Knights were failures in every way. He could see it in their walk, hear it in their talk, and he was determined to change it.

Colonel Nieson handed him a sword. "I want you to use this, Cadan."

It was beautiful. A silver grip with a round sapphire pommel decorating the hilt. On the blade, there were light etchings of a script of language he was not familiar with.

"Thank you," Cadan offered back. "I don't understand, though. This seems to be a special sword."

"It is my old sword," he answered. "I haven't used it in years, and it should be put it to good use. I'm sure one day you will find a blade of your own, but for now consider this yours."

"The edges are sharp, though. Can I use it?"

"Josiah placed a temporary spell on the edges for this session. The blade won't actually puncture anything in the simulation, so you can't accidentally kill anyone. Once the session is over, the spell will be broken and the blade will be as sharp as ever."

"Thank you again."

"Just make me proud," he mouthed low, so that the rest of the people in the room couldn't hear.

Cadan and Nieson joined the others on their side of the room. Nate watched out the window in his usual sullen fashion. It didn't seem to faze him much that Cadan would be joining the battle.

The door opened again, and Tomas entered the room, wearing his training uniform. It looked as brand new and fresh as his own did.

"What is he doing here?" Anthony spoke first. His tone sounded like he was spitting.

"I invited him," Cadan spoke up.

Tomas looked as if he wanted to retreat into his shirt like a turtle. His face was red and his head hung low.

"Absolutely not," Nate turned from the window.

Josiah ignored them all. The old man was smiling brightly at Tomas. "I'm glad you decided to join us, Tomas. We would be glad to allow you to participate in the scrimmage."

"No way," Nate continued.

"Young man, that is not your decision," Josiah warned him.

"But Josiah, that will have two extra players," Anthony protested.

"Are you scared of losing to the Knights?" Josiah asked with a glimmer in his eye.

"Of course not!" Anthony responded.

"I have an idea," Jude said, stepping forward.

"Do tell," Josiah nodded.

"Nate can fight with the Paladins."

"What?!" Nate and Anthony said simultaneously. Natalie and Darius shared a look of utter horror.

"It's no secret that Nate doesn't like us," Jude explained. "And that would even the teams."

"It wouldn't even be a fair fight," Anthony said. "We already pulverize you, and now you want to give us the only decent person on your team?"

Jude met his gaze. "If you're so confident, why do I hear your voice shaking? Is that liquid running down your leg, Anthony?"

Josiah stifled a laugh. When Anthony shot forward, Josiah held up a hand of caution.

"Who would lead the Knights?" Nate asked.

"Cadan will."

The Paladins chuckled.

Cadan turned to Nieson and Tregellos. Both had smiles on their faces and Nieson gave him a slight nod of approval.

"Cadan," said Nieson. "Do you agree to this?"

"Yes," Cadan answered immediately.

"It's settled then," Josiah said with a mischievous smile. "Nate shall join the Paladins. Tomas shall join the Knights, with Cadan as their leader."

The knot in his stomach returned. What had he gotten himself into?

Chapter Thirteen

The inside of the training room was colder than he expected. Natalie mentioned that they had to keep it that way because of all of the machinery, but later in the match, the ruhk-fire would heat the place up fast.

They took their positions on the slightly raised platform at the right side of the room. Cadan was in the center towards the front. The others assembled behind him and spread out. They were a motley crew of dysfunctional soldiers preparing themselves for their first battle together as a new team.

He looked to his left and right and gave each of his teammates a nod. Jude and Madison were thrilled to begin the match. Bryce and Tomas looked petrified, and Darius and Natalie were somewhere in between.

"So what's the plan?" Darius leaned over and mumbled out the side of his mouth.

"We'll have to wait and see."

"What?" Natalie hissed. "You said you had a plan."

"I'm going to shield them – or most of them."

"What do you mean most of them?" Jude asked. For the first time, he looked a little concerned.

"Carmen and Anthony are fairly powerful, and Russell is nearly as powerful as me. I didn't count on Nate, which sort of throws it all off."

"So can you shield them?" Madison asked.

"At least three of them," Cadan answered.

"That will have to work," Darius said, perking up, determination appearing on his face as he stared straight ahead.

"Let's see who I can shield first and then how they react," Cadan explained. "We need to get Darius in the air in the beginning while we can provide some cover."

"What if they shield us first?" Tomas asked.

"That's not going to happen. I think Russell is the only one that can shield any of us, and I don't think he can get one around me. Not to mention, he's the main one I'm throwing a shield over."

Tomas didn't look confident. "If he can't shield you, what makes you think you can shield him?"

"Just wait and see," Cadan told them.

The sounds of the machinery in the walls hushed them all. The simulation was about to commence.

"Okay, soldiers." Nieson's voice was coming from the small earpiece in his ear and through speakers over their heads. "Prepare to begin the scrimmage. We've added a few surprises to make this afternoon entertaining."

What was that supposed to mean? The hum of the machinery behind the walls got louder. Cadan's stomach felt like it was going to drop out of his body. When he turned to look at Jude, his eyes were wide. The goose bumps running up his arms made Cadan feel even worse. Jude shook his head at him in utter astonishment. Even from across the room, Cadan could see the Paladins shifting awkwardly.

Something was about to happen.

Cadan readied himself. He could feel ruhk-magic being drawn from five members of the Paladins. Behind him, Tomas was tapping into the power. Cadan was surprised that he had drawn so much despite his trembling hands.

Cadan noticed that Natalie had not bothered to prepare herself. He turned and looked at her straight in the eyes. "You can do this, Nat. Remember everything the Paladins have ever done to you. This is your chance to get them back for all of it."

Her troubled face suddenly brightened, and a smile appeared. Her shoulders went back and her posture straightened. As a violet glow began surrounding her, he knew she was ready.

He didn't dare draw on the power. He opened himself up to the small intangible repository in his chest. The heat of the ruhk radiated just on the surface. He was so close he could almost touch it, but he resisted the urge. To draw any for the spell he would use would just tip his hand. Cadan had trained with Simon countless hours, probably more than the Paladins ever had, and he was ready for this. He could pull ruhk-magic and perform any spell before Russell could throw a hand back.

"Um, what's going on Cadan?" Jude leaned towards Cadan. His roommate was a low-level ruhk-wielder but of sufficient enough power that he could tell when someone close to him was using the power.

"Don't worry about me," Cadan mumbled back. "You make sure we take them out one by one, and I'll worry about cutting them off."

Jude couldn't reply because Nieson's voice came on the intercom with just one word. "Begin."

The first few seconds were slow motion in Cadan's mind. Even replaying it, he could remember every millisecond. He had experienced heightened senses, such as sight or smell, when using the ruhk-magic. But in this case, he may have used so much power that he thought it actually may have slowed time, or at least made him more acutely aware of time's passing.

Russell threw both arms up. He was sending a shield their way.

Cadan turned his body towards Jude, and in one rapid motion, he drew power, extended his right arm, whirled back around to the Paladins, and sent a shield their way.

Cadan caught sight of a small, nearly invisible field coming at him, but his own larger shield had enough momentum to swallow it like a whale eating a minnow.

Russell recoiled as the kickback from his failed spell was forced onto him. He screamed as an invisible shield found its way over him. He could still pass through physically, but he was cut off from the power.

Cadan's shield managed to envelope Anthony, Nate, and Carmen, as well. All three stared at him in disbelief until anger returned and the two men drew their weapons. They would fight any way that they could. Carmen stood there, surprised at what had just occurred, gripping the sides of her head in confusion.

Heather was the only one he had not been able to trap within the spell. He wondered if it was some sort of subconscious act because he felt sorry for her or something. Even as she stood there on her platform, the only ruhk-wielder left on her team, she appeared lost. She stared back at him with the same longing look on her face.

He pulled the sword from the sheath at his side. Jude had his staff ready, and Madison had her bow up with an arrow knocked.

He turned his head slightly to the right and muttered quietly. "Go, Darius."

Darius's uniform was identical to theirs, except he had a large tear away strip in the back of his shirt. From that hole, two large wings sprouted up and out in each direction. They were lush and full, like a giant eagle about to take flight. The deep blackness of his plumes only accentuated their beauty.

As his wings spanned, he bent his knees and pushed off from the ground, flying into the air faster than Cadan had thought possible. It was the first time he had ever seen Darius fly with such confidence.

Cadan jumped down from the platform and made his way toward the center of the room. Jude and Madison were right behind him; Natalie and Tomas followed more slowly. Bryce stood his ground. He had actually unsheathed his mace and looked ready to use it. That was some progress, Cadan thought.

Nate, Jason, and Clay were meeting the Knights in the middle from the other side. Anthony, Carmen, and Russell were preoccupied with finding a way to break through the shield. He had tied the spell off well enough that the battle would be long over before they figured a way out. Heather was descending the platform behind the men.

When they neared the middle, Nate drew his sword and charged.

Cadan sidestepped his first lunge, but didn't lose his footing. Nate was more of a skilled fighter than Cadan would have given him credit for. He needed to give him an equally formidable display. Nate pivoted back towards him, so he lunged hard. His sword came down and met Nate's, and he put all of his strength in the strike. Cadan could see Nate's arms lock, and he knew he felt the force in his shoulders. Before Nate could react, Cadan pulled back and came from underneath. Again Nate blocked it, but this time Cadan used the strength of both his arms and legs, and Nate couldn't resist the power of that drive.

Nate tumbled back. Cadan caught a glimpse of Madison pummeling Clay with arrows, but the dwarf was able to block each one with his shield. He had much faster reflexes than Cadan had expected. Jude was parlaying with Jason. The half-troll's sword and strength were almost too much for Jude to handle with his staff, but luckily the half-elf was nimble enough to dodge any significant blow.

Heather threw ruhk-fire in their direction. Natalie and Tomas were on it before Cadan could react and blocked them all. They continued sending and blocking volleys of fire. Just as Madison had said, the room had already begun heating up.

"Darius," Cadan yelled, motioning towards Clay. He was still flying overhead and Cadan could see the seraph prepare for a dive.

Just then two large metal bars came swinging from opposite walls, near the ceiling. Darius screamed out and had to take evasive maneuvers to avoid both. Just when he cleared those, two more came protruding from the two opposite walls. Cadan didn't remember anything like this from the last session, so this must have been part of Nieson's "entertainment."

He turned his attention back to Nate, who paid no mind to what was going on above him. He was determined to take Cadan down.

As they traded blows with their swords, he heard a hum of machinery from beneath them. Cadan braced himself for another surprise; but nothing could have prepared him for what came. Large guns appeared on the opposite wall from the monitoring area. Suddenly large balls began shooting towards them.

At first Cadan almost laughed, until one made contact with Clay's back and sent him flying twenty feet or more to land against the glass on the opposite wall. Cadan ducked just in time to dodge one and backed away from Nate. His opponent was retreating as well. He turned to make sure that Madison was okay, and Heather slammed him hard with ruhk-fire.

Cadan was off his feet and flying backwards towards their platform. His vision went black momentarily as he tried picking himself up off the ground.

He felt two hands lifting him up and saw Madison and Jude on each side. Checking to make sure that the shield spell was in place, he looked around. Russell had managed to produce only a small amount of ruhk-fire, as most of the shield was still intact, but there was enough give that his opponent managed a small spell. Tomas stood in front of him, meeting him blast for blast. Natalie was just a few feet away from them, blocking Heather from coming any closer.

"We need to regroup," Cadan told them, as he saw Anthony and Carmen descending the platform. Both had swords drawn and were ready to fight. "We need to finish this."

Jason shrieked as he surprised Natalie from the side. He had his sword raised in one hand, his axe in the other, and was descending on her at superhuman speed.

A roar vibrated the entire room, as Bryce descended the platform. He had two maces drawn and was coming up on Natalie from the opposite side. She ducked just as Bryce jumped over her and smashed one mace against Jason's sword and the other against his axe. The two men were locked in a struggle as Natalie backed away and resumed her ruhk battle with Heather.

Cadan descended the platform with Jude and Madison once again, and met Anthony, Carmen, Nate, and Clay head on.

Carmen drew her sword and came towards them. "I got this bitch," Madison called out as she drew her long dagger and crept towards Carmen.

"I got Nate," Jude said as he approached their former leader from the right.

"That leaves us, girly boy," Anthony chuckled as he came towards Cadan.

He didn't give the Paladin leader's statement the credibility of a reply.

Anthony struck first. Cadan blocked his swing with Nieson's sword. Again and again Anthony hacked at him. At first he made defensive maneuvers only. Cadan waited until his fifth swing, and then reaching out to the ruhk, he shot a bolt of ruhk-fire.

It was enough of a blast that Anthony lost his footing, and Cadan brought his sword down towards his opponent's face.

"That's hardly fair," Anthony said, as Cadan stopped just short of his nose.

"Just a little taste of what you put the Knights through in past scrimmages."

"You're weak," Anthony said as he knocked Cadan's sword back with his. Cadan could have taken him out then and there, but he was angry with the

Paladins for the manner in which they had treated the Knights in the past. From what Jude had told him, they were never content with a simple victory and relished finding new ways to humiliate them. Cadan wanted to continue toying with Anthony, hoping that he would grasp the point Cadan was trying to make.

He stood up and began striking at Cadan again. This time Cadan only allowed him two swings, before he took an offensive stance and began hacking at Anthony with his sword. Simon had always taught him to make sure that every swing counted.

"So I heard that you're looking for your parents," Anthony chided as they continued their fight. Cadan didn't respond. "They must have left when they realized what a miserable son they had."

He realized that Anthony was only making comments to get under his skin and distract him, but at that moment Cadan was furious. He felt that making a fight so personal was repulsive.

Out of the corner of his eye, Cadan noticed Clay coming up from behind him with his axe bared. Cadan didn't think he could take them both on at the same time with just one sword. A blur appeared from the sky and suddenly Darius was there lifting Clay into the air. They travelled up twenty feet and then Darius dropped him. The dwarf landed in a heap on the ground, unconscious or worse, but Cadan didn't care.

He noticed two of the balls that had hit Clay before were a few feet behind Anthony. Cadan knew that this was his chance. The large, almost spherical, objects appeared to be made of stone.

Gripping his sword with both hands, Cadan began wide strokes with his weapon, slicing and chopping. Anthony was a formidable opponent and was able to counter each time, but the force behind each one was pushing him backwards. As his left foot retreated behind him, it made contact with the spheres on the ground.

He lost his footing and waved both arms, including his sword arm. It would only take him seconds to regain his footing, but that was sufficient time for Cadan. He rotated his sword so that the flat side was towards his opponent, and with one swing directly into the side of his head, Cadan knocked Anthony unconscious.

Cadan scanned the room to see his teammates take down their opponents one by one. With the fall of their leader, the Paladins had lost their determination. Carmen and Nate were in a heap on the ground in front of Jude and Madison. Natalie tied Heather up with a spell, and Bryce had sent Jason flying into a wall, after which the half-troll surrendered.

Tomas sent a force spell against Russell, knocking him back to the platform. Russell fell to the floor, trying his best to hold himself up with his arms.

They came together in the center of the room to congratulate each other. Jude's white teeth were showing behind his gaping smile, and Madison looked even happier than when she had watched the roller derby match. Even Darius's typical grumpy demeanor had dissolved.

"You bastards!"

They turned towards the Paladins' side of the room. Russell had managed to stand, and he was clenching the ruhk-fire in his hands. Apparently Cadan's shield was loose enough that he could pull a larger degree of power.

Cadan's shield was still intact even though it had loosened somewhat when Heather had hit him earlier. The agonized look on Russell's face was pure fury, and he was ready to strike.

Cadan performed a quick spell and then another shield was over the Paladin, only this one he could not walk through. He had no idea what Russell was capable of in his state of madness. He didn't want to take any chances. He had two shields over Russell now, one that was impermeable and would not allow him or his magic outside of it, and another that made a filing attempt to cut him off from the ruhk. Cadan was much stronger in the former, so he dropped the latter. His hope was to contain Russell, but his full abilities had returned.

With another scream of rage, he loosed his ruhk-fire. The energy was mainly contained within the shield Cadan had created, but some residual power seeped through. He threw up a shield around himself and the other Knights. Only Jude, Natalie, and Tomas could see the shield in place, so the others flinched when the ruhk-fire swirled around them.

"I hate being trapped!" Russell yelled again, as another wave of power pulsed from him. This time Cadan felt the sheer strength of his spell as it pressed against his shield.

"Stop, you crazy freak!" Jude yelled at him.

Another wave struck. This time Cadan almost lost his balance, but Jude and Darius were there to help him stay up.

Josiah's voice called over the intercom. "Russell, release the ruhk-fire at once."

Another pulse of ruhk-fire exploded.

Josiah didn't bother with another message. The door to the training area opened and Josiah, Helena, and Benton entered the room. The door slid shut behind them, and a locking mechanism followed immediately.

The trio of senior mages slowly made their way towards the enraged Paladin. Benton and Helena placed shields over the fallen Paladins to protect them from Russell's tantrum. Josiah placed a shield over the three adults.

By that time enough of the ruhk energy from Russell's spell had seeped through Cadan's shield and was swirling around the room. He had never seen such an effect, and he was scared at what might happen.

Josiah turned to Cadan. "Remove yourself and your team from the training room."

"I can't keep my shield up from outside the room."

"I will place a shield over yours, and then you can release and leave." Cadan nodded his acknowledgement.

Before Josiah could perform his spell, the largest pulse of power yet belted through the room, shaking the entire area. Cadan could still see Russell's eyes behind the aura of the magic, and they were red. He had completely lost his mind.

"Russell!" Josiah yelled. "Stop this at once! You are about to destroy yourself and all of us!"

"What do we do?" he asked Josiah from across the room. "If I don't release my shield, he'll destroy himself with his own power."

"But if you release it, we are all surely dead. Give me a moment to place another one on top of yours."

Again Josiah lifted his arm to perform the spell, and again another wave of energy was sent around the room. This time everyone standing in the room toppled to the floor.

Cadan was at a loss about what to do. Did he release the shield and endanger everyone else, or maintain Russell's shield and potentially allow Russell to kill himself? As he looked at his teammates and their pained expressions of fear, he made his choice. He didn't want Russell to die, but he would never allow him to kill everyone else – especially his new friends.

And then it happened. The shield around Russell turned shades of red and purple as the ruhk-fire inside boiled. They heard Russell scream one last time as his own ruhk-fire coursed through his body.

The scrimmage was over.

Chapter Fourteen

Several minutes passed before Cadan released the shield protecting the Knights. The trio of elder mages had dropped their shields and was already inspecting the platform where Russell had once stood. Jude gripped his shoulder and whispered quietly that it was okay to let go. Cadan could see the smoke coming from his own mouth, an after-effect of using so much power.

The heat in the room outside of the dome was staggering. The Knights instantly began sweating. He walked over to the Paladins' platform to the spot where Josiah had kneeled. Russell's magic had incinerated any evidence that he had ever existed. Not even his clothes were left.

Tears were welling in his eyes, and it seemed like something deep within his chest had left him forever. He felt numb and empty as he stared at the charred metal platform.

Josiah's face was grim as he stood back up. Helena looked furious while Benton scratched his balding head.

"Cadan," the Administrator said as he approached. "This was not your fault."

Cadan couldn't think of a response. Did he feel responsible? Of course he did. This whole scrimmage was his plan and execution. He had shielded the ruhk-wielding Paladins and was the determining factor in the Knights securing their first victory. Could he have done anything different? He had embarrassed Anthony in front of everyone, and the humiliating defeat of Russell's team had left the man with only two options: surrender or keep fighting.

He felt a hand slip around his waist and heard Natalie whisper a thank you. Darius placed his hand on Cadan's shoulder as a silent sign of comfort. Tomas stood there with a baffled look on his face and Jude and Madison stood behind the twins, lost for words.

Helena walked away from the group and began checking the fallen Paladins for serious injuries. Tregellos and Nieson ran into the room, followed by Sheila, Hazel, and Wendell. All five were cursing as they assisted Helena in checking on the injured students.

The training room itself was something from a disaster movie. Burn scars were set deep into the walls. The floor was uneven in several places. Smoke was billowing up from most of the charmed areas. The effects of Russell's outburst were everywhere.

Josiah addressed the Knights. "It does not appear that any of you are suffering from serious injuries. Despite the awful catastrophe that occurred here today, I still want to congratulate you on your victory. You all fought well as both individuals and as a team, and that makes me immensely proud of all of you." He sighed heavily. "I would ask that you return to your rooms to change and rest. You will all receive a respite from classes until further notice."

They returned to the dormitory level and went their separate ways to their rooms.

Cadan set his Link down on the nightstand, and plopped down on his bed. Jude was behind him and kicked off his shoes plopping down on the bed. Neither said a word for quite some time.

Jude finally broke the silence. "You feel responsible, don't you?"

"Of course I do."

"Well, you shouldn't."

"How could I not? The whole plan was my idea."

"But it wasn't your plan that made Russell do that."

"I don't want to talk about this anymore."

"Fine." He could tell by Jude's tone that he was pouting. "We should go shower and change."

Cadan grabbed a bundle of clothes and a towel and followed Jude out the door and down the hall to the men's shower area. They set their clothes down in individual stalls and then walked to the shower area. Bryce and Darius were already there, and a few minutes later, Tomas joined them.

Other than nods of greeting, no one said a word. The only sound was that of the showers spraying water and the hum of machinery behind the walls.

Darius finally spoke. "I saw Hazel in the hall on our way in."

"What was she doing on our floor?" Jude asked.

"She was getting clothes from the Paladins' rooms. She said that they'd be in the infirmary for a few days."

"Did we really beat them up that bad?" Tomas asked.

"She said their main injuries were from Russell's ruhk-fire. Some of the magic hit them before Helena and Benton could get them shielded."

"I should have shielded them, too," Cadan said quietly.

"Are you done with your pity party?" Jude wheeled around to face him.

"What?" he asked.

"I asked if you were done blaming yourself for what happened. How could you have shielded the Paladins too? You already had Russell and all of us shielded, which is more than what anyone else I know could have done."

"I wish I could have done more." He placed his palms against the tile of the shower and let the water hit his face. The barrage of the hot water somehow eased some of the tension he felt in every part of his body.

"Are you blaming yourself?" Darius asked.

Before Cadan could say anything, Jude answered. "He is."

"Man, you should not be thinking like that," Darius told him. "They were a bunch of arrogant assholes who couldn't handle the fact that we finally beat them."

"Well said," Tomas added. "Anthony was upset that someone could match him in sword skills, and Russell was even more upset that he was no longer the most powerful student here. What could you have done differently? What could have possibly happened differently that was within your direct control and would have provided a different outcome?"

They were all right. Everything they said was spot on, but for some reason he couldn't shake the guilt. His actions, whether direct or indirect, had led to Russell's death. He had a hand in the Paladin's demise.

As if reading his mind, Jude spoke to him through his. *It's okay to feel like crap about this. But just know that it was not your fault. We all know it.*

I killed someone today.

No you didn't. You protected everyone from an idiot. You protected me. You are anything but a murderer.

Thank you. It was good that the conversation was mental and the water pouring over his face helped to disguise the tears.

Cadan turned the shower off and found his clothes. He and Jude quickly dressed and returned to their rooms. They dropped their dirty clothes in the hamper and met the others in the lounge down the hall.

The girls were already there. They both tried to force small smiles as he entered.

"How are you?" Natalie asked.

"I'm okay." It was a lie, but as Jude had pointed out, Cadan had to end the pity party.

Even Tomas joined them in the lounge for a few minutes, before returning to the Library to finish up on some work. The conversation was light, as no one really wanted to dredge up any of the day's events. Even the victory was bittersweet; nobody wanted to make a reference to the scrimmage. Jude made a few attempts at joking, and there was a little brief laughter, but the mood was definitely somber. They stayed in the lounge for an hour or so, and then went as a group to dinner.

Cadan awoke from slumber with a start. A loud siren filled the room and a light in the upper corner of their bedroom was flashing yellow. He looked at the clock on their nightstand and it showed just past 11:00 pm, only an hour after they had went to bed.

Beside him in his own bed, Jude was sitting up and rubbing the sleep from his eyes.

"What's going on?" Cadan asked over the noise of the siren.

"Ah crap," Jude said. He leaned his legs over the side of the bed. "Some medium level emergency. If it were high level, it would be flashing red. Either way it's loud and hurts my head," he growled.

"Has it ever flashed red before?"

"One time," he answered loudly, trying to be heard over the annoying commotion. "Two ogres broke out of the pens and made it all of the way to the cafeteria. Any time there is an immediate threat to our lives on site, then it's considered red. If it were red, we would have to get our weapons and prepare for battle immediately. Yellow means that there is no immediate threat to our lives, but there's still crap in our fan."

It took him a moment to realize that Jude meant that *crap was hitting the fan*. For living such sheltered lives in a government installation, the Knights sure knew their fair share of colloquialisms. That said a lot for their heavy television watching, except for the fact that Jude managed to butcher the expression.

"What do we do?"

"We dress and then report to the Command Center."

They dressed in under a minute and retrieved their weapons. He still had Nieson's sword, and hooked its sheath to his belt. They left the room and made their way to the elevator. Along the way, they were joined by the other Knights. Darius was in a worse mood than normal, and Natalie looked liked she was sleep walking.

When they reached the Command Center, Cadan noticed soldiers running everywhere. It looked like one of those war movies where someone just yelled for everyone to man their battle stations.

The Command Center was a large room that reminded him much of the monitoring area in the Training Room. There were computer terminals and machinery everywhere. The center of the room held a large railing in a perfect circle that stood about waist level. As they passed by the central construction, he noticed a digital map in the center.

There were two rows of seats that ringed the circumference of the room, the outer of which was raised about two feet higher than the inner. Instead of seats, there was an extended bench for each row.

In the center of the room, Josiah stood with Helena and Wendell. Hazel, Benton, and Sheila stood on the far side from the Knights. A little behind

Josiah stood a man that Cadan had never seen before. The man's face had hardened into a scowl that appeared to be permanent, and his hair was a deep, unnatural red that reminded him of Daphne's hair. His eyes were the most severe feature of all; they looked as if they outlined with thick eyeliner, and they watched Cadan as he entered the room. He wore a purple robe with intricate designs on the yellow edges.

Jude saw Cadan staring. "That's Lars," he explained. "He's our resident fairy and the main mode of transport in and out of this place."

"What?" he asked, confused.

"Fairies have the ability to open portals that connect one place to another. Lars is one of the best and the one assigned to this facility."

There were at least a half-dozen soldiers in the room on the opposite side from Josiah and the other ruhk-wielders. At the front, an older man with a green uniform stood firmly near the center railing, his hands clasped together behind his back and his feet spread apart. His smooth, short white hair was a stark contrast to his tanned, well-worn skin.

"That's General Rieken. He's in charge of military personnel within DOMA." Jude shook his head. "Stay away from him. He is mean and doesn't care much for anything of the magical variety."

"Isn't he in the wrong line of work?" Cadan asked.

"He sees it as a paycheck and a way to keep magical people segregated away from the tax-paying public."

Josiah noticed the Knights enter the room. "Please come in," he beckoned with the hand not holding his cane. "I will explain everything shortly."

All in attendance looked as if they were still asleep, especially Wendell. Everyone but Josiah appeared to have been roused from sleep just minutes before.

He noticed the absence of the Paladins. They were probably still in the infirmary recovering from their failure in the scrimmage earlier. Tregellos and Nieson joined them soon after. When they entered, Josiah began the meeting.

"It pains me to say, but something unspeakable has occurred today."

Was he talking about Russell's death?

"First I will mention the death of a student. Russell was a formidable fighter and one of the best students we had in the program, but his rage got the best of him today. His death was his own fault. No one else is to blame for the atrocity, and if there are any opinions to the contrary, I would advise you to keep them to yourself. Any spoken judgments regarding the matter will be dealt with in a very harsh manner." He paused and looked around the room, his eyes settling on Cadan for a few seconds longer than everyone else.

His words were only mildly reassuring.

Josiah continued. "Approximately thirty minutes ago, I contacted the Los Angeles Facility and received no response. We assumed it was a communication breakdown, so Lars transported Benton and Helena to the other facility to render aid. The facility was abandoned – ransacked. Everything of value was gone."

"What about the Pens?" Nieson asked, concern already evident on his face.

"Empty," Josiah gritted his teeth. "Helena ran a diagnostic on their computer system and there was no sign of significant life in the Facility."

"Where did they go?" Tregellos asked.

"We are not sure. I checked with Durham in Nebraska to see if this was part of some higher order, and he knew nothing of it."

Cadan turned to Jude and whispered, "Who's Durham?"

"That's Josiah's boss," he explained. "The head honcho of DOMA."

Cadan nodded.

"What about their tracking beacons?" Sheila asked.

"Their signals are gone. We don't know if they've removed the devices or not, but we do know that they have been completely disabled."

"Do you think Nolan is behind this?" Rieken asked. "Or is this an outside operation?"

"I fear that this could only have come from the inside," Josiah explained. "There are fail-safes within each Facility that would make it nearly impossible for anyone but the Administrator to orchestrate something of this nature."

Jude spoke next. "What of his Paladin team?"

"His current roster is at three, all ruhk-wielders, one of whom is three quarters elf and an augur. I do not know if they are a part of this, but I have suspicions."

What's an augur? Cadan asked Jude telepathically.

Basically an elf who has visions of the future, he explained.

"How many senior staff were stationed there?" Hazel asked, her hand still over her mouth.

"Four," Josiah answered. "One of which is the Facility's resident fairy."

Rieken spoke again. "So if they decided to go rogue, we are looking at a fairly threatening force. Four experienced mages, three mid-level threats, and a fairy. Nor should we take the augur elf lightly either. If we're not careful, the augur will see our response before we can act. Not to mention the creatures from the pens if they can control them. Have you checked their most recent inventory list?"

"We are working on that now. From what I remember, there were at least eight goblins, two trolls, and an ogre."

Sheila gasped out loud. The pencil in her hair actually faltered momentarily.

"What is your planned course of action?" Rieken asked.

"I want to send a force to the LA Facility to perform a thorough search of the entire premises. Rieken, you will take a dozen soldiers, and I will send Helena, Benton, and Wendell. I would like to send the Paladins as well, despite the fact that Helena hasn't actually released them from the Infirmary yet. That will leave the remainder of the senior staff, half of our Knights, and another dozen soldiers here to protect this Facility should Nolan make the poor decision to attack."

"What do you mean half of the Knights?" Jude asked quickly.

"In the middle of trying to figure out what was happening, we received an urgent call from Tyler Knox in LA. He was approached last night by Nolan, and initially had no reason to suspect anything was wrong, but then decided to contact us to make sure. I would like for Jude, Madison, and Cadan to pay him a visit in person and see what they can learn."

Jude shook his head in frustration.

"Tyler Knox?" Cadan asked. "Isn't he that kid that starred in all of those teen movies?"

"Yes, the one and only."

"Why would we visit him?"

"He's an elf. It's fairly obvious if you look at his physical characteristics. I'm surprised that the public thinks he's normal. He doesn't have any magical abilities at all, so DOMA allows him to work in show business as long as he gives them a cut of his revenues. Just like the Femme Fatales."

"I would like for the three of you to leave immediately," Josiah advised them. "Once you have finished questioning him sufficiently, contact us and Lars will open a portal back here. I don't want you out there for any longer than you have to be."

"Time to go," Jude said as he stood up. Cadan wasn't sure where they were going, so he just followed Jude and Madison as they descended into the center of the room.

They approached the fierce looking Lars, who addressed Cadan. "Since this is your first conscious trip by fairy portal, you will probably be really sick. Just do as I say, and I will do my best not to kill you."

Chapter Fifteen

He exhaled sharply as Lars turned. The senior mages behind him parted and made an empty space in the middle of the room. Lars threw up both hands and a tiny vertical slice of red light appeared. It was similar to ruhk-fire, but somehow different. The small slit began to widen and crackle and in seconds there was a doorway. Cadan bit back a moan as he stared at the glowing fuchsia colored gateway, standing open before them like a hungry mouth ready for a snack.

"Take my hand," Jude reached out. "It'll be easier this way for your first time."

Cadan reached out and gripped Jude's hand. Together they stepped through the portal, and he could hear Madison right behind them.

He would never forget his first time through a fairy portal. His stomach felt like it was exploding and the rest of his insides seemed to be switching places inside his body. His head was scrambled and his vision faded in and out. Even his teeth felt loose in his gums.

As they exited the other side, his legs were weak and wobbly. Jude still had his hand, and with his other hand, he reached around Cadan's waist to steady him. From behind Cadan, Madison gripped his shoulders.

"The feeling will pass," Jude said, and when he saw that Cadan could stand, he let him go.

"Where are we?" Cadan asked. They were in a hallway somewhere, with several doors in sight.

"Just outside of Tyler's apartment," Jude explained.

He turned and knocked on the nearest door. A few seconds later, Cadan heard someone unlocking the door and at least two deadbolts.

Unexpectedly, Cadan was star struck when the door opened. Tyler Knox was standing there in the entryway. The actor had bluish eyes like his and there was no mistaking the elven characteristics once he knew what to look for. His hair was brown streaked with blonde and swooped down over his forehead, not quite reaching his eyes. Cadan would never admit it out loud, but he sort of liked Tyler's movies. Raney was completely obsessed; she thought he was the hottest thing that walked the earth, and Cadan watched each film with her. His excuse was that they were catchy movies.

"What are you doing here?" Tyler asked. So hospitality wasn't his strongest suit.

"We are here to ask you some questions," Jude answered. "Aren't you going to let us in?"

"Can we talk out here?"

"Why?"

"Because Shannon is sleeping in the other room."

Jude and Madison both laughed. "So you're still keeping that charade up?" Madison asked.

"Of course. If I have a girlfriend, it affirms to people that I am heterosexual, therefore I earn more money for my movies than I would if they knew the truth."

"Well, you don't have a choice, Tyler. Let us in."

The movie star obeyed and beckoned them inside.

He led them over to the couch, while he plopped down in a chair on the other side of the coffee table. Cadan had always envisioned apartments as small one or two bedroom places that people rented when they didn't want or couldn't afford a house. But Tyler's apartment was luxurious, and from what he could see from the front room, enormous as well. The uncomfortably modern couch was low to the floor, and Cadan nearly knocked over a giant vase that contained plumes of green plastic plants.

Jude began the questioning. "So how are things with Shannon?"

"Are you trying to be funny?" Tyler asked. "I doubt you came to ask me about my love life."

"Shannon is hardly your love life. She is just the little fictitious life you set up. And I should remind you that you have been granted this opportunity by DOMA. You know that we could take you back in and the world would never hear from you again."

"I know that, but I've done nothing wrong here. I make much needed revenue for the Department, and I follow every rule to the letter."

Cadan knew that Jude was putting on an act to make sure that Tyler was scared enough of them to give honest answers, but it still surprised him. This was a part of Jude he had not seen before.

Something else bothered him. As they argued over the merits of Tyler's 'freedom' here in Los Angeles, something in Cadan's mind tingled when he looked at him. Cadan subtly opened himself to a small amount of ruhk-magic and then reached out towards Tyler. He allowed a tendril of his magic to slip over the celebrity.

And there it was. Tyler had the ability to use ruhk-magic! Why would they allow him to live outside of the Facilities when he had such power?

Maybe he had somehow managed to hide it from Josiah and the rest of DOMA. How was he able to do this?

He was tempted to out him right then and there, but after thinking about his own predicament and family, he realized that this was a better life for Tyler. If Cadan revealed what he had discovered, the actor would be thrown into a pen in one of the Facilities, if not punished more severely. Cadan couldn't bring himself to turn him in.

You know my secret.

Cadan was surprised that Tyler could tell. He was even more surprised that the boy decided to admit it.

Yes. Cadan replied back after a moment.

I was a fool for not shielding my power from you. Are you going to say something?

He was talented. Tyler was still carrying on a conversation with Jude and Madison and talking to him telepathically.

I don't think so.

Why?

I wouldn't wish this life on anyone. At least this way you have some semblance of freedom.

Thank you.

Just please cooperate with Jude.

I will.

And with that their mental conversation was over.

"So what all did Nolan ask you last night?" Jude was asking him.

"He wanted to know if I would join him on a mission."

"What mission?"

"He wouldn't say unless I agreed to go with him. He did mention something to one of his Paladins named Cody that he needed my help opening something up."

"Opening something up?"

"Yes," Tyler nodded. "Something about a ship."

"A ship?"

"I guess. I have no idea what that means."

"Is that all he said?"

"He asked if I knew of any fairies in LA."

Jude looked perplexed. "Why would he ask that? He should know of all of the fairies. All administrators have access to that information."

"Maybe he thinks there are some DOMA wasn't aware of."

"Do you know of any?" Jude asked suspiciously.

"No," Tyler shook his head. "I know of the Femme Fatales, but other than that, I have no idea if there are any more."

"What else can you tell us?"

"That's all he said that was important. He spent most of the time trying to convince me to join him."

"Why did you tell him no?"

"Why?" Tyler seemed surprised by the question. "DOMA is gracious enough to allow me to live this life and I'm grateful for that. I have fame, money, and everything I could ever want."

Jude still seemed suspicious. "Any other reason you said no?"

"I'm not an anti-establishment kind of guy. DOMA is going to wipe the floor with Nolan, and I don't want to get caught under that mop. I'm fine with my place at the table."

"Hmm." Jude as still not fully convinced.

"Can you guys go now?" Tyler asked as he glanced at the bedroom door.

"Sure," Jude smiled as he stood. "Don't want to wake the missus." He beckoned for Cadan and Madison to follow. Before walking out the door, he turned back to Tyler. "If you think of anything else, or if he contacts you again, you should call us immediately."

"Will do," Tyler mumbled as he slammed the door behind them. All of the locks clicked in a quick successive motion.

"What was going on with you?" Cadan asked Jude.

"What do you mean?"

"You were a little mean to him. And what was with all of the cold references to his girlfriend?"

"That's not his girlfriend," Jude and Madison chuckled. "He's faking more than the fact that he's an elf. Shannon is just his hired beard."

"A beard?"

"Yes, he prefers the company of the same gender, which, I should add, I don't have a problem with whatsoever, but the fact that he goes to such lengths to disguise that fact is repulsive."

"How is that different from disguising the fact that he's an elf?"

"Much different," Jude replied. "He's hiding the fact that he is an elf because, for one, the government is requiring him to do it, and two, it would open up all kinds of cans that would affect us all. The fact that he's lying about Shannon and his proclivities is something that he isn't required to lie about, or some secret that could prove disastrous to humanity. He's lying because he's scared that it will hurt his fame and fortune."

"In other words, he's chicken shit" Madison said, only she wasn't laughing. "For some reason, society ignorantly places undue emphasis on who we love, and creeps like him just further that paranoia."

They were right, Cadan guessed. Someone had to take that step.

"So how does he pass as human?" he asked. "Has no one noticed his pointy ears?" Granted, it was hard to see his ears with the mop of hair on his head, but surely someone would notice.

"He had them surgically removed years ago," Jude answered.

"Wow," Cadan said as he grabbed his ears. That must have hurt. Tyler seemed like a desperate person to go to such lengths to hide who he really was.

Jude reached into the bag hung over his shoulder and removed his Link. He hit a button on the glass front and the device sprung to life.

"Josiah," he called into the device.

"Yes, Jude," came the older man's voice.

"We've finished our interview with Tyler."

"Anything important?"

"Just something about asking for his help to open something. Nolan tried to convince Tyler to help him, and he asked if Tyler knew of any other fairies in LA, other than the Femme Fatales."

"That is disconcerting," Josiah said and there was a long pause. He finally continued. "We need to dispatch someone to the Fatales' manor, but we currently cannot spare anyone. Would you three kindly visit them and warn them about Nolan and his people?"

"Sure," Jude answered.

"I wish we could spare some security for them, but the majority of our forces are currently at the LA facility taking inventory of everything that was removed. Do you remember where their residence is located?"

"I sure do," Jude said.

"Then please hurry. And give me an update once you have arrived."

Without saying goodbye, Jude hit another button, turning the device off.

Madison looked pleased. "So we get to go traipsing all over Los Angeles at midnight?"

Jude smiled. "Looks like it."

They turned and hurried towards the elevator. Cadan was just glad that they didn't have to ride the fairy door anywhere this time.

Chapter Sixteen

Jude's bag also contained a pouch of money. They crammed into the back of a taxi cab, which stunk worse than Cadan's barn back home. After a half hour and some grinding traffic, they pulled up to a large iron gate positioned along a long white stone wall.

They got out of the taxi, and after Jude handed the driver two twenties, the cab sped off.

"How are we getting in?"

"We knock," Jude answered as he pressed the intercom button on a panel next to the iron gate. After Jude introduced himself, the gate quickly swung open.

The walk up the drive took nearly as long as the cab ride over. Jude explained that the Fatales kept the area around their manor densely forested to prevent anyone from discovering their true identities.

Cadan didn't know any of their names, which was unusual for someone in high school. He was sure that Raney could have recited their names and all sorts of useless trivia. The Fatales were a widely popular group. Even before finding out that they were really creatures of magic, he could see through their illusion. The lead singer had a good voice, but the rest of them just danced around and gyrated on whatever objects were closest. Jude helped him identify them based on their hair color. Apparently they all had flaming red hair, which was the most telling trait of any fairy, but they each dyed it a different color as part of their act.

The graveled drive was surrounded by a dense canopy of enormous trees. When they turned a corner on the drive and entered a clearing, the manor stood in front of them, looming as large as any home Cadan had ever seen. The white stone of the manor seemed to give off its own light and the façade was interrupted by several large windows. A grand staircase led up to the front porch, which extended across the entire span of the mansion. The door stood gaping open and four women were standing there with their arms crossed.

"What are you doing here?" the one with brown hair said. Cadan remembered that her name was Malina.

"Not happy to see me?" Jude asked, obviously trying to flirt.

The blonde Fatale, named Tina, actually smiled when she replied. "You are ever so cute, dear, but DOMA showing up on our doorstep unexpectedly doesn't bode well for the evening."

"So again, what can we do for you?" The one with black hair, Corina, seemed even more upset than Malina.

"May we come in?"

"Of course you can," Sabrina, the one with red hair, beckoned them inside. She seemed the most normal of the four.

"I thought there were six in the group," Cadan whispered to Madison.

"They're probably inside. Katina and Batina are the twins, and they're usually drunk and passed out somewhere in the house."

Sure enough, Madison was correct. The twins, one with blue hair and the other with purple, were laying half-conscious on the couch in the main sitting area. There were at least another dozen people, both men and women, lying about the room.

"We didn't mean to interrupt your party," Jude said sarcastically as he looked around the room.

Cadan made a mental note of everyone there. They all looked fairly normal, but his eye caught one young man in particular – probably no older than him –

standing in the back by a window. The boy watched them wearily. His hair was the same flaming red as Sabrina and Lars.

"No problem," Corina said as she clapped her hands. Everyone left the room, including the red-haired boy.

"Now," Malina began as she sat down. "What can we do for you?"

"Has Nolan or anyone else from the LA Facility come to visit you recently?"

"Why?" she asked after picking up a glass of wine and taking a long swig.

"We need to know, Malina. Has anyone come to visit?"

"Yes," she answered. "Nolan paid us a visit two days ago."

"What did he want?"

"I'm not really sure. He was here for dinner and hung out with us for a little while and then left. He didn't say much."

"Is that unusual for him?"

"Not really. He comes by about once a month just to check in." She folded her arms and stared at Jude, as if to ask why any of it was his business.

"But Josiah is your main contact within DOMA, right? Why would Nolan be coming to visit? Does Josiah authorize the visits?"

"I'm assuming that he authorizes them. Honestly, I don't really care."

"Well, you should. This is vitally important to DOMA's security, and we need your cooperation."

"How can we be more cooperative?" Sabrina asked.

"Tell me what he said."

It was Tina that spoke. "He did make a comment that he wished he could figure out who all of the fairies were in LA."

"Did he say why?"

"He just said that he needed to know who all of the fairies were. That was it."

"And nothing else?"

"Nothing else," she answered plainly. None of the Fatales seemed pleased with the conversation.

"Well, Josiah seems to think that you need additional security in case Nolan comes back. We can't spare the manpower at the moment, so he wanted me to warn you to be extra cautious."

"We can take care of ourselves," said Sabrina. "We don't need DOMA guarding us."

"We have security here," added Corina.

"But Nolan has forces that will cut through humans like a hot knife through butter," Madison informed them flatly.

"But there are at least six fairies waiting for him inside this house," Malina said as she made a fist.

"Two of which are passed out," Jude mumbled.

"We can still take care of ourselves," said Tina.

"Please promise me that you will call if he shows up again. Even if you think you can handle it."

"We'll see," Tina smirked.

There was more behind the conversation that Cadan was sure he was missing. The Fatales had been on their own away from DOMA for a few years now, and their relationship with Josiah, Jude, and the other DOMA agents was very complicated. From what he knew of Jude, he seemed incapable of fear, but as Jude turned to look at him, Cadan could see that he was afraid.

Any further conversation was interrupted by a beeping noise in Jude's bag. He removed the communication device and with the click of a button, Josiah's voice came through.

"Jude, where are you?"

"Still with the Femme Fatales."

"We have a situation. I need you to have one of the Fatales transport the three of you to a location off of Highway 15 outside of LA."

"What's going on?"

"Someone just called in to the San Bernardino Police that there is a twenty foot creature at the intersection of Highway 15 and Cleghorn Fire Road. This could be either a random ogre that has just now appeared or it could be Nolan's work. He had an ogre in his pens, and this may be part of his plan."

"Will any other personnel or agents be meeting us there?"

"I'm afraid that reinforcements will be a moment. Lars is returning from the LA facility and Rieken's men are transporting some of the abandoned equipment back here. I need the three of you to get there now and make sure that no civilians are injured. I will send aid as soon as I can."

"Sure thing."

"And please be careful, you three."

The device shut off as Josiah ended the call.

Jude turned to the Fatales. "Who can take us there?"

"I've been there before," Malina told them. "I won't go with you, but I will open a gateway for you."

Jude saw the baffled look on Cadan's face.

He explained, "Fairies can only transport to places that they have been before or can see." He turned back to Malina. "Please, make the portal."

Just as Lars had earlier, she raised both hands and created a glowing red slit in the air. Red flame-like energy poured from the opening. As she spread her arms wider, the line extended out and made a portal.

Cadan and Madison followed Jude through. He had no idea what to expect on the other side, but this was his first real mission for DOMA, and his heart was filled with an unusual mixture of trepidation and excitement.

Chapter Seventeen

H is second trip through a fairy portal was only slightly better than the first. The speed in which he recovered from the dizziness was in large part due to the giant ogre that stood on the bridge of the highway.

The hour was late and the area was nearly deserted of all light. The stars and the glowing globe of the moon loomed behind the ogre, who was hunched over a car that held a screaming woman. The ogre towered at least twenty feet high and that wasn't even standing straight up. His skin was a light, scaly green and he wore a patchwork of brown fabrics around his groin. His face only appeared human in the way his features were arranged. His nose stuck out disturbingly far, and his wide mouth bared teeth as sharp as swords and at least a foot long.

Other than the one under the ogre, there were only three other vehicles nearby. The three Knights had arrived in time before any more traffic could pile up on this stretch of roadway. Malina had deposited them onto the shoulder of the highway just a few dozen feet from the bridge. They were close enough to the ogre to hear his low snarl. Cadan could even see the slobber that was dripping from the right side of the beast's mouth.

"What do we do about those people?"

"We save them first and then take this ogre down," Jude said as he sprung forward. "We'll save damage control for when the reinforcements show up." Cadan knew he was referring to the mind magic it would take to make these people forget this tragedy.

They ran along the shoulder of the road. Once on the bridge, they cut across the highway. Jude pulled his staff from behind his back and as he stopped on the opposite side of the car, he was in his battle stance. Cadan unsheathed his sword and was prepared to use it. Madison's bow was already nocked with an arrow.

"What's the plan?" Jude turned to Cadan.

"What? I don't know what I'm doing!"

"You're our leader."

"You could have told me this before we got here."

"I'm telling you now."

What the hell? He wanted to scream at Jude. There was no time to figure out how he was going to lead. Instinct kicked in.

"Madison, take cover behind the car, and pump arrows into the ogre's face," he said to her without looking over.

"Unless I can get a good shot at his eyeball, the arrows won't pierce his skin."

The hood of the woman's car was smashed in. The ogre had been using it for boxing practice. He slammed his fist into the hood again, and the rear tires of the car left the ground.

"They don't need to pierce his skin. You're just providing cover. Jude, when the ogre is distracted, get that woman out of there."

Cadan ran towards the left and away from the ogre. He went around an abandoned van and approached the ogre from behind. It was dark and the street light on this side of the highway was gone, so his presence went unnoticed.

He swung his sword back and then towards the ankles of the ogre. The edge of the sword made contact with the ogre's Achilles tendon, but was unable to pierce the skin. The creature was busy with the annoyance of arrows hitting his face. Both of his arms were up to block them. He looked like he was simply swatting flies away, not even noticing the tiny human hacking at the back of his ankles.

Cadan's heart was racing. He was actually fighting a creature almost four times his height and more bulk than an elephant. If the creature took one step back, Cadan would be squashed.

To some degree, the fight with the ogre elicited memories of sparring matches with Simon. Sword training began at a young age, and when Cadan was younger, he would go up against Simon, who was nearly double his height. The man formerly known as his father had told him the best strategy against a much larger foe was to use that foe's weight against them.

He continued hacking at the back of the ogre's ankle. Out of the corner of his eye, he saw Jude helping the woman out of the driver's side window. The door was caved in so far that it was nearly impossible to open. He and the woman disappeared into the night.

How were they supposed to take this creature down? Swords and arrows were no use. Guns wouldn't be any better. Maybe that was why DOMA didn't bother much with modern weapons.

He could try ruhk-fire. There were still a few people running around who would see him using magic, and that would just be more for DOMA to have to cover up. But then again, it would be a feat to cover up a twenty-foot monster on the highway.

Madison had run out of arrows. They were all lying in a pile around the ogre's feet where they had fallen.

The creature stopped flinching and turned his head each way as if looking for something. His head dropped in Cadan's direction – and the ogre noticed him.

With a roar that could be heard for miles, he stomped his right foot. He was pissed.

Cadan stepped back a few feet and the ogre crouched as if ready to lunge for him. All of the civilians were far enough away that they would be safe if the ogre occupied itself with him.

He turned and ran for the edge of the bridge – the first pounding of a foot on the pavement told him that the ogre was chasing him. He reached the guard rail and could see the slope of the ground underneath that led to the road below. He could make the jump, but it would definitely hurt.

He glanced back and saw the ogre take a swing in his direction. He clutched the guard rail with both hands and propelled himself over the side.

Once he hit the ground, he began rolling. Pain shot through his left arm the minute he hit the slope and his sword slipped from his hand. His body didn't stop until he hit the pavement of the road under the bridge.

Cadan tried to pick himself up as quickly as possible, but his movements were sluggish from the fall. The ogre had not followed him over the side, which was a relief. He needed to find his sword and get back up there in case Jude and Madison were in trouble.

He heard a noise behind him. He whirled around and was confronted by several dark figures of various sizes. One figure appeared human and was flanked by two shapes at least twelve feet tall. There were several smaller forms closer to him. The dreams from the past week came back to Cadan in that instant, and he was reminded of that night in New York when he feared someone had been following him.

"Who are you?" Cadan called out.

"We are not here to harm you, Cadan." The voice was male. Cadan didn't recognize it.

"Then what do you want?"

"Our master Nolan Burrell requests your assistance on a certain matter."

"Did you bring the ogre?"

"Of course."

"Why?" Cadan asked.

"To get you here," the shadow answered.

"People could have died."

"Oh, people will most certainly perish in the coming days, my dear boy. What lies ahead is for the benefit of magic kind only."

"What does Nolan want?"

"Your help. You must come with us to discover specifics."

"Why would I go with you without knowing first what you need. That would be stupid."

"I am asking you nicely," the man warned, his patience waning.

"And I am telling you a little less nicely."

166

"No one denies our requests, boy. If you tell us no, then we have no choice but to force you."

"How would you do that?"

The man laughed; the noise was deep from the throat. He raised his left hand in the air. Suddenly green ruhk-fire burst forth in all directions. The energy lit up the area under the bridge, and Cadan could see for the first time.

The man talking was older, with short graying hair and glasses. He was average height. The towering figures on each side of him looked just like the troll that had chased Cadan in Manhattan, and the half-dozen shapes crouched in front were unmistakably goblins. All of them were growling and slowly moving in his direction.

"What would be stupid, Cadan, is for you to turn this offer down. If you do not accept this offer, then my friends here will share you for a light snack."

"Piss off, Robert," Cadan heard a voice behind him. Jude stepped forward with Madison next to him. Cadan knew the name as one of Nolan's senior staff members.

"So you honestly think that the three of you can take down my force here?" Robert challenged.

"Of course we can," Jude goaded. "But we will give you a chance to surrender first."

"Surrender to three miserable whelps?"

Jude shrugged. "It's either that or get hurt."

"Where's the ogre?" Cadan whispered to Jude out of the corner of his mouth.

Jude grabbed him by the arm and the three of them dove to the ground, just as the ogre charged from behind and towards Robert and his forces. The creature's roar sounded like a hurricane wailing and his arms were swinging wider than the road. The ogre ignored the Knights and continued forward to meet the goblins, who were hissing and backing away. Cadan was completely confused.

Then several figures stepped out of the darkness behind the ogre. Tomas was the first. He had a large golden stone in his upraised right arm. He followed the ogre, never once looking in Cadan's direction. Natalie, Darius, and Bryce were right behind him.

"The cavalry has arrived," Jude told Cadan as he hauled him back up. "Let's go."

Jude held his staff tight, and Cadan found his sword on the ground nearby. They charged after the ogre to join the battle.

The two trolls decided to tag team the ogre. The first troll came at the ogre from the front, but the smaller creature ended up being picked up by his legs and then pummeled against the concrete, as the larger creature swung him around like a doll. The second troll jumped onto the ogre's back and began punching away at his spinal column.

The goblins scattered and came around the sides of the ogre to face Cadan and his friends. He readied his sword for their attack.

He didn't have to wait long. The lead goblin held his axe high and began barking orders in a language that Cadan did not understand. When his comrades began inching towards the Knights, and their leader was satisfied with his orders, he turned, and in one quick motion, lunged towards Cadan, who sidestepped the goblin's reach and brought his sword down towards the creature's arms. The goblin was quicker than Cadan and brought his axe back towards himself, wasting no time in taking another swing. All around him, the rest of the Knights were fighting other goblins.

Cadan saw Tomas in the center with a goblin approaching him. Whatever he was doing with the golden stone and the ogre, the task consumed all of his attention. The battle raged around him and he was oblivious to the goblins near him.

"Protect Tomas!" Cadan yelled.

Each Knight maintained focus on their opponent, but slowly began backing towards Tomas. Cadan took a break from his own opponent long enough to dive towards the goblin that was coming up on Tomas. By the time he reached the snarling beast, the goblin was inches away from a killing blow. Cadan had never killed anything before, but Tomas' life was in danger, and he didn't hesitate. He planted his sword into the unsuspecting goblin's back. A yellowish liquid like pus came bubbling out of the creature.

Cadan had to fight back his emotions. He had just killed another living creature, and while he was fully aware that there had been no other choice, he still couldn't stop the tears that began to pour as he turned his attention back to the goblin leader.

The goblins were not much of a match for the Knights. Bryce had both of his maces barred and was pummeling a goblin on each side of him. Cadan had never seen him fight so ferociously. He kept one eye on his two opponents and the other eye on Natalie. Natalie was creating small shields and throwing them at goblins that came near her. The clear, pulsing spheres pummeled her opponents like a game of dodge ball. Her brother had his wings spread wide and flew a few feet off the ground, taking his foes from above with his two short swords.

Madison's goblin was lying on the ground with several arrows sticking out of its chest. Cadan turned to see Jude make the final blow to the side of his goblin's head with his long staff.

The battle was not over though. Robert came sweeping towards them, his robe flowing in the cool night breeze. Brandishing ruhk-fire in each hand, he began sending bolts of the magical energy in the Knight's direction.

Natalie threw up a shield to cover herself, Darius, Bryce, and Tomas. Cadan noticed that her block was proving less of a problem for her.

Madison and Jude leapt out of the way, dodging each barrage as it came towards them.

Cadan stood his ground. Using his own magic, he was able to deflect each chunk of ruhk-fire with a small amount of his own. Unless the agent was holding back, he knew that he was much stronger. Robert may have more experience, but Cadan knew that he could outlast the older man in stamina, and he could out-handle him in a duel.

The other mage realized it too. Instead of direct ruhk-fire, Robert began sending a variety of spells in his direction. The older man tried to place a shield on Cadan, but he was strong enough to prevent that. He then switched back to ruhk-fire, which Cadan deflected.

With his right hand, Robert reached inside his robe. When he pulled it back out, Cadan saw a shiny silver revolver in his hands.

"No!" Madison yelled out, as she sent an arrow his way. The arrow stuck into the mage's wrist, and sent the gun flying.

"Enough!"

Cadan turned to see Josiah. Behind him were the rest of the senior staff, Nieson, Tregellos, and Rieken. All of the mages held swirling ruhk-fire in their hands.

"So, Robert, you have joined your Administrator as a traitor to the Department?"

"So the old windbag, Josiah, has come to the rescue," the other mage taunted.

"What are you doing here? Why did you bring these creatures out here in the middle of nowhere?"

"Do you think I would be stupid enough to answer your questions?"

"You can answer them now, or when we begin the interrogation. I can promise that Nieson and Rieken won't be as nice as I will."

"You assume that I will be going with you."

"Of course you will."

"But I won't."

A red doorway appeared behind him. It was unmistakably a fairy portal, but this one was much larger than the two Cadan had seen earlier in the night. Using a complicated spell that manipulated the air, Robert snatched the trolls from atop the still struggling ogre and drug them through the portal behind him.

Then they were gone.

The ogre stopped, and with a few words from Tomas, the creature sat down and was still.

"Are you all okay?" Josiah asked, as he walked over to them.

"Yes," Cadan said, as the older man helped him up.

"Sorry we could not come sooner. We had no idea that this was more than just an ogre."

"Or that Nolan was behind it," Nieson added.

Rieken still had his gun in hand and looked furious. "We need to get the senior staff to spread out and clean up this mess. Josiah, have you thought of a cover story?"

"We need to position the vehicles to make it look like they were in a wreck. Nobody was hurt, so the news will think this was some sort of miracle. Track down all occupants of these vehicles and wipe their memory of the evening."

"That should be sufficient," the general agreed.

There was something unethical about their conversation, but Cadan knew that there was no other way.

"We need to get back to the Facility immediately," Josiah told them all.

"Is something wrong?" Jude asked.

"With the events of the past few hours, I believe that we can expect a direct attack on the facility any time now."

Chapter Eighteen

Cadan's left arm was still sore as he sprawled on his bed. Jude was sitting next to him, and held an ice pack to his shoulder. The throbbing of pain was in time with the fast pace of his heart. The adrenaline from the past few hours was still pumping through his veins and while he felt exhausted, he knew that there was no way his eyelids would shut.

"How are you feeling?" Jude asked.

"Better now," he answered, looking up at his roommate. Cadan remembered the question that he wanted to ask him. "What was that stone that Tomas used?"

"It's a garnet numina stone," he explained. "They're used to control creatures of lesser intelligence than humans. A spell is woven between the garnet and the creature. We use them a lot when trying to take down an ogre, troll, or dragon. Tomas must have brought one with him."

"Good thinking on his part."

Jude had that look like he wanted to ask a question. "I heard Robert ask for you by name," he said.

Cadan nodded silently.

"Do you think Nolan told him about you?"

"I don't know," Cadan answered. "It was strange. Nolan was there when Josiah and I had that talk about finding my parents."

"And what did Robert ask you?"

"Just a variation of the same thing he asked Tyler Knox and the Femme Fatales. He needed my help with something."

"Did he say what?"

"No, and they wouldn't tell me unless I agreed to go with them."

"Did you tell Josiah?"

"I haven't had the chance. Should we go now?"

"I would wait. He's still making preparations for an eventual attack."

For some strange reason, his thoughts drifted back to his family. He pictured Simon and Daphne sitting in the living room, wondering where he was. Or would they be out looking? Simon wasn't the type to just rest if something needed to be done. And what about Derrick and Raney? They didn't deserve the departure that he had given them. He was so focused on finding out about his parents, he never stopped to consider them. They had just found out that their brother was not their biological sibling. Cadan had completely ignored that fact on the day he left.

Cadan was meant for a quiet life on a farm of his own somewhere near Simon's. As much as he liked his new friends, he wanted to go home. Fighting trolls and mages, running from ogres, and killing goblins was more than he could handle. He could still see the amber-colored blood pouring from the goblin's back as his sword found its way in between two of the creature's ribs.

"Do you think that they could attack this Facility? We took out most of the creatures that were inventoried in their pens. They should only have a group of mages and two trolls."

"I heard one of the soldiers talking when I went to get you a bag for the ice. It seems that the inventory logs for the pens were inaccurate. The logs showed that he had one ogre, two trolls, and eight goblins. When they checked his shipment receipts, he was bringing in four times the amount of food that would have been required to feed them."

"So what does that mean?"

"That means that he has been gathering more creatures and not logging them in his inventory."

"So he was probably planning this for some time."

"It seems like it."

"I wonder if they can find out how many he has with him now."

"I don't know, but I bet Josiah is working on that."

"Can we enlist the creatures that are in our pens?"

"Definitely not," Jude shook his head. "Those in the pens are deemed unable to reside outside of their cells. Some are in the process of being rehabilitated and go through a certain type of therapy, but those in the maximum and medium level security pens are in there for a reason. They have no business outside of these walls." He shivered just thinking about it. "But we probably won't need them. Nolan would be a fool to attack the Rocky Mountain Facility directly. Other than the goblins, trolls, and ogres, he only has himself, five other mages, and a fairy. If he came against us, he would have to contend with eleven ruhk-wielders, two dozen soldiers, all kinds of others, and me. We would take him down easily."

"Then why would Josiah expect him to attack? If I were Nolan, this would be the last place I would attack."

"What do you mean?"

"It's like in soccer," Cadan explained. "If you have the ball and need to take it downfield towards your opponent's goal, you don't go straight through the center where all of your opponents are huddled and waiting on you. You find a weak spot and exploit it."

"So what would our weak spot be?"

"I don't know," Cadan said as he shook his head.

And then it hit him. Robert *asked* him first if he would join him. But then he said that if Cadan did not come willingly, they would just take him anyway. Who else had they asked? Tyler Knox and the Femme Fatales.

"Jude, we have to warn Tyler and the Fatales," Cadan said as he sat up.

"Why? What do you mean?"

Cadan explained his theory.

"You may be right," he said as he slipped his shoes back on. "We have to go tell Josiah."

They rushed from their room and took the elevator towards the top of the facility to the Command Center. The room was bustling with senior staff and soldiers, all trying to make sense of what was going on around them.

The center console in the room had a holographic 3-D map of the southwestern portion of California hovering above it. Josiah seemed convinced that something was going to happen in that area. He was leaning over the railing, deep in conversation with Rieken, Helena, and Nieson. Tregellos was behind them watching a wall of monitors with the technical guru Benton and three other soldiers.

"Boys," Josiah said as he looked up. "You are both supposed to be resting."

"Cadan thought of something," Jude said.

"Oh really," Josiah said, making a poor attempt to hide his smile. "Please tell us what you have thought of."

"It was something that Tyler Knox and the Fatales both said," Cadan explained. "They both said that Nolan requested their assistance." He took a deep breath. "Under the bridge, Robert asked for my assistance as well, as if I should cooperate with him. I told him no, of course, but then he said they would just make me."

"So you are thinking that Nolan will return to Tyler and the Fatales?"

"Yes," he nodded. "He was targeting us specifically."

Josiah turned to Tregellos. "Please send two agents to retrieve Tyler and his girlfriend. Tell them both that it is a matter of security that pertains to his celebrity status, but I want them both taken to one of our safe houses. I'm not sure what exposure that boy represents for us, if any." He turned to Helena. "As for the Fatales, I want them brought here. Six fairies is a much larger liability than a talentless elf-child."

The Administrator was interrupted by a monitor sounding on the wall. A soldier turned to Josiah and said, "Administrator, a call is coming in from the Fatale Mansion."

"Bring it up on the screen."

Malina's face appeared on the monitor. "Josiah," she said through her tears.

"What is the matter, Malina?"

"Something has happened," she said between sobs.

"Please try to calm down and explain."

"Something has happened to Sabrina. We ran out of alcohol in the house, so Sabrina took two security guards and was going to get more. Just on the inside of our main gate, the car was attacked. The security guards were killed and Sabrina was taken."

"How could the attackers have gotten inside the walls? I have placed wards on your perimeter –" He stopped and then he growled. "Malina, was anyone else granted access through my wards?"

"Yes," she nodded.

"Nolan?"

"Yes."

"Why?"

"He was coming to visit us, and he was nice to have around. We gave him access so that he could come and see us anytime."

"You foolish girl!" Josiah yelled into the monitor. "Damn fairies and your notions that life is nothing but one giant game! You have placed all of yourselves in extreme danger and probably gotten your sister killed."

"We didn't know!" another voice said from behind Malina. Tina appeared on the monitor and was even more upset than Malina.

"We need to get you here immediately. Since none of you know the spell to open a portal through our wards here, I will send a team to come and get you. Now, go and tell the others to be ready to leave within the next fifteen minutes. And you are not bringing your little debutante entourage with you either, so don't even bother asking."

He reached up and turned the monitor off.

Jude asked. "So should we suit up?"

"No," Josiah shook his head. "The Paladins are back up and asking to join the festivities. They seem a little banged up still, but I think they can handle this. I need the Knights here in case something else comes up."

"Sure," Jude nodded, but Cadan could tell he was disappointed.

A few minutes later, the five Paladins entered the Command Center; Nate was bringing up the rear. None of them would even so much as look at Cadan or Jude. Despite their anger, he could see the pain behind their eyes. They were a nasty bunch, but they had loved their fallen teammate. He actually felt a little pity for them.

"Thank you for coming Paladins," Josiah greeted them. "Lars will transport you to the Fatales mansion. Please see that they pack a week's worth of clothes and necessities and then bring them here. I want them back as soon as possible."

Anthony nodded, and they walked to the other side of the room to Lars, who formed a gateway for them. A moment later, the Paladins were gone.

Josiah turned back to Cadan and Jude. "I am hoping this little mission will help bring their spirits back up."

He was interrupted again by a noise coming from one of the monitors.

"Josiah," a soldier called to him. "We have a signal on Sabrina. Her tracking beacon has been tampered with, but there is a very faint signal coming through."

"Where is she?" the Administrator asked.

"We have pinpointed her location. She is at a gas station off of Highway 40 just outside of Ludlow, California."

"What?" Josiah looked baffled. "What is Nolan playing at?" he said to himself. "Call the rest of the Knights here. I am sending them in."

"Is that a good idea?" Nieson asked. "We don't know how many of Nolan's people are there, or if Nolan himself is there."

"I saw the Knights battle Robert, and I am confident that they can handle anything short of his entire force. If there are more there, then we can send in reinforcements. I will also send Benton and Hazel to assist."

A few minutes later, the other five Knights arrived at the Command Center. Josiah addressed them. "It appears that Sabrina is at this gas station. Your mission is simple. Find and secure her, and then contact us to bring you back. That is it. If at all possible, do not engage Nolan's people if they are there. If you are outnumbered, contact us and we will either pull you back out or we will send reinforcements. Understand?"

They nodded simultaneously.

He pulled several strips of leather from a box sitting near one of the many computers. He handed the straps to Jude and added, "You know how these work. If you get a chance to capture any of Nolan's people, I want them brought back here."

"Yes sir," Jude nodded his head. He turned to Cadan to explain. "These block the ruhk-wielder from using their magic. We can place it around their neck, leg, or hand, and it will cut them off."

Cadan shivered at the thought of being blocked from the ruhk-magic.

"Lars, ready their gateway," Josiah said.

As they approached Lars, Cadan wondered if the fairy ever tired from making gateways. When Cadan got up close and saw the bags under man's dark eyes, his question was answered. The night was taking its toll on everyone.

In the span of a few hours, he had travelled through three fairy portals. Just as Jude promised, each time was less upsetting. This time the dread in his stomach had nothing to do with the gateway and everything to do with the disaster that was waiting for them on the other side.

Chapter Nineteen

The gateway opened onto a deserted Highway 40. Cadan wasn't as disoriented as the three previous trips, but it still took him a moment to adjust to their new surroundings and gauge where they were.

The gas station was just a few hundred feet directly in front of them. He had to admit that Lars was fairly good with where he placed his portals, as there was a large brown stone outcropping that would have prevented anyone in the gas station from seeing the red gateway.

The lights were on inside the station and he could just make out two figures standing outside it. There were two cars parked on the side of the building, and he surmised that they were not patrons. Someone shouted from outside the store and a bolt of ruhk-fire hit the side of the building.

"A standoff," Hazel whispered quietly. "But what's keeping them from going inside?"

"What's the plan?" Jude asked Cadan.

"We still don't know the situation," Benton said before he could speak. "We must assess and then Hazel and I will formulate a plan."

"Cadan is the team leader. Josiah said you were only here to assist, not lead."

179

Benton stared down at him. "You may feel comfortable placing your well being in the hands of some inexperienced runaway, but I do not."

"Are you mad that he's twice as powerful as you?"

The Knights chuckled.

"Power is secondary to skill, you whelp. Show some respect or I will call Josiah and have you sent back to the Nursery immediately."

"We should move closer," Hazel said, ingnoring the argument.

Moving between various barriers of streets signs and rock formations, they moved closer and closer towards the gas station. Once their group was within a hundred feet, Cadan could see the two figures on one side, plus two more on the other side, all standing around the building as if trying to get in.

There was a flash of movement on the inside, and then one of the outside figures shot another charge of ruhk-fire towards the store. This time glass shattered in several places.

"Come out of there, Pedro! You cannot take us all!"

Hazel and Benton glanced at each other nervously. She whispered quietly to the older man. "Do you think he's talking about *the* Pedro?"

Benton saw Cadan behind them and quickly hushed Hazel.

"We should attack from two sides," Benton explained. "We have them outmanned and can easily overpower them."

"What about the two *in* the store?" Cadan asked.

"What?" the older man looked baffled.

"You didn't feel the two ruhk-wielders inside the store? They may be the enemy, but more likely they're the reason Nolan sent people here."

Benton was befuddled. "I didn't think that –"

"What do you think we should do?" Jude asked Cadan, trying his best to hide a smile.

"I think we need people to get inside the store. If Nolan is trying to get to the two people inside, then we should get to them first. We need two people who are quiet and quick. Once we have them in the store, the rest can cause a distraction, and then the four in the store can join the fight. You say we can easily take them now, but with two more ruhk-wielders aiding us, we won't even break a sweat."

"What if the two in the store aren't happy to see us either?" Hazel asked.

Benton hushed her again.

Cadan continued. "It won't matter much. I would assume that we and the people in the store have a common cause against Nolan. They should be our allies."

"Good point," Benton nodded. "You and Jude go around the perimeter and come in through the back. You are both of elven blood, so you are made for this sort of thing. But be quiet. You have ten minutes."

Silently he and Jude crept around the south side of the gas station away from the highway. Using a dry creek bed for cover, they followed the path away from the building. When they were comfortable enough with their distance, they left the confines of their naturally placed cover, and continued towards their destination.

They overshot the target by a hundred feet, so once they were on the direct opposite side of the station from their teammates, they moved towards its rear.

They heard the faint echo of a shout from the front of the store, but the back was quiet. He searched the darkness behind them but could see no one. Cadan opened himself to the ruhk-magic, letting a small bit flow through his body and searched once again. His heightened vision allowed him to see a lone dark figure standing two dozen feet from the back door.

Someone's standing there, he told Jude through their minds.

He's a ruhk-wielder?

Yes. Means that you probably can't get close enough with your staff.

I don't think so.

He turned back to the figure shrouded in darkness. He would have to take him out with ruhk-magic from a distance, but use a small enough amount that the others in the front wouldn't be alerted to their presence.

Cadan found a large rock on the ground behind him. With his mind, he lifted the rock into the air until it was level with the back of his enemy's head. With a slight degree of force, he sent the rock into the dark shape.

His target toppled to the ground with only a muffled grunt. He and Jude both jumped from their hiding spot and ran towards the mass of limbs lying there in the dirt.

"It's Cydra," Jude explained as he saw her face. "She's one of the senior staff members at the LA Facility."

"Is she unconscious?" Cadan asked.

"Yes," he answered.

"We should get inside," Cadan told Jude as he followed him to the rear door.

Cadan turned the knob and the old metal door swung open quietly. The back room was dark, thankfully, so no light was let outside. He slipped inside, waited as Jude followed, and then shut the door behind him.

The room they were in was piled high with boxes of all sizes. Reaching out with his power, he couldn't feel anyone close to them.

They moved through the boxes towards the opposite doorway. Reaching the edge of the boxes, Cadan could see that the doorway led into the retail area. Some of the small shelves had been knocked over and merchandise littered the floor. He couldn't catch sight of either of the two figures in the store.

Suddenly there was a shout from outside. He sensed the use of ruhk-magic from over a half dozen sources and knew the ten minutes was up. Benton was commencing with the distraction.

Cadan crept past the boxes and into the store itself. He didn't move more than a foot when he felt someone tackle him.

He felt a fist planted in his side, then Jude was pulling his attacker off.

"We aren't here to attack you," Jude yelled at the man.

Cadan's rib still hurt from the blow as he leaned up into a sitting position.

A dark-skinned man well past his middle years was staring at them with a confused expression on his face. His gaze was eerily focused on Cadan.

"Who are you?" he asked finally. His Hispanic accent was thick.

"We are here to help you," Cadan explained.

"I know you boy," the man said, his eyes widening in recognition. "You look just like your father."

Father? The man must have him confused with someone else. Either that or he must have lost his mind.

"My name is Cadan," he introduced himself.

"I am Pedro, an old friend of your father's."

Maybe there was some truth to what he was saying. "How do you know my father?"

"There is no time for explanations," Pedro stood up. "DOMA is here to take us all in. After fourteen years of running, they have found me."

"Pedro, listen to me." Cadan stood up and placed a hand on his shoulders. "This is not DOMA attacking you. Well, they were with the Department up until this evening when they went rogue."

The older man finally understood. "Then you are with the Department now?"

"Yes," Cadan nodded.

"But I thought you got out and your father escaped as well?"

"My father was a part of DOMA?"

"You don't know your father?" Pedro asked him.

"No," Cadan shook his head. "He died when I was young."

Pedro's eyes started watering as he stared at him for a moment. "He was a good man. Helped me and Rafe's mother escape."

"What do you know about my father?" Cadan asked. "Can you tell me anything else about him?"

"There's no time," Pedro shook his head. "I wish there was, but everything is happening so fast."

Cadan turned to see a boy at least three years younger than him standing there. His eyes were a piercing grayish-blue, which was a stark contrast to his tanned skin.

"This is my son, Rafael," Pedro introduced them.

"Nice to meet you," Cadan said, as he extended a hand.

"He can't hear you," Pedro explained. "He is deaf, and doesn't talk."

But I talk with my mind.

It was odd to hear the boy's voice in his head. Aside from Jude and Tyler, this was only a trick he had ever used with his family.

That's a better method anyway. Cadan smiled, and Rafael returned it with one of his own.

He turned back to Pedro. "Will you help us deal with the rogue agents?"

"I will," Pedro agreed. "But I require one thing in return." He paused and looked over at his son with sad eyes. "If DOMA catches me, I will suffer a fate worse than death. Rafe's mother died four years ago, and I'm all he has left."

"Why would DOMA harm you?"

"It's a long story," he shook his head. "If I help you with these sons of bitches outside, do you promise to watch over my son? It may seem strange of me to ask this of you, but you are Alexander's boy, and anything but a stranger to me. In a sense, we are like family. That makes you and Rafe family now."

"Why do you just call me 'Alexander's boy'? My father's name was Gordon Stone. Maybe you have me mistaken with someone else."

"I know exactly who you are. I need for you to give me your word you will look after him."

This whole thing was strange. The man sounded so sure of himself that he knew who Cadan was, but 'Alexander' was not his father's name.

"This is a little weird," Cadan admitted. "I'm not even an adult myself."

"I'm not asking you to adopt him," Pedro said. "Just take him under your wing and teach him everything you know. And take him with you wherever you go. He's a special boy and most would lose patience with him since he can't hear and won't talk."

"Where are you going?" Jude asked.

"By the end of this night, I will have reunited with my wife."

Cadan knew what he meant. Whatever happened when they left the station, Pedro was confident that he wouldn't survive.

"Do you agree?" he asked again.

"Yes," Cadan answered. He didn't know if it was because he claimed to know his father, but he felt an immediate kinship to Pedro and Rafael.

"Thank you," he said as he put a hand on Cadan's shoulder. He walked over to his son and the two embraced. Cadan could feel the ruhk-magic emanating from them and knew that they were having a silent conversation. The boy's eyes watered as he removed himself from their embrace, and he glanced once over at Cadan. He nodded to his father that he understood whatever had passed between them.

"Now we fight," Pedro told them as he moved to the front of the store. They all followed the older man to the main doors. He reached behind a counter and retrieved a sword and a hand gun. He stuffed the end of the gun in the back of his jeans, and brandished his sword in front of him as if he were ready to strike right then.

Cadan could see that a battle was already underway. Benton, Hazel, and the Knights were just outside the light from the station, and they had placed a protective shield around themselves.

Nearer to the gas pumps, he could see Nolan, flanked by three ruhk-wielders on each side. One of them was Robert, and the other, a girl with flaming red short-cropped hair could only be the fairy Sofia.

"What's the plan?" he asked Pedro.

"We light up the night sky," he said gruffly, as he kicked the double doors completely off their hinges and stepped outside.

Chapter Twenty

Cadan wasn't quite sure what the best strategy was to defeat Nolan. In fact, he didn't think that beating Nolan was possible; he just wanted to get the Knights out of there in one piece.

The Knights' forces were split on each side of Nolan's group. Cadan could see his teammates across the lot, just within the boundary of the gas station's enormous lighting system. There were at least a dozen goblins coming at them from both sides. Madison fired her arrows in quick succession, while Bryce stood defending the group from the other side with his battle axes. The four armed man was locked in combat with Cody, and Cadan couldn't escape the feeling that their fight held an undercurrent of personal rage.

Natalie and Tomas were behind the senior mages. Benton and Hazel were sending ruhk-fire in Nolan's direction, but each time the bolts of fire were deflected and a volley returned in their place.

Nolan's strategy became clear as the fighting intensified. Each of his ruhk-wielders drew closer to the gas pumps, knowing that their opponent's ruhk-fire would have to be accurate for fear of blowing everyone up.

Pedro was the first Cadan's side to join the fray. His sword was drawn as he met Robert in battle. Monroe and one of the Paladins named Steven ran over to join the fight. Cadan lifted his sword, and he and Jude came to the Pedro's aid.

As Steven tried to swing at Pedro from the side, Cadan threw his body and his own sword in the way, blocking the force of the blow. Steven snarled at him, and brought his sword back for another swing. Cadan met that one as well, pushing his opponent back.

Nolan realized that his team was surrounded. Cadan saw the red ruhk-fire out of the corner of his eye. It was too late to produce a shield, but just before the fire reached him, a shield appeared to protect him. He glanced back to his right and saw Rafael standing there with his arms stretched upwards.

Cadan nodded his thanks and returned to his fight with Steven. Powerful swings drove his opponent back towards the gas pumps. He tried swinging from different angles, but Steven's prowess matched his own.

Two of the goblins from the other side must have grown tired of dodging Madison's arrows because they ran past their leader and came towards Cadan and Jude.

His roommate was busy blocking the sword attack from Monroe. The older mage was hacking away at Jude, but each swing was either blocked with the staff or dodged altogether. Jude was so lithe and limber; he would have no trouble getting a job as an acrobat

Across the way, Natalie and Tomas had finally joined Benton and Hazel in their ruhk-fire battle. It was a little strange to watch them throw small bits of ruhk-fire that were only a fraction of what Cadan knew they could each perform. The fear of blowing up a gas pump was dictating the battle.

He wondered for a moment where Darius was, but then he saw a whirl of black flash over a goblin. When the flying figure was gone, so was the goblin.

His own opponent was trying hard to get the best of him. Steven sent an uppercut; Cadan had to pull his arms up next to his body to keep from having his forearms cleaved off. There was no relenting either. Steven came at him again with another swing, and though Cadan was able to keep the blade from hitting his face, the pressure of the blow almost made him eat his own sword.

He didn't give Steven time for a third swing. As soon as his opponent pulled his sword back, Cadan swung his own blade wide from the right. Steven had to struggle to maintain a defense. Finally gaining the offensive, Cadan began hacking away at him, over and over, in quick, successive strokes.

Next to him, he felt Jude hold a small portion of ruhk-magic. He knew his roommate was a ruhk-wielder, but he had never seen Jude use the power for anything other than a telepathic conversation. From what little he used, Cadan could tell that he had great potential. He made a mental note to bring it up later.

"We need to get across to your friends," Pedro said from behind him.

"Isn't it better that we attack them from both sides?" Cadan managed between sword thrusts.

"Not when you are trying to get the hell out of here," Pedro replied. "You kids need to leave because I don't think we can take them down without losing some of ours."

He nodded, knowing full well that Pedro was right. But how would they get past Nolan and his force? The most obvious way was to just run around the gas pumps in a wide arc, but that would be time consuming and if Nolan repositioned his own forces while they tried it, they still might not even be able to join with the others.

Cadan had an idea. The pole holding up the enormous metal awning over the gas pumps stood just several feet to his left. To free himself of his battle, he swung his sword high at Steven. When the other tried to deflect the blow, Cadan reached up with his right leg and kicked him in the softness of his stomach. Steven fell back against the concrete, and Cadan gained the time he needed.

Careful not to hit the pumps, Cadan sent a wave of ruhk-fire at the metal support structure. It took only a moment for the pole to split in half; the noise from the awning overhead was deafening. Despite the loss of one of its six pillars, the awning still held.

But the distraction proved successful.

"Come on," Cadan yelled at his three companions on his side. As he passed Steven, who was trying to get back up, he planted his shoulder into him, sending him sprawling back to the ground. They ran past a pump on the opposite side from Nolan. With his fear of causing a massive explosion, they were able to pass by without incident.

They reached their friends on the other side. Madison, who never took her eyes away from her arrow firing, showed relief at their arrival by a simple nod and half grin. Benton furrowed his eyebrows as he glanced at Pedro disapprovingly. From the look on the other's face, Cadan could tell that neither one was very happy to see the other.

Nolan's forces had regrouped near him. When they were convinced that the covering would hold, they pressed forward with their attack.

"Pedro, you and Rafael take the right side," Cadan called to them. "Madison, Bryce, and Jude, you take the left. Benton and Hazel, maintain a shield. Natalie and Tomas, be ready to back them up on that shield."

Ruhk-fire of different colors came at them: twin red columns from Steven and Nolan, gray and green from Monroe and Robert, and yellow and orange from Marcia and Cody. Benton and Hazel both threw up shields, and yelled for everyone to get behind them. The barrage of ruhk-fire was intense, and the Knights could not return any of their own. The pumps stood there near the rogue agents, as if they had a giant bullseye plastered on their shiny metal surfaces.

As the pounding ruhk-fire beat against the shield, the Knights stooped behind Benton and Hazel, who stood defiantly against the attack. Cadan searched around for some way to gain the upper hand and help his teachers out. He noticed the opposite side of the awning was off to the left past Cody and Robert, who were both lost in their fire-creating spells.

Cadan had made ruhk-fire curve before, but it was quite difficult to perform. It would be nearly impossible under this much pressure. He knew he had to try it though.

As he flicked his left arm up, a column of ruhk-fire shot from his hand. It passed around Benton's side of the shield, arched around Cody and hit one of the two poles on that side. The force of the blast split the column in half. The blue fire moved through the metal like a hot knife through butter.

The two pieces of the column tumbled to the ground. Cody and Robert had to take several steps back, and for a brief moment, they dropped their attack.

Benton saw their respite and used that moment to send a volley of his own orange ruhk-fire in their direction. Cadan watched to see if their foes would be able to block the blast, but something else broke his concentration.

Benton and Hazel's shield was rocked by another blast. Nolan had been watching as well, and had noticed Benton's break in concentration, and used that to his advantage. The rogue Administrator's red fire pounded the shield like rain on a skylight.

The initial blast caught the senior mage by surprise. The force hit Benton so hard that his shield exploded, the ruhk-magic that comprised it flew through the air in all directions. The old man was thrown back, past Cadan and the Knights, and onto the ground at least twenty feet behind them.

Natalie screamed out and ran towards him. Tomas looked around for just a moment and then threw his arms up and replaced the shattered shield with one of his own.

"Make sure he's okay," Cadan called to Natalie as she disappeared into the darkness to check on her mentor.

"I don't know how much longer I can hold my shield," Hazel said over her shoulder.

Pedro finished off the goblin that was attacking them from the side. "I can take over the shield," he offered.

"Nevermind, I'm fine," Hazel said coldly, never making eye contact with him.

"Jude," Cadan turned and looked at his roommate. "Call Josiah and get us a portal. We need one now!"

He noticed Hazel's arm began to vibrate; the strain of the shield was getting to her, and despite her protest to Pedro, he knew she couldn't hold onto it much longer.

"Josiah said that Lars will have a portal open in 20 seconds," Jude said as he stuffed his Link back into his pocket.

Cadan was about to mentally call to Rafael to back up Hazel when her shield exploded just as Benton's had, sending her body flying into in the darkness behind them.

Once her shield was gone, Tomas's broke apart as well, and everything plunged into chaos.

Nolan and his forces came so fast, their bodies, their weapons, and their magic lunging at the Knights more quickly than Cadan thought possible. He didn't know whether to defend with his magic, attack with his sword, or command his teammates to take action.

When the two forces met, the sound of steel against steel resounded throughout the station. They held their lines, just as Cadan had warned them to earlier, and met the charging force. It seemed the mages had produced more goblins, as there were over a dozen now. He wondered where Nolan could be getting such an endless supply of the creatures.

Robert met Pedro in battle, Cody met Bryce, and Steven met Jude. Madison had to brandish her short sword from the sheath at her side to defend against the fierce Marcia.

Nolan wanted Cadan for himself. But he didn't charge; his sword stayed in its scabbard, and he used ruhk-fire instead. Red flames lapped at Cadan's arms; he had to step back and produce small shields to keep them from burning his exposed flesh. When he managed to fend off the fire sufficiently enough to find a few seconds of free time, he sent his own blue fire towards Nolan.

The former Administrator fluffed it off easily with his own shield, and then sent another wave of red fire.

Cadan knew that he had to do something. Even when the portal finally opened, they would have a hard time gathering together, not to mention getting through it. They needed a distraction.

"Darius!" he yelled out. He felt the wind at his back and knew that his teammate had landed. "Go help your sister with Benton and Hazel. Get them ready to go through the portal when it opens."

"Sure thing," he said, disappearing into the darkness.

By Cadan's estimation the portal should have opened already. Something must have gone wrong back at the Facility.

He needed to distract their opponents. There were still four support beams holding the awning up over the gas pumps: two in the center and one on each side. If he could eliminate the two in the middle, he might just be able to topple it.

After deflecting a large blast from Nolan, he called forth ruhk-fire in each fist. This time when he sent it in Nolan's direction, he made each column of fire fan out around the man in a circular direction. At first Nolan defended himself, thinking they were both aimed for him, but then he saw each one pass by his face. He turned momentarily to stare at the splitting support beams and knew exactly what Cadan had done.

As the awning groaned and shifted, the weight of its mass moving towards the middle, Nolan began to back away towards the entrance of the gas station. Cadan used this moment of hesitation to take down Robert and Steven with ruhk-fire, relieving two of his teammates.

"The portal," Darius said as he appeared with Benton over his shoulder. He was pointing off towards the road along the north end of the station's parking lot.

"Where's Hazel?" Cadan asked.

"I'm bringing her," Natalie said as she dragged their teacher into the light.

The awning finally gave in to the weight in its center. In a massive, ear shattering cacophony of chaos, it fell. Heaps of debris settled noisily to the ground. Nolan had been able to get to the other side before it had crashed. His allies scattered away from the Knights, lost in the confusion of the cave-in, waiting for their baffled leader to give them more orders.

"Bryce," Cadan called out. "Get Hazel from Natalie."

"You've got to go," Pedro said to them.

"Come with us," Cadan pleaded.

"As I told you before, DOMA would not very happy with me. Go! And take care of my son!"

Rafael's eyes were wet. He knew what was coming. There was time for one quick, final embrace.

Nolan screamed when he saw the fairy gateway. He ordered his minions to resume their attack, and suddenly there was ruhk-fire everywhere.

"Go!" Cadan screamed. Everyone, with the exception of Pedro, darted for the doorway. Cadan grabbed Rafael's small arm and ran for the portal. As they retreated, he had to throw up small temporary shields to block lances of various colored ruhk-fire. "Thank you," Cadan said to Pedro as he passed him. Cadan hated to leave the man stranded there alone, but if Pedro was hiding from DOMA, his punishment upon being caught would be severe. The older mage was doing what he had to do to protect his son. Cadan admired him for that, and imagined that his own father would do the same.

"No, Cadan, thank you. I can tell you are already becoming the man your father was, and someone that he would have been proud to call his son."

"Thank you," Cadan said again.

"Now go," he barked. "I will hold a shield to protect your getaway."

"Cadan!"

He turned and saw Jude standing in almost the exact spot he had been before the retreat. There was a cloudy substance around him and his hands were pressed up against the surface. He was being shielded.

"Jude!" he called back.

"Oh shit," he heard Pedro say. The man was pointing towards Nolan.

The rogue agents had stopped their attack with ruhk-fire, and instead were concentrating their magic on the nearby gas pumps. Robert had formed a shield around the small group, and Cadan guessed he was responsible for the one around Jude as well.

"You have to go, Cadan," Pedro said. "He's about to blow this place up."

"That would be stupid," Cadan said.

"They have a shield," Pedro said. "Now go."

"But Jude—"

"Go! He's shielded, too!"

Cadan wanted to protest, but there was no time. He glanced over and saw Darius and Bryce passing through the portal with their charges, and the other Knights were directly behind him.

Then the pumps exploded.

Cadan wanted to scream out. He wanted to run to Jude and protect him.

But his entire body felt the pain from the wall of heat and his entire line of sight was blocked by a fiery inferno. He whirled and started for the fairy portal, and saw that Madison was next to him.

In one moment, they were both lifted off their feet by the blast and the pink and purple incandescence of the portal flew at them like a missile.

Chapter Twenty=One

Cadan observed two things before all went black: Pedro's body being consumed by fire and Jude trapped in a shield several feet from them. He was not able to move, but at least he was protected from the fiery ball of fire that was consuming the entire area around the gas station.

He felt Madison holding his arm as they were blasted through the fairy portal.

His state of consciousness was somewhere between deep sleep and that place where dreams are most vivid. Two faces flipped back and forth between one another – Jude and Simon. For a moment one was there, and then the other. After a few rotations, they both stopped.

And then another face appeared. The one from his repressed memories – his father. Now in his dreams he could recall the name Alexander. His father had a name. Simon had told him another name, but he knew now that his true name was Alexander, just as Pedro had said. If Simon had lied about his name, then he must have lied about his mother's name as well. Maybe one day he would get a chance to ask him what her name really was.

His heart seemed like it would burst from his chest as he thought about his father. *Why didn't you tell me, Simon?* Were he awake, the tears would certainly be flowing. He screamed out in his mind. He called to Simon.

His life was full of lies. Simon had lied about who he was and who his family was. When he left, Cadan found another family, and had to lie to them about who he was. There was no place in his life where truth reigned. He screamed out to Simon again, this time cursing at him, something he would never have done before.

As his eyes fluttered open, he expected to see Josiah or the crisp sterility of the Facility, but instead he was looking up at the same night sky he had viewed just moments before.

Madison was there next to him, her hands just a few inches from his arm. Her eyes were closed and she was lying in the soft sand. She would have looked peaceful were her limbs not contorted behind her. He rolled over and checked her pulse; she was okay.

He picked himself up and groaned. There wasn't a bone or muscle in his body that didn't hurt. Blood was coming from the side of his left arm and thigh, and his shirt was gone, burned and torn away in the explosion at the station.

Surveying the area, he found Darius helping Natalie off the ground; both seemed okay. Rafael was behind a large shrub near him, and Bryce had come to a stop on a stretch of highway just a few dozen yards away.

"What happened?" Madison said as she stood up and began looking around, rubbing the back of her head. Her shirt had torn and was hanging on by one shoulder. Her pants had several rips and tears down the side.

"I don't know," He shook his head.

"The explosion must have interfered with the gateway," Tomas answered as he came over a ridge. "We didn't make it to the Facility."

"Is everyone accounted for?" Darius asked, looking around.

Jude, Cadan thought to himself.

"Where's Jude?" Madison asked, as if reading his mind.

"He's not here," Cadan answered. "He didn't make it through the gateway."

"Did he die?" she asked.

"No," he shook his head. "I saw him surrounded by a shield before we were thrown through. He would have survived."

But my father didn't.

Cadan turned to see Rafael standing there with tears in his eyes.

I'm sorry, Rafael.

He died so that we could escape.

Yes, he did.

He always taught me that dying for a good cause is one of the most honorable things you can do.

He was right. But you are safe with us, okay?

Rafael nodded.

Natalie came up behind Rafael and wrapped her arm around his shoulder. The boy flinched at first, but then settled in and accepted the comforting gesture.

"What do we do?" Darius asked.

"First we have to find Benton and Hazel," Tomas said. "They came through with us, so they must be around here somewhere."

"Where are we?" Madison asked.

"We can't be far from the gas station," Cadan answered. "Our surroundings look almost identical."

"I don't see the explosion," she countered.

"We were probably unconscious for a little while. It could have died down by now."

"I found them," we heard Tomas call from over a rise.

Cadan and Madison turned and ran over the short hill and found Tomas checking Benton's pulse.

"Are they okay?" Cadan asked.

"They're both alive," he answered. "But still unconscious. We need to get them back to the Facility."

Cadan reached into his pocket and grabbed his Link. Just as he had seen Jude do several times, Cadan punched a button on the side. For several seconds, there was no response. He knew that something was wrong. Josiah had always answered very promptly before.

Finally a voice crackled from the speaker.

"Are you all okay?"

"For the most part," Cadan answered. "Who is this?"

"It's Sheila," she replied. "Why are *you* contacting us? Where are Benton and Hazel?"

"Benton and Hazel are still alive, but barely," he explained to the magic-wielding math teacher. "We need immediate evacuation. Jude has been taken by Nolan's people."

"That is not possible at the moment," she said after moment of hesitation. "That explosion came through Lars's portal. The entire Command Center was destroyed along with parts of the Hangar and the storage area above Josiah's office. Josiah, Lars, and most of the others are unconscious as well. Nieson and I are the only two awake right now."

"Ask her about the other Facilities," Tomas urged. "Contact one of them to come and get us."

"What about one of the other Facilities?" Cadan asked.

"Impossible," she replied. "All of our communications are down. We are only talking because Helena's Link happened to be one of the only things not obliterated."

"What do we do?" Cadan asked.

"The Paladins never made it back from the Fatales' mansion, so they should still be there. Rendezvous with them at the mansion and then await transfer to the Facility."

"What about Jude?"

"We'll have to wait for Josiah's command when he wakes up," Sheila explained. "Now I need to go help Nieson with the wounded."

The communicator went silent.

"So what do we do?" Natalie asked.

"I guess we go to the Fatale mansion," Cadan shrugged.

"What about Jude?" Madison said.

"We don't even know where he was taken," he said.

"Our only choice is to go to the Fatales like Sheila told us," Tomas explained. "Maybe Josiah will be awake by then and help us get Jude back."

"This is bullshit!" Madison growled as she kicked dirt in the air.

"Calm down," Cadan told her, putting an arm on her bare shoulder. He leaned in and said quietly, "Let's go with this for now. As soon as we learn Jude's whereabouts, we go after him. I promise."

She turned and smiled at him with a devilish grin.

"There's something I need to tell you," she said. She patted the small brown leather satchel at her side. Part of the strap looked tattered, but the bag itself was fairly unscathed from the blast.

"What is it?" he eyed her curiously.

She slipped the strap of the bag over her head and then threw the bag towards him. He caught it and immediately opened the top. Inside he found several familiar objects. His journal was on the top, which he pulled out and flipped through to see that everything was still intact. He peered back in the bag, and saw his gold encrusted dagger lying there, the blade wrapped in a small sliver of white cloth. Nestled in the cloth were two stones – one green and the other clear. His numina stones.

Memories flooded back to him. He had only been with DOMA a little over a week now, but it seemed like another lifetime since he was back on the farm with his family.

"Why do you have these things?" Cadan asked.

"That night in Manhattan when we captured you," she reminded him. "Nate told me to search you for any weapons. When I looked and found these things, something told me to hide them for you. I hid them in my own bag. Only Jude saw me, and he kept quiet about what I did."

"Why would you steal from me?"

"It was in your best interest," she replied. "DOMA does a much more thorough search, and if they had found them instead, they would have been confiscated."

Tomas was looking over his shoulder. "And by the looks of it, you would have had a lot more explaining to do."

Cadan didn't know what to say. Yes, she did steal from him, but if Josiah had read this journal, he would know a lot more, including information about his family. He slipped the journal and dagger into his own bag.

"Did you read my journal?" Cadan asked.

"Of course not," Madison said with a smile. "Jude wanted to, but I wouldn't let him. I told him that if you decide to tell us your secrets, then we would know, but we weren't going to pry to find them out."

"Thank you," he said. Something about having his personal items back, especially the dagger that belonged to his father made him feel more connected to Simon and his family. With the jade, he could summon an easy spell and contact any of them in seconds.

"You have two numina stones?" Tomas asked. "If I'm not mistaken, that's a diamond and a jade."

"Yes," Cadan nodded.

"So?" he asked, waiting for an explanation.

"I've had the diamond since I was kid. A man who was taking care of me for a while told me that it had belonged to my parents."

"And the jade?" Tomas asked. "Each jade is specifically tied to a group, and they're used for communication with the others in the set."

"I don't want to talk about that," Cadan answered, knowing full well that his refusal to answer let his teammates know that he was hiding something.

"I respect that," Tomas nodded.

"We should be going," Darius said, changing the subject. Cadan could see his wink even in the darkness.

"How do we get back to LA?" Natalie asked. "We don't even know where we are."

"I can see lights off in the distance," Madison told them. "Some sort of building."

"Let's head that way," Cadan told them. "Bryce and Darius, can you bring our teachers?"

"Sure," they both grumbled as they hoisted their load.

The lights Madison was referring to was a motel out in the middle of nowhere. There were a half dozen cars out front, and the only light came from the office. Cadan told everyone to wait outside by the highway while he and Madison crept through the parking lot. The motel was a U-shaped building with two floors of rooms that occupants entered from the front.

He had an idea. The second vehicle they checked turned out to have what he was looking for. The black, older model Suburban had an aftermarket navigation system stuck to the front windshield with a lick-and-stick suction cup. Not the most stylish to go cruising through Los Angeles in, but it would have to do.

"How are we going to drive this thing?" she asked.

"Hot wire," Cadan told her.

Thankfully the rear passenger door was unlocked. He waved the others over. "Get in," he told them as he ran around to the driver's door.

Madison crawled from the back seat into the front and unlocked his door before settling into the passenger seat. Bryce opened the rear hatch and laid the two unconscious mages in the back area, before climbing in to sit beside them. Tomas, Natalie, and Rafael slid into the rear seats.

Cadan fumbled with the wires underneath the steering wheel for a moment, the whole time thanking Simon for never buying him a newer vehicle. He and Derrick had had to hotwire the old truck every other time they drove it, so the task was not that difficult for him. He was also thankful that the Suburban was old, making it that much easier.

"Tomas," Cadan turned to him. "When we get to the Fatales', will write down the license plate so that Josiah can make sure that the owner gets it back?"

"Sure," he nodded.

He started the SUV up, and threw it into reverse. They were out of the parking lot and onto the highway before anyone at the motel knew what had just happened.

The navigation system told them where they were. Madison checked the system and found that they were only a few miles west of the gas station, and the highway they were on would take them right into Los Angeles. Less than two hours and they would be at the Fatales mansion. They were all silently hoping that everything would be okay. Heading down the deserted highway with a sky full of stars, there would have been no way to guess that everything was about to get so much worse.

Chapter Twenty-Two

The Fatale mansion was silent as they drove up the long driveway to the front doors. All of the lights were on, but they didn't see a single person stirring inside. Cadan stopped the Suburban behind a black Escalade and put it into park. Turning the keys, he glanced over at Madison, who had the same grim expression on her face.

"Nothing's moving in there," Madison pointed out.

"We go in slowly," Cadan told them.

They got out of the SUV and made their way towards the front door. He gripped his sword tightly, prepared to swing. Madison had her bow, but no arrows, so she was effectively weaponless. Bryce still had both of his maces, so he and Cadan were the only ones armed.

The front door was ajar, and he pushed it with the tip of his sword. It swung open a few feet and then stopped, something behind it blocking the way.

He peered around behind the door to find Malina, the brown haired Fatale, lying motionless on the ground. Reaching down, he checked her pulse and was relieved to find one.

"Is she alive?" Natalie asked. He nodded.

He continued to survey the front room. There were two more unconscious bodies lying in the foyer. Taking the four steps down into the living room two at a time, he found at least a dozen more people lying on the floor and strewn about over the furniture. He recognized Katina and Batina with their blue and purple hair. Both were clutching each other on the sofa and neither was moving, but he could see their chests rising in time with their breath.

Several of their entourage were among the bodies, and not all of them had a pulse. And then he saw Anthony. The Paladin leader was still holding his sword, but his body was lying back against the large stone fireplace. Blood was coming out of the back of his head and his eyes were closed. Cadan checked his pulse, and he was still alive.

"Jason and Clay are over here," Darius called over. He was in the doorway leading to the kitchen. "They're alive, but down for the count."

"Heather and Carmen are over here," Natalie said from the far side of the room. "Same thing."

"They must have been attacked," Madison said, stating the obvious. "And it's fresh."

"Definitely very fresh," Cadan agreed. "Anthony's wound is still bleeding and none of the blood has dried."

"Where's Nate?" Darius asked. They all shrugged. His body wasn't among those in the living room.

"Nolan's team must have just left," Tomas guessed. "We should probably get out of here."

"They are long gone," Cadan told him. "Or we would have already been attacked."

"Why did Nolan come back?" Natalie asked.

"It seems like they're systematically taking out our resources," he explained. "First they try to take down the Knights and destroy the Facility, and now they take down the Paladins. They're trying to weaken us."

"I don't think that's it at all, Cadan," Tomas shook his head. "It would be a fool's mission to try to take down DOMA, even one piece at a time. There are other Facilities just like ours and many more agents. They haven't even bit off a fraction of DOMA's resources."

"They're playing at something," Darius agreed. "And it's not taking DOMA out, that's for sure."

"Then what are they doing?" Natalie asked.

"They wanted something here," Tomas told them. "See the way everything is disheveled," he pointed out. "Every pillow is cut and the stuffing has been pulled out. Every drawer is open and its contents are on the floor. They were looking for something."

"What could possibly be here of value besides the Fatales?" Cadan asked.

"A garnet numina stone," Tomas explained, looking around the room. "I remember reading a report recently that detailed where the secret numina stones were located. Wendell had asked me to file in the low level classified section of the archives."

"The what?" Madison asked. "Why would they have secret numina stones?"

"We don't have much time, so I'll make this brief," he said as he started look around the room. "All of the ruhk-wielders in DOMA are relatively evenly matched. Josiah and Cadan are among the most powerful, but with the other ruhk-wielders considered, there is no one that is really undefeatable should the need arise. With numina stones, an individual could make themselves powerful enough to be nearly unstoppable. The stones are rare though, so DOMA has spread them out evenly among the Facilities and the staff. For those with specific and important purposes, they have them hidden in other places, such as the Fatale mansion."

"Isn't a garnet numina to control a creature?" Natalie asked.

"Precisely," Tomas said as he turned and ran down the hall. They all followed to finish hearing his explanation.

"So you think Nolan is going to try and control some creature?" Cadan asked.

"Yes," he nodded, as he rummaged through a chest of drawers. "You said that Tyler mentioned something about a ship. Well, the garnet that is supposed to be in the Fatale mansion controls a dragon that guards an airship."

"A dragon? An airship?"

"Yes, an actual dragon is guarding the airship at Area 51."

"The one that Josiah's mother came over from Andaloria on?"

"Yes," Tomas nodded. "The Area 51 Facility surrounds it now. To get inside and to the airship, you have to have the garnet numina to control the dragon so that it will allow you to pass. Without the numina, you'd just be a snack for the beast."

"Why would they go to the airship?"

"I don't have a clue. Nobody has any idea what's on that ship. It must be something important because DOMA commissioned an entire complex around the ship and even went to the trouble of placing a dragon there. Whatever's in there, they don't want anyone having access to it."

"So Nolan probably has the garnet now and is making his way there, and we have no way of warning Josiah."

Tomas stopped and looked at the bed. "The garnet is gone."

Cadan followed his gaze and saw the metal box on the bed, which had been opened. Inside was a smaller case which was open as well. Inside the smaller case, there was a small foam cushion with a perfectly hollowed-out center, just right for a gem-sized object.

"That is what the numina are kept in," Tomas explained. "Nolan has taken it and they are gone."

"We can follow them," Cadan said triumphantly. "We know where they are going and we can rescue Jude."

"We couldn't even take them down at the gas station," Natalie pointed out.

"We take them by surprise," Cadan came back.

"I'm with Cadan," said Madison.

They heard a scuffling noise from the next room over. Everyone stared at each other with wide eyes.

Cadan raised his sword and slowly walked out into the hallway, towards the next room. He crept as quietly as he could. Bryce and an unarmed Madison were right behind, but the others stayed near the first room. He found the door to the next room just a dozen or so feet down the hallway. Pushing it open, he peered inside. The room was empty.

Then he heard the noise again. It was coming from the closet. He tiptoed over to the closet and motioned at the door. He pointed to Madison. She nodded.

She crept up to the side of the closet door and put her hand on the handle. He nodded. She threw the door open and he threw his sword up, ready to swing.

"Don't hit me!"

A red-haired boy, lying in a ball of clothes on the floor, was holding his arms up to shield his face. Cadan remembered him from his and Jude's earlier trip here.

"What are you doing in here?"

"I'm sorry!" he shrieked. "Just don't kill me!"

"Shut up!" Madison yelled.

"Please stop screaming," Cadan told the boy. "We need you to answer some questions."

"I will do whatever you ask if you promise not to kill me."

"We're not going to kill you. Did you see the people that came in here just before us?"

"You're not with them?" the redhead asked.

"No, we're not," Cadan explained. "Those people took a friend of ours and something else valuable. Did you see or hear anything?"

"No," he shook his head. "I was in this room when I heard them come through the door. They started yelling and threatening everyone inside, so I hid in the closet. They never checked in here. I heard them banging around in the next room over, and then suddenly they were gone."

"Is anyone else here? Anyone else not dead or unconscious?"

"I haven't been out of this closet since I heard the commotion."

"Cadan," Madison sighed. "We don't have time for this. We need to get going now."

Cadan turned around and began to walk out of the room. He heard the red head behind him get up and walk towards them.

"Where are you going?" the boy asked.

"Can't tell you," Madison answered as they walked back into the living room.

"I can't find Nate anywhere," Bryce said. "I scanned the rooms and couldn't find him.

"I want to go with you!" the redhead said.

Cadan ignored him. "Darius," he said as he turned to his teammate. "Can you and Bryce scan the perimeter outside and find Nate? He may have been attacked outside." He turned to Tomas. "Do you know where the Facility is located?"

"Vaguely," he answered. "I've seen photos, so once we get close, I should be able to locate it."

"How long will it take us to get there?" Cadan asked.

"A few hours," he replied.

"Not quick enough," Cadan said. He rubbed the back of his head as he looked around in thought. "He's probably already there."

"I can get you there faster."

Cadan turned and stared at the redheaded boy. "How so?"

"I'm a fairy," he revealed.

"What's your name?"

"Gabe. I can get us almost anywhere you want to go."

"Have you been to Nevada?" Cadan asked.

"I've been to Vegas. I can get us there."

"Not close enough. Where else have you been?"

"Where are you trying to go?"

"Area 51."

"What?" he almost laughed. "You want to go find some aliens or something?"

"No, we need to get to the government facility there called Area 51."

"Well, I went to Crystal Springs. I don't think it's far from Area 51, because I remember an alien gift shop there."

"That's close," Tomas nodded.

Darius and Bryce returned. "No sign of Nate," Darius said.

"We've decided to go to Area 51. Gabe here is going to take us."

"Um" Gabe pursed his lips and pointed towards Cadan's torso. "Not that we're going to a fashion show or anything, but you guys may want to consider finding some new clothes first."

Cadan had forgotten about the fact that he didn't have a shirt. His pants were ripped, as well. He looked around at the other Knights, and their clothes were just as ragged and filthy.

"The Fatales should have some clothes for the girls," Gabe offered, "and I can get some clothes for everyone except that big guy with all those arms."

The guys followed Gabe into one of the rooms and he found each of them a shirt and pants that were close to their sizes. Other than being covered in grime, their boots were all wearable. The blue button up shirt Cadan got was a little snug and confining. He had to roll the sleeves up past the elbow to free his arms for better movement. He was certain that his sword arm would be tired before the morning. The pants were khaki, and even better, they were clean. A shower would have been nice, but clean clothes were an adequate consolation.

They returned to the living area and soon the girls joined them. Madison's blue top hung off her shoulders and her tight jeans that hung so low on her hips they were nearly inappropriate. Natalie wore jeans that were equally as low and a shirt that, much to the open chagrin of her brother, bared her midriff. There was some difficulty in finding a shirt for Bryce, so he settled for keeping his old one on despite the two large tears in the back. Darius and Rafael had changed into simple t-shirts and jeans.

"Are we really taking this fairy?" Darius grumbled.

"Hey," Gabe said as he whirled around, one hand on his hip and the other in the air. "What do you mean by that comment?"

"Uh," Darius stammered. He obviously hadn't understood the word's potential double meaning.

"He didn't mean anything by it," Cadan told Gabe, trying to soothe the escalating tension. "And yes, Darius he is going with us."

"Why?"

"Because he is going to take several hours off our trip. Simple as that."

"But we're going to have to protect him! He can't fight for himself."

"You don't know that," Gabe said as he folded his arms across his chest. He closed his eyes and brought his feet together. His face contorted so slightly that Cadan almost missed it. Pink and purple particles – almost like dirt or dust – spewed from his back. Objects that looked like flaps sprung out behind him, separating and extending in four different directions. When Gabe was done, he looked up at the others and his four wings – two large upper wings and two smaller, lower wings – sprouted in all directions. The wings looked like they came from giant dragonflies, and had beautiful intricate designs all over, with shades of pink and purple glistening in between.

"Wow," was all Cadan could say. Rafael was the only other person who seemed surprised by what they had witnessed. It must have been more commonplace for the others, since they didn't even bat an eyelash.

"So," Darius shrugged. "You going to slap a goblin with a wing?"

"Don't patronize him, Darius," Natalie chided her brother. "You heard Cadan say that he is coming."

"And that is all that needs to be said," Madison added.

"What do we do about Benton and Hazel?" Tomas asked. "They're still in the back of the Suburban."

"Josiah will come here first, right?" Cadan asked.

"I would think so," Madison said, still glaring at Darius.

"Then we leave them here with the Paladins," Cadan answered.

"But they could wake up and help us if we take them," Tomas suggested.

"I don't want to take that chance," Cadan explained. "What if they don't wake up? Then we have to keep an eye on them and make sure they stay protected."

"How are we going to get past the dragon?" Madison asked.

"I have a plan," Tomas said, as he reached into his brown leather bag. He pulled out an amber colored numina stone. "I still have the garnet I used back under the bridge. I'll try to use it to calm the dragon."

"But it's not the numina stone tied to the dragon, right?" Cadan asked. "How will it work?"

"Well, a garnet always works best when it's the one linked with a particular creature. But any garnet will give you some degree of control or influence. I can probably keep it occupied while we pass it, or persuade it to not attack us."

"Probably?" Madison threw her hands up. "I'm not willing to become rotisserie for your probabilities."

"I'm almost certain it will work."

"Whatever," Madison mouthed, as she shook her head.

Cadan turned to Gabe. "So how are you going to get us to Area 51?"

Chapter Twenty-Three

Gabe's plan began with them driving the Suburban out of the main part of the city and into the outskirts. Since it was the middle of the night, they missed most of the horrendous traffic for which LA was notorious for. Cadan estimated that he had been awake for at least twenty hours and that exhaustion lay just on the other side of the adrenaline pumping through his veins. He stifled a yawn and kept his eyes focused on the roadway.

Everyone was quiet for most of the ride through town. His thoughts settled on Jude. He wondered what Nolan would be doing to him right now. Nobody had any clue what they even wanted with their teammate, but they apparently wanted Nate as well. Something was located at Area 51 that Nolan wanted, and Cadan was going there not only stop him, but to rescue his friend as well.

Even as Cadan said the word 'friend' in his mind, it sounded strange. He and Jude had begun with a strange relationship of mentor and mentee, with a mutual respect for each other's strengths. The world of magic that Jude was so familiar with had been thrust upon Cadan and at times it was overwhelming, but his roommate navigated the choppy waters of life at the Facility with ease. Despite teasing from the Paladins, tension on his own team, and the unpredictable personalities of the staff, Jude kept a smile on his face the whole time.

He was clearly an expert on all things DOMA, but he had quickly deferred to Cadan and his leadership skills and prowess with ruhk-magic. Jude was the textbook definition of cocky, yet he unquestioningly believed in Cadan's abilities.

Somewhere during the events that brought them to this point, they had become friends, even though they never vocalized it. It had just seemed a very smooth and swift process. Settling his mind with the idea that he was now a part of DOMA was a difficult process, but Jude's constant quips and irreverent attitude towards everything made it much more bearable.

Gabe leaned up to the front seat. "This should be good enough."

Cadan pulled over to the side of the road. He was so lost in his thoughts that he hadn't realized they had passed the city limits some time back. The side of the highway was deserted. The only lights were from their own vehicle.

Cadan got out of the SUV and stretched his legs, looking around for any sign of other people. He was about to ask how the transport process was going to work, when the communicator in Tomas's bag beeped. He pulled it from the leather satchel and tossed it towards Cadan.

He clicked the little button to turn it on and Josiah's voice greeted them. "Cadan."

"Yes, Josiah."

"Where are you?"

He hadn't even thought about this eventuality. If he told the Administrator the truth, Josiah would immediately forbid what they were going to do. At all costs, Cadan knew they had to save Jude from Nolan and his followers.

"We're at the Fatale Mansion," he lied.

"Where is everyone else?"

"They're all here with me," he answered. "The Paladins and Fatales are all unconscious, but Nate and Sabrina are missing. Jude was taken at the station, and Benton and Hazel are still out of it." What a gloomy assessment, he thought to himself.

"Oh, dear," Josiah said quietly into the device. "This is a very grave situation." There was a long pause on the other end. "Our communication system that we utilize to contact the other Facilities has been disabled beyond repair and Benton is with you, so we have no way of re-establishing the systems here. The injuries that Lars suffered were more severe than we originally believed and while Helena has healed him, it will be some time before he has enough strength to make a gateway to reach you."

"Will the other Facilities check in when they don't hear from us?" he asked.

"They should," he explained. "We have a rotation system where we check in on each other every four hours. That is still nearly two hours away."

"What do you want us to do?" he asked.

"Stay right where you are," the Administrator answered.

"Josiah, we figured something out."

"Go ahead."

"Nolan is making his way to Area 51. There's something there that he wants."

"How do you know this?"

"He has the garnet numina stone from the Fatale mansion. Tomas remembered its location and function from a report he filed. Now the stone is gone, and we think he is headed to Area 51 to your mother's airship."

"He must be stopped at all costs," Josiah sighed.

"We can do it," Cadan volunteered.

"I cannot put you and the Knights in that kind of danger. You do not have the training nor the power to take down an entire Facility."

"We can try."

"No, you cannot. You are to stay right where you are. We will be there as soon as we can, and once you are all back here, we will contact the other Facilities and formulate a plan to stop him."

Then it hit him. They had to tell Josiah where they were going. If he didn't divulge their plan, then how would Josiah know where they were if something went wrong? Besides, Josiah would show up at the Fatale mansion and find them absent anyway.

"Josiah."

"Yes."

"Don't be mad, but we are on our way to Area 51. I have a plan. Please trust me."

"Cadan –"

He flicked the button to disconnect the call and threw the Link back into the Suburban.

"So how are we going to get to Area 51?" Cadan asked Gabe.

"I have to confess something," Gabe smiled weakly. "I'm not really that good with making portals. Since we're pretty close, I'm sure I can get us to the right place. I just can't make the doorway that large and can only hold it for a minute."

"Can you get the SUV through?"

"I think so," he nodded. "I'll stand outside and hold it open. Drive the Suburban through slowly, and then I'll come through behind it."

"Will this work?" he asked the fairy, throwing a suspicious stare.

His nod was not that confident. "If I make this gateway, I won't have the strength to make another one for a few hours at least. I'm not that strong."

"It's our best option," Cadan said. "Now let's get moving."

The fairy nodded and ran up the road a dozen feet to prepare his gateway. Cadan jumped behind the steering wheel of the vehicle and turned the engine back on. The communicator was beeping obsessively and he finally had to bury it in the glove box to help preserve his sanity.

A purple slit appeared in the air in front of them. The violet luminescent glow was beautiful against the pitch black of the night. Resembling an aurora borealis, the line first extended up and down until it reached about eight feet in length, and then began extending out.

When Gabe was satisfied that it was wide enough for the Suburban, he motioned them forward. Everyone was tense when Cadan let up off the brake and the vehicle lurched towards the portal. Their transportation made it through the opening fairly easily. He felt only a very mild disorientation from the trip. The only problem they encountered was the sharp drop off as they passed through as if the ground on one side was not level with the other. He fell forward and narrowly missed hitting his face on the steering wheel. The front bumper scraped the concrete on the other side.

He checked the mirror to make sure that the rear bumper was out of the portal and then stopped. Gabe came through shortly after, then turned and closed the gateway by bringing his hands together.

As the fairy climbed back into the vehicle, Cadan surveyed their surroundings. Other than a stark lack of plant life, their new location was eerily similar to the old one. There were a few lights far off in the distance.

"That's Crystal Springs," Gabe pointed out.

"Now how do we get to Area 51?" Cadan turned and asked Tomas.

He was looking around and scratching the top of his head. "We're on the highway that runs southwest, so that should take us much closer. Once we get near the compound, we should make the rest of the trek on foot."

"How far is it?" Madison asked.

"No more than a thirty minute drive," he answered.

The drive to the secret DOMA complex was quiet; no one really knew what to say with the impending confrontation looming over their heads. Tomas was correct and just under a half hour later, he motioned to pull over.

"Where's Area 51?" Bryce asked, as he scanned out the rear window. "I don't see any buildings or lights."

"It's mostly underground," Tomas explained. "It wouldn't be wise to pull up to the gate and drive on into the parking lot."

"So no gift shops?" Madison chuckled. Cadan suspected that like Jude, she also used her irreverence to stifle her own insecurities and doubts.

"No," he shook his head. "We're on foot from here. There's a barbed-wire fence not far over that hill there. The complex is another mile on the inside of it. We're going to sneak in through the loading docks."

"Won't someone see us?" Darius asked.

"With the dragon guarding the only entrance into the truly valuable area of this facility, there's no need for any serious security. There's minimal protection around the building, mostly security cameras. The guards are instructed to contact Josiah if they see anything suspicious."

"But Josiah is unreachable at the moment," Natalie noted.

"Precisely," Tomas smiled. "So we won't have much to worry about."

"But the guards seeing us will still be a problem," Cadan said.

I can take care of that.

He was a little surprised to hear Rafael's voice in his head again. He didn't even know the boy was following their conversation. He must have been reading their lips to understand the discussion.

How can you take care of it? Cadan asked him.

My father taught me a spell that bends light. We were able to sneak past security cameras and sometimes even people's own eyes if they weren't paying close attention. It should work if they just have cameras and we don't actually come in contact with another person.

Rafael's plan might work. Cadan had never heard of such a spell and didn't know if Simon even knew the trick, but it sounded plausible to him.

"Are you two talking?" Madison asked him. She was watching as they stared wordlessly at each other.

"Yes," Cadan said. "Rafael knows a way for us to pass by the cameras undetected. He knows a spell that can bend light."

"Really?" Tomas looked surprised. "Wendell told me that he knows that spell, but apparently it's extremely difficult. He tried to teach me once; I was having so much trouble, and he has so little patience, that we just abandoned the project altogether. I would be fascinated to see him produce it."

The boy looked very pleased with himself. Even the team know-it-all Tomas couldn't do something that he could.

By the way, call me Rafe. That's what my family always called me. You can tell the others too.

Cadan passed along the message. "He also wants me to tell you to call him Rafe."

They opened the doors to the SUV and started filing out. Darius clapped Rafe on the back. "Way to earn your spot on the team, little man."

What did he say? Rafe must not have caught his lips to understand what he said.

He said that he appreciates your assistance with this and that you are doing well to earn your spot on the team?

So I'm on the team?

It's not my decision, but I will definitely give you a good referral to Josiah. Cadan smiled and Rafe nodded.

A realization came to Cadan suddenly. His world had been turned on its head. His quest had begun as trying to find out who he really was and who his parents were. He was an orphan with no knowledge of his own heritage. Rafe was an orphan now, as well as all of the Knights, whom he had come to know as friends. He hadn't stepped back long enough to look at it and let it fully sink in. He was exactly like them. Whatever pain and anguish he felt over being alone in this world was shared with the tiny group of people standing around him. But everyone was willing to put aside their feelings of self doubt and challenge a force at least ten times their size to rescue a lost friend. He wasn't actually alone at all.

He was still mortified at the prospect of what lay before them, but at least he was with people that he was growing to care about. And he honestly felt like they cared about him in return.

Leaving them near the car, Cadan walked down the road about ten feet to get a moment of privacy. He reached into the left pocket of his pants and found his jade numina stone. He knew that this would somehow connect to four other stones, all in the possession of the four people formerly comprising his 'family.' Simon never went into much detail on how to use the green stone.

He gripped the numina in his fist and whispered into it. "Simon, I want you to know that I love you. Please tell Daphne, Derrick, and Raney that I love them as well." There was no response. He didn't know if Simon could even hear what he said. He decided to add, "I don't know if I'll be coming back from where I'm about to go and just wanted to let you know that I'm sorry for the way I left things between us. I really do appreciate everything you have done for me."

A tear rolled down his cheek. He wiped it off and returned to the group, hoping that they hadn't seen him cry.

"What were you doing?" Madison asked.

"Nothing," he replied. "Just thinking."

He paused and surveyed the Knights. They stood in a line awaiting his direction. Before he had arrived, Nate had been their leader and sucked at giving direction. Cadan was never the cocky sort, but as he stood watching them, he was proud of his apparent leadership skill.

"We'd better get going," he told them as they crossed the road and a small culvert that ran along the pavement. "It may already be too late to stop Nolan."

Chapter Twenty-Four

For the first few minutes they thought they were heading towards a hill or a mountain, and it was the largest site looming object in the night sky. The moon shone over the deserted landscape and the stars were as bright as Cadan remembered from back home in Texas. Vegetation was scarce, so they followed Tomas as he meandered among the natural stark landscape. The only noise was the wind sweeping among the varying rock formations. It was eerie, considering their rambunctiously blaring battle at the gas station and the cacophony of Los Angeles that they had left only an hour before.

The barbed-wire fence proved only mildly frustrating. He and Tomas levitated the other Knights over the fence using a basic spell, and then they took turns magically helping each other over. Cadan considered using ruhk-fire to burn his way through, but Tomas warned that the ruhk-fire would warn any mage within a several mile radius that they were near.

When they came closer to the base of the mountainous hill, they changed courses and began trekking around to the west. They were almost upon a large metal structure before he realized what he was looking at. As they approached, Cadan had assumed that the structure was part of the chaotic craggy formation of the natural landscape.

He had expected a more impressive Area 51 than what lay before him. Tomas said that the vast majority of the complex lay underground. Despite that, Cadan didn't anticipate such a dismal collection of small metal buildings.

The main building was only double the size of his home back in Iowa Park. There were a few other buildings the size of houses attached through circular turrets. The bases of the buildings were concrete and the sides and tops were flat metallic sheets. Even from a distance he could see the patchy weld job on most of the walls.

There was no hint of movement anywhere.

Once they were within sight of the Facility, Tomas stopped.

"Past this point we'll be within range of the cameras."

Cadan turned around to face Rafe. *Are you ready?*

Yes. I'll tell you once I've finished cloaking all of us, and then we can head over there.

Rafe closed his eyes as he bowed his head, raising both arms until they extended out at a perfect ninety degree angle to his body, palms up. Other than a slight tingle of the hairs on the back of Cadan's neck, there was nothing to tell that the spell was in place.

I'm done, he said as he raised his head and opened his gray eyes.

Unsure of themselves, the Knights looked around at each other for a few seconds. Cadan stared at Tomas and then raised a questioning eyebrow. He simply shrugged.

Cadan led the way towards the government compound. He was surprised at the lack of grandeur an entrance into Area 51 would have. Maybe he was expecting guards to come out blazing their guns and commanding them to lift their arms in the air. Or maybe the President of the United States would walk out and greet them. But they simply walked over to one of the garage bays and stopped.

Standing about five feet in the air, the bays were closed, but not locked. There was a stack of metal crates over to one side, which they used to make a couple of steps for easy access. He and Darius jumped up first, and with a lift of a handle, the door slid up on its path with a sharp clank.

They searched for any sign that their entrance had been noticed, and after a few brief moments of nothing, they turned and helped everyone else up into the bay area.

Tomas leaned in and whispered, "I think I remember the schematics for this Facility. I only saw them once, but they are very simple, so I'm sure I can find the entrance to the underground area."

"I'm right behind you," Cadan told him.

They passed through a doorway, into a hallway and turned right, the little group of misfits trying their best to stay quiet. There was very little lighting in the passageway, and only a glimmer of light from somewhere far behind them.

He heard Tomas grunt and stop suddenly.

"I just kicked something," he mumbled.

Cadan slid up beside him and kneeled down – it was a body. Turning his palm up, he conjured a very small burst of ruhk-fire to provide a light source. Tomas had kicked the body of a fallen soldier, who was lying in the fetal position across the expanse of their intended course. A few feet beyond him, a woman in a matching uniform was laying face down, blood trickling out around her head. The man didn't have a pulse, and he guessed that the woman wouldn't either.

"Nolan killed them," he surmised.

"Bastard," Madison hissed.

"So we put a cloaking spell up for nothing?" Darius asked.

"Who knows if there are soldiers in the other rooms?" Tomas explained. "It was better to be safe than sorry. Not to mention that the video surveillance is recorded, and I don't know about you, but I would prefer there be no evidence that I broke into Area 51."

"I agree," Natalie added. "Let's go find Jude and get out of here. This place gives me the creeps."

"The entrance to the underground area is just up ahead, at the end of this hall," Tomas said. "There should be a staircase."

They cautiously stepped over the lifeless bodies and made their way to the end of the hall. Just as Tomas had predicted, there was a spiral staircase. Beyond the first few steps there was nothing but a hungry chasm of blackness. A damp coldness bit at Cadan's face, seeming to emanate from out of the pit.

He shivered at the unexpected sensation and goose bumps shot up on every inch of his skin.

"We're going down there?" Madison asked

"Yes," Cadan answered.

"How far down is it?" Darius asked.

"From what I remember of the schematics, the lower level is at least three hundred feet underground."

"So three hundred stairs?" Natalie groaned. "You could have warned me back at the Fatales mansion when you saw me come out in heels."

"You knew we were going into battle – you picked those shoes," Darius pointed out.

Before Natalie could come back with something, Madison put her hand up. "Hey girl, you got to look good, right?" She winked at her friend. Natalie winked back, but shot her brother a nasty glare.

Cadan turned his palm over again and produced a small flame of ruhk-fire just above his hand. The flame wasn't very bright because he didn't want to warn Nolan and his forces that they were coming. He just needed it to be bright enough to make sure that none of them tumbled down football fields worth of stairs.

Since he had the light and the sword, he went first, followed by Madison and Rafe, then Darius and Tomas. Bryce brought up the rear with Natalie right in front of him, providing them both light with her violet colored ruhk-fire. She knew to keep the flame on a low intensity to keep it from being spotted.

The descent was excruciating. For the first few steps, they were buffeted by rocky, jagged earth on all sides. Before they had finished the first two dozen steps, the earth around them had disappeared and there was nothing but blackness in all directions. Once during the trek down, he intensified his flame so that the light extended out several dozen feet, but still he only saw emptiness.

Cadan tried to soften his steps as his feet made contact with the metal underneath, but he could still hear clanking echoes as they descended. If one of Nolan's people were around, they would definitely hear the Knights' approach.

Without any warning, his ear drums were filled with the most shattering noise he had ever heard. The piercing cry was something akin to two wolves side by side, one howling and the other growling, both in front of a microphone hooked up to a stadium's surround sound.

His flame disappeared, and he put both of his hands up cover his ears, stooping down to the steps. Natalie screamed behind him and her flame disappeared as well.

"It's the dragon," Cadan heard Madison mutter. Her voice was trembling.

"Great," he heard Gabe sputter, and Cadan thought the poor boy was close to tears.

The noise came again, and even though it was the second time, it was still equally as unnerving. He felt his arms tremble with fear.

"What do we do?" Darius asked, his voice stuttering.

"We are sitting ducks up here," Tomas advised. "There's a good chance we're on a suspended staircase in the middle of the dragon's lair."

"Are you serious?" Madison asked. "Why didn't you tell us that?"

"I didn't think I had to! Where do you think they keep a dragon – in a crate?"

"We need to get down to the bottom and fast!" Cadan told them as he stood back up and relit his makeshift torch of ruhk-fire.

"Or get back to the top," Natalie said under her breath.

"Let's go." Cadan began descending again, taking the steps two at a time.

And then the noise came again, only this time something large struck the staircase as well. Their feet came out from under them and they plummeted down the metal steps, their bodies like rag dolls as they fell. His shoulder hit the frail railing, and he tumbled at least five or six more steps before coming to a stop around the curve. Tomas nearly fell on top of Cadan as he stopped himself.

"He's trying to take us out," Bryce said.

Cadan wasn't sure what to do. His entire team was ready to mutiny as their unseen opponent was creating waves of hysteria. Without a word he stood up and threw both arms in the air. Summoning every bit of ruhk-magic he could manage in a short span, he sent waves of ruhk-fire in every direction, lighting the space up. If Nolan was there, he would know the Knights were too.

The breath left his body when he saw that they were in a spacious cavern that seemed to go on forever. The ceiling of the cavern was about fifty feet above them and Cadan caught a glimpse of earth another two hundred feet below. In the distance, there was a small hill, and behind that was blackness. A gigantic green tail disappeared behind the hill, and he caught an even briefer glimpse of a wing over the top. It was definitely the dragon.

He brought the ruhk-fire back in and once again they were surrounded by blackness.

"Did you see that?" Darius screamed out.

"The dragon," Tomas nodded.

"Do you have the garnet ready?" Cadan asked.

"It's in my pocket and accessible. I need to be closer to him to control him."

"I didn't see any sign of Nolan or his people," Madison said.

"Then we need to get to the bottom fast," Natalie said, urging them down.

They began descending again, this time making no effort to mask their noise, and doing their best to take them two or three steps at a time.

He could tell without talking to Rafe that the boy was scared because he clung to the sleeve of Cadan's shirt.

The end of the staircase couldn't have come soon enough. They reached the last step and Cadan almost screamed out in relief. At the bottom, they heard the dragon's shrill cry once again.

"Look what I found," Tomas said as he waved his handful of ruhk-fire over the wall. Cadan walked over to the rear of the staircase where an electric box was mounted to the central column of the stairs. He opened the front cover to reveal a switch.

"Flip it," he told Tomas when the mage hesitated.

He did and the room lit up. The ceiling was at least three hundred feet up and there were several large lights mounted in various places, shining at different angles.

The room seemed to be so enormous that he struggled to find anything to compare it to. They were standing on a ledge that divided the cavern in half, starting with the staircase and curving around the promontory he had seen the dragon disappear behind. The ledge was no more than eight feet wide. On each side there was nothing but darkness. Even the lights overhead failed to penetrate its depths.

"They couldn't put some railings down here?" Darius asked dryly.

"At least you can fly," Madison mumbled.

"Do we keep going?" Natalie asked.

"Yes," Cadan answered her. "We need to get Tomas closer to the dragon. Since the beast doesn't seem to want to oblige us and make it easier, I say we keep moving forward."

"He's trying to get us to the middle so that we can't escape," Bryce said. His matter of fact tone was not refreshing.

Chapter Twenty-Five

The walk to the promontory was about a hundred feet. The ledge widened a good deal and the hill Cadan had seen earlier was no more than a raised extension to the side of the ledge. They had not seen the beast since coming off the stairs, but deep in the blackness underneath them, the cavern walls echoed with its cry.

"If I can stand on that platform up there, I think I can get a good view and try the garnet on the dragon," Tomas said.

"But you'd be right out in the open," Cadan warned.

"I have to try."

He turned to the others. "I'm going with Tomas. I saw a small outcropping about two dozen feet ahead. That should provide you some cover if the dragon tries to attack. Go there now, before we get on the ledge."

"I'm going with you," Darius said.

"There's no need to be brave," Natalie chided him.

"He's right," Cadan told her. "He can fly, just in case the worst happens."

"Actually the worst that could happen would be for the dragon to appear and use his fire breath to incinerate us," said Tomas.

Cadan was taken aback. "I thought fire breathing was only a myth."

"Oh no, it's what the myths are based on. A dragon's teeth secrete a chemical that reacts with the molecules of his breath to actually produce a really hot fire."

"Wow," was all he could say.

There was no time to take their positions. The cavern echoed with the sound of the beating wings and as soon as the dragon's head came into view, it let out another cry.

"Run!" Cadan yelled at the others.

Tomas pulled the garnet from his pocket and clambered up the promontory to take his position. Cadan and Darius were right behind him.

As Cadan pulled himself up the rest of the way onto the platform, He saw that the hill was actually the dragon's perch. The enormous creature landed with earth-shattering force onto the promontory, and he saw some of the sides of the ledge break away and fall. Out of the corner of his eye, he spotted the others dodge under the outcropping.

The dragon was exactly as Cadan had imagined – straight out of a movie. On four massive legs, the mammoth beast was towering before them. Its head was raised in the air, while its tail disappeared down the side of the cliff. As close as they were, he could see the large, shimmering green scales coating its skin like armor.

Tomas held the garnet in the air, and Cadan could see the glow of the ruhk-magic all around him. He was powerful, and he was using all he could to ensure that the garnet worked. Although the numina stone wasn't synced specifically with this creature, Cadan hoped it would still work.

The dragon didn't have to move its body to come closer – it simply swung its head in their direction. Tomas was still working the spell, and was almost face to face with the beast.

"Tomas," Cadan warned. His sword arm was ready to strike for whatever good it would do.

The dragon peered at Tomas for a moment and then its head retreated back. He thought for a moment that the spell had worked, when suddenly the dragon whirled its head and came at Tomas from the side. The mage grunted loudly as he was thrown up into the air.

Cadan watched his teammate plummet over the side and into the darkness beyond.

"I'm on it," Darius yelled, as he jumped up, ripped off his shirt, and disappeared over the side behind Tomas. Just before he was out of sight, Cadan saw his great black wings spread wide.

He didn't have much time to think about Tomas because the dragon whipped its tail around to lash at the outcropping where the others were hiding. The four Knights scrambled and Bryce caught Natalie before she fell off the side.

The creature turned its attention to Cadan. He held his sword low with his right hand and held a bolt of ruhk-fire with his left. He knew it was only doing its assigned job and didn't want to cause it any undo harm, but he wouldn't let it hurt any of his friends.

"Run!" Cadan yelled at the others. The dragon's tail was swinging around again to hit them.

Bryce stopped on the stony causeway and pushed Gabe, Rafe, and the girls past him. Planting his feet on the ground he lifted all four arms and braced for the force. The dragon's tail hit the big man square in the chest – any other person would have been crushed by the intense physical pressure, but Bryce was simply pushed back a few steps.

The dragon realized its rear opponent would be harder to knock aside, so it turned its attention back to Cadan. Its blazing red eyes glared at him. As its nose sniffed, a cloud of gray smoke puffed from each nostril. The smell of sulfur and ash permeated the air.

With a growl that produced a gallon of saliva on each side of its mouth, the creature's head darted towards him, as if trying to head butt. He jumped to the left and tumbled across the ground, narrowly dodging the strike. Face down, his body was on the rocks, and his legs dangled over the ledge. With as much upper body strength as he could manage, he pulled himself back up.

He turned just in time to see the dragon go for a second head butt. With both legs, Cadan kicked himself sideways, as far from the lunge as he could. He had cut it so close that the tip of the dragon's nose brushed against his feet, but it was enough to cause a loss of balance. He fell onto his upper back, and expected his head to hit rock, but there was nothing – his head was hanging over the edge of the precipice. He gripped a rock to hold himself in place.

"Watch out," he heard a voice from somewhere under him. He glanced to the side and from out of the darkness, Darius appeared, his large black wings flapping, his right arm extended into the air, and his other hand down by his side. Tomas was hanging on to his left arm for dear life.

As Darius flew by, the wind from his wings gave Cadan the extra bit of leverage he needed to pull himself up. The dragon was stepping towards him, growing closer.

A large rock hit the dragon in the face. Madison was there beside him, pulling him by the shirt sleeve away from the edge.

"Come on, Cadan," she urged.

He followed her, trying to stand, halfway crawling towards the walkway beside the promontory.

He jumped down onto the stone walkway, and landed next to Madison and Bryce. Natalie, Gabe, and Rafe were taking cover behind the big man. Darius set Tomas down and then landed behind him.

"We're in a little trouble," Cadan grumbled.

"No, we're in really big trouble!" Tomas pointed up at the dragon.

The beast was rearing its head back with its mouth closed tight.

"What's he doing?" Darius asked.

"He's getting ready to have a barbeque," Tomas explained.

"We need to get the hell out of here!" Madison screamed.

"Cadan!"

A new voice echoed through the immense chamber, coming from the stairs.

Cadan knew the owner of the voice before he turned around, having heard it on so many occasions throughout his life.

He whirled around to see Simon and Daphne coming towards them. This must be dream, he thought. How could the two people, who up until a week ago he thought were his parents, travel from Texas and magically appear in the middle of the desert in Nevada?

"What are you doing here?" he asked them. The dragon was all of a sudden the last thing on his mind.

"You kids need to move now," Simon yelled back.

"Simon—"

"I said move!"

The dragon roared. Like a bunch of scared school children, the Knights ran towards Simon.

The ground trembled under his feet as he stumbled towards Simon. The dragon, following them, stepped down onto the ledge. The weight of the creature was causing swathes of the stony façade to slide off into the black beyond.

"Grendell!" Simon yelled at the dragon. His tone was the same as when he was reprimanding Derrick for sleeping late.

The air around them seemed to stop as the beast halted where it was. There was a strange eeriness to the exchange.

Simon continued talking to the dragon. "That's a good girl. Just calm down." He was cautiously approaching the enormous, scaly creature, both hands extended, and a smile of recognition forming on his face.

Cadan looked questioningly at Daphne.

She shrugged in response. "I guess he knows it."

"She is not an it," Simon told us. "This is Grendell. We're old friends."

Cadan guessed that whomever had named the beast must have had a thing for Beowulf.

A sound emitted from the dragon's mouth – a deep, throaty groan that came from her stomach. Raney had a cat back home so Cadan knew the dragon was purring.

"These are friends of mine, girl, so please don't eat them."

And with that, Grendell leapt into the air and was gone.

Simon turned to Cadan and asked. "What are you doing here?"

"What are *you* doing here?" Cadan returned the question. The warm feelings of seeing Simon and Daphne also brought a reminder of their last conversation.

Simon explained. "We felt your pain through our jade numina stones. You words didn't come through very clear because we never taught you kids how to use them the proper way, but the pain was clear enough."

"But how did you find me?"

"The stone can act as a tracking beacon to help us find you."

"But you got here from Texas in less than a half hour."

"Your stepmother is a fairy."

The revelation hit him hard. Since meeting Gabe and the Fatales and learning a little about fairies, he should have put it together. Her unnaturally red hair should have been his first clue.

Daphne smiled warmly and waited on his reaction. Cadan tried to smile back.

Simon didn't bother waiting. "Now tell me what you are doing here? Who are these people?"

"These are my friends," Cadan explained. "I went to Manhattan to find information on my parents, since you wouldn't tell me, and government operatives found me there."

"DOMA?"

"How did you know?"

"I once was a DOMA agent," he answered. "Are these kids agents?" he asked, pointing to the Knights.

"Yes, we are," Madison answered. "How did you get away from DOMA?"

"That's a story for another time young lady," Simon said. "Needless to say, we escaped. That's why I couldn't tell you much about your past, Cadan."

"Why?"

"Because your father and I served together as agents."

"With Pedro?"

"What? How do you know about Pedro?"

"I met him earlier tonight."

"Where is he? I lost contact with him years ago."

"He died a few hours ago. This boy here," Cadan indicated Rafe, "is his son."

"He was a friend," Simon said. "And a good man. I'm sorry for your loss boy."

"Cadan," Natalie interrupted. "What's going on here? Who are these people?"

"I can't tell you right now, Natalie. Please trust me that they won't hurt us."

"You must tell me everything, Cadan. But we'll have time for that after we're away from this place," Simon said

"I can't go with you," Cadan told him.

"What?"

"A DOMA Administrator has gone rogue and taken a friend of mine. We're going after him."

"Are you here on DOMA's orders?"

"No, Josiah told us to stay at our previous position, but we disobeyed and came here to save Jude."

"Josiah." Simon almost laughed when he heard the name. "That old windbag is still breathing?"

"Watch it, old man," Madison eyed him. "That's our boss."

"Well you all won the lottery with that one. But Cadan, you have to leave with us. This is not the place for any of you to be."

"No chance, Simon. I have to save my friend."

"You've only been gone a week. Could you have really grown that close to someone already? You would risk being trapped with a crackpot government cover-up and never seeing your family again?"

"We're going, Simon."

"Then we're coming with you."

"I can't ask you to do that. You have to think about the other two." Cadan was intentionally cryptic. He and Daphne had already placed themselves in jeopardy by coming there, and Cadan couldn't risk bringing Derrick and Raney into this.

"You're not asking. We're coming."

"If you're sure, then okay. But we should go."

"Three questions first."

"Shoot."

"Who is this rogue agent?"

"Nolan."

"Nolan Burrell?" Simon whistled. "He was a loon back when I was around. I can't believe they made him an Administrator. DOMA must be hurting if they had to pick Nolan and Josiah as Administrators. What kind of force does he have waiting on us?"

"Four senior mages, one of which is a fairy, three Paladins, and no telling how many ogres, trolls, and goblins. One of his Paladins is an augur as well. What's your next question?"

"You must be a Paladin team – who's your leader?"

"We're not the Paladin team," Cadan answered him. "We're the Knights, the team in training. Our Paladin team was taken out earlier tonight. And I am the leader."

Both of Simon's eyebrows shot up and he tried to keep from smiling. The unmistakable look of pride covered his face. "Just a week and you're the leader?"

"You taught me well." Cadan smiled.

"That I did." He gave Cadan a wink. "They have an augur and we've been making a lot of racket. I'm sure they know we're here. Now let's go whip Nolan's ass so we can leave."

Chapter Twenty-Six

C adan's mind was racing in so many directions and his perception of the night became so cloudy. A multitude of extraneous ideas were flying through his head all at once and colliding like galactic bodies in the depths of space. Simon's lies and his own were coming around full force and his new friends were somehow caught in the middle.

His ancestry was a lie and for the most part still unknown to him. He could stop and ask Simon now, and Simon might tell him more since the DOMA secret was out in the open, but Cadan couldn't wait any longer to find Jude. For the past week, he had insisted to his friends that he knew little of his past and had been living on the streets, fending for himself. Each one knew now that it was a lie, yet they didn't say a word to him.

The web that entangled the relationships of their rescue party was secondary to his immediate drive. Jude was somewhere close, and Cadan had to save him.

Tomas and Simon led the way across the remainder of the rocky walkway suspended in the center of the cavern. The dragon had left, and there was no sign of her anywhere. Behind them the rest of their group followed. He noticed that Gabe took an immediate liking to Daphne once he learned her secret and walked as close to her as possible without being creepy. They chatted quietly together, even once giggling softly.

After passing the dragon's perch, they found the doorway leading out of the chamber only a few dozen yards away. Wooden slats about six inches wide were held together by two iron bars and comprised the enormous door at the end of their path. There was a large iron ring in the center of the door.

"It's not locked?" Cadan asked.

Simon shrugged. "Why lock it when you have a dragon guarding the room?"

"That makes sense."

With a groan the door swung inwards. Simon held up his hand and produced a gray flame of ruhk-fire, giving them light. Beyond the door was a hallway lined with stone bricks of nearly actual shape and size, stacked even with traces of mortar here and there to fill in the gaps. In the distance the hallway curved, so they were unable to see what lie ahead.

Simon took the lead as he seemed to be familiar with the place. There was slight ascent to the hallway as they proceeded. The darkness was so overpowering that it was impossible to gauge how long they travelled before coming to another door.

"Are we there yet?" Gabe giggled quietly.

"Shut up," Madison hissed.

"Sorry."

They paused before the door and nobody said a word for at least a minute. Once in the next room, the battle would begin. Nolan and his forces would be on the other side waiting to ambush them. At least Jude would be there, Cadan thought.

"Are you ready?" Simon asked.

Cadan nodded. "What's the plan?"

"You're the leader here," he replied. "What *is* the plan?"

"We don't really know what's going on in there and once we open the door, they'll know we're here. I think we should go in fast and take down anything that moves."

"Sounds good to me."

Simon grunted as he raised his right foot and kicked the wooden door in. The hinges kept a tight hold on the door, but it swung open into the room with a bang.

The next chamber was surprisingly well lit. Large halogen lights on the high dome ceiling gave the impression of a stadium. It was not quite as large as the previous cavern, and the ground was rocky, but still relatively flat. The air was stale and dry, and he felt a pressure in his body he assumed was due to being so far underground.

A large vessel was perched precariously on the edge of a chasm. It looked so much like a Seventeenth Century Dutch frigate that Cadan expected pirates to be onboard. The masts rose high towards the ceiling and sails still hung in various places like curtains on a dilapidated house. The wood looked brittle and was splintered in various places along the hull. The bottom of the ship disappeared beneath the rubble of the floor.

Behind the ship, a trench formed what was likely the path of the crash. He imagined Josiah's mother and her parents on board and how scared they must have been when they landed here.

'What is this?" Darius asked.

"It's an airship," Simon replied.

"It's the same one that Josiah's mother came over from Andaloria on," Cadan added.

"Wow," Simon turned to him. "You've learned some things."

"Just a little," he answered. "I don't know what we're doing here."

"And where's Nolan?" Bryce looked around suspiciously.

To the right side of the room, there was a bank of computer terminals and desks in a half circle that looked out over the main area of the airship.

"The lights are on," Tomas noted. "That means someone has been here recently."

"I can feel traces of a recent fairy portal," Daphne advised.

"We must have just missed them," Tomas said.

"What do we do now?" Madison asked.

"What if they're in the ship?" Cadan asked.

"I doubt that very much." Simon shook his head.

"What makes you so sure?" He was suspicious.

Simon explained. "Josiah's mother, Mariam, came over on this ship, just as you pointed out. When she left this ship, she placed a really strong spell over the entire vessel. The spell would only allow her son or one of his progeny to enter."

"So only Josiah can enter the ship?" Cadan asked.

"No," he shook his head. "At first the spell only allowed her access. When her first son was born, she altered the spell so that he could enter. Josiah was her second son, but she never granted him access."

"There must be some reason we're here," Natalie said, the irritation heavy in her voice.

"Maybe it's a trap," Madison looked around suspiciously.

Bryce grunted. "If it were a trap, they would have already sprung it."

"They're not here," Simon told them. "We are alone."

"Simon," Tomas said quietly. "Did you say that the progeny of Mariam's first son are allowed access to the air ship?"

"Yes," he answered.

"What is Mariam's first son's name?" he asked.

Simon didn't answer at first. Something strange was happening; Cadan could have cut the tension with his sword.

Finally, he spoke. "I don't think that's important now."

"But I do," Tomas kept on. "What was his name?"

After a long pause, he answered. "Alexander."

Cadan's mind reeled – he almost fell over when he heard that name. Balance was hard to maintain as he tried to convince himself that it was just a coincidence.

Cadan, that was the name my father spoke. Rafe had been there for the conversation with Pedro. He was the only one in the chamber that knew his father's name.

"Simon," Cadan managed to say. "Pedro told me that Alexander was my father's name."

Again there was a long pause. When Simon finally turned to face him, Cadan could see the tears streaming down his cheeks and into his beard.

"I didn't want you to find out like this," he spoke softly. "You are still too young to handle this knowledge."

"Handle what knowledge?" Cadan asked, making little effort to hide the anger in his voice. "Quit trying to protect me and tell me!"

"You father was Alexander Ogden," he said, breathing very deep once the words were out. He could almost see the physical manifestation of the weight leaving his shoulders. "Stone was just a name I made up so that you wouldn't learn the truth."

"When were you planning on telling me?"

"I don't know, just not now. It's so complicated, Cadan."

"Try me!"

"You're Josiah's nephew," Tomas pointed out. He seemed to be lost in his own little world, trying to reason out the ramifications of the recent revelation.

"Alexander made me promise him that I would attempt to raise you as normally as possible. The Ogdens are a family of great power and great responsibility. I thought that if I kept this knowledge from you, then I could keep all of the heartache that has plagued the Ogden family from you, too."

"Only to have it come crashing into my life like this?"

"I couldn't have predicted this Cadan, and I am sorry for that."

"Why didn't Josiah tell me?"

"Honestly, I don't know, Cadan. You look identical to your father. There's no way the thought couldn't have at least crossed his mind."

"I don't mean to interrupt this," Madison cut in. "But we need to either come up with a plan or get the hell out of here."

"Why are we here?" Darius asked.

"I can get in the airship," Cadan said, realizing it for the first time.

"What's in there?" Bryce asked, eyeing the airship with a hint of wariness.

"No one knows," Simon answered. "Though I'm not sure that entering it is such a good idea."

"It could play into Nolan's plan," Madison said.

"Or it could be the exact thing that he doesn't want to happen," Cadan argued. He turned to Simon. "Do you know how to get in there?"

"No," he shook his head. "For someone given access by Mariam, it shouldn't be too difficult."

Without another word, Cadan stepped towards the airship.

Chapter Twenty-Seven

As he approached the airship, Cadan didn't have the first clue how to get inside. He didn't want to ask Tomas or Simon – this was something he felt he should accomplish on his own. The vessel grew larger as he got closer. When he was within a dozen feet, he stopped and marveled at its greatness. It was the size of a commercial jetliner, possibly bigger.

His heritage lied within. The legacy of his family was somewhere within those walls. Since finding out that his childhood had been a lie, he had searched for his true parents. Even though they would not be inside, he knew that somehow he had found them. When Tomas had recounted parts of the Ogden legacy, he had been both excited and jealous. Now, he was connected to those stories.

The thought wasn't a conscious one, but the diamond numina seemed to call to him in a subtle, almost indiscernible way. Reaching into the neck of his shirt, he gripped the stone and pulled the silver chain over his head. Raising it into the air, he closed his eyes and focused on his connection to the source of the ruhk-magic within his spirit.

Was it a spell that held the ship tight? There was no way to be certain and no one to instruct him. He called out to Mariam, his grandmother. He spoke the name of Alexander Ogden, and he reached out with his power and touched the side of the airship. Countless voices whispered to him. Though the words were indecipherable, he knew what they were asking. They wanted to know who he was. He identified himself. Not as Cadan Stone, but as Cadan Ogden, a member of the great dynasty of heroes from Andaloria. It felt great to say that, even if was just to a mass of wood and iron.

Nothing seemed to happen, but he could feel his entire body tingling. He felt a hand on his shoulder.

He let the power go and slipped the diamond numina back around his neck. When he opened his eyes, a doorway on the side of the ship had opened. The top had disconnected from the ship and folded out, creating a ramp.

"I'm going inside," Cadan announced.

"Do you want us to come with you?" Tomas asked.

Cadan didn't reply, but simply walked up the ramp.

The first room was large and empty. There were two passageways leading off from each side. Something inside him pointed to the left. He followed his instinct. The hallway was simple, and he ignored the first few small doors, all of which were closed. The same instinctual impulse that had directed him left continued pushing him further.

He stopped at the fourth or fifth door – he had lost count and didn't really care. He could hear the faint trace of footsteps behind him, and knew that at least one person had followed.

The door was already ajar, so he pushed it open the rest of the way. He walked into the room, which was dominated on one side by a large bed and on the other, a large armoire, with a seating area in the center. Other than a thick layer of dust and grime, the room looked untouched.

He sat down on the nearest chair and leaned back, taking in his surroundings and letting the ghosts of his ancestors flow through him. For some reason he knew that this had been Mariam's room when she was a young girl. His grandmother, his grandmother, had once stayed in this room. In fact, she had crossed over from her homeland and crashed on earth in it.

His cheeks became wet, as several tears managed to escape. The emotional intensity of the recent revelation coupled with the discovery of a location rich with his family's history was too much for him to handle. He felt truly connected to something. Growing up he had felt a connection with his 'family,' but the feeling from being in this room was something altogether stronger.

Cadan sensed a presence in the room with him. When he turned, Simon was standing there, tears flowing down his cheeks as well.

"Your father's name was Alexander and your mother's name was Lorelei," he began. "They were the best two people a man could know. I could tell you many things about them, but the most important one is that they loved you more than anything. They would be so proud to see you now."

"I just wish you had told me."

"I wanted you to have a normal life, Cadan. If you only knew what Daphne and I, your parents and so many other people have gone through, you would understand. Life in DOMA is difficult and anything but normal. Per regulations, our children were to be raised in the Great Lakes Facility by strangers. We were only allowed scheduled visitations with our family. DOMA wanted to train you all to become warriors, and they felt that contact with birth parents would only inhibit the process. In the beginning, your father and I, and even your mother and my first wife were so focused on being the best DOMA agents we could be. We were having the time of our lives, but when we had children and those rules were applied to our new families, we felt differently."

"How did they die?"

"Protecting you," he answered. "They died trying to escape DOMA."

"Who killed them?"

"I don't know. I wasn't there."

Sitting atop the table was a small leather book, about the size of his hand and only a little thicker. Cadan reached up and flipped through the pages, only to find them all blank. Other knick knacks littered the room.

"There's an armory of sorts across the hallway," he heard Madison say. "Would you care if I took a couple of bundles of arrows?"

She hadn't had any arrows since she spent all of hers back at the gas station, and he knew that it left her feeling practically naked. Her bow sat lonely around her shoulders. His first reaction was to tell her no, since all of the items in here were his family heirlooms, but he figured that a bundle of arrows in an armory couldn't be too sentimental.

"Sure," he finally told her.

Cadan stood up and walked around the room. The dresser on one side had a few small boxes sitting askew across the top. He picked the first up and opened the lid, only to find it empty. He reached over and picked up the other one. Inside were several tiny jewels, each one attached to a silver chain much like the one around his neck.

"Your grandmother's numina stones," Simon whistled. "She must have left these. They are yours now."

In the palm of his hand, he held the four stones – two diamonds, one pearl, and a sapphire. The diamond and pearl stones would enhance the ability of the wearer, but he was clueless about that sapphire stone.

He looked questioningly at Tomas, who just shrugged. "Only two sapphires are known to exist. One legend says that the sapphire granted a mage entrance into their order's headquarters. Beyond that there are no other practical applications."

"Natalie?"

"Yes, Cadan," she answered, as she walked over to him.

"I want you to have this diamond," he said, handing her the first diamond.

"I can't take this, Cadan," she said quietly while shaking her head.

"Consider it a loan," he said. "We may yet end up in a battle with Nolan's people, and I want you to be prepared. Please wear this for now." She nodded.

He handed the pearl to Tomas and the other diamond to Rafe. "Same agreement, this is just a loan." They both agreed.

He crossed the room to the armoire and opened the top drawer. Inside were several dusty leather-bound books strewn about. They looked as if they had been stacked neatly at one point, but the crash had left them in disarray.

"This is like a museum," Simon said looking around.

"Nobody has been in here since my grandmother crashed?" Cadan asked.

"Not that I know of," he answered. "She sealed it up and never came back."

"But she was only ten when she crashed," Tomas mentioned. "How could she have performed such a task at that age?"

"She was a powerful ruhk-wielder," Simon said. "If I remember correctly, she started training with magic at the age of seven. That's very rare. I started teaching Cadan here at about seven; he was an early bloomer like his grandmother."

"What's in the top part of the armoire?" Daphne asked. "Can it be opened?"

There was a tiny silver lock on the front of the armoire, preventing the large doors that took up the top three quarters of the front surface of the armoire from opening. He reached up and tried to pry the lock off, but it wouldn't even move. It was as if it was frozen in the air right where it was.

"It's stuck," Cadan said, as he tried looking underneath for some sign of how to get inside. Most locks had a keyhole on the front, but this one looked like it was just a chunk of silver hanging there. He watched the bright silver lock for a moment, and suddenly the silver flashed a light shade of blue. The effect was like a dull light bulb going off behind a sheet, and had he blinked, He would have missed it completely.

It occurred to him that the key to opening the armoire would be in the room. He reached back into his pocket and removed the sapphire numina stone he found seconds before. He held the stone up to the front of the armoire, leveled it with the lock, and not sure what else to do, he called a small portion of ruhk-magic forth to aide him.

The blue shade of light appeared again, but didn't blink out this time. It continued to grow brighter and clearer, until the lock finally snapped. He reached up, took the lock off of the armoire and set it on the table nearby. With a deep breath he opened the two doors.

He expected the interior of the cabinet to have shelves, but instead there was a single chamber. The inside was empty, except for one object hanging on the back – a sword.

The blade was bright, reflecting the bit of light that was able to reach the back of the cabinet. The sword looked as new, as if it had just been forged. The cross guard and grip were darker silver, and the pommel was light, metallic blue, several shades lighter than the sapphire numina. Above the cross guard were several jagged pieces of metal that stretched towards the tip of the blade, giving the abstract appearance of fire.

"What is this?" Cadan asked Simon. "Was this her sword?"

"I can't believe this," Simon stood beside him and peered inside of the armoire. "We always thought this was a myth."

"Oh my gods," Tomas said, equally as astounded. "I didn't think the stories were actually true, either."

"What is it?" Cadan asked, frustrated that they would only stare at the weapon.

"It's the Sword of Ogden," Simon answered. "Also known as the Sapphire Blade."

"The what?" Darius asked before Cadan could.

"The Sword of Ogden," Tomas answered.

"They get their own sword named after them?" Madison asked dryly.

"It's a long story," Tomas explained. "A really, really long story. To sum it up, on Andaloria, the goddess Achama was cast from the Pleroma, and a man named Ogden, who would later spawn the Ogden family, took up a sword and became her champion. The gods imbued his sword with all sorts of magical power and abilities, and the sword was passed down from generation to generation."

"This makes sense now," Simon said. "The Ogdens came over from Andaloria about fifty years before Mariam and her family. Alexander told me once that Mariam had told him a story of the Ogdens leaving something behind in Andaloria when they crossed over to earth. Mariam and her family were charged with bringing that item to the Ogdens. So when they crashed here, they were looking for the Ogdens, and your grandmother not only found them, she married one."

"She must have been referring to the Sword," Cadan said. "You think she was bringing the Sword over?"

"Must be," Simon shrugged. "But she eventually married your grandfather, who was an Ogden. Why she didn't give *him* the Sword is beyond me."

"What do we do with it?" Cadan asked.

"It's yours, Cadan," Simon told him. "You are the rightful heir to the Ogden line, so it's yours."

"What about Josiah?" Cadan asked. "He's older than me."

"He's a second son, but you are the son of a first son," Simon explained. "You are the rightful heir."

"I don't know what to do with it," he shook his head. "If I take it, DOMA would only come in and take it from me. They wouldn't let such a powerful artifact out of their hands."

"You're right," Simon said. "That is why you must take the Sword, and we must leave."

"I have to save Jude," Cadan reminded him.

"Then take the Sword, let's save this Jude kid, and then get out of here before Josiah and the rest of his cronies arrive."

"Technically, we're Josiah's cronies too," Madison said to Simon.

Simon turned and looked at her. "No, you are a bunch of confused children who have been programmed all of your lives with how to feel and think. You are anything but cronies, and one day I think you will all see that."

"Pick it up, Cadan," Tomas urged.

Cadan reached in and touched the grip. A tingling sensation like electricity shot through his fingers and up his arm. He jerked back in reflex. Taking a deep breath, he reached out again and took the grip in his right hand. This time he didn't pull back, but let the power run through his arm and fill his entire body.

The Sword came off the brackets easily, and he removed it from the armoire. It felt strange to just stand in the middle of the room and hold it. Everyone watched with grim anticipation, not sure of what to think or do.

"Will it fit in your scabbard?" Simon asked him.

Cadan removed Nieson's sword from the scabbard at his side and set the weapon on a nearby table. When he slid the Sword of Ogden in its place, the fit was snug, but it still felt like it belonged.

"Cadan!" a familiar voice called from the doorway.

He whirled around and in the doorway, Nate was staring back, wide-eyed.

"What are you doing here?" he asked the Paladin. Everyone else was asking questions too.

"I tried to stop him," Nate moaned. His eyes looked like he was on the verge of crying. "They took me prisoner back at the Fatale mansion and made me help them. I didn't know what to do."

"What are you talking about?" Madison asked.

"Nolan is here, and he has Jude."

"How did you get away?"

"I didn't," he lowered his head as he said it. "He sent me in to get you."

"Then we'll fight him," Cadan said.

"We can't," Nate shook his head. "He has Jude and he told me to tell you that if any of us make a move towards our weapons or call for ruhk-magic, he would kill Jude on the spot."

"Are they outside?" Cadan asked.

"Yes."

"Could Daphne or Gabe teleport us out of here?" Darius asked.

"If you escape, he'll kill Jude," Nate answered.

"What do we do, Simon?" Cadan asked.

"We don't have much choice."

Nate walked into the room and over to the table where he had set Nieson's sword. "He told me to retrieve this," he said indicating the sword.

Cadan immediately saw Nate's mistake, as did the rest of the Knights. He decided to play along. He used his left arm to hide the pommel of the one in his sheath. "He was after the Sword of Ogden the whole time," Cadan said, looking over at Simon. "This was all a plan to get me to come open the airship and get the Sword."

"And now Nolan will have it," Simon moaned. "We should have known, Cadan."

"Nate," Cadan pleaded. "Do not give him that sword – it's very powerful and he could destroy us all."

"I'm sorry, Cadan." He lifted Nieson's sword and held it there, looking it up and down, his eyes wide in awe. Finally he let the sword drop to his side. "We should be going. Nolan is waiting for us."

Chapter Twenty-Eight

Nate stepped out into the hallway first but stopped just a few feet past the door. He was counting to make sure that all of Nolan's prisoners were accounted for. Something struck Cadan as odd about his behavior. He and Madison walked out and then stopped. He could still see the former leader of the Knights gripping Nieson's sword like it was his most precious possession.

When they reached the hall, Nate stood there, as waiting for something.

"What's wrong?" Cadan asked.

"Someone's missing," he said, looking around, trying to figure out who was gone.

"Sorry," Tomas came bolting from the room, a nervous look on his face.

"What were you doing?" Nate asked.

"I saw a pile of books that looked interesting. Sorry," he mumbled.

"You were always ridiculous," Nate spat and turned to walk towards the exit of the airship.

The Paladins, and a few of the Knights, had never cared for Tomas because he always had his nose in a book or his head in some fantasy world he created in his mind. When Nate spoke then, there was only a thin veil over his hatred. Something wasn't right. In the room, their former leader seemed scared, but now that the sword was in his hand and they were almost to the exit, his former loathsome self had returned.

"Let's go," he said as they entered the main room that led outside. "You first, Cadan."

Cadan stepped out onto the ramp and began walking down. His heart dropped to the ground when he saw what they were up against.

Nolan stood in the center, just a few dozen feet from the bottom of the ramp. Next to him was the man Cadan recognized as his second in command, Robert; the man who spoke to him under the bridge was now holding Jude in one arm. Jude stared back at him with a look of horror. He looked bad; Cadan could see several bruises on his arms and one on his face. His eyes were red and puffy from tears. When Jude saw him, his face brightened a little and he nodded in Cadan's direction.

The LA Administrator was flanked by two fairies, Sabrina on one side, and Sofia, the LA Facility's resident teleporter on the other.

A dozen feet to Nolan's left, his other two senior staff members, Cydra and Monroe stood. She must have recovered from the blow of the rock back at the gas station; she didn't look very happy with him. The snarl on her face told Cadan that she was itching for payback. Monroe looked to be in his late thirties, with glasses sitting atop a hawk nose. His chiseled features and short, dark hair only intensified his formidable appearance.

The LA Facility's Paladin team stood off to the right. Their leader Cody was in front, with Marcia and Steven positioned behind him to each side. All three looked ready to clobber their prisoners once Nolan gave the word. Marcia and Steven both had dark hair, but Cody's was a light blonde and his features gave away his elven heritage.

In a ring behind the ruhk-wielders and fairies, at least two dozen goblins, several trolls, and an ogre were poised waiting to strike. Their various weapons were drawn, and their stances said that they were ready for battle. All of their sharp teeth were bared and they eyed Cadan with an insatiable hunger. He descended the ramp.

"It took you long enough to get here," Nolan said. "We've been waiting for two hours."

"Sorry to make you wait so long," Cadan responded.

"What do you want, Nolan?" Simon asked.

"Simon," Nolan seemed surprised by his presence. "What brings you here? And I see the lovely Daphne has returned as well. I'm sure the Department would be very happy to get reacquainted with you both."

"Right now, I think Josiah would rather see *you*," Cadan said. "He is gathering the forces of all of the Facilities and will be here soon. You may want to leave now."

"Oh, I must applaud your bluffing skills, boy, but I know that our strategically planned explosion at Pedro's gas station has knocked out all of his communications. If Facilities are responding, it's to clean up the mess we've made all across California and Nevada. Our little exchange here will go uninterrupted."

"Jude, are you okay?" Cadan called out to him.

He only nodded.

"Nate, bring me the Sword," Nolan yelled out.

"Don't do it, Nate," Cadan begged him. "Just give it to me, and I can save us all."

"That would be foolish, Cadan," Nolan chuckled. "You could possibly save most, but you will certainly not save Jude here. One suspicious move and Robert will obliterate any trace that this miserable brat ever existed. I warn you not to try anything."

Nate walked past Cadan and handed the sword to Nolan, who gripped it with both hands. His mouth turned up on each side in a wide smile that reminded Cadan of a comic book villain. He turned the blade over and over, inspecting each side and studying the weapon. He slid the sword into his own sheath at his side.

"What are you going to do with us?" Cadan asked.

"You are the only one of use to me, Cadan. The rest of this drivel you brought with you can all burn in hell for all I'm concerned."

"What do you want with me?"

"That will all be explained in time. First I want to give each of you a chance to join us."

"Join you in what?" Madison asked.

"Josiah and DOMA have grown soft. We have hidden in secrecy for thousands of years, and we have always lived on the outside of humanity or in the dark recesses of a generation. Our greatest accomplishments are some of the most pivotal events in the history books, but never do we receive credit for anything. Leaders in the world think that they control what happens, and none of them realize that they are only responding to what we magical people have put into place. Modern humanity seeks to explain everything with science and anything of the supernatural is relegated to myth or fiction."

"It's best that way," Simon said. "Humans would not understand, and we would only incite fear."

"But we are more powerful than they are," Nolan continued. "Darwin first made use of the term 'natural selection,' or more commonly 'survival of the fittest.' It is time that we take that concept and apply it to our own people."

"You want to eradicate mankind?" Simon asked.

"No," he shook his head. "We will become their rulers. The powerful shall inherit this earth."

"Megalomania doesn't become you," Daphne hissed.

"You won't get away with this," Cadan added. "Eight ruhk-wielders against the entire world? Not very good odds."

Nolan laughed. "This is much bigger than what you see here in this room, boy. Don't think the odds are stacked so far against me."

Cadan.

It was Jude, talking to him through their minds. *Are you okay?*

Yes. Distract him.

How?

He's insecure.

Cadan understood what Jude meant right away. He knew what to do.

"There's something I need to tell you, Nolan."

"What could you possibly need to tell *me?*"

"On that day when I first met you in Josiah's office, the Administrator later called me back after you left. He asked me if I found you as weak as he did. At first I was embarrassed to admit that I had sized your ruhk-wielding ability up, but I finally confessed."

"You lie."

"No, I'm not lying. He said that he regretted the decision to make you the Administrator over the Los Angeles Facility and had always thought that Robert was the better choice."

"What?" Robert looked befuddled, but slightly happy.

"It's not true! He's trying to distract us."

"It's true," Natalie spoke up. "Benton told me the same thing one day. He said that Josiah was planning on closing down the LA office but couldn't quite figure out how to disperse you all to the other location without ruining things there."

"Josiah thought so little of you," Cadan continued. "And now you're proving him right. He found you unstable and most of the meetings between Administrators didn't include you. The other leaders felt the same way as Josiah."

"You lie! Shut your mouth now!" He actually looked unnerved.

"One more thing," Darius threw in. "He was always worried about leaving goblins in your pens because he thought you were having sex with them."

"Enough!" Nolan screamed, spit flying in the air in front of him. He held his sword up and walked towards the Knights, ready to strike.

Robert's grip on Jude loosened a little as he tried to calm his leader. "Nolan, you must calm down. Do not react out of anger."

Suddenly a poof of pinkish violet dust burst in front of Robert. Daphne was there one moment, grabbing Jude and tearing him away from the senior mage's clutches and pulling him to herself. Then she was gone again.

She and Jude appeared next to Simon. Cadan was overcome with emotion at seeing his friend again.

"No!" Nolan screamed, realizing that his leverage was now gone. "Kill them all!"

Cody unsheathed his sword first and led the charge from the right, with a pack of goblins following right behind. Cadan, Simon, and Bryce, were there to meet the wave of attack. The LA Paladin leader sought Cadan out, and he unsheathed the silver sword from its scabbard and brought it up to counter the strike. Cadan expected magic to burst from the Sword, and was a little surprised to find it function much like a typical weapon.

The goblins charged from the other side and came towards their little group. Jude armed himself by grabbing a sword from one of them, and joined the fight with Darius and Madison, who was firing off arrows at a heavy rate of speed.

Natalie, Gabe, and Rafe held back with Daphne. The four of them backed up towards the ramp. Tomas put himself in front of them and stood guard.

Out of the corner of his eye, Cadan saw Nolan charging him, but he didn't have his sword in the air. Instead, the Administrator's left fist was upturned in the air and he was conjuring ruhk-fire. His red fire matched that of his eyes and his blood thirsty ego.

Cadan turned away from the battle with Cody and moved to meet Nolan head on. As soon as he turned his attention, Nolan shot a bolt of ruhk-fire. Cadan was quick enough to block the attack with one of his own. But Nolan's second wave, although much smaller than the first, was enough to knock Cadan back and almost over.

They continued back and forth a few times. Robert stepped up next to Nolan to join him, and sent a bolt of green fire. Natalie appeared beside Cadan though, and used her violet colored ruhk-fire to block the second enemy.

All around them, the Knights were battling the goblins, the former gaining the upper hand and the latter falling fast. A troll charged the right flank and Bryce met him, knocking the axe from the beast's hand. The troll dodged a few of Bryce's swings, but the fourth time, he wasn't fast enough. The four-armed man's right mace clubbed the troll on the side of the head. With a splatter of blood, the troll toppled over on top of two goblins.

Rafe joined the fight, and using his gray colored ruhk-fire; he took aim at Steven. Even when the DOMA-trained ruhk-wielder fired back, the boy held up well. Pedro had charged Cadan to watch over him, but he wasn't sure the boy needed much looking after.

Daphne and Gabe joined in the battle as well. She was opening up fairy portals under the goblins' feet, sending them to places unknown. She was teaching Gabe how to work the spells as she fought, but he was having difficulty recreating them. At one point a goblin got close to them, and Daphne brandished two daggers from her boots. With several quick movements, the goblin was dispatched to the ground in a heap of unmoving flesh.

Tomas and Cydra were sparring with ruhk-fire on the other side, leaving Monroe free to attack. Simon turned from fighting goblins and sent a volley of gray fire towards the man.

The ogre had held off initially from assaulting, which showed a moderate level of intelligence, seeing as how he would have stomped over more of his own comrades than anything. With everyone spread out now, he charged, coming straight for the center.

"I got him," Jude called as he moved to meet the ogre's rampage. The creature saw him and sped up, now having a target in sight. When the gigantic beast was within range, he swung a fist down. Jude nimbly stepped aside and brought his stolen sword down on the ogre's wrist. The creature howled in pain and brought his other arm around in a swinging motion. Jude hopped in the air, onto the passing fist, and used his leverage to jump up and slam the flat of the sword into the ogres face before returning to the ground.

The creature reared back and screamed, and Jude ran straight at him. Just as the ogre was about to lean back down, Jude brought his sword up and struck again between his legs.

"Move!" Jude yelled as the ogre toppled over on his side, taking out three goblins and Monroe. Tomas and Cydra narrowly avoided being crushed as well.

Nolan and Robert continued sending ruhk-fire in the Knight's direction. Cadan and Natalie were able to block it each time. Nolan raised his sword and slowly began to advance. Cadan was about to raise his sword as well when a bolt of ruhk-fire from Robert slipped past his magical barrier, and struck Natalie in the chest, knocking her back several yards. When she hit the ground, she didn't move. Darius was immediately at her side to make sure she was alright.

Most of the goblins had been beaten. Madison was collecting her used arrows as she continued to fire more off.

Nolan turned around and yelled, "Sofia! Reinforcements!"

The side of Sofia's mouth raised in a twisted expression that somewhere between a smile and a sneer. While one hand stayed on her hip, she casually put the other in the air and snapped her fingers. A wide gateway opened in the room behind her. From out of the gateway another two dozen goblins came charging.

"We can't keep this up!" Simon yelled at Cadan. "We need to retreat!"

"Daphne!" Cadan yelled at his stepmother. "Prepare a gateway!"

"I don't think so!" Robert yelled as he shot a bolt of ruhk-fire towards Daphne.

Simon screamed and jumped to block the force. He managed to block a great deal of it, but some blew past him, striking his wife and sending her tumbling.

"No!" Simon screamed. He spread his arms wide, screamed again, and brought them together as hard as he could. When his two hands made contact, one of the biggest bolts of ruhk-fire Cadan had even seen shot towards Robert.

When the fire faded, there was no trace that Robert had ever existed, other than a small pile of ashes.

"You bastard! You killed him!" Nolan was stricken with grief.

He called forth an equally large amount of ruhk-fire and sent it flying back towards Simon, who wasn't quite ready to deflect such a force. Cadan knew it and ran towards his foster father. As quickly as he could manage, he threw up a shield large enough to block most of the onslaught.

As Nolan's column of ruhk-fire blasted against his shield, he fell to the ground. Still he held his shield. He could feel a trickle of blood come out of his left nostril as smoke seeped from his mouth. His arms hurt when he started to pick himself up.

Tendrils of the administrator's power flowed around the shield and shot out in different directions. One of these tendrils of fire hit Cydra in the back while she wasn't looking. Her body flew against the side of a large rock and a small amber colored object flew out of her hands. Tomas reached down, picked it up and stuffed it in his pocket.

Cadan and Nolan continued exchanging volleys of ruhk-fire as both of them moved closer and closer, each with their sword held ready to strike. The look on Nolan's face betrayed his surprise at Cadan's skill. Like everyone else within DOMA he had encountered so far, Nolan assumed that his skill would be much lower than his own. When they were within striking distance, their swords were up and metal clashed. Nolan was fighting with anger, and Cadan could feel it in his arms each time their swords met. He was definitely fighting defensively.

"Take him down!" Jude yelled from Cadan's left. He glanced over and saw Nate approaching Jude from behind, his sword high in the air, preparing to swing.

"Jude, watch out!"

Jude turned around in time to see the strike coming towards him, and he threw his goblin blade in the air, blocking the thrust. Jude tumbled backwards, but kept his sword up and was able to block as Nate hacked away, trying to break through Jude's defenses. It was obvious that he was aiming to kill.

Cadan wished he could help, but Nolan was not letting up. He was still backing away; the older man's strikes were more powerful than he would have expected.

Cadan's heel made contact with something behind him. Glancing down, he saw that he was at the ramp of the airship. If he wanted to go any further, he would have to go into the airship. A fight in close quarters was not something he wanted to chance.

To his right, Tomas was helping Natalie off the ground, whispering something in her ear. She stood up and started immediately for the exit. Maybe Tomas was organizing a retreat, which would have been a good move, considering their state.

Cadan blocked two more of Nolan's strokes, and on the third the Administrator overextended himself. Cadan raised his Sword quickly, stepped back, and then brought it down towards the older man. Nolan blocked his swing, but now Cadan was on the offensive. He struck one time after another, bringing his sword towards Nolan from different angles, but each was blocked in turn..

In the midst of Cadan's attack, Nolan turned to his Paladins and yelled one word. "Ruhk-fire!"

Cody, Marcia, and Steven all conjured ruhk-fire and began throwing it at Cadan and the other Knights. Simon shielded himself and Daphne, who was still lying on the ground. Madison dodged them each time, and Tomas and Rafe brought up shields to protect the others.

With his left hand, Cadan had to conjure shields to block stray bolts of ruhk-fire while maintaining his fight with Nolan with his right. Jude was still fighting Nate off towards the rear of the cavern. He had positioned himself with Nate between him and the LA Paladins, so he didn't have to worry about the fire.

Cadan struck out at Nolan again, this time his sword aimed at the man's neck. Nolan blocked, quickly lifted his right leg and kicked Cadan in the thigh. He couldn't block it nor could he maintain his balance.

All of the wind escaped his lungs as his back met the ground. His head hit a rock as he landed. Upon contact, everything went blurry. His vision faded in and out of blackness and it was impossible to keep his eyes open, much less focused.

He managed to pick his head up and open his eyes. Nolan was standing over him, and he was holding his sword upside down, prepared to drive it into Cadan's chest.

There was nobody near enough to save him.

Chapter Twenty=Nine

Nobody was coming to save him. Everyone was preoccupied with their own battles and had not noticed that he was about to die. He had lost his own battle, and Nolan would be victorious.

When he closed his eyes for a brief second and reopened them, Nolan had moved his sword and was staring straight ahead. His face was contorted in fear. Then Cadan felt the ground quake beneath him.

Nolan backed away and glanced around the room.

Cadan picked himself up and turned around. Grendell was clambering out of the narrow passageway that connected the two chambers. She let out a loud bellow as she trampled three nearby goblins. Natalie was standing next to her, the violet aura of her magic surrounding her, an amber stone in her outstretched hand.

Cadan flipped back around, grabbed his sword, and swung it upwards toward Nolan. He deflected the blow and backed away. Breathing was still difficult, but Cadan managed to pick himself up off the ground.

Even with Grendell there, he knew that their odds were quickly dwindling. Sofia could open another gateway for their endless supply of goblins, and Grendell could only manage so much in such close quarters with nowhere for her to fly.

The Sword called to him. He knew it was the only way. He didn't know what spells it would produce or the limitations of its magic, but he knew that with it he could defeat Nolan.

Cadan raised the Sapphire Sword in the air and opened himself to the ruhk-magic at the same time. The essence of the magic flowed through his body, into his arms and further into the Sword. Even as the energy left his fingertips, he could still feel it, as if it were a part of him. The weapon became an extra appendage and the power continued to flow – more than he had ever held before.

"What are you doing?" Nolan looked confused.

"Using that which you seek against you," Cadan told him.

"But Nate brought me the Sword."

"No," he shook his head. "He didn't pay close enough attention. The sword you carry is one that Colonel Nieson let me borrow."

Nolan backed away, whirled around, and ran towards Sofia, and screamed, "Retreat!" The goblins continued fighting along with the last remaining troll. The three LA Paladins, Monroe, and Cydra backed away from their fights and were heading towards Sofia.

"Stop them!" Simon yelled to Cadan since he was closest.

Cadan focused the ruhk-magic into the sword and sliced a stream of energy in their direction. A bright blue column of power cut through the air and the cavern wall behind Nolan exploded. Sofia produced a fairy portal that Cydra and Monroe disappeared into, the latter carrying Sabrina over his shoulder. Nate saw what his new friends were doing, stopped his fight with Jude in mid-swing and ran towards the portal.

"Cody, get through the gateway now!" Nolan grabbed him by the sleeve and pushed him through. "Steven, Marcia, hold here until Nate is through."

Again Cadan cast a slice of ruhk-magic out of the sword, through the air, and towards the portal. The magic flowed like liquid, but crackled and snapped like electricity. He ran towards them, the Sword in the air. He had to stop Nolan before he crossed through the gateway.

"Cadan!" Nolan screamed. "Watch as your family's possessions burn!"

Nolan hurled something small and black across the cavern. The tiny object sailed over Cadan's head and hit the airship with a small thud. Less than a second after contact, the entire airship burst into flames. The vessel and everything in it was an inferno in a matter of moments.

Cadan couldn't stop to mourn the loss – Nolan was about to get away. As he approached the gateway, Nate appeared and dove through head first. Nolan backed slowly away from his two Paladins, inching towards the gateway. Cadan was almost to them, when Nolan grabbed both Steven and Marcia, and before he could swing the Sword one last time, they were gone.

Exhausted and emotionally drained, Cadan's body went numb and he started to fall. The Sword clanked against stone and slid down next to him. His knees hit the ground, and he used his hands to catch himself. Sweat was rolling off the back of his neck and onto the ground.

"Cadan, are you okay?" Jude came over and knelt next to him. Behind him Madison, Bryce, and Simon were taking care of the remaining goblins.

"Jude," Cadan mumbled as his friend knelt close and wrapped his arms around him in a hug. Cadan couldn't even lift his head. "We got you."

"Yes, you got me," Jude said as he embraced him tighter. "Thanks for coming after me. Madison told me that you wouldn't even let them stop to pee until you found me."

"Jude," Cadan fumbled for the right thing to say. "I'm so glad that you're alive."

Jude finally let go and leaned back against a rock. Cadan lifted himself up and saw that his friend was actually crying.

"I'm serious, Cadan," he said quietly. "Thank you for coming for me. You're a lightsaber."

"You mean life saver?" Even in his condition, Cadan had to chuckle.

He laughed too. "Yeah, I guess I mean life saver. Thank you though."

"Anytime," he patted Jude on the shoulder.

"Is Daphne okay?" Cadan asked Simon as the trio joined the rest of the Knights.

"She's going to be okay," he answered. "She woke up, but I told her to stay down and rest for a minute. We'll need her abilities in just a moment."

"Simon, this is Jude. Jude, this is Simon," he introduced them. They exchanged a handshake and 'nice to meet you.'

Simon turned to him. "So now that we've rescued your friend, are you ready to go?"

Cadan looked around at the Knights, and they were all watching him. He thought about the past week and all of the hell that he had been through. The Knights had to be the most dysfunctional group of people that he had ever met, and they would need a lot more work to be able to function better as a team. Jude was staring at him intently. Cadan looked into his eyes and knew what he had to do.

"Simon, I have to stay."

"Why?" he asked. The blazing flames had already begun to recede, the crackling still echoing in the enormous cavern. The hulking mass of the airship was reduced to ash and small bits of rubble.

"My new friends need me," Cadan answered.

"We can take them all with us," he offered.

"We have tracking beacons on," Cadan told him. "They would find us no matter where we went."

"Hmm," Simon considered that. "They didn't have those when I was in DOMA."

"We do now," Cadan said.

"And you have one too?"

"Yes," he answered.

Cadan could see his foster father's heart sink. Simon pulled him closer and talked so that only he could hear. "DOMA is not a good place for anyone, Cadan. Now you know that Josiah is your uncle. It will be nice for you to have a living blood relative, but Josiah has been known to be a tad on the shady side. Be careful putting your trust in him. Some really heavy stuff went down fifteen years ago, and that's when your parents were killed. I don't know everything that happened or who was or wasn't behind it all, but if Josiah is now one of the top dogs over there, then that should tell you to be really careful."

"What do you mean?"

"I don't want to say more, other than you must be careful. Another thing to think about is that once DOMA finds out who raised you, even if they don't find us, you will be in a lot of trouble."

"They won't find out anything about you. I promise."

"What if one of your friends here let something slip?"

"I'll have to take that chance."

"I wish there was a way to get you to come with us or some way we could stay longer, but Daphne and I need to get going. DOMA will be all over this place any minute now."

"Go," Cadan told him. Simon pulled him in for a hug. He felt a hand on his back and turned to see Daphne was there. They pulled her in.

"Take care, Cadan," she told him, tears streaking down her face. "I love you."

"I love you too. And I'm very sorry for all of the things I said to you. You two were the best parents a kid could ever ask for. Tell Derrick and Raney that I love them."

"I'm sorry we lied to you, Cadan," Simon said. "You know where the house is if you ever get away from this damn place."

Jude walked over to Cadan and the Mercers. "I see you're about to leave," he said to Simon and Daphne. "I just want to thank you both for everything."

"No problem," Simon patted him on the back. "Take care of my boy."

Jude put an arm around Cadan's shoulder. "Don't worry, I'll take good care of him."

Simon turned to the rest of the Knights. "Good job, all of you. You are all fine warriors."

He got a few waves and smiles from the others. After hugging Cadan again, Daphne produced a violet gateway, and the people he had always thought of as his parents disappeared.

He had no idea if he would ever see them again.

Chapter Thirty

Cadan turned back to the smoldering ruins of what was formerly his grandmother's airship. The spell that had been broken had allowed him to enter, but it had also dropped any protection the ship had, which resulted in its ruin. There were items in the ship that he wanted to go back and sift through. He had hoped that there was something inside that would give him a connection to his parents and the rest of his family.

"Sorry about your grandmother's ship," Tomas said.

"Was that a grenade he used?" Cadan asked.

"It was a hematite numina stone," he answered.

"I've never heard of a hematite stone."

"It's because they are one of the rarer types," he explained. "Hematite stones are very dangerous – the user can funnel quantities of ruhk-magic into the stone for storage. Once it's reached full capacity, it takes on explosive characteristics."

"I can't believe he destroyed the airship," Madison said as she patted Cadan's back.

Tomas turned and smiled. "Have you ever heard of a jacinth numina?"

"I remember Simon mentioning them, but I don't remember what they're used for."

"It's basically another form of storage. Each one is a key to a tiny little pocket dimension that the wearer can use to store items. I have one in my possession that has the storage capacity of a small room."

Cadan smiled. "So that's what you were doing when we all left the room and Nate was looking for you?"

"Yes," he nodded. "I only had a few seconds, so I grabbed what little I could."

"What did you get?"

"I got the dresser, the armoire, the bed, the chairs in the center of the room, and some loose objects laying around."

"You got all of that?" Cadan was amazed. Tomas grunted as Cadan gripped put his arms around the librarian and squeezed. "Thank you!"

"I also went across the hall with Madison when she went to get the arrows. I was able to get most of the weapons in there, as well."

"That's amazing! Thank you!"

"You may want to put your new weapon in here too."

"Why?"

"If you don't, DOMA will take possession of it. We should probably put the numina stones in as well."

"Can a jacinth hold other numina stones?"

"It can hold anything, except for living beings."

Tomas pulled a red stone from his pocket and held it about waist level. The jacinth glowed brightly, and a few seconds later, a small red disc appeared about six inches away from the stone. Tomas pulled the pearl numina from around his neck, placed it into the red opening and it disappeared. Natalie and Rafe pulled the diamond numina stones from their necks and placed them into the circle.

"How did you get furniture into that tiny little hole?" Cadan asked.

"If you know what you're doing," Tomas explained. "You can adjust the size of the jacinth's opening, and can also move it around to secure a larger object."

"I better hide my numina stones, too," Cadan said as he pulled the stone from around his neck and the jade from in his pocket and placed them into the red opening. He added the sapphire stone and the Sword of Ogden in as well, and they too disappeared.

"Thank you, Tomas."

He nodded.

All of the Knights were staring at Cadan questioningly. Now that Simon and Daphne were gone, he was sure they had many questions to ask him. He had lied to them. "I guess I owe you all an explanation."

"You don't owe us anything, Cadan," Natalie told him. "If you need more time before you confide in us, you have every right to take it."

"Yeah man," Darius added. "We owe you for believing in us. Before you came along, there was no way we could have done half the stuff we did tonight. We know you got some stuff that you haven't told us about. But truth be told, with DOMA breathing down our necks, I'd keep it a secret too."

"No," Cadan shook his head. "Natalie, you told me your and Darius's story on the first day I met you. The least I could do is give you my story." He took a deep breath and began. He told them about growing up with Simon and Daphne and finding out a week ago that they weren't his parents. He described how much he loved his siblings Derrick and Raney, and how despite the lack of blood relation, he still considered them his brother and sister. He recounted his journey to Manhattan to find information about his parents. The only detail he omitted was the location of his home.

"Maybe you'll be with them again one day," Jude told him.

"But there's no leaving DOMA," Cadan said.

"You never know." He smiled.

"Well, your story is safe with me," Natalie spoke up. "As far as I'm concerned we followed Nolan here to the airship to save Jude. We never made it in because Nolan blew it up before we could. It was just us and nobody else."

"Yeah," Bryce agreed. "Who's Simon?" he asked sarcastically, actually breaking a smile.

"Cadan, we got your back," Darius added.

"What about you two?" Jude asked Gabe and Rafe.

Rafe shrugged and Gabe said, "I don't really care. I know I'm stuck now. I should be pissed about being locked up with DOMA, but you guys are pretty cool."

"Madi?" Jude asked her. "What say you?"

"You know I don't give a crap," she laughed.

Suddenly there was purple and red flashing all over the room. In one corner Josiah appeared through a doorway. He was followed by Lars, Helena, Nieson, and the rest of the senior staff and nearly a dozen soldiers. Another portal opened on the other side, and a group of strangers walked out. The leader of that pack was by far the most bizarre. Her hair was big, blonde, and curly, and pulled up on top of her head. She wore a giant gray fur coat that pushed up against the side of the high collar of her dress. Her gait was something Cadan would expect from a queen. Behind her stood an odd collection of others – one guy had blue hair that was spiked up at least a foot high; a dark-skinned girl had a long dreadlock mullet with her hair shaved on the sides. He was so entranced by her hair that it took him a few moments to notice that she had four arms like Bryce.

"That's the Alaska team," Jude indicated.

"Where is Nolan?" Josiah asked, as he hobbled brusquely over to the Knights.

"He left, and the rest of his team got away as well. Robert was killed in the battle."

"Oh dear," Josiah put a hand over his mouth. "Who killed him?"

"I did," Natalie piped up first, taking the heat for Simon.

"Why would you kill him?" Josiah asked.

"He was shooting ruhk-fire at us and trying to kill us," Natalie explained.

"I'm sure he deserved it then, the damned traitor."

"He did," Cadan agreed.

Josiah's demeanor changed completely once he knew the Knights were okay. "What were you thinking!" he began yelling, his voice boomed through the cavern. "You disobeyed direct orders. I told you all to stay at the Fatale's mansion, but you came here. I want a full explanation from all of you!" He noticed the charred remains of the air ship.

"Oh no," Josiah mumbled. "What happened?"

"Nolan destroyed the ship right before he left," Cadan apologized. "I'm sorry, Josiah."

"It is not your fault, Cadan. It's just that it has obvious sentimental value for me."

"I understand," Cadan nodded. "For me as well."

"What do you mean?"

"I know who my parents were. I figured it out when I opened the ship."

He was startled enough by the revelation to momentarily forget about the ship. "I wasn't sure if it was true. I had my suspicions, but I didn't want to put voice to them until I was sure."

"That makes you my uncle."

"And you are my nephew. Nothing could please me more. We will definitely have to take the time to get to know each other better. I have mourned the loss of your father for fourteen years, and it is a nice consolation to have you in my life." He turned back to the airship. "Now you say you were able to get inside the ship?"

"Yes," Cadan answered. "I made it up the ramp and then Nolan attacked us, so I didn't have a chance to explore inside."

"That is unfortunate."

"Was there anything important inside?" Cadan asked.

"We don't know," Josiah answered. "Nobody has ever stepped foot inside. I would have liked to have seen where my mother stayed on her journey here."

The blonde woman strolled over to stand near them. "So do we have all of this under control now Josiah?" she asked blankly. She didn't look very happy to be there.

"Kyla, this is my new student and nephew, Cadan. Cadan, this is Kyla, the Administrator of the Alaska Facility."

"Nice to meet you," Kyla extended her right hand. He noticed her eyebrows perk up when Josiah had said his name. Cadan thought she wanted him to kiss her hand. That seemed a little strange to him, so he just turned his hand sideways and shook hers in greeting. She giggled.

Josiah continued. "The rest of the teams are cleaning up the mess that Nolan left all over California."

"We should get the children back to the Facility, Josiah, so that I can examine them further," Helena said, interrupting their conversation. "You can question them there."

"You are right," he nodded. "Kyla, you may take your team back to your base. We will all return to our Facility to recuperate."

"Thank you, Josiah," she nodded. "Let us know if we can be of service."

"Thank you, Kyla. We will." He turned to the Knights. "Let the soldiers handle the clean up; we must be going." Sheila retrieved the garnet from Natalie and stayed with the soldiers. She was tasked with getting Grendell back to her lair.

Lars opened a portal for the rest of them to return to base. Cadan retrieved Nieson's sword from the ground where it had fallen, and followed the Knights over to the portal. As he stepped through, he took a deep breath. He hoped more than anything that he had made the right decision.

Chapter Thirty-One

The meeting with Josiah was long and nerve wracking. The story the Knights had all agreed to was full of lies and deceit, no matter how simple they had tried to make it. Jude said the best story was the one with the fewest lies. So all they had to omit was anything to do with Simon and Daphne or with items from the airship, which was basically the entire story.

Josiah was deeply upset by Nolan's treachery, and even more upset by the death of Robert, whom he had considered one of his colleagues. "I should have seen this coming, Cadan," he sighed. "About eleven years ago, Nolan and his wife had a child. What should have been a joyous occasion became nothing short of a tragedy. Their child was born a goblin. They pleaded with the Great Lakes Administrator and Truman Durham to allow their baby to live the most normal existence possible, but when the child was only two years old, he bit another child's arm nearly in two. There were several other less severe incidences around the same time. Durham made a hard decision to have the child sent to the pens below this very facility. Try as they might, some creatures can never escape their nature."

"So that's why he rebelled against DOMA?"

"That was the beginning," he continued. "His wife was so grief stricken that she died within the month. Nolan went through intensive counseling, and his psychiatrist cleared him. We had always assumed that he was healed, but apparently we were wrong. I'm sure he felt helpless in his situation and thought that because his child could not pass in the regular world, we put him in the pens. Which, by the way, was not the case. Goblins are put in pens because they are dangerous to humans." He paused and leaned back in his chair.

"He has been plotting this for some time," Josiah explained. "The LA Facility has been collecting goblins and trolls and lying about their numbers. We checked their food orders, and the amount they were ordering was way over the amount required to feed their reported numbers. We should have recognized that and inquired further. We still can't adequately estimate what his force has grown to or the location of their new base of operations. One thing is clear – Nolan is building an army."

Cadan looked confused. "One thing puzzles me though. Nolan spoke with the Fatales and Tyler Knox about locating more fairies. It was obvious that he was trying to find more to build a larger army. But he asked Tyler about helping him. What could he have possibly wanted from Tyler? And why did he take Jude and not me?"

"I have thought about that too. When you came to visit, I shared with him that I thought you might be my nephew. I have suspected that fact since the moment the Knights brought you through the fairy portal from Manhattan, but I had no way to be certain. He knew that Alexander's child would be the only one with the ability to open the ship. He may have suspected that I was on to his plan, and by telling him about you being my nephew, he may have thought I was trying to throw him off the scent. So he went for Tyler or Jude as possibilities. He had to have the son of Alexander, since his other option was a little more difficult to get to."

"His other option?"

"Your sister."

"My sister? I have a sister?"

"Yes, a twin sister, actually. Her name is Caira. She is an agent in our New York Facility. I have contacted Jackie, the Administrator there, and we are making arrangements for her to come here for a while so that the two of you can get to know each other."

Cadan wanted to jump up and scream. He had a twin sister! He had become so accustomed to the idea that he would never have a biological family, but now he was blown away.

"What is she like?"

"She is cut from the same block as us. Incredibly powerful and a great leader. In fact, she leads the Paladin team at her Facility, which is the main reason we are having trouble getting her here."

"So how was I taken from DOMA and she was not?"

"Your parents left here when you were both young. It's a difficult thing to talk about because, for one, it is a painful period for me personally, and also, it is highly classified information. Basically, all I can tell you is that at one point in time, many people escaped DOMA in a break out. They were unhappy about certain issues and left, taking what they could. Your mother and several other agents left with you, and your father died in an attempt to free Caira."

"Who killed him?"

"One of the human guards. His name is classified."

"How did my mother die?"

"I do not know. A little while after she left with you and the other agents, a source informed us that she had died. There was no word of the other agents. In fact, the biggest reason I doubted that you were my nephew is that you had spent your time in foster care and on the streets. I had assumed my nephew would have been raised by one of the agents who had escaped." Suspicion flashed across his face for a moment.

"I never knew any of the other agents nor do I remember anything about them. They could have used mind magic on me to make me forget it."

"I suspect that is what they did. I can tell without probing deeply that your mind has been tampered with."

The meeting was interrupted a few times by the construction that was commencing since the attack at the gas station. One corner of Josiah's ceiling had a gaping hole that lead into the command center above. The explosion had caused much damage, but at least it was confined to a specific area.

Josiah was saddened by the news that Nate had been working for Nolan, and that he was still out there somewhere. The other Paladins had been recovered from the Fatale's mansion and were all in the care of Helena. Part of Josiah's remorse came from the fact was that he felt he had let Nate down. The rogue agent's issues with self-esteem and fitting in with the others had been identified when he was very young, and Josiah felt that there was more that he could have done to help him with those problems.

Josiah still wasn't sure what to do with Rafe and Gabe. He was surprised to hear that Rafe was the son of Pedro, a former agent of DOMA who had gone AWOL before the advent of homing beacons. He also seemed a little sad about Pedro's death. Rafe and Gabe would remain at the Rocky Mountain Facility for a short while, but Rafe would eventually be transferred to the Great Lakes Facility until he reached the age to become a full fledged agent. Gabe would be transferred to a Facility that was in need of a fairy.

Cadan and Josiah agreed to regular meetings and meals together so that they could get to know one another. Both of them were excited to actually have a living relative so near. Cadan left the Administrator's office, and once he walked through the doors and towards the elevator, he felt a strange sense of relief.

The room that he and Jude shared was full. The Knights were all in the sitting area of their room, and were silent as he entered.

"How did it go?" Jude asked first.

"How do you think?" Cadan sighed. "Way too intense, for sure." Maintaining a lengthy lie created more than a little stress.

"It's all over now," Madison said, trying to cheer him up.

"Thank the gods," he muttered as he plopped down in the open spot on the sofa next to Jude. "So how did your meeting go?"

"My meeting was brief," Natalie said. "And Bryce's meeting was like two minutes."

"Literally," he said with a giggle. His cheeks turned red and he looked down. It was so confusing that he was so shy even with just so few in the room.

"I didn't say anything in my meeting," Darius said. "I just clammed up and acted traumatized."

"He told me in my meeting that I will probably get transferred in a few weeks," Gabe said. "I hope he changes his mind, because I really like you guys."

Me too. I don't want to go to the Great Lakes. Rafe hadn't left Cadan's side since they had returned to the Facility. Cadan suspected that it was a mixture of being somewhere he had always been told was a bad place, and mostly still grieving for his father.

We'll talk to Josiah later about keeping you.

Thank you.

"Thank you all for keeping my secret," Cadan told them. "That means a lot."

The conversation turned lighter, and everyone talked for a few more minutes before returning to their rooms. They had not slept in over twenty-four hours, and they were in much need of it.

Once everyone was gone, Cadan changed into pajamas he borrowed from Jude, and got ready for bed. Jude was already in his pajamas and lying down. Cadan had expected him to be asleep, but he was wide awake, staring up at the ceiling.

"You okay?" Cadan asked him, as he walked back into the room.

"Yeah, man, I'm good."

"Just making sure." He pulled back the comforter and sheet on his bed and slipped in between. He glanced one more time at Jude lying on his back, still staring straight into the air. He reached over, turned the lights off and settled in for sleep.

A few seconds later, Jude spoke. "Are you asleep?"

"Not yet. Why, what's up?"

"Can I tell you something? You have to promise to not tell anyone."

"Sure. I promise."

"I'm scared to sleep. I don't want to dream about what happened last night."

"What part?"

"When I was with Nolan."

"What happened when you were with him? Did he hurt you?"

"Not really. They hit me a few times, but most of what they did was psychological."

"What did they say?"

"I'm not sure I'm ready to talk about it right now. Maybe another day."

"All in your own time, Jude."

"Thanks, Cadan."

"No problem."

There was a long pause. Jude finally spoke. "I hated the feeling of being helpless. I've always been a man of action, and for several hours I couldn't do anything. I just kept thinking that you and the rest of the Knights were in trouble, and there wasn't a thing I could do about it."

"You'll get through this, I promise. I'll be here for you."

"I appreciate that. I appreciate you staying with us. I know you'd rather be with your family, but instead you chose to stay with us. Thank you, Cadan."

It sounded weird hearing his name. Even just his first name sounded strange, though it had been his name his entire life. In the past week, he had gone through three last names: Johnson, Stone, and finally, Ogden. He felt like he became a new person with each new name. Johnson represented his innocence, Stone represented his search, and Ogden represented his new life. A life that involved a sister.

What would happen now? Since being captured by the Department and conscripted into their little agent program a week ago, he wanted nothing more than to escape. He now recognized that it was no longer that simple. The Knights were his friends now, and he had to consider them in any decisions he made. Outside of Cadan's own family, Jude had become the best friend he had ever known. Rafe was now his charge. There was more at stake now than his own simple desire to escape. Getting out of DOMA and taking the Knights with him would be his new goal. He also had a sister to think about. Even before meeting her, he knew he would need to help her too. They were both the children of Alexander and Lorelei Ogden.

He loved saying their names. He had said them more than a hundred times in his head since learning of them.

He rolled over onto his side, facing Jude, wondering if his friend had finally managed to fall asleep. His thoughts turned to the dark figure that had plagued his dreams recently, and he wondered if he would come back that night. Nolan would definitely be there, but somehow, for some reason that escaped him, Cadan knew that the rogue Administrator was not the dark man from his dreams. Was Nolan the one that followed him in Manhattan before the Knights apprehended him? There was no way to be sure, but Cadan didn't think that he was responsible. Something else lurked about on the periphery of the light, waiting patiently to pounce when his guard was down.

He thought back to what Jude had said before. Why had he chosen to stay? Simon could have surely found a way to disable a stupid tracking beacon. But he hadn't hesitated with his decision. He loved his family, but for some reason he just couldn't go back to his previous life.

And then it hit him. A sense of purpose was what he had always been missing. In school and at home, he was restless and always searching for a greater feeling of worth. Despite Simon's warnings about the dangers of DOMA, he knew that this was where he wanted to be. He had friends and now, and just as importantly, he had a sister and an uncle.

Cadan was an Ogden.

DOMA: Betrayal of Magic - Reference Sheet
Dramatis Personae

ROCKY MOUNTAIN FACILITY

Staff
JOSIAH OGDEN, Administrator, ruhk-wielder
LARS, Fairy
HELENA LANG, Chief Healer and ruhk-wielder
WENDELL WINTERS, Chief Archivist and ruhk-wielder
BENTON MARKS, Chief of Technology and ruhk-wielder
HAZEL HANKS, Teacher and ruhk-wielder
SHEILA BROWN, Teacher and ruhk-wielder
TOMAS REIS, ruhk-wielder and assistant archivist
GLADIOLA, gnome
HADRIAN, faun
ESTELLE, pixie
IRION, centaur
TREGELLOS, centaur
COLONEL NIESON, human and head of training
GENERAL RIEKEN, head of human military

Paladins
ANTHONY WALKER, ruhk-wielder and team leader
CARMEN FULLER, elf and ruhk-wielder
HEATHER MILLER, ruhk-wielder
CLAY VERNER, dwarf
JASON PADDOCK, half-troll, half-human
RUSSELL SUTHERLAND, ruhk-wielder

Knights
NATE CARTER, ruhk-wielder and team leader
CADAN STONE, ruhk-wielder and half-elf
JUDE BISHOP, ruhk-wielder and half-elf

MADISON RILEY, elf
BRYCE BECK, quad-arm
NATALIE GIBSON, ruhk-wielder
DARIUS GIBSON, seraph

LOS ANGELES FACILITY

Staff
NOLAN BURRELL, Administrator, ruhk-wielder
ROBERT CLARK, ruhk-wielder
CYDRA GRADY, ruhk-wielder
MONROE LAFFERTY, ruhk-wielder
SOFIA, fairy

Paladins
CODY COOKE, ruhk-wielder and augur
MARCIA WILSON, ruhk-wielder
STEVEN CARR, ruhk-wielder

OTHER CHARACTERS

Iowa Park, Texas
SIMON MERCER, ruhk-wielder
DAPHNE MERCER, ruhk-wielder
DERRICK MERCER, ruhk-wielder
RANEY MERCER, ruhk-wielder

Los Angeles
TYLER KNOX, elf
SHANNON, human
SABRINA, fairy
TINA, fairy
CORINA, fairy

MALINA, fairy
KATINA, fairy
BATINA, fairy
GABE, fairy

Acknowledgments

There are many people to thank, but only so much room in which to do so.

To Onaje, your talent for the arts is stunning. To Lisa, thank you for your ear – no one has ever been a better sounding board. To Jenny, where do I start? How you put up with my insanity, I will never know.

To my mother, thank you for introducing me to the gift of reading, and encouraging me along with all of those trips to the bookstore when dad was out fishing. And to my father, for introducing me to the world of fantasy fiction.

To Darren, I want to thank you for everything that you are and everything that you do. There is nobody else I would rather have at my side on this journey.

About the Author

Brian Dockins is the author of the DOMA: Department of Magic series. He has been writing since he could pick up a pen, and *Betrayal of Magic* is his first foray into publishing. He currently lives in Texas, where he received his Bachelor of Arts in Historical Studies and a Masters in History at the University of Texas at Dallas.

To learn more about the author and the DOMA series, please check out his blog at www.departmentofmagic.blogspot.com or follow the Department of Magic on Facebook.

About the Illustrator

Onaje Beal is an Art teacher, graphic designer, illustrator, and painter. She received her Bachelor of Arts Degree in Painting and Graphic Design from Savannah College of Art and Design, Atlanta. Born and living in Dallas, Texas, her work consists mostly of detailed realistic oil paintings and multimedia designs.

Website: www.wix.com/obvisual/Onaje

Shrouded Island

The Department of Magic prepares to counter the rogue Administrator Nolan Burrell and his ever increasing army of rebels. The Facilities come together to begin formulating plans to stop the spread of insurrection, but a new threat looms in the distance.

The Bermuda Triangle has been one of the biggest mysteries of the century, and even the secret, magical specialists within the Department are clueless as to the reality that lies beyond the mists. After an entire Paladin team disappears in the Atlantic, Josiah and the rest of the Department's leaders decide to send a larger force in to investigate.

Cadan finds himself at the head of the force made up of members of three Paladin teams. While taking on the responsibilities of leadership, he must also juggle his own secrets, a sister that he has never met, and a surprising, blossoming love. But nothing compares to what he finds in the mists of the Bermuda Triangle.

Here is a special preview of Chapter One of Shrouded Island....

Chapter One

Until today, Hannah Cooper had never believed in the paranormal.

It started just like any other. She arrived at the hospital at 5:40 A.M., just twenty minutes before her shift was to begin. With barely enough time to get started, she stopped by her office and set her coffee on the corner of the desk. She found her clipboard in its usual place, and after throwing on her long white coat, she began her rounds for the morning.

There were patients to see and death sentences to hand out. Initially working in the cancer wing at Boca Raton Memorial Hospital had left her emotionally drained on a constant basis, but after only three months, her sensitivity began to dull. You could only tell people they had mere months to live so many times before compassion began to be replaced by mundane repetition.

She enjoyed her profession, though. Working in the medical field was a constant adrenaline high. There was no better afternoon than one spent studying x-rays and other diagnostic tests, searching for an answer to some biological mystery. The people aspect was not as much fun as the research, but Hannah had always felt a constant need to help people. Although delivering bad news was not exactly her idea of helping people.

There had to be a way to help the terminal patients. Their death certificates were virtually already signed, and they were just waiting on their final moments to pass. Short of a miracle, Hannah couldn't do a single thing about their impending doom. This fact frustrated her more than afternoon traffic on the freeway.

Her first patient of the day was Mildred Schoonover, age fifty-six, with a husband, four children, and her first grandchild on the way. She was diagnosed with pancreatic cancer two years ago, and with remission now out of the question, and the rest of her health failing fast, Hannah had estimated that she would be lucky to live through the week.

She had given the news to Mr. Schoonover and his oldest son just two days ago, albeit in a much nicer way, and the family had accepted Mildred's eventual death with a resounding calmness. They were thankful that she had lasted this long, as this type of cancer usually claims its victims within a year after diagnosis.

Hannah entered her room to find Mr. Schoonover seated in a chair next to his wife's bed. From a picture in her file, Hannah knew that Mildred had been a healthy size – not obese, but not thin by any interpretation of the definition. The woman laying in the bed now was skin hanging loosely over bones. He reported that Mildred hadn't eaten much in the last few months and when she did, she would throw up soon after.

Hannah closed her eyelids for a moment as if to put a dam up to prevent the tears from falling. Acutely aware that her ability to sympathize had lessened, she still found the Schoonovers' story heartbreaking enough to make a statue cry.

"Hey, Mr. Schoonover." Hannah reopened her eyes and forced a smile. Her right hand was gripping her clipboard, but her left hand was balled tight into a fist inside her pocket, as if that would help keep the emotions at bay.

"Dr. Cooper," he returned the smile as he stood to come shake her hand. "Thank you for coming by so early."

"No problem," Hannah nodded. She leaned in close to him and whispered, "Mildred is actually one of my favorites."

They both chuckled softly.

"Are you two laughing at me?" Mildred said from the bed as her weak eyelids fluttered open.

Hannah turned. "Yes, Mildred, we were laughing at you. I was just telling your husband how awful that hospital gown looks on you, and how we really need to get you out of here."

"Oh honey, this hospital gown looks much better than that awful white coat you are so fond of wearing." She laughed around the feeding tube jammed down her throat.

Hannah went and stood next to her bed and leaned down. "How are you feeling this morning?"

"Same as always," she answered.

"I just wanted to stop by and make sure everything was okay, and to see if I could get you anything." It felt odd asking her if everything was 'okay.' Obviously it wasn't 'okay.' The woman was dying.

"Well, my I.V. has slipped out a little."

Hannah checked it and sure enough, the top of the needle had fallen out slightly. A little blood trickled underneath the clear bandage around her wrist.

"I can replace that for you real quick. Won't take me but a minute, and I will do my best to make it not hurt."

"You know," Mr. Schoonover interrupted. "I could really use some coffee. Hannah, would you be a dear and stay with her long enough for me to run downstairs to the cafeteria and get a cup?"

"Of course," she said. "I should be done by the time you get back. *Poor Mr. Schoonover*, she thought. He was resolute in his attendance to his wife, but the sight of blood always made him tremble. Each time blood was going to be visible, he would find an excuse to leave.

Hannah turned back to Mildred and took her right arm. She began unwrapping the bandage that held the I.V. in place. Just when she was about to pull the needle from her arm, a sensation shot through Hannah's chest. She had felt this a few times before over the past several years, and each time would immediately check her blood pressure.

This time it was different. She couldn't describe how she knew, but this time the feeling was more urgent. The sensation travelled around the inside of her abdomen and radiated through her hands. Her head shot up straighter as the tingling moved up her spine and into her brain. *What is happening to me?*

"Honey, are you okay?" Mildred asked.

Hannah looked down at her patient, but instead of seeing the Mildred she had come to know, she saw something that looked more like a biology textbook photo. As if in some sort of trance, Mildred's room became foggy, and Hannah's eyes focused in on her patient's body – and then suddenly *into* her body.

Hannah could see her patient's heart, the lungs on each side, and even the stomach just underneath. Instinctively, her probing moved to the area just under the stomach, and she searched for the source of this woman's doom. She knew what cancer looked like in a CT scan and had seen several tumors in cadavers and a few in patients she had performed surgery on, but gazing upon a functioning tumor inside of an unopened body was something she could not have prepared herself for. There it was – the parasitic misgrowth of cells that had formed on Mildred's pancreas, choking the life from this sweet woman.

In the trance, her hands didn't work, but in her mind, she had an invisible appendage, almost like an extra limb. She had no frame of reference to explain what was happening to her, but somehow she knew she could touch the cancer. And she did. The tumor was within her grasp, and somehow, using that inexplicable inner energy, she destroyed the cancer just as it had intended to destroy Mildred.

"Dr. Cooper?"

Hannah shook her head vigorously and once the blurring disappeared, she saw Mildred once again. The older woman's eyes showed concern and her arm was still in the air, waiting for her new I.V.

"Are you okay, Dr. Cooper?" Mildred asked.

"Yes ma'am," Hannah finally answered. "I had a late night last night reading some medical journals. I'm really sorry."

"No problem, honey," Mildred said with a smile.

As she replaced the I.V. feed back into the woman's wrist, she began thinking about what she had just seen. Was it all just a vision or had she really travelled into Mildred's body and removed the cancer? How was that possible? There was no explanation available, except that she had been hallucinating. It was the only possibility.

But what if it had actually happened? Had she had defied the laws of nature that she had spent so many years studying and supernaturally killed the cancer that was in Mrs. Schoonover's body?

There was only one way to find out. "Mrs. Schoonover, I'm going to order a CT scan for you, if that's okay?"

"Why would you do a thing like that? Let's be frank, you know that I could die any minute now. It would be a waste of your time, my time, and the poor tech who has to do it."

"There's something that I want checked out. Since I am requesting the CT, I'll make sure that it isn't billed to your account. I hope it's not too much of an inconvenience." She couldn't tell Mildred the truth. For one, it would be plain cruel to give a terminal cancer patient false hope, and it would make her sound completely nuts. She was a medical professional who took the Hippocratic Oath to take care of people, not some tarot-reading, incense burning, New-Age guru.

"If that's what you think we need to do, then let's do it," Mildred agreed.

Mr. Schoonover returned shortly after, and Hannah quickly hurried out so as to avoid any questions from him regarding the CT scan request. She stopped by the nurses' station and ordered the test for Mildred, and pleaded with one of the nurses to make this her top priority.

Three hours later she was finally able to return to her office for a brief respite from her rounds. There had been nearly a dozen other patients, two of them with terminal cancer that gave them less than a month to live. Those were the two that Hannah had performed her new mental experiment on, and each time the result was identical to what occurred with Mildred's case. In her clouded trance, she saw her invisible "hand" squash the life from the tumors. The repetition of the procedure came easily to her for some reason. Doing it once somehow made it become a natural part of her, just like brushing her teeth or clipping her nails.

Both times she ordered a CT scan on the patient. One was a case of stomach cancer and the other was lung cancer. Hannah hoped to have the results within the next few hours.

She walked down the long hallway and back to her office, thoughts of Mildred's cancer and her vision into the woman's body stuck in her mind. Her coffee was cold by the time she got back, but it was still caffeine and she needed all the help she could get.

Sitting back in her chair, she let out a long sigh and closed her eyes. What could have caused these visions? The only odd thing that had ever happened to her had been the tingling sensations in her chest. When she had checked her blood pressure each time, the results came back normal. She had spoken with her colleague, Dr. Jones, about this, and his immediate diagnosis was stress.

Hannah had always been stressed. A foster family had finally decided to take her in when she was eight, but they were never exactly warm towards her. She suspected that they were only after the stipend from the state government and had little actual interest in raising a child. She threw herself into her schoolwork. The first full year of school with her new foster family, she had passed through three grade levels. Math and science came easily to her, and her reading comprehension skills often surpassed even her teachers'. Her eidetic memory made memorization of the biological components of the human body easier than learning to tie her shoe laces.

By the time she turned ten, she was nearly through high school and had begun applying to colleges. She got some media attention for her genius level intellect, and scholarships were easy to find. Her foster family let her leave for college with little fanfare, and that had deeply upset Hannah. They never showed much interest in her, and praised her even less when she advanced to a new grade level. One of the only aspects of her family that she found reassuring was that they never attempted to exploit her.

But Hannah didn't need a family; her books and her learning were her family. She was driven to be a doctor even before her foster parents had taken her in. Even in serious medical schools, students like to partake in revelry, but she would have none of it. She was fortunate enough to secure a dorm with no roommate and thus was able to study effectively and with little interruptions. When she turned fifteen, she graduated medical school and began her internship at Boca Rotan Memorial in Florida.

The doctors who oversaw her residency quickly began giving her additional responsibilities. They saw that she could handle it and her skill surpassed others who had been in the field for decades. A few months ago, the board had changed her from a resident to an actual full-fledged doctor at the hospital. Other than Doogie Howser and crazy television specials on basic cable, becoming a doctor by the age of seventeen was unheard of.

She heard a knock on her door. She bid the person enter and looked up to greet them. The nurse walked in and set a manila folder on her desk. Hannah thanked the nurse profusely for expediting the scan, and shook her hand, before the woman left. Hannah saw the name "Mildred Schoonover" across the top and knew that the CT results were inside. In two years she had never gotten a CT scan report back so quickly.

She opened the folder and began reading the reports, and the reason the report had been so prompt was evident. There were several small images of the scan attached to the report. Usually the radiologist viewing the CT scan would write up their findings and then have a clerical associate dictate the report, before it was sent to the doctor. Looking down at the page of hand written notes, she saw that the writing was Dr. Hubbard's. He was a friend of Hannah's and would have been well acquainted with Mrs. Schoonover's case. The results had excited him enough that he hadn't taken the time to have them dictated, but instead sent the information to Hannah directly. She would owe him lunch for this, she thought to herself, placing the idea on her long mental to-do list. All findings consistently agreed on one fact. Mildred's cancer was gone.

Hannah dropped the folder onto her desk and held her hands to her eyes as to stop the flow of tears. Was it possible? She didn't know who to tell or how to tell them. If she told anyone the truth, she would be considered a raging psycho. She considered whether or not to tell the Schoonovers. What if the CT scan was wrong? But the reports were detailed, and the image that she was looking at was clear in that there was no trace of a tumor.

It took one phone call down to the lab to verify with the technician that she was indeed looking at the right report. The technician had remembered Mildred's case, and even though they were not allowed to diagnose cases, the tech was still fully aware of the terminal aspect. Fortunately, he didn't pry too much with questions about how the cancer was suddenly gone, but Hannah could read his curiosity over the phone line.

Before she could decide how to proceed, the CT scans came back for the other two patients. Each report was clear – the cancer was completely absent from their bodies.

One question played over and over in Hannah's mind – *Have I just cured cancer?*

The next day Hannah stood in the Schoonovers' empty room. Since arriving that morning, she had not had a moment to herself. Her colleague, Dr. Jones, and several other doctors from all over the hospital had filled her office with questions and objections to the three cases of disappearing cancer. She had thought up a decent story to tell them, but it didn't matter anyway because they didn't stop long enough to let her tell it.

Most of her morning had been spent with the board going over the three cases, and still she hadn't had the opportunity to say much on the matter.

After the recess for lunch, Hannah had returned to the Schoonovers' room. They had checked out late the previous day after Mildred had successfully eaten lunch and dinner, and had also managed to keep it down. Once Hannah had destroyed the cancer, the physical manifestations of her recovery were immediately evident. Her jaundice disappeared and her blurred vision had cleared by lunchtime.

The Schoonovers left the hospital only after hugging Hannah so much that they nearly broke her ribs. Mildred and her husband both wept openly throughout the entire check-out process. She had walked them to the elevator and with a tearful goodbye and promises to return for regular checkups and tests, then they were gone.

Their old room was quiet now. The technicians would be in soon to clean and sanitize the room to make way for a new patient that would surely come through the doors. There were just so many sick people dying every day.

Hannah sighed and walked back out of the room. She walked to the nurses' station and picked up the clipboard which would detail her next several hours. Before she read the first page, a nurse interrupted her.

"Dr. Cooper, you have visitors. We've sent them to your office, and they're waiting on you."

"Who are they? Did they say who they represent?"

"I don't have their check-in information, but I think they are from the Department of Health and Human Services," the nurse answered.

"That's odd," Hannah mumbled to herself. She turned back to the nurse. "No more details? I'm not expecting anyone. It's quite odd for them to show up unannounced."

"Yes it is," the nurse agreed. "But they didn't provide us any more details."

Hannah was sure that they had already heard about the three miraculous cures that had occurred over the past twenty-four hours. Attention was something that she had always wanted to avoid, especially now. Her 'cure' that she had provided was something that she couldn't explain medically, but the gravity of her discovery would soon catch many an unwanted eye.

She decided to forgo the rounds long enough to find out what the HHS reps wanted with her. She slipped the clipboard back into its appropriate slot and walked in the direction of her office.

As she turned a corner, she crashed into a man coming the opposite direction. She hit his chest and then staggered back against the wall. She was able to catch herself against the railing.

"Sorry about that, ma'am," one of the two men standing in front of her said.

She got a better look at them. They were not men – they were boys, no older than she was. Both were dressed in simple button up shirts and khaki slacks. They were both blonde, although one blonde was a shade darker, and they were both very handsome. She had never cared to make accommodations in her life for romance, but if she did, these two seemed just the type of guy she would go for, even if they were a little on the young side.

"I'm so sorry," she said as she pulled herself up.

"It's my fault," the one on the left said. "I really should watch where I'm going."

"Actually," the other boy pointed out to his friend. "It's probably her fault, since she was walking on the wrong side of the hallway."

She was taken aback. *What a jerk!* The boy she ran into seemed sweet, but this other one seemed more than a bit on the a-hole side. Her best bet, she decided, was to give them as little of her time as she could manage. There were still the HHS reps and the patients to see.

"I would love to stay and chat, but I have things to do," Hannah said suddenly as she tried to move past them.

The nice boy looked down at the name tag on her coat. "You're Hannah Cooper," he said to her, the surprise registering in his tone.

"Aren't you a little young to be doctor?" the other one asked.

"Who are you?" was all she asked.

"We're with the US government," the nice one explained. "And we need for you to come with us."

She sucked in air sharply. Hannah knew that various organizations would be calling on her shortly to answer questions regarding her patients' recent success with their illnesses, but she had no idea that the government would resort to arrest or even detainment. Charts were still stacked against the nurse station and there was plenty yet to do before she could call it day.

"I don't have time for this," she finally said. "If you want to discuss something with me, you can set an appointment."

"*We* don't have time for this," the arrogant one let out a sigh.

The nice one laid a hand on the other's arm. "What he meant to say was that your particular situation requires a degree of urgency. For your own sake, please come with us."

"I need more if you want me to trust you."

The nice one leaned in close to her, so that only the three of them could hear what was said. "We know what you did to your patients here and we know how you did it. We just want to talk to you."

Her heart plummeted to the linoleum floor just as her legs started shaking. Anxiety gripped her by the throat and she looked around for somewhere to hide.

There was only one safe haven for her here. She turned back the way she had come. "Nurse, I'm going to my office. Please contact security and see that these two men are removed from the premises."

"Yes ma'am," the older woman behind the counter picked up her phone to dial the guards.

"Dr. Cooper –," the nice one began.

"I told you I don't have time for this, now please leave me alone." She brushed past them, her shoulders bumping into theirs.

At the end of the hall, she turned and made her way to her office. She never bothered to turn to see if she was being followed, and she didn't really care. Her office would give her at least a moment of peace before the feds called in back up.

Just as she reached her door, she remembered the reps from the Department of Health were waiting there. Maybe she could have them reschedule. As she caught sight of her door, it dawned on her. The HHS was part of the federal government, and there were two agents behind her. What if the ones in her office were in on this whole thing?

When she opened the door, there were two men waiting for her. They weren't dressed like HHS representatives, and they weren't much older than her.

The brown haired one stood immediately and approached her, and the blonde one was right behind her.

"May I help you two with something?" she asked.

"Ma'am, we're with the federal government, and we would like for you to come with us."

Oh, hell. Why were the feds suddenly sweeping down on her?

Shrouded Island

By Brian Dockins

Coming Summer 2011

Don't miss these other exciting works by Brian Dockins

DOMA: Department of Magic

Book 1 – Betrayal of Magic

Book 2 – Shrouded Island

Book 3 – Rise of the Witch

Book 4 – Magic of Heroes

Book 5
Hounds of the Himalayas

Book 6
Second Exodus

Book 7
Hidden Relics

To learn more about the Department of Magic and learn of updates to the series, check out Brian Dockins' blog:

www.departmentofmagic.blogspot.com

Also Available - DOMA Origins Short Stories

Learn more about Cadan's teammates in the new companion series to the Department of Magic. Each one is a short story that details how each of the Paladins became associated or apprehended by the Department. They are sure to provide entertainment and deepen your love for the characters.